PRAISE FOR THE LAWL

"I love Lexi Blake. Read *Ruthless* and see why."

—*New York Times* bestselling author Lee Child

"Smart, savvy, clever, and always entertaining. That's true of Riley Lawless, the hero in *Ruthless*, and likewise for his creator, Lexi Blake. Both are way ahead of the pack."

—*New York Times* bestselling author Steve Berry

"*Ruthless* is full of suspense, hot sex, and swoon-worthy characters— a must read! Lexi Blake is a master at sexy, thrilling romance!"

—*New York Times* bestselling author Jennifer Probst

"With *Ruthless*, Lexi Blake has set up shop on the intersection of suspenseful and sexy, and I never want to leave."

—*New York Times* bestselling author Laurelin Paige

"The love story that develops will touch the hearts of fans. . . . A welcome and satisfying entry into the Lawless world."

—RT Book Reviews

PRAISE FOR THE NOVELS OF LEXI BLAKE

"The sex was hot and emotionally charged in many beautiful ways."

—Scandalicious

"A book to enjoy again and again. . . . Captivating."

—Guilty Pleasures Book Reviews

"A satisfying snack of love, romance, and hot, steamy sex."

—Sizzling Hot Books

PRAISE FOR THE PERFECT GENTLEMEN SERIES
BY SHAYLA BLACK AND LEXI BLAKE

"Hot and edgy and laced with danger, the stories in the Perfect Gentlemen series are just that—perfect."
                        —*New York Times* bestselling author J. Kenner

"While there are certainly incendiary sex scenes at the top of this series opener, the strength is in the underlying murder and political mystery."   —RT Book Reviews

EVIDENCE

of

DESIRE

LEXI BLAKE

JOVE
NEW YORK

A JOVE BOOK
Published by Berkley
An imprint of Penguin Random House LLC
1745 Broadway, New York, NY 10019

Copyright © 2019 by DLZ Entertainment, LLC

Library of Congress Cataloging-in-Publication Data

Names: Blake, Lexi, author.
Title: Evidence of desire / Lexi Blake.
Description: First Edition. | New York : JOVE, 2019. | Series: A courting justice novel ; 2
Identifiers: LCCN 2018028541| ISBN 9780399587481 (paperback) |
ISBN 9780399587498 (ebook)
Subjects: | BISAC: FICTION / Romance / Contemporary. | FICTION / Romance /
Suspense. | FICTION / Contemporary Women. | GSAFD: Romantic suspense fiction.
Classification: LCC PS3602.L3456 E95 2019 | DDC 813/.6—dc23
LC record available at https://lccn.loc.gov/2018028541

First Edition: January 2019

Printed in the United States of America
1 3 5 7 9 10 8 6 4 2

Cover design by Alana Colucci
Cover photo by Claudio Marinesco

ACKNOWLEDGMENTS

I want to thank everyone who made *Evidence of Desire* possible. Thanks to Kate Seaver and her whole team at Berkley for believing in this project and helping to make every book as good as it possibly can be. Thanks to Merrilee Heifetz at Writers House for championing this project and Kevan Lyon at Marshal Lyon Literary for helping to shepherd it through. Thanks to my personal team—Kim Guidroz, Danielle Sanchez, Jillian Stein, Stormy Pate, Riane Holt, Kori Smith, and my super-supportive husband. And thanks to the best lawyer a writer could have—Margarita Coale.

ONE

It was always the roar of the crowd he heard first. It came out of nowhere. Like the world was quiet and still, and then a joyous chaos slapped him in the face. How many times had he stood outside the locker room, waiting for that moment when he moved from the darkness and into the brilliant light? When he went from being something small to being the center of the world?

It was odd though because now he wasn't surrounded by laughing teammates, their camaraderie usually buoying him in the face of those questioning, demanding lights. He wasn't bouncing in his cleats, pumping himself up by messing around with the running back or joking with his line. Sometimes they would bump hard against one another as though prepping for the hits to come, to remind each other—I am invincible.

Now there was only him standing in the shadows, waiting for that moment when he would be called to glory.

Why the hell was he in a suit? He looked down and there wasn't a football in his hand. Instead he carried an elegant briefcase. He felt leaner, his body not as ripped as it was supposed to be. He needed the muscle, needed the strength. Here only the strongest survived. Only the most willing to sacrifice made it to the field.

The announcer's voice shook the stadium, calling out number thirty-four.

This was wrong. He knew it deep in his gut. This was wrong and he wasn't going out there. He would stay in the shadows. Being small didn't mean being wrong. Except his feet were moving and there it was, the roar that seemed to shake his soul. Had he once thought that was the sweetest sound in the world? Now he could hear the hunger behind the cheers, the craving for something to take each fan away from their ordinary lives. Blood would do. Bones cracking and miracles performed, every player would feed the need of the crowd that jubilantly screamed now, but oh how it could turn when things went wrong. One misstep. One fumble. One missed chance and that jubilation would turn ugly and he would feel it in his soul.

He found himself in the middle of the field, all lights on him. Blinding lights. He'd wanted this? He'd once needed this like he needed his next breath. These lights, that crowd, those voices proved he'd climbed out of the cesspool of poverty he'd been born into, lifted up through gift and discipline, through blood and pain.

He held his fists up, dropping the stupid briefcase. He didn't need that. He didn't need pads or helmets. He needed discipline and the ability to ignore pain. That was the sacrifice. What were a few broken bones compared to the glory he could find here?

And then everything stopped. No more cheers. No more lights. He was alone and yet not because the crowd had gone, but something was coming for him. Silence and darkness, and he realized it was close. It was coming for him in that sullen night, a quiet locomotive that bashed past all precautions.

He waited, bracing himself for the final tackle.

~

David sat straight up in bed when the phone rang, the sound splitting the deep gloom of his dream. His hands were shaking, and it took him a moment to remember that he was here in his nice Chelsea apartment that cost more than a thousand of the trailers he'd grown up in. He was safe and functional, and he was a lawyer, not a Sunday soldier.

Fuck. He hated that dream. Why couldn't he dream about serial killers stalking him? He was a damn criminal defense attorney. He'd met with some of the creepiest human beings on earth. Surely he could come up with a few nightmares about them. It would be less disturbing.

He glanced at the clock. Barely five A.M. on a Saturday. Damn it. He had exactly two days to sleep in. Not to not work. He worked seven days a week, but at least on weekends he got a couple of extra hours of sleep. Everyone knew that.

His cell trilled again, the sound not as close in proximity as it should have been. Had he turned the ringer down?

His heart seized a little because everyone did know that he slept in, and that meant this was likely an emergency. He scrambled to get to his phone.

Where was his phone? He could hear the fucker, but where was it? Why wasn't it sitting on the nightstand where he always put it?

What the hell had he done last night?

He turned on the lights and walked into the living room, where the sound was louder. Yeah, now he remembered. He'd gotten together with friends and ordered takeout to celebrate the end of a case. Margarita and Noah had come to his place. They'd started out by going over the jury polling and ended up drinking way, way too much tequila.

He was too old for that shit. How had he gotten talked into it? And Margarita could seriously drink some tequila. They'd laughed about it the night before, the amount of tequila going into their Margarita. Naturally she'd been the completely steady one. She was the one who directed him to go to bed when it got late, and promised to see Noah home. God, he hoped Noah hadn't hit on her. That was the last thing they needed. Margarita Reyes was one of the single smartest legal minds he'd ever met. She split her time between his New York firm, Garrison, Cormack, and Lawless, and the software company 4L, owned by the incredibly wealthy Drew Lawless. David was almost certain Margarita had been initially sent by Drew to watch over the youngest of his siblings, Noah, as he embarked on his career, but two years in she was a part of the team and not someone's watchdog. Either that or she was a terrible watchdog because she instigated most of the parties.

Where the hell was his phone?

It had stopped ringing. He was going to feel so damn bad if that was his mother and something had happened to his dad. With the way things had been going, it could be anything. Since the Alzheimer's had progressed, his father had been known to wander off, thinking it was still the eighties and looking for his toddler son.

He hoped things had changed since he'd started paying for a full-time nurse. He would do almost anything to help his mother out. She was aging herself and he wanted her to enjoy her golden years instead of worrying about a husband who was rapidly forgetting who he was.

There was a tapping on his door, lightly, as though the person knocking knew how pissed off New Yorkers could get when something interrupted their weekend sleep.

It was Grand Central here this morning. Everyone wanted a piece of him. Without bothering to find a robe, he strode to the door and looked out the peephole. He sighed and started the long process of unlocking the door.

Noah stood in the doorway, and David thought seriously about punching him in his perfect, nobody-can-tell-I-spent-the-night-finding-the-bottom-of-a-bottle-of-tequila face. He was dressed in a designer suit, his *GQ*-ready face all fresh and youthful.

David was fairly certain he'd never looked that young in his life. "What? Do you have any idea what time it is? Did Margarita lose you on the way home? Did you find some model's bed and now you need a place to hide?"

The way Noah went through women, it was a plausible scenario.

Noah's eyes widened. "Is that any way to greet the man who is about to make your entire year? You said you wanted a big case, I've caught us a whopper. But seriously, you're going to have to wear more than those boxers. Let's get you dressed and moving, my man. I've got a car waiting for us."

He strode in and David closed the door behind him. "What case are you talking about, and can it wait? I need to find my phone. I think my mother might be calling."

"It was me. I thought I'd warn you I was coming up." Noah set his briefcase down and moved to the kitchen. "Go and shower and change while I make you some coffee. I would have gotten some at Starbucks, but I know that's too froufrou for you."

"I'm not trying to be a jerk. I just like plain coffee, and there's nothing plain about theirs." Why couldn't coffee be coffee flavored? When he asked for coffee-flavored coffee, the baristas stared at him like he'd grown two heads. Which he kind of felt like he had today, and both of them were throbbing. Damn tequila. "Why am I getting into a suit on a Saturday morning?"

"Because we're going to have to wade through an army of reporters at some point, and you know you like to look your best," Noah said from the kitchen, where he proved he'd spent far too much time here. He went straight for the coffeepot and started it brewing. "Seriously, we have to hurry. I want us there when they arrest him. According to his personal attorney, they've still got him at his place. They haven't transported him yet, but that's what you get when you're a star. Kid-glove treatment."

"Arrest who?" David knew he sounded irritable. He was irritable. "And if this is such a big case, why isn't it Henry you're bugging at this god-awful hour of the morning?"

"Because Isla requested you personally," Noah replied.

"Isla?" He knew the name vaguely. A vision of a petite woman with brown-and-gold hair floated through his brain. She was a few years younger than him. He remembered her as smart and a bit on the somber side. "Are you talking about Isla Shayne? She used to work with the New York Guardians in the front office, right?"

The Guardians were one of the state's many professional sports franchises, this one a football team with a storied history of winning championships.

Noah nodded. "Yes, that's Isla. I know her from school. She was a couple grades ahead of me at the girls' school when I was a fresh-man at Creighton. I knew her fiancé. He was a senior at Creighton."

Austin Kendrick, son of Guardians owner, Carey Kendrick. Aus-tin had been an up-and-coming quarterback until he found out he had non-Hodgkin's lymphoma at the age of twenty-three. Austin Kendrick was proof that money and privilege couldn't always avert tragedy. Now he was curious. Isla was known for being a workhorse. She'd worked for her would-have-been father-in-law for years before she started her own practice. David had heard she was the go-to girl for wealthy athletes and celebrities who needed someone to look at every single item they signed. She was highly sought after.

And apparently she had a client in trouble. If that client could afford to hire Isla Shayne, this might be a seriously high-profile case. Was his Armani clean?

"Who are we talking about?" David asked, the smell of coffee lifting some of the fog from his brain. *Be a basketball guy or a Holly-*

wood actor. Be a baseball player or some dumbass reality star. Anyone but an athlete from that world he dreamed about.

"It's Trey Adams." Noah held a mug in his hand, and his eyes were lit with ambition. Sometimes he was certain this was the real reason Henry had brought in Noah. They needed someone young and hungry, someone who hadn't already been ground down by the system, who still thought that being king of the world would bring him some happiness. That kind of drive fueled a great firm.

"Adams?" David's stomach did a deep dive, and he once again wished he hadn't partied with the youngsters the night before. Damn. He wasn't even forty and he still felt old around those two.

"Trey Adams, the quarterback saint of the football world, allegedly killed his wife in a fit of rage in the early hours of this morning, and we're going to defend him. This is it, my man. This is the O.J. trial of our time and we've got the case. We're about to catapult into the stratosphere. It's everything we've been waiting on."

Trey Adams was a legend. Trey Adams had led the Guardians to three Super Bowl titles during his twelve years as a professional quarterback. He'd married model and activist Portia Adams, and they'd been the world's power couple for more than a decade. After his retirement fifteen years ago, they'd settled here in Manhattan, where he'd done color commentary for five years and then suddenly quit, saying he wanted more time with his wife and kids.

But there were rumors. Rumors that he couldn't remember where he was at times. Rumors that he could get violent. Rumors that he was addicted to pain meds.

David knew what it all added up to.

"Portia Adams is dead?" He felt a little numb even as Noah handed him the mug.

Noah's eyes softened. "I'm sorry. You knew him? I should have thought of that, but you've been out of the game for a long time. You rarely talk about it."

"I've met him a few times. We were never on the same team. His wife was a lovely woman. She ran a lot of the charity works for the league. Smart lady." He took the coffee. It looked like he was going to need it. "I'll get changed. How bad is the press coverage at this point?"

"David, maybe I should call Henry," Noah said, sounding hesitant for the first time. "He's out on the island with Win, but I can hold down the case until he gets here."

"I thought they wanted me." He knew what Noah was doing, giving him an out. He wasn't going to be cowardly enough to take it. Because Noah was right. If this wasn't an open-and-shut case, it would be *the* case. Hell, he could make something of it no matter what the evidence showed. Even if there was clear proof that Adams killed his wife, there was likely a defense. A defense no one had ever used in a case this big.

CTE. Chronic traumatic encephalopathy. Every athlete's nightmare.

Who better to bring it than a man who might suffer from it one day?

"She does want you," Noah replied. "She asked specifically for you. You're perfect for this case. It's not easy finding a Harvard-educated lawyer who also played in the NFL. And I don't think the press coverage is bad yet, but the minute the sun comes up, you know the vultures will start to circle. I wanted to try to be there if they take him into custody."

"Don't you mean *when* they take him into custody?"

Noah shrugged. "I'm trying to be optimistic."

"Stop," he shot back as he started for the bedroom. No time to shower. That would have to wait, and he needed to get into battle mode. He would be stepping into those lights today and there would be nowhere to hide. "I don't need Suzy Sunshine as my second. I need Dour Dan."

Noah frowned in a way that looked silly on that matinee-idol face of his. "I can be that. And they're definitely hauling his ass down to the station. The question is how they do it. We should hurry if we intend to mitigate the damage."

"All right, then. This is my case." He said the words, allowing them to sink in. "I'll get dressed. You figure out what kind of shit storm we're walking into, and have Margarita start writing some statements about the victim. I want her to get the clerks working on everything we know about Trey Adams and his state of health, both physically and mentally. If he's popping pills, I want to know where they came from. If he's seeing a shrink, I want the phone number. And everything on their marriage. If there's a single rumor of someone cheating or even thinking about leaving, I want to know. Go through every gossip rag for the last two years. They suck, but there's sometimes a kernel of truth to those stories and they'll give us a place to start. But the medical records are the key to this case. You understand?"

He would need all the medical records, and there would be tons of them. Over the course of his career, Trey Adams would have been injured many times. But it was the head injuries that David was particularly interested in. Could decades of small traumas to the brain have turned a hero into a killer?

Noah was already on his phone. "Margarita, I need you to get up. What do you mean? You've already made breakfast and been to the gym? What'd you make?"

He opened the closet and started pulling on his new uniform. It was still a form of armor. He was going to need a very thick skin to come out of this one whole.

⁓

Isla Shayne glanced at the clock. Five forty. How much longer would she have? How much longer could she stand here in this apartment where she'd come for parties and dinners and remain calm and cool?

How in all that was right with the universe could Portia Adams be dead?

A hand reached down for hers, a slender body leaning, and she felt a silent sob go through Miranda Adams's body. Isla squeezed her hand. Miranda was barely twenty but she was holding up like a champ. She'd been the one to phone Isla after her father had called her at her dorm at Columbia University. Miranda had been the one who met her in the lobby of her parents' building.

But it had been Isla who'd made the long ride in the elevator, who'd used Miranda's key to get in, who'd walked into a bloodbath.

"When will they take her out?" Miranda asked.

Her. Her mother. When would they take her body away? "It could be a while, sweetie. The medical examiner just got here a couple of minutes ago and the district attorney isn't here yet."

"Should Dad be talking to the detective?" Miranda straightened up, her shoulders squaring.

"I'm trying to keep things civil right now. I don't want to risk them hauling in your dad. If we play the game right, we might be able to avoid parading him in front of the press, but I need his defense attorney here."

"Why can't you handle it? Isla, we trust you. You know us."

"I do, but David Cormack knows criminal law and I think he'll be very good at talking to your dad," she replied quietly. "I'm good at handling a lot of different legal situations, but I have no experience with this."

None, or she wouldn't have taken a single look at the scene and ended up vomiting in one of the elegant large planters that decorated the penthouse. Yeah, she'd had to explain that to the police. She glanced across the room to where the detectives were speaking to her client.

"So you woke up and she was dead?" Detective Campbell was a tall man in an elegant suit. He had midnight skin and eyes that had seen way too much of the world. And yet his voice was soft as he stared at his subject.

Trey's eyes were unfocused, bleary. "Portia? Portia's dead?" His face went blank for a moment and then his jaw tightened. "I knew that. I knew she was dead."

They hadn't allowed him to clean up yet. Trey Adams still had blood on his hands and his shirt. He'd tried to get up and hug his daughter, but the police weren't allowing him to do anything but sit in the living room.

He had gotten bad. Much worse than the last time she'd seen him, and she had to wonder what they would find in his tox screen. "Detective, I would prefer to wait for his attorney."

Campbell turned his stare on her. "I thought you were his attorney."

"She's a good lawyer," Trey said, nodding her way. "If you're looking for one, you can't do better than our Isla. Known her since she was a kid and now she looks out for us. Doesn't she, Randi? Isla's the best. For me and . . . I know she's dead." He ran a hand through his hair.

Miranda moved in closer to her father, speaking to him in soothing tones.

The detective drew Isla away, taking her out of earshot of Miranda and Trey. "I thought you told me the antianxiety meds would make him better."

"He is better. He's talking and not crying. We managed to get him to let her body go," she replied. And that had been a close thing. She'd had to talk him down because she couldn't let Miranda see her mother's body, couldn't let her know how much blood had spilled. She had to hold it together until David Cormack got here. That was all she had to do. Keep things from falling apart until the big guns arrived. Her job was to not screw up and let her client incriminate himself.

And not break down because it was truly tragic.

What happened to him?

That's not the Adams I know.

The cops were all whispering. These were New York's finest, career cops who rarely blinked, but it was easy to see that even the most hardened officer was off his game today. Being in the presence of a living legend was bad enough. When that living legend turned out to be a fragile, broken version of the man they'd once called the greatest to play the game, it seemed to have thrown some of them for a loop.

"Gentlemen . . ." Campbell's deep voice had them scrambling to get back to work. The detective gestured for her to move with him, slightly out of Trey Adams's earshot. Two officers took up watch on the suspect—how could he be a suspect?

"I'm trying to handle this as delicately as possible," Campbell said. "But I need you to explain his situation right now. Will I be able to question him?"

"Yes. He has good days and bad days. You'll absolutely be able to question him. But I can't promise you he'll remember what happened."

"I think we can come up with some ways to help him along," a deep voice said.

She turned and was facing a blond-haired man in a superexpensive suit. One she knew well. "Hello, Royce. I don't suppose you're here for a social visit."

Royce Osborne was born to work in the district attorney's office. He had Superman good looks, the ability to convince people he cared, and the dark soul of a true amoral demon. He was all about the win, and his record showed it. If he thought he couldn't win, he would drop the case no matter how desperate the victims were.

She couldn't believe she'd dated that walking hairpiece, but then she'd let herself be set up on a blind date, and at first he'd seemed nice. That had changed over the course of their relationship. It was two months of her life she wouldn't ever get back, and she was fairly certain at some point he'd stolen her moisturizer. She was never again going to date a guy who spent more time getting ready than she did.

Royce smiled, his teeth definitely too white to be natural. "Not at all. I'm here to lay the groundwork and to talk to the public. This is going to be a big case. I want to make sure no one screws it up, but it looks like you're not doing the same, sweetheart. You're not a criminal lawyer. Decide to play with the big boys, have you? Do you think that's smart?" He looked around the room, his face becoming a mask of disgust. "What the hell happened? Jesus, he looks like shit. Are we sure he's the perp and not the victim?"

"Keep your voice down, Royce. His daughter is here," she said under her breath. She looked over and it seemed like Miranda hadn't heard him.

The assistant DA shrugged. "Should she be here? Shouldn't we clear all the nonessential people out? Speaking of that, should he still be here? Detective, is there a reason you haven't arrested this man?"

"Well, ADA Osborne, I tend to prefer to figure a situation out before I rip apart families and force potentially innocent suspects to do a perp walk in front of a thousand cameras," Campbell replied laconically. "Tell me something. Did you smile for your close-up? I bet you didn't come in the back way."

Royce smiled dismissively. "The public needs to know they have the best representing them. My talking to reporters reassures the people of New York that the DA's office can handle this. Now, Detective Campbell, I must insist that you do your job. Arrest this man. I want him outside in handcuffs in thirty minutes. We can do this down at the station."

Campbell frowned. "There is no point in humiliating the man.

I'll be honest. I'm not convinced that he has the mental capacity to know what he did, if he did it. I've been trying to get him to cooperate with processing, and I think he'll do that more readily if he's in a familiar place."

"Force him," Royce insisted.

"He's not trying to be uncooperative," Campbell replied. "He's confused and scared. I'm trying to do this in a way that doesn't further the trauma."

"I don't care about his trauma," Royce replied. "It's an election year and my boss is running on a law-and-order platform. We care about the victim. I'm not going to allow this to turn into fucking O. J. Simpson, do you understand? We will show the world that New York doesn't care if you're a celebrity. You come here and kill someone, you get treated like the thug you are."

"Whatever happened to innocent before proven guilty?" Isla asked.

"The fact that you can even ask that question with a straight face proves my point," he replied. "You shouldn't attempt to represent this man, Isla. I'll tear you apart and I won't think twice about doing it. I would rather we did something more pleasant. Why don't you call in one of the big boys and let them handle this, and when I've got some free time, maybe we can go to dinner and I'll fill you in."

Or she could punch him. She was pretty good according to her self-defense teacher. This was sort of self-defense. He was offending her greatly with his mouth and she could shut it with her fist.

"Well, well, look at that, Noah. You see, that is what we call a triple threat," a new voice said. "He's managed to violate our client's rights, sexually harass the females, and bring into question his own police department's competency. This one's going to be easy, brother."

"I love it when the DA does our job for us," Noah Lawless said.

Noah was an old friend and a welcome sight. If he'd been irritated to be called to work early in the morning, it didn't show on his face. Noah looked young, his blue eyes shining as he smiled her way.

David Cormack was different. He didn't look young and shiny, but there was a competence about the man that called to her. His dark hair was cut ruthlessly short. His suit was fashionable, but she could tell this wasn't a man who spent endless hours on his skin care regimen. Nope. He spent that time in the gym. No amount of expensive suit could cover those muscles.

She held out a hand, welcoming Noah. "I'm grateful you're here." She caught Miranda's attention, calling the younger woman over. "Miranda, these are the men I was telling you about. They're very good."

The cavalry was here. Thank god. Noah looked like a knight on a stallion, swooping in to save the damsel in distress. Normally she didn't think of herself that way. She was strong and smart and able to handle almost anything thrown at her.

Except blood and death and heartache.

"It's nice to meet you, Miranda." The man who'd spoken to Noah stepped up. Now there was a white knight. "I am sorry for your loss. My name is David Cormack. I'm going to be looking out for your dad."

Isla watched as Miranda shook his hand. It was startling how he changed from the man who'd stared at Royce with a hint of disdain. Now he looked down at Miranda with the kindest eyes. He wore a suit to rival Royce's, but the difference was already apparent. He hadn't said *I'll be representing your father* like almost any other lawyer would. He'd said he would be looking out for her father. This was a man who knew that words mattered, that intent was important.

"Thank you," Miranda said quietly, releasing his hand. She looked back up at Isla. "I should go soon. I hate to leave Dad, but I have to get to Oscar's place in Brooklyn. He's not answering his phone. My brother sleeps in most weekends and nothing wakes him, but I don't want him to open the door when he goes out for coffee and get besieged by reporters. I need to get there before they find out where he's living."

David looked over his shoulder, but Noah was already on the phone. He nodded Miranda's way. "You can take our car. It should be ready for you in five minutes. He'll pick you up in the parking garage and go out through the service entrance. The herd is thin there."

Noah hung up. "He'll also stop and pick up an associate of ours. Her name is Margarita Reyes. You don't need to be alone right now. She'll keep reporters off your back, but she'll also give you all the space you need."

Miranda looked up at Isla, an expectant look on her face.

Isla nodded. She trusted Noah. They hadn't been close, but Austin had liked him and she liked his sister, Mia. They'd met at social functions and charity balls. "I need to stay here to monitor things with your dad. You go on. They'll take care of you—and, Miranda, I'm so, so sorry. We all loved your mother."

Miranda sniffled and started to turn. She moved over to where her father was sitting, tears streaking down her face as she spoke to him.

"Are you letting her go?" Royce asked. "We should probably question her."

Detective Campbell frowned. "A few minutes ago, she didn't matter. Make up your mind. And do you think I haven't questioned her? She's given a full report on everything she knows. She wasn't the one who found the body." He called over a female officer. "Benson, please escort Ms. Adams down to her car. She needs to inform her brother of their mother's passing and she would like to do it before the press does."

The blonde nodded and then put a hand on Miranda's shoulder. "Come on. Let's get you out of here."

At least someone was showing some compassion.

"Detective." David held out a hand. "How are the wife and kids? Last time we talked, Devon was sweating his SATs. How'd that work out?"

A genuine smile crossed the detective's face. "Top five percent of the country, Counselor. My boy's heading for the Ivies."

"Could we deal with the situation at hand? I love a good reunion as much as the next person, but I would like to know why the suspect isn't in custody." Royce had puffed up, like an overstuffed peacock trying to get the attention back. "I want the suspect cuffed and carted out of here in less than half an hour. Do I make myself clear?"

"This is my crime scene," Campbell shot back, staring the ADA down. "I understand this is a big case for you, but I don't walk into your office and tell you how to handle juries. There is something wrong with Trey Adams both physically and mentally and I will handle him as I see fit."

"And if the detective does as you ask and hauls my client out in front of that sea of press, I will have great grounds to move the trial to someplace less media obsessed," David pointed out. "I'll make sure the judge knows that the DA's office wanted to taint the jury pool."

"Taint the jury pool?" Royce asked. "By arresting a suspect? Wow, you are really digging deep, aren't you, Cormack?"

Watching the new guy stand up to Royce made her spine straighten. She was Trey's advocate. She needed to stop being emotional and get her head in the game. "I assure you a judge will not look favorably on the fact that you chose to take an incredibly famous man who is struggling with mental illness, keep him in blood-soaked clothes, and parade him in front of Manhattan's press corps, and you chose to do this knowing you are sensationalizing a crime that doesn't need any help. If you perp-walk him covered in blood, that will make the cover of every magazine in the country. No one will care about the facts of the case. That picture will seal the verdict. All you're doing is putting it in people's heads that he's a monster. And we will move for a change of venue." She looked at her new partner. "Perhaps the suburbs."

David shook his head. "Too close to the city. I was thinking upstate. Someplace rural, where they don't much care for the press and a man can get a fair trial."

She liked the way he thought.

Royce's cold eyes rolled. "Yes, that's also where the yokels think football players are gods and anyone in a suit is suspicious. Very clever." He turned to Campbell. "You make sure Adams is cleaned up after you get him through processing and take him out as quietly as possible. I want this trial happening right here in the city. I'm not having it moved because of some photos. Do I make myself clear?"

"As crystal," Campbell replied with a long sigh. "I'll start processing his clothes now. Johnson! Let's get things moving. The press will have us surrounded in a few hours."

Royce leaned in, lowering his voice as he spoke to David. "And you are here on the sufferance of my boss. The only reason you're allowed to walk in this place is because we don't want you outside talking to the press. Watch yourself. One wrong move and you'll be the one hauled out of here."

Royce moved away, marching toward the back of the house, likely to get an idea of the crime scene.

"Giant ass," Campbell said with a shake of his head. "He'll be giving a press conference before he even reads the initial reports."

"And that would be a good time to get Trey out of here," Isla pointed out. "He needs to be in a hospital, not a prison."

Campbell held up a hand. "He's not going anywhere but the station. I need to question him and I can't do it here. We'll process his clothes and body and then transport him. I'm sorry, David. You know what a football fan I am, but this isn't looking good. Adams is on some serious drugs, but we've got no signs of an intruder. They kept separate bedrooms and hers was the only room in the house that got trashed. She was killed with a knife. I won't know how many stab wounds until we get the ME report, but it was a lot. This was a rage killing, and I would bet a lot of money the person who killed her also loved her. Nothing professional or cold about this one."

David nodded. "Noah, would you please stay with Mr. Adams while they process him? I want everything documented. We'll need to move somewhere private."

"Of course." Noah followed the detective.

David turned to her, holding out a hand. "Ms. Shayne, it's good to see you again, though I hate the circumstances."

She'd met him before. Somewhere in the back of her brain she realized that, but she'd never noticed how handsome he was, how warm his eyes were or how broad his shoulders. Of course, she'd been in a deep freeze for a few years following Austin's death. She seemed to finally be coming out of it and her hormones were working overtime. But this was not the time nor the place to flirt. "Thank you for getting here quickly. Obviously I'm in over my head. I handle Mr. Adams's business and minor legal issues. I've never practiced criminal law. I hope you'll help me keep up. This family is important to me."

"What do we know? Noah wasn't able to tell me much. I can easily see the DA's office is already salivating," he said with a frown. "That might make my job easier. They're going to be impatient, and Osborne is more politician than lawyer. Speaking of getting everything in order, does Mr. Adams know he has new representation?"

"I have power of attorney in case of . . ." It felt wrong to say the words. She should be colder than this.

"In case of Portia Adams's death, you have Mr. Adams's power of attorney, so you have the legal right to retain me."

She nodded. "I'm sorry. I'll pull it together."

He reached out and put a hand on hers, squeezing slightly. "Relax. I'm here and you are no longer an attorney. You're a family friend and you've suffered a terrible shock. What can you tell me?"

"Ms. Shayne?" Noah was back and slightly out of breath, his eyes trailing to where he'd come from. "We're having trouble with Trey. He's having a hard time understanding the officers and it's upset him. I think you should come in here and try to calm him down."

She turned. She should have expected this when she'd sent Miranda out. Portia could cover for him, make him appear almost normal. Without Portia's steady hand, Isla had no idea what Trey would do. "He has trouble remembering where he is sometimes."

She walked down the hall, her heels clicking on the marble floors. David and Noah were behind her. The detective had been patient and shown some compassion, but he could only go so far. Now that Royce was here, he would have to move a bit more quickly.

"Mr. Adams, I need you to calm down," the detective was saying.

She turned and found herself in the downstairs office. It looked like they were trying to process his clothes. They'd managed to get his shirt off, but now Trey paced across the floor.

"Where is my wife?" Trey asked, his eyes bloodshot.

"Mr. Adams, if you do not comply, I'm going to have to make you comply," Campbell was saying. There were three officers surrounding Trey. All of them had their guns out.

Isla stopped, taking in the scene and the fact that there was something in Trey's hand that shouldn't be there.

Oh, god. They would kill him or he would kill himself.

"Why does my client have a gun?" David asked. He reached out as though he was going to pull her back.

If he got a hand on her, he would likely haul her away. She could already tell she was dealing with a save-the-women-and-children kind of guy. Noble, but it wouldn't solve the problem. She stepped away before he could get hold of her.

"Trey, it's me. It's Isla," she said, giving him a hint of a smile. It was all she could manage. "I need you to calm down."

"He grabbed the gun when my officer was trying to take his shirt, and don't think someone's not going down for allowing that to happen," Campbell said, his voice tight. "Ms. Shayne, you better get him on board and fast, or I will tase you and have you hauled out of here if you get too close."

Behind her, she could hear a crowd gathering. Royce was saying something about taking the problem out. She had to ignore everything but the man in front of her.

"Where's Portia?" Trey asked.

Her heart ached. She remembered when this man had been a god walking the earth. He'd been the darling boy of the Northeast and now he was ruined, his mind in tatters. "Trey, I'm sorry. Portia is dead. Please give me the gun. The police need to do their job. They have to find out who killed Portia."

Her heart was breaking because he was obviously confused. This giant of a man had been brought so low in the last few years that she couldn't imagine he could go lower, but here they were.

He stared at her, his eyes seeming to clear for a moment. "Who killed Portia?"

"We don't know. We have to find out, but her blood is on your clothes and the police need them. I need you to cooperate with them." Her voice sounded tiny in the big room, so shaky. It couldn't stand up to the tension of the place. That tension was a living, breathing thing and it felt like it was growing. She had to find a way to beat it before it burst and took down all of them. "They need your clothes as evidence."

"Isla, did I kill Portia?" Trey asked.

She could hear David Cormack curse under his breath. Oh, he might curse her name at the end of this. Royce likely had his phone out, recording everything. He would use this all against them. Every word that came out of Trey's mouth would make David's work harder.

But she couldn't think about that now. This situation was visceral, and nothing would matter if she couldn't find her way out of it. She shook her head. "No, Trey. You couldn't have hurt her. You love her. Please don't say anything else. Please."

His once handsome face grimaced in pain. He was still big and muscular, still capable of destruction. She was worried he was going to destroy himself.

"I'm nothing without her. Without her I am nothing. Nothing." The words came out of his mouth in a hard monotone.

"Ms. Shayne, please back up," Campbell said, his voice hushed. "I'm going to try to bring him down."

"Please don't hurt him." She wasn't sure his children would survive losing them both.

"I love you, Portia," Trey said.

The gun came up and chaos broke out.

Every cop in the room tensed. She watched in horror as he brought the gun to his forehead. And then she was whirling, her body twisting and turning, not of its own accord. She found herself pressed up against the wall, David's big frame covering hers, ready to take a stray bullet for her if he had to.

A loud bang crashed through the room, and David went rigid above her.

She heard shouting and then the unmistakable sound of electricity going through a body. The air around seemed to crack and fizzle as the Tasers did their job.

"He's going to be all right," David whispered. "But don't move until we're certain. I don't want you caught in some adrenaline-fueled crossfire."

"He's alive?"

"The shot went wide." David's voice was calm in the storm. "He's alive, but this is bad for us. We need to talk."

She understood exactly what he meant. Her client was alive, but the fight had begun and they were already behind.

TWO

David paced the floor of the hospital, his loafers barely making a sound. It was quiet. Too quiet. The silence in the hallway made it far too easy to hear the only sounds that anyone was paying attention to. The nurses' station was full and every eyeball was peeled to a TV monitor showing a glossy morning anchor, her perfect face solemn as she delivered the salacious story.

"According to police sources, longtime Manhattan resident and world-famous philanthropist Portia Adams was found dead in her Upper East Side apartment early this morning. She died of multiple stab wounds. Her husband of twenty-five years, former New York Guardians quarterback Trey Adams, was in the home at the time. Here is assistant district attorney Royce Osborne with an update."

He turned away. That massive ass. Osborne had done his impromptu press conference from the hospital steps. And he'd done a far better job of kissing the DA's ass than of telling the public anything they needed to know.

"Any news?" Noah looked over at the nurses' station. "Well, any news that's not being handed out by a douche canoe?"

"The doctor hasn't come out yet. It could be another hour. They're being very thorough. The detectives decided to take a lunch break," David explained. "I think it's a ploy to get us to do the same. They would love to get in there without his lawyer present. One of us needs to be here at all times."

Noah frowned, his face slightly panicked. "But what about food?"

Poor little rich boy. He pointed to the ramshackle vending machines and their nonstop offerings of stale chips and too-sweet candy. There was an ancient coffeepot that held coffee-flavored coffee, so Noah would hate that. "That's where your next meal is coming from. Buck up, buddy. Where's Isla?"

She'd ridden over with them. He wasn't sure she'd noticed but she shook for a good thirty minutes after Adams had attempted to commit suicide and nearly taken her out instead. He'd had to restrain himself or he would have reached out to hold her hand in the car.

He'd forgotten how pretty she was. Or maybe, when he met her the first time, he hadn't been ready to see her. He'd stood there in the middle of a crime scene, and all he was able to think about was how plump her lips were, how her hair brushed her breasts. He was an asshole. She was hurting and his dick was thinking of a million and one ways he could comfort her.

"On the phone," Noah replied, his shoulders sagging. "Are you sure we can't have pizza delivered or something? Maybe some Chinese. I don't think well without food and I skipped breakfast."

"I have a protein bar in my briefcase," he offered. "It's all yours."

For a second he looked like a puppy who'd been kicked and hard. "Real food is important. I need bacon and eggs and pancakes."

"Do you honestly get up every morning and cook a full breakfast?"

"Well, I don't but someone does," Noah admitted. "Usually who-ever I brought home with me, but if my sister's in town, I go to her place. The point is I'm not used to going without food that looks and tastes like food."

He stared at his young partner. "Go get a hot dog, then. I'll wait."

Noah huffed. "Jeez, and they say Henry's the intimidating one. Any idea how long they'll take? They've been in there for hours. And what exactly is wrong with him? What kind of drugs is he taking?"

The elevator doors opened and Isla stepped out. She wore a pair of faded jeans, a T-shirt, and a sweater that was far too big for her. Her hair was up in a ponytail and her face was free of makeup. She looked far too young to be an attorney, much less a high-powered one. She looked like she'd rolled out of bed and gotten dressed in a hurry.

And walked into a nightmare. He hated the fact that he would be the one to take her back to the moment when she'd found the body.

Her gaze went to the nurses' station and she flushed as she caught sight of the monitor, her jaw tightening before she turned and walked over to them.

"The news stations are broadcasting as the ME moves Portia's body," she said, her words clipped and terse. Anger was there in her eyes, but also a helplessness. "They're showing the gurney and the white sheet. Her children could be watching. How could they do that?"

She was obviously in shock or she likely wouldn't have asked the question.

"It's what the press does," he replied simply because getting angry about the press helped no one. It was a reality of life. "If we would allow them in, they would film the crime scene and do a whole report standing over the dead body. Are you all right?"

She slipped her phone into her purse and took a deep breath. "Yeah. I'm okay."

"How long has Trey Adams had CTE?"

He had his answer in an instant as she went from flushed to pale and her eyes widened. Oh, not the timeline answer, but what he'd really been looking for. Confirmation. The family knew what they were dealing with.

"CTE?" Noah asked.

"How did you know?" Isla looked around as though trying to make sure they were alone.

He could have told her no one was paying attention. They were all watching the news with the singular exception of the cop guarding the door to the room where Trey Adams was being housed. "There have been rumors for years that he left his color commentator job because he couldn't handle it mentally anymore. Oh, you've done a good job of covering, but the rumors are still there. Some people think he's addicted to drugs, likely painkillers from using them when he played, but no one's sent him to rehab, not even a quiet, private one. There are other rumors that he has early stage dementia, that he has problems with memory. But I know the truth. He has all of it. Drug problems, dementia, the whole wide range of what we call CTE. Chronic traumatic encephalopathy."

"So this a brain injury?" Noah asked.

"It's thousands of brain injuries," Isla explained. "Over the course of a professional football player's career, it's been estimated he could sustain thousands of asymptomatic subconcussive hits. These aren't the kinds of concussions that put a player on the injured reserve list. The player likely wouldn't even realize the injury had occurred. Over time, the brain injuries trigger the buildup of an abnormal protein in the brain tissue. It leads to all sorts of brain problems, and you saw a few of them today. Confusion. Memory issues. Depression. He takes a lot of meds. They help keep him calm, but they don't help him remember or control his impulses."

Impulse control. It was a serious symptom of CTE. Violent

episodes. Paranoia. Had Portia done something to upset her husband? Some minor infraction that his damaged brain built up into something worth killing over?

"He's been diagnosed?" It had been only recently that CTE was acknowledged as a problem that could affect football players and other athletes. Before the work of Dr. Bennet Omalu, who had formally identified the condition, it was known as dementia pugilistica, or in more informal terms "punch-drunk syndrome," and was thought to be confined to boxing. It was only in the last few years that a diagnosis could be made on a living brain.

"As much as we can diagnose," she replied. "He started to have trouble concentrating years ago. Even at the end of his career he was starting to show signs. We kept it quiet at first because we weren't sure what was wrong. After we were sure, Portia didn't want the press to know. It would have put a strain on him. As you can see, dealing with the press can be stressful."

He wanted to ask if she thought it was possible that Trey Adams had killed his wife, but that was one question that would never pass his lips. It didn't matter if Adams was guilty or innocent. All that mattered was putting forth the best defense possible. Typically that would mean talking to the client. He was starting to get worried he might not get to have a stable conversation with this particular client. In this case, he would have to investigate Trey Adams from the outside. He would need Isla.

In the hours since she'd nearly gotten herself killed, he'd done a bit of research on her. She'd been Trey Adams's personal attorney for years. She'd interned for the Guardians' front office to get some business experience under her belt and then gone to work for Trey straight out of Yale Law. From what he could tell, she'd become very close to Portia Adams over those years, and when Trey left the league, she left with him. She had a total of six clients, but Trey was absolutely the most important person she represented and the one she spent the most time on. She also represented two other football players, an MLB pitcher, and a famous competitive ice skater, and she handled a team owner's personal business.

She knew this family inside and out. She was going to be invaluable, but he had to make sure she trusted him.

"This is why you wanted me to get the medical records." Noah shook his head. "I thought that was weird when you asked me to do that this morning. I should have known you had a reason."

"I need to keep all our options open." Even one where he used CTE as grounds for an insanity defense. He turned back to Isla. "How many people know Trey has CTE?" He was surprised they'd managed to keep it quiet this long. From what he'd seen, Trey was pretty far along in the disease.

She bit her bottom lip and her eyes shifted as though she was counting mentally. "Not many. Maybe ten people. His medical doctors, his psychiatrist, Port . . . obviously his wife knew, and Miranda and Oscar, his kids. I'm fairly certain a couple of his old teammates know, but I don't think they talked to him about it." She took a deep breath. "Carey Kendrick."

That was interesting. "The owner of the New York Guardians knows about the diagnosis?"

She nodded. "He's not a bad man. I know he's flamboyant, but he cares about his players. Portia went to him when it first became clear something was wrong. Carey was the one who brought in the doctors. He was very concerned. I've already talked to him today. He offered to pay your fees, but Portia was careful with the money Trey made. There's more than enough for his defense."

She likely would have said more, but the door to Trey's room opened and a doctor came out.

He turned toward the doctor, determined to find out something. Anything. Noah stepped up beside him.

"Doctor?"

The white-haired doc stopped, folding a clipboard against his side. "You must be the defense attorney."

"Yes, David Cormack, and this is my associate, Noah Lawless. When can I talk to my client?"

"Doctor, when can we talk to Mr. Adams?" Osborne strode up, and David had to wonder if someone had texted him. "It's imperative that we get some information out of him. I also want a full toxicology report done. I want to know every single drug that man is on."

Noah frowned at the ADA. "You can't talk to our client without one of us in the room."

Osborne looked positively smug. "I don't know that he's your client, Lawless. I'd like to hear that from him. From what I understand, Cormack here hasn't even had a conversation with him yet. Also, he hasn't asked for an attorney, so we'll have to see about that."

Isla stepped up. "I have the right to hire representation for him. I have his power of attorney."

Osborne frowned at her. "We'll see about that. Doctor, what's wrong with Adams? How long before the drugs leave his system?"

The doctor shrugged. "I don't think it's going to be safe to let the drugs leave his system. According to the medications he's on and what his personal physician told me, that could be dangerous. He's asleep right now. When he wakes up we'll have pysch come and evaluate him."

"I need to get my forensics team in," Osborne complained. "We weren't able to finish processing him. I don't know if he's got defensive wounds or DNA under his nails."

"You can bring them in," the doctor said. "He's heavily sedated at this point. The room is large enough that you can have a witness in there as well. We've taken blood and tissue samples. I will tell you he's got some cuts on his feet, one of which was significant and needed several stitches. I don't know when it occurred. I had to suture the wound to stop the bleeding."

Osborne shook his head. "I bet you fuckers planned this. I bet you told him to pull that stunt to get the body evidence thrown out."

"I certainly didn't, but I will absolutely bring that up when we get to court." David would use anything and everything he could.

Noah picked up on his line of thinking. "How many cops hit him? You know you can't use his clothes now as evidence. They've been compromised."

"Compromised? Because officers had to put your guy on the ground? He wrestled a gun away from an officer. How many cops should I have allowed your client to murder?" Royce asked.

"He was only a danger to himself." Now, that he was not completely sure of, but he wouldn't let the ADA know.

"Or he's actually quite smart and he and his attorney planned things out this way." Osborne stared at Isla like she might grow fangs and bite him at any moment.

"What is that supposed to mean?" Isla settled her purse over her shoulder, facing down the ADA.

He nodded to someone behind David and his hand came out, gesturing for them to join the group. "It means it's time to start getting to the bottom of this. Officer, please escort Ms. Shayne to the station house. Take her out the front."

David stepped in front of her. "Excuse me? What exactly do you think you're doing? Are you arresting her? Under what charges?"

"I don't need a charge," Osborne said. "She's a material witness. She's the one who found the body, and I'm going to find out if she's the one who scrubbed evidence and made certain her client knew exactly how to get potential evidence against him thrown out. And you better hope I can't connect her to you, Cormack, or I'll have your license, too."

Isla's blue eyes had gone wide and she tried to pull away from where the officer had taken her elbow in his big hand. "If you have questions, I'll answer them. I've already talked to Detective Campbell."

Osborne shrugged. "I don't think Detective Campbell is focusing on what he needs to focus on. I don't think he's seeing the bigger picture."

"And I think you're very into crazy conspiracy theories," David shot back. "Or you want to distract me so I can't get in there with my client when the time comes."

It was right there, the impulse to drop absolutely everything and deal with her. The minute Osborne had threatened her, he'd practically forgotten she wasn't his client. He'd gone into hyperprotective mode.

He could stay here and protect his client, or he could go with Isla and protect her. Because of the state of his client's mental capacity, he could easily see Trey Adams getting confused and telling the ADA anything he wanted to hear.

Or he could block the ADA another way.

"Noah, call Henry. Have someone file an emergency motion to have Trey Adams evaluated for mental and medical competence. I want him kept out of gen pop and placed in a medical facility where they can take care of his condition."

Osborne shook his head. "I assure you the doctors at Rikers have handled drug detox before. They'll take good care of him."

"I bet they've never handled CTE," David shot back. He started to follow the officers currently dragging Isla toward the elevators. "Tell Henry to hurry. We fear not only for our client's health and well-being, but also for the well-being of those around him."

The ADA looked confused. "Are you talking about the same thing that took out Junior Seau? You telling me Trey Adams has that?"

"Yes, that is what I'm telling you, so let's can the adrenaline and calm down." He needed to lower the testosterone in the room. He also needed to get to Isla.

Osborne wasn't having it. "You're bluffing. Two minutes in and you already have a defense. I should have known you would do this.

Gentlemen, let's get down to the station, where we can have a nice chat with Ms. Shayne." He pulled out his cell. "Kenny, yeah, you're going to need to read up on everything you can about CTE. I want to know how we keep a CTE patient in with the general population and out of a psych ward. What do you mean you don't know what that is? Yes, there was a Will Smith movie about it, but that's not going to help you in legal discourse." He cursed under his breath. "No, you don't have time to fucking watch it. Get me someone else. Someone with half a damn brain."

Noah was already on the phone and had taken up a place near Adams's room. He nodded David's way, giving him obvious permission to go and meet Isla.

The cops had her at the elevator. He raced to catch up with her. The elevator doors closed before he could. He cursed under his breath and pushed the button to call another one.

And vowed to find a way to get a pizza delivered to Noah. He was going to need it.

~

Yep, this was a side of the law she hadn't meant to get closely acquainted with. She preferred the type of legal drama that required her to negotiate multimillion-dollar deals and then celebrate with champagne. She liked princess law.

This was criminal law and it smelled like stale coffee, body odor, and serious regret. Like hyper-bad-life-choices-style regret. And feet.

She found herself in a police procedural, like the ones on TV, and it was apparent she had been cast in the part of suspect for this particular episode.

She glanced up at the two-way mirror and wondered if Royce Osborne was enjoying his day. Was he planning on breaking protocol and questioning her himself?

And it was cold in here. She glanced at the clock. How was it only a bit past one in the afternoon? It should be much later. What a horrible day, and now she was alone and she would have to make things worse because she wasn't about to talk to the police without an attorney present. They'd taken her cell phone and locked her in this freezing room after parading her in front of that army of reporters.

She wiped away a tear, trying not to think about how scared she'd been as they muscled her through a sea of press. She was supposed to be tougher than this. She'd better be because they might shove her in a cell when they realized she wouldn't talk without a lawyer. Oh, she would get the whole routine—why do you need a lawyer if you haven't done anything wrong—but this was too important. She was shell-shocked. Emotional. She needed someone watching out for her rights.

At least David would take care of Trey. Maybe he would send someone down here for her. It had all happened so fast she'd barely managed to look at him before they hauled her off.

He'd been staring down Royce and looking big and manly compared to Royce's slender metro masculinity. David Cormack was solid. He looked like a man she could count on.

He reminded her a little of Austin before the disease had ravaged his body.

Naturally she would think about him today. Today she'd seen her second dead body.

She didn't want to think about that. No. Not today. She couldn't break down again. How long could they hold her? Technically they couldn't keep her in custody unless there was no other way to gain her testimony. She was willing to comply, so she might be able to argue her way out of a jail cell for the night. If she was willing to give her statement, she could argue that if they could secure her testimony by deposition, they couldn't legally detain her as a material witness. She intended to cooperate fully, but she didn't want to be taken into custody.

The door opened and Detective Campbell stepped in, followed by his partner, a woman he'd introduced as Detective Garza.

So Royce was staying behind the mirror. Coward.

She turned to the detectives. "I would like to speak with an attorney. Until I do I'm exercising my Miranda rights."

"Where'd the obnoxious one go?" Garza asked, glancing back. "The ADA's been up my backside for an hour and now he disappears?"

"He said something about coffee," Campbell replied before looking at her. "You know this is merely a witness statement. I'm not sure why you think you need an attorney, Ms. Shayne."

"Because she's far too smart to say a word in a police station without someone protecting her constitutional rights." David Cormack walked through the door carrying his briefcase and clutching a disposable cup of the aforementioned stale-smelling coffee. She'd kill for a Starbucks tall vanilla latte.

But suddenly she wasn't weary, because he was here. She couldn't help how her body seemed to relax now that he was in the room with her. Her thoughts, jangled and ragged moments before, were much clearer because David was here. How could she trust him that way in the brief time she'd known him? "Is Noah with Trey?"

David nodded as he set his briefcase down on her side of the table. "And Henry should be there by now. Our partner Margarita Reyes is drafting an emergency motion and we've found a judge who'll hear it this afternoon. She's contacted his personal physician and he's going to testify. Though, at this point, he hasn't been arrested for the murder. He has been arrested for the scene with the gun, and they do have him on a 5150 hold. But I think we can keep him in a private facility."

Unless the judge was completely heartless, Trey would likely be held at the hospital for a few days. Isla had been terrified at the thought of him being shipped out to Rikers if they arrested him. He had trouble remembering at home lately. She couldn't imagine what would happen in a chaotic, foreign environment. "Thank you. And thank you for coming. I know you can't represent me, but I appreciate you being here."

He could advise her. He could make sure she didn't say anything stupid.

"I'm looking out for you, and quite frankly, I'm ready to hear a few actual facts about the case." He looked down at his cup and frowned. "I only got one. Do you want it?"

She shook her head. "I'm fine."

He smiled and his whole face lit up. "Good, because this is the best coffee I've had in a while."

Garza shook her head. "Are you insane? That tastes like motor oil, and not new motor oil. Like the kind that's way overdue for a change."

David sighed and looked younger than before. "It's perfect."

He had horrible taste in coffee, but she was happy to see him. She turned back to the detectives. "All right. What can I help you with?"

"I'd like you to state for the record your name and relationship to the victim," Campbell said, getting down to business.

Victim. How was Portia the victim? "My name is Isla Shayne and I am the personal attorney to the Adams family. I do everything from managing their business deals to helping them find real estate for the various retail operations they're invested in to advising them on school choices for their kids. I'm a legal girl Friday."

"How did you come to be at the penthouse in the early hours of this morning?" The detective stared at her with world-weary eyes.

David stood up and shrugged out of his coat. "Here, you're shaking. It's cold in here, but I've always run a little hot."

He placed his suit coat around her shoulders and she was immediately enveloped in warmth. Some of his body heat clung to the designer coat, making it toasty and warm. And it smelled like him. She forced herself not to sniff the wool.

"Thanks," she said, turning back to the detective. "I received a call at a little after two A.M. from Miranda Adams."

"That's the victim's daughter?" Garza asked.

"Yes, she's the younger of their two children. Oscar is their son. Miranda is a junior at Columbia University and Oscar is an aspiring artist who lives in Brooklyn. I think they would say not living on the island is his way of rebelling."

David put a hand on her arm, just a pat, and she realized she was rambling.

Stick to the facts. Stay calm.

"Miranda called and told me she'd had a distressing phone call from her father. She couldn't tell what he was saying but she was worried. She asked if I would meet her at the penthouse."

"And you said this was after two this morning?" Campbell asked.

"That's easily verifiable with her phone records," David pointed out. "I assume you've already taken her phone."

She flushed. "I shouldn't have given it to them. I know that."

"You're insanely tired. You've had no food and you're practically in shock. That's what they're counting on. And that's why I'm here. To make sure this meeting doesn't go on for hours. Ms. Shayne will give an initial account, but I'm walking her out of here in an hour and I'm taking her home. She'll be available to the police again after she's slept."

Garza's eyes hardened. "Or we can arrest her as an accessory after the fact. Some people think that's exactly what happened."

She could hear Royce saying all those things.

David started to stand. "That's an entirely different conversation. We will need to obtain proper representation. Until then, she will be at her home."

Campbell held up a hand, the obvious voice of reason. "Garza, don't let that ADA get you in a froth. Can we get a timeline, please? We're all tired. I don't want to be here any more than you do. Could you please continue, Ms. Shayne? And I personally thank you for letting us examine your phone. It certainly goes a long way to make me believe you're telling me the truth."

She looked at David. She didn't want him to think she was a total idiot. "It was my personal line. I have two cell phones. One is purely business and the other is for friends and family. They would have pried my business phone out of my cold, dead hands no matter how tired I am."

"I wasn't judging."

But he should. She got back to the issue at hand. The faster she got through this, the quicker he could be out of here and back to his life. He'd had to practically hold her hand all day. She wasn't this girl. "So I got dressed and took a cab. I still have the receipt. He dropped me off at roughly two forty-five and the doorman let me in. Miranda was already waiting, but I decided to go up first."

"Why?" Garza asked. "If those were my parents, I would have gotten up there as quickly as I could."

"She's twenty and her father has health issues." Mental problems. Sometimes he didn't recognize his own daughter. Sometimes he scared Miranda. "I asked her to wait for me. I didn't want her to walk in and see something she couldn't unsee."

"Are you saying her father is violent?" Campbell sat back.

"She's already stated that Trey Adams has health issues. She's not his doctor," David said. "And I believe this interview is about what she witnessed this morning. Could we stick to that?"

The detective's disappointment was a palpable thing, but he nodded for her to continue.

"I went up in the private elevator."

"Is that locked down?" Garza asked.

"Yes, but it's not the only way in. I know there's a delivery entrance and there are stairs that connect the penthouse to the rest of the building. You'll have to talk to the doorman. When I got there the door wasn't locked and no, that's not normal. Portia is careful about security and they have a high-tech system."

"With cameras?" Campbell had a notebook out despite the fact that they were recording the interview.

"There are cameras around the building but not around the penthouse. The only thing Portia valued more than security was privacy. You'll see me before I get into the elevator and on the elevator, but once I get off, there's no tape." And she was grateful for that because what happened next was something she wasn't proud of.

"Why didn't you call the police when you realized the door was open?" Campbell asked.

David leaned in. "I thought we were dealing with the timeline, not questioning her. Again, if we're going to do that, I'll stop the process here and now and get her an attorney."

"You're acting like she's guilty, Counselor." There was no small amount of provocation in Garza's tone.

"Like I said, my clients value their privacy. I wasn't about to call in the authorities until I knew what I was dealing with. We were trying to keep his condition quiet," Isla replied. "For all I knew Trey had been out and he'd forgotten to close the door, and before you ask, yes, he did forget things. I tried calling both Trey and Portia, but I couldn't get either to answer. Again, not surprising since it was early in the morning and they should have been sleeping. I called out but it's a big place. I didn't see anything wrong until I got to the second floor."

She didn't want to talk about this. She didn't want to remember. God, how had it been less than twelve hours? It seemed like this was something that had been weighing on her forever. The world had flipped and she wasn't sure how to handle it.

"Isla, we can leave if you need to. They obviously aren't charging you with the crime and the material witness statute doesn't apply here. You're not leaving town and you're willing to talk to the police and the DA's office," David said quietly. "He's being an ass, but there's not a lot he can do here."

She shook it off. She had to get through this because she was the only one who could. No one else knew what she'd seen, could explain what had happened in those moments. "I went to Trey's bedroom first." She knew the question that was coming. It was none of their business, but Portia's precious privacy was gone, eliminated in the act of her murder. It was the sad truth of the crime. Portia would be a victim twice. Her very life had been taken from her. And then her *life* would be ripped apart, vivisected and examined by people who couldn't understand the uniqueness of how she passed her days. Every choice she'd made would now be judged, her life a measure of the way she died. All to answer the question everyone asked and no one voiced, that secret fear—did she deserve it? It was a natural thing. People blamed the victim, found a way to distance themselves so they never had to think that kind of death could come for them. "They'd had separate bedrooms for years, but it doesn't say anything about their marriage except that Trey snored."

"All right," Garza allowed. "Was Mr. Adams in his bedroom?"

She shook her head. "No, but that was when I heard something. I heard someone crying. I followed the sound. There was one lamp on, but it was in the living room. It was dark up the stairs. That was odd because there are sconces in the hallways that are usually on at night. I found my way down the hall to Portia's bedroom."

This was where everything went dark. One long breath and then another because she didn't want to be in this place, didn't want to think about or see this again.

Someone was crying. The sound was guttural and low, as though the voice that held the sorrow had been decimated. As if the soul it represented couldn't take much more. That was what she heard. The pain registered in her very ears. Isla stopped in the middle of the hall. It was dark, but there was light ahead. Portia's bedroom was open. Isla could close her eyes and see that pretty, feminine bedroom. Sometimes she would sit in there while Portia dressed, taking notes and discussing business. They would have coffee if it was morning. Tea was for the afternoon. If she happened to be there after five, wine or a martini would be served. Portia enjoyed the ritual of days and god, she so loved each holiday.

Why was her door open at this time of night? Why was that sound, that terrible sound, coming from her room? It was the sound of a wounded animal.

She knew she should be running toward that sound. If she was the person she thought she was, she should race to it, try to help, but something deep inside her, some internal instinct knew that wasn't a sound that called for help. It was a sound of death. It was beyond help. It was despair, and she would know despair if she walked into that room.

Yet she forced herself to keep going. If she didn't step into that room, Miranda would. Someone had to. Someone had to know and it couldn't be a person who didn't care. Someone from the family had to step up, to begin to chronicle how that sound had come to be.

She walked, her feet slapping against the marble floors. Every step seemed hard, but she wouldn't back down. She moved down the dark corridor and into the light. She turned into that room she knew well and she stopped.

If something could be overturned in the room, it had been. Portia's perfectly organized outer room was complete chaos. Her Theodore Alexander desk had been turned over, the drawers pulled out and tossed around like children's toys. Someone had taken a knife to her chaise. Her precious books had been pulled from their shelves and thrown out like trash.

The lights were all on. Why would they be on at this time of night?

She moved past the small living room section of the suite. Someone was sobbing. Call the police. Walk back out and let someone else deal with this.

She kept going, her feet on the plush carpet because she'd moved from marble in the hall to the luxury of the bedroom. She moved because she could do nothing less. Portia was her friend. When her own parents hadn't believed in her, Portia was there.

You don't have to marry someone to make your life meaningful. Quite the opposite. Make your life meaningful and then you'll be ready to love someone fully because you'll love yourself.

She couldn't walk away.

But that sound. It was visceral. A low cry that came from someone's soul.

"Trey?" There was a quake to her voice she wished wasn't there. She sounded like a scared child, but then she felt like one, too, because she knew this didn't end well. This didn't end in some kooky adventure where Portia had sprained her ankle because her heels were so high. This was no sitcom.

She moved past the bed. It had been slept in at some point. The silky cover was pushed back and the pillows had indentations in them. Her slippers were still on the floor as if waiting to be used, her robe draped on the edge of the bed.

She turned, the world seeming to slow. Light spilled out from the bathroom and that was when she saw it. For a moment it didn't quite register in her brain. As she stood there, she wondered how they would get that dark stain off the milky white marble. Had Portia gone crazy and decided to play around with hair dye? There was so much of it. It was almost to the carpet. Should she get some towels and sop it up?

It was blood. Some practical part of her was still thinking, still capable of reason. That was blood, so much blood that whatever body it came from had almost certainly released the soul it held.

She started at the sound of another animalistic groan.

If she stayed here, she wouldn't have to see it. If she stayed here, it wouldn't haunt her.

If she stayed here, she would be a coward.

She stepped around the blood and saw a sight that would be with her forever.

"Do you need a break?"

David's quiet question broke through her memories and she realized she'd been talking for a while. She shivered despite the warmth of the coat around her body.

The detectives were staring at her expectantly.

If she took a break, she might never come back. She shook her head. "I want to get it over with."

"You stepped into the bathroom," Garza prompted.

She had to divorce her emotions. She forced herself to look at the detective. "That was when I found Trey and Portia. He was holding her."

He had his arms wrapped around his dead wife like holding her could somehow bring her back, like she could absorb his life's energy and somehow find a way home.

"She was dead at the time?" Campbell asked.

"Oh, yes. There's no question in my mind. I couldn't see much of her because Trey wouldn't let go, but she was covered in blood." Her skin had been like the marble, contrasting starkly against the dirty, almost muddy color of the blood.

"Did you speak to him?"

She shook her head. "Not then. I . . . I turned and ran back out to the hallway. I'm not proud of it, but I threw up. There are several large potted trees on that floor. I threw up in one and then I called the police."

Campbell looked down at his file. "Our records show you called the police at 3:14 A.M. That's when 911 logged the call."

She wasn't sure of the exact time. "Okay. I'm sure that's right."

David tensed beside her and she knew something had gone wrong.

Garza glanced back at her notes. "We have the elevator log. You went up the private elevator at 2:50 A.M. Are you telling me it took you twenty-four minutes to get from the elevator to that moment when you called the police? Because that must be a very big house."

Had it taken her that long?

"This interview is over." David stood up. "Detectives, if you want more from her, call my office."

Campbell shut his notebook. "I think we have what we need for now, but we'll be in touch."

She was sure they would.

As David led her out of the interview room, a door down the hall came open and Royce stepped out.

All the way down that long hall, she could feel his eyes on her.

THREE

"You don't have to walk me up," Isla said as the car stopped in front of her building. She wanted him there, right beside her. Over the course of one day, she'd come to view the big, gorgeous lawyer as something of a teddy bear. Could she call him an emotional support attorney and take him with her everywhere? David had been smart and, beyond that, kind and patient with her.

Which was precisely why she needed to be a big girl and let him get on with his life.

It had been hours since she was released from the station. They'd gone to the hospital, where she met the other two lawyers aside from Noah in David's firm. Margarita Reyes and Henry Garrison seemed solid. Reyes had successfully argued that Trey Adams should be held in the hospital until he was well enough for a physical and psychiatric evaluation.

They'd waited for a while, hoping Trey would wake up long enough for them to speak, but he'd been heavily sedated and didn't seem like he would come out of it any time soon.

Everywhere they'd gone there were press. She'd had to fight through them at the station and the hospital. She was worried about the rest of the family. It seemed there were reporters camping out close to Miranda's apartment, but they hadn't found Oscar yet.

They would soon enough, but for now the kids were safe.

Tomorrow might be another story.

"I thought we could talk," David said. "We've avoided the subject, but there's no way we'll get around it forever. Unless you don't want to talk to me. Do you have a lawyer you prefer?"

"No, of course not," she said. "Please come upstairs. I'll tell you anything you need to know. I think I still have some lasagna leftovers."

"Food and information. What more could a man ask for?" He said something to the driver and then followed her out.

The black sedan drove off.

"Did your driver want to come up, too?" She hated the thought of the poor man driving around and around Manhattan.

"I gave him the rest of the night off. I'm only a block away from here. I can walk home." He nodded as the doorman let them in. "I believe they're going to arrest Trey in the morning. The ADA is hungry and this is a red meat case."

"They don't have any evidence."

"Not that we know of. That's kind of why I want to pick your brain." David stopped at the elevator, pressing the button to call it down. "I'm worried given Trey's state of mind and overall health that they're going to railroad this through. Is there any way he might be able to take the stand? Not that I would do it. I would prefer not to, but I have to be able to question him."

The doors opened and she followed him in, selecting her floor and watching the doors close.

"Some days he's perfectly coherent." She needed him to understand something. "He couldn't have killed her."

"It doesn't matter. I don't care if he's guilty or innocent."

"He's innocent." She knew it deep in her heart. Trey hadn't done this. She looked up at David, willing him to understand. The elevator that seemed roomy most of the time now felt the slightest bit cramped. He took up a lot of the space, but in a good way, an I'm-safe-with-this-man way.

"I'm glad he has someone who believes in him, but that's not my job." David stared down at her, but his eyes seemed kind. "I know it sounds harsh, but my job is to put on the best defense for him, to get the absolute best outcome we can given the circumstances we're in."

"And you don't think that's an innocent verdict."

He shook his head and looked back at the doors. "I think it's too soon to make any kind of call, but trying to kill himself this afternoon certainly didn't help. It's already all over the news."

The elevator opened and she led him out, pulling her keys from her bag. "I hate that the kids are hearing this on the news."

"What's their family dynamic like?" David asked. "Are they happy?"

"As any family, I suppose. But if you're asking if either of the kids had a problem with their mother, I would say no. Oscar is embarrassed by his father, but he was close to his mother."

David seemed to have stiffened beside her. "Embarrassed because of the CTE?"

She brought the keys up to the lock, deeply grateful she wasn't walking in here alone. Her hands were still shaking. Damn it.

"Allow me." David stepped up, took her keys, and swiftly had the door open. "After you."

She tried not to think about how her skin had warmed where he'd touched her, how close he was as he held open the door. She stepped inside. This was her sanctuary. At least it had been. Now she wondered how long it would be before she felt safe again. Despite what the police believed—what David probably thought—she knew Trey hadn't killed his wife. Someone had done that to Portia. Someone had snuck in and watched her while she slept and then took a knife and ended her in a viciously brutal fashion.

How long had she suffered? How much pain had she been in? Isla tried to shake it off. "I'm sorry. I'm not usually this fragile. I would have told you I was tough. I guess today proved me wrong."

"You're close to these people." David set his briefcase down on her coffee table. "You can't expect to see something like that and not fall apart. I would think you were a little cold if you didn't."

She'd done worse than falling apart. "I froze. I froze for twenty minutes. Well, when I wasn't puking my guts out. How could that have happened? How could so much time have gone by and I didn't even realize it?"

"You were in shock, but they'll use this against us if they can."

Her mind was still whirling. Ever since they'd left the police station she couldn't help but wonder why Royce seemed determined to put her in some kind of a corner. "Use it for what? To prove I was in on it? Or that I covered something up?"

She'd promised him food. She'd made that lasagna to eat for the next few days, but she could share. She moved into the kitchen.

He followed. "You wouldn't be the first attorney to help a wealthy client get away with a crime. Some people would say private lawyers are also known as excellent cleaners."

"Well, there goes my career, because I was terrible at it. If I was going to cover up his crime, why would I let the police catch him covered in his wife's blood? I at least should have made him shower." Had she done everything she should have? She'd panicked and gotten emotional. She'd known Miranda was downstairs, known she would have to be the one to tell her that her mom was gone.

"Or you're brilliant and wanted the scene as contaminated as possible." David leaned against her bar. "If I wanted to fuck things up for the police, that's what I would have done. The scene was too bloody. You have two ways to go—you clean or you use all that blood in your favor. First you ensure that the police won't be able to find the murder weapon. In this case, they think it was a chef's knife. You clean it up and hide it among the knives in the kitchen. They might find it, might not, but as long as there's no DNA, it could be hard to prove. As for the actual blood on the suspect, well, it's a reasonable thing for a man to want to hold his wife. I can argue that's where the blood came from, not the crime. Showers are iffy. If you don't get every single bit of her DNA off him, it could come back to haunt you. Then what Trey did with the police, well, that was a very physical fight. After the Taser, they tackled him good. Any injuries he had could have come from that fight. How can we know? It could be enough for reasonable doubt."

She stared at him for a moment, her skin chilling. "You honestly believe I did that?"

His face softened. "Not at all. Isla, I'm sorry if I offended you. I'm a defense lawyer. I sometimes think in very cold terms."

And that was why he was good at his job. When she was negotiating a contract, she wasn't thinking of the other side of the contract. She would go in and get absolutely everything she could for her client. "Sorry, it's been a long day. For the record, I wouldn't do that. I know there are people out there who would, but that's not me."

"I believe you, but the DA is going to use those twenty minutes against us. You said the scene was chaotic?"

She hated thinking about it, but the scene was right there. If she closed her eyes, she could see it easily. "Her bedroom had been ransacked. I got a glimpse of her closet and it was the same. It looked like whoever killed her was searching for something."

"We'll get a full accounting of everything in that room," David promised. "I assume there's an inventory."

It had been one of the first things she'd insisted on when she'd become the Adamses' attorney. She didn't want insurance to fight them in case of a loss. "We've got both a paper inventory with receipts and provenance where applicable, and a video inventory. It covers everything she had insured. All the jewelry, the art. She had a couple of designer pieces that would be considered worth a lot of money. Some of the furniture was scheduled as well. And there was cash in a safe she kept hidden, but I don't know where that safe is. They kept a good amount of cash on hand. I don't know if the kids know."

David was a large, masculine presence in her sunny, feminine kitchen. It reminded her of how long it had been since she'd invited a man into her place. "I'm sure we can find it. If we can establish something was taken, we can potentially argue that this was a burglary gone wrong. Is it possible that someone could have broken in? Would a camera have caught them?"

"I don't know. Despite the security at the front, there are always ways in. There's a back entrance that delivery people use. The service elevator goes straight to the kitchen for deliveries, and it's helpful when they would have parties. They could bring the catering staff up that way instead of parading them through the party space. But there should be a camera on that entrance, and you would need a code to get into the back door if no one was there to let you in."

"How often did they have parties?" David asked.

"Portia loved parties. Even with Trey having all his problems, she still held parties and charity events at the penthouse at least once a month or so."

"And how often would she change the pass code?"

Isla winced. "She wasn't good at that. Trey used to take care of things like that. When he became unreliable, she kind of gave up. She wasn't good at remembering things like security codes. So now we have what might be a lot of people who could have had access."

But that was a good thing. Any argument David could make that went against Trey being the only suspect was a good thing.

"All of that should be fairly easy to get our hands on. Sit down. You're exhausted. I can microwave lasagna, despite what Margarita will tell you. I can't believe she showed up at the hospital with a full meal for Noah." David stepped up to the refrigerator.

"I thought it was impressive, and Noah seemed perfectly happy." The bright and attractive lawyer had brought what she called snacks but what everyone else in the world called a three-course meal. Noah had practically melted at her feet. "It was nice that she thought about him."

And it was nice to talk about anything except the case. How long had it been since anyone was in her apartment? Much less a gorgeous, nice, intelligent man who could microwave lasagna for her. It would be even nicer if he was here for a date and not as her client's attorney.

"Margarita thinks of everyone, but Noah in particular. I like her a lot. I don't want her to get trapped in that weird web he seems to spin around women." He pulled out the baking dish that held the lasagna. "I think it's the puppy eyes. Or the billionaire brother who is quick with the cash. Was he always such a manwhore?"

"Noah? Oh, no. In school he was superquiet. He tutored Austin in computer programming and they became friends. Noah was a sweet kid." That seemed like another world. "The plates are above your head. Do you want some wine? I'm fairly certain this is one of those times when we should drink."

"Sure, I could use one," he agreed. "Do you know of any problems in their marriage?"

And they were back to the issue at hand. "Beyond the fact that he's been slowly losing his mind over the last twenty years? I know you have to ask all the questions, but I'm telling you they still loved each other. They didn't have a typical celebrity marriage. They didn't like to be apart."

He cut two slices and placed them on plates. She knew she should be the one playing the gracious host, but he was right. Exhaustion was taking its toll on her. She sipped her wine and watched him. Even through the material of his dress shirt, she could tell the man was cut. He was the all-American type. He was her type.

Yep, she was way too tired to make any kind of decision. She was hollowed out inside and searching for some solace.

He pressed the button to start the microwave. "I'm going to need you to get me a list of everyone who's spent time with both Portia and Trey in the last few weeks. Did she have a particular friend she spoke to regularly?"

"She was close to her sister. Cressy is with the kids right now." Trying to protect the privacy of Miranda and Oscar was paramount. She'd spoken to Miranda while they were waiting at the hospital, and she and Oscar were heading to their aunt's place out in the Hamptons.

"I'd love to talk to her." The microwave dinged and before long David placed a heaping plate of comfort food in front of her. "I'd also like to know if there was anything coming up in the future they might have been stressed about."

He sat down next to her, a plate in front of him. Yeah, she was going to have to rethink her meal plans for the rest of the week. He was a big guy.

"There was something she was planning for, but I wouldn't say she was stressed about it," Isla admitted. "She was excited about the party."

"Party?" He put a forkful in his mouth and his eyes closed. "This is incredible. Do you know how long it's been since I had real food? I eat takeout and drink protein shakes. You're a woman of many talents, Isla."

Ah, she'd always known the cooking thing would come in handy. Her grandmother had been all about food. "Thanks. It's an old family recipe. As to the party, I was talking about Trey's birthday. Portia was planning a huge party to celebrate. We recently signed a contract with the Four Seasons for their ballroom and she was having a mini documentary made. I hadn't seen her this excited since Trey made the Hall of Fame on his first ballot."

Blue eyes flared and he nodded enthusiastically. "Three Super Bowl rings, four-time league MVP, record holder for highest ever QB rating; damn straight he made it on the first ballot."

She sobered a bit because that had been yesterday's thinking. She had to deal with today. "Unless this scandal hurts him."

"O.J. is still enshrined in Canton," he pointed out.

"O.J. was inducted long before he was accused of murder," she replied with a sigh. "We'll have to see. You played pro ball for a few years, right?"

He nodded. "I did. I went to Harvard at the tender age of seventeen. I made the team there and got drafted to play for Seattle when I graduated. I think I'm one of the only Ivy Leaguers in the last couple of years to make it. I was solid and cheap. Played for seven seasons though I spent a lot of time on the bench the last three years and then tore my ACL. It wasn't repairable, so I got early retirement and a one-way ticket to law school. It's probably for the best. I was beat to hell by the time I made it to the pros. I played QB in high school and we had no line whatsoever. I got sacked fifty-two times over my high school career. I switched to safety in college because they thought I was too short to play QB. That year there was a dearth of talent at my position. If it had been two years later, I probably wouldn't have been drafted at all and my law career would have started a lot earlier."

He'd played. He certainly had the build for it. And he wasn't short. The man had to be six foot two. "Sorry. At one point I'm sure I would have known that. I kind of grew up around it."

"Nah, I was inconsequential."

"You made it to the pros. That's hardly inconsequential. That's the top of the world. Well, that particular world."

Though even in the pros there was a vast difference between the superstars and the men like David who'd likely made league minimum or close to it. If he'd been a second stringer, he would have made an excellent salary, but even that could be eaten away. She knew far too many players who came out of the game without much money left. Though, given his suit, she wouldn't be surprised if this man had taken care of what he'd made.

He turned to her, taking the glass of wine she offered. "Why did you ask for me? I would think you would want Henry."

Henry Garrison was known as the Monster of Manhattan when it came to defense lawyers, but someone she trusted had been very sure of who they should go with. "I contacted Carey after I called the police. He said no one would handle it better than you. I didn't ask him why at the time. I remembered that you seemed nice and competent, and I called up Noah."

"Well, I'll have to thank Carey. I'll be honest, I'm a little surprised he knows who I am." He turned serious. "I need you to be prepared. This is not going to be easy. We'll have two trials."

"The first by the press and the second in a courtroom." She'd lost her appetite but forced herself to eat something. He was right. The first battle had already begun and they were in a bad position. The press would want the most salacious story possible. Trey as the killer would bring in far better ratings than Trey the grieving husband. Once it got out that Trey was suffering from CTE, it would be difficult to convince anyone he didn't have a hand in his wife's death.

That first public excoriation would influence the second trial because it wouldn't matter where the potential jury members lived, they would have heard of Trey Adams and his wife's murder. It would be human nature to come in with preconceived notions, and the press would set those in motion.

There wouldn't be anywhere she could go, any channel she could turn on or radio station she could listen to that wouldn't be discussing and dissecting the crime. Portia and her life would be stripped down and examined to see where she'd "gone wrong."

"You're close to this family. It might be easier if you stepped back and let me investigate. I'm going to do some of it myself, but the majority of the heavy lifting will be done by my firm's investigators. We use McKay-Taggart. They're quite good at what they do."

She had the feeling he was trying to tell her something without actually saying it. "You don't want me to work with you?"

She was surprised at how much that hurt. Despite the atrocities of the day, she'd liked being around him. He was the first man in a long time she'd felt something for, and she was self-aware enough to admit that this felt like rejection.

He reached out and put a hand on hers, the sensation nearly electric. "I didn't say that. It would help enormously if you went with me on these interviews. I need to get into their world, and you're the perfect one to guide me around, but this will get nasty. Some of the people we contact won't want to talk to us. The family will start to take sides, and that's when the nasty surprises arrive. You might find out things you'd rather you didn't know. Every marriage has its secrets, and I'm giving you the chance to not have to live with that knowledge. You could stay with the kids and advise them and start to shift the company and assets over to them for a smooth transition. You could isolate yourself so you only have to deal with the press when it's totally necessary."

Was he really giving her an out because he thought she could get hurt? Was he trying to treat her like he would one of his clients' family members? Or was he thinking his life would be way easier without the girl who knew nothing about criminal law trailing after him?

"I'm only trying to spare you pain, Isla," he explained. "This could get messy and you're intimately involved. I meant what I said. You would be marvelous at easing my way. You know this world in a way I don't, but I can work with all of that if it makes your life a little easier."

"I'm not some delicate flower." She didn't like the idea of him thinking she was fragile. She'd been keeping up. It was a terrible day and she was still standing.

He pulled his hand back, leaning away from her. "Again, I didn't say that."

She missed the warmth of his hand on hers. "I don't want to drag you down, but I also don't want to be left out. You're right. I know their world better than anyone else. People will talk to me. Trey can't help you. I owe it to Portia to do this. If you think I can't handle it, you're wrong."

He stood up, taking his empty plate to the sink. "I never said you couldn't handle it. I said maybe you shouldn't."

She was too emotional and she wasn't listening to him. The last thing she wanted to do was annoy the man she'd brought in to save Trey. "Can I sleep on it? I'm making this far too personal. I think I want to be involved. I think it would be hard for me not to be, but I shouldn't make any kind of decision today. Tonight. God, it's been a long day."

"Of course." He was quiet while he washed off his plate and placed it in the sink. "Do you have anyone you can call?"

"Call?"

He looked back at her as though trying to decide if he should pursue his line of thought. "I don't think you should be alone tonight."

She hadn't even thought about it. What would happen when she was alone again? When she closed the door behind him and she had to think about everything? Right now she was running on adrenaline and it was easy to put things out of her mind, but when she was all by herself and the place was silent, would she hear that cry again?

Tears immediately sprang to her eyes. Damn it. She'd held it together all day. "I don't . . . I work. I work all the time. My parents are gone. I don't have anyone."

Austin was gone. She'd dealt with that though. That had happened long ago. It wasn't affecting her now. Was it?

It struck her forcibly that she'd shut down all those years ago, shut out people who might have offered her friendship or more because she'd watched Austin die. She'd loved him and he was gone, and she hadn't truly lived since that moment. She wasn't in love with him anymore. It had been too many years and they'd been children, but his death was still holding her back. She'd buried herself in work and held herself apart. She'd gotten involved in her clients' lives because she didn't have one of her own. It was easier to care about them, to find a way to make herself a part of their families because they were safe.

Except they hadn't been safe. Her "safe" family had blown apart over the course of a single day and she was alone again.

"Hey, it's going to be okay." He started to move toward her.

She backed away. "Don't. If you touch me, I'm going to fall apart."

His face softened, a fact that didn't make him any less manly. The truth was he'd shown his compassion over and over that day, and it had drawn her in like nothing else could have. "Would that be so bad? I've found you can't put yourself back together properly until you've fallen apart."

"You don't even know me." Though it sounded a lot like he did.

"I know you're kind. I know you're hurting and I know you're human. If you want to talk, I'm here. What you've been through—

only a few people in the world know the horror of having to see a scene like that. It affects us all even if we have no idea who the victim is. If you care about the victim, well, it changes everything. Don't feel bad. Why don't you go and take a shower? Cry there if you can't do it out here with me. Let it out and you'll feel better. Your head will be clearer. If it's all right with you, I'll bake those place-and-bake cookies I saw in the fridge and when you're ready, we can work on a schedule for tomorrow."

She wanted nothing more than to walk up to him, have him open his arms, and wrap herself around him. Something about David Cormack was solid and safe. But she couldn't give in to the instinct. He would view her differently, see her as something less. Most men in her profession did. "I will take you up on the shower. And thanks for staying for a while."

He nodded but there was almost a sense of disappointment coming from him. Still, he gave her a half smile. "It's only eight o'clock. I'm typically a night owl. Besides, you have way more in your fridge than I do. Do you mind if I make those cookies?"

"I can do you one better. I baked peanut butter bars last night. They're in the container by the fridge." She frowned. This could be a deal breaker for their future partnership. She wasn't sure she could work with a nonaddict. "Unless you don't like peanut butter."

"I love peanut butter. It's one of my favorite things in the world." He'd already turned to go back to the kitchen.

Well, it was easy to see how to get to that attorney. Feed him. And by *partnership* she meant that in a work way. Not in an every-time-he-touches-me-my-skin-comes-alive way. Not that way at all. Besides, he was only being kind to her. He hadn't shown one drop of physical attraction, and that was a good thing because this wasn't the time to have feelings for someone.

She closed the door to her bedroom behind her, thankful he was still there.

One righteously hot shower later and she still couldn't cry. She'd stood there, hot water flowing, and she hadn't been able to summon a single tear. They'd been right there all day long and when she could finally let them flow—nothing. It was odd, but she'd wanted what David had promised her. If she gave up the waterworks, maybe her chest wouldn't feel so tight. Maybe she wouldn't feel as heavy as she was now. Grief weighed her down, and not in that incidental way that came later. This was a road she'd been down before. Later, the grief would be a sweater she wore—easy to forget when the temperature was right, easy to remember when she got too warm but couldn't take it off. No, this was a smothering blanket that covered every inch of her body. She felt numb, and maybe that was okay for now. All that mattered was breathing.

She put on a pair of pajama pants and a tank top and left her bedroom to talk to David. It wasn't fair to keep him here no matter how much she wanted him. Here. In the apartment. Because she didn't want to be alone. That was all.

She would let him know she wanted to work on the case, make plans to meet with him in the morning, and then let the poor man go home. By tomorrow he would realize that this day was a one-off and she could be a professional. After some sleep, she would be back on her feet and ready to be the tough lawyer she was.

Stepping out of her bedroom, she heard the news playing softly in the background. A woman was speaking. Isla moved into the living room. David sat on the couch, leaning forward, his focus on the television in front of him. A picture of a young Portia floated across the screen, followed by others. Some Isla had seen before, others must have been sent in by Portia's friends and the designers and photographers she'd worked with over the years. It wouldn't be hard to put together a video montage of a woman as famous and photographed as Portia.

Portia Adams was a figure in her community. Emigrating from her

*native England as a teen, she rapidly became a staple of New York Fashion
Week and she parlayed that fame into a decades-long career where she
championed body positivity in the modeling field. She once famously refused
to work with a designer who wouldn't consider a plus-sized line. She married quarterback Trey Adams at the age of twenty-five and together they
built a foundation that serves New York City's children. From sponsoring
intramural sports leagues to housing the homeless to funding STEM classes,
Portia Adams used her money and her celebrity to make the world a better
place. She is survived by her husband and two children and a world that
will miss her.*

Isla stopped, the simple words of the reporter gutting her in a
way all the salacious reporting never could. Portia was gone. Trey
was lost.

It wasn't fair. They'd only had twenty-five years together. It wasn't
enough. They should have had a lifetime. A lifetime of health, of
love, of time to do the things they'd been born to do.

Tears came, her numbness gone in a storm of pure sorrow. It
wasn't fair. Portia had been kind. She'd done everything right and
some animal had taken her apart like she meant nothing. Someone
had walked in and ruined everything, and now those kids had to go
on without a mom and Trey would be alone, lost in his head without
Portia's steady hand to pull him back out.

David stood up, turning to her. "I'm sorry. I wanted to get an
idea of what the press was saying."

She shook her head. It didn't matter. She knew she should turn
away, go back to the bedroom and collect herself. She couldn't let
him see how broken she was.

"Isla, it's okay," he said, his voice a little shaky. "It's okay to mourn.
It's all right to cry for them. They deserve your tears."

All she had to do was take one step forward and lift her arms and
he was suddenly there. Big strong arms wrapped around her.

"It's going to be okay," he whispered. "You're going to be okay.

Maybe not tomorrow or the day after, but I promise you'll get through this."

She sobbed, clutching him as though he was the only thing real in the world.

~

David felt his heart break a little as she wrapped her arms around him. All day he'd watched her, saw how she held herself together in the face of all that pain. When he'd walked up here, he knew that he wouldn't leave unless she had someone she could call, someone to watch over her this first night.

And damn him but he'd been happy she hadn't.

He was a bastard for that reaction, but he didn't want to leave her. He acknowledged that he wanted to be the one holding her. Like he'd wanted to be the one to feed her. It had only been the easy task of heating up something she'd already made, but in that moment, he needed to do it.

He moved until he was able to sink back into the sofa, taking her with him. She was sobbing against his shoulder, her tears making his shirt wet, but all that mattered was that she was finally getting some relief. And that she trusted him enough to let him comfort her.

If there was one thing he'd learned over the course of the day, it was that Isla Shayne was a woman he wanted to know, wanted to be close to. It had taken every good instinct he had to tell her she didn't have to help with the case. He'd thought about it the whole long while they sat together at the hospital, waiting and hoping to speak with Trey. He'd thought about how emotional the case would be, how personal it was to her. He'd weighed it against the fact that all he wanted was to keep her close. Somewhere deep down he'd decided that the case could be a reason to stay near her. It was much more simple than asking her out and trying the dating thing. He could be near her every day for months and months at a time. This kind of case could turn into a 24-7 job and she would be there the whole time. It would be damn near impossible to not get to know her.

But he'd seen her sorrow and known he had to give her an out.

Maybe she wouldn't take it. Maybe she would trust him enough to know he would take care of her.

He sat there on the couch, stroking her hair and feeling closer to her than he had to any human being in a very long time. He'd missed this, missed being needed in a physical way. She wasn't asking for sex, but there was a deep intimacy in what they were doing.

"I was scared," she whispered when the sobs finally died down. "I hate that my first reaction was fear."

She was being far too hard on herself. He sighed, breathing in her scent. Her hair smelled like citrus. Even when he'd sat with her in the gloom of the police station, there was a light about her. "You're human. I would have been afraid, too. And I would have thrown up."

She shook her head and moved back a little so he could see her face. "You would not have. I'm sure you've seen terrible things in your time."

She didn't cry pretty and yet her emotion made her all the more lovely in his eyes. Her face was red, her eyes swollen, but it was the pure portrait of a woman who felt things deeply. He couldn't help himself. He stroked back her hair. "I threw up on national television once. It was during the playoffs and I tackled a guy coming at me. I hit him just right and his leg snapped and there was a bone coming out and I lost it. It was one of the last games I played. I still hate the fact that I caused that injury even though the guy is a good friend of mine and doesn't blame me. Seeing something that visceral, hearing the pain in someone's voice and knowing there's nothing you can do, is one of the roughest things you'll ever go through."

She winced. "I remember that. I was working with the Guardians at the time and the guys would watch it in the media room over and over again. I even remember them laughing about the guy who threw up. I can't believe that was you. I thought they were horrible for laughing about it."

This he could explain to her. "Guys are different. Especially athletes. We either laugh at it or we get scared of what could happen. It's better to laugh. It's a rough business. We do what we have to in order to survive."

"I still think it was mean." She almost laid her head back down, but she pulled back at the last minute. "I should get off you. I'm sorry."

He pulled her closer. "Don't. Not unless you truly want to. I had a rough day, too. This is the best I've felt all day."

She sighed, a weary sound, but she cuddled close to him. "I know I shouldn't do this, but it feels right."

It was right. He knew that deep in his gut. Isla might be right for him, but he wasn't going to push it. "It does."

"This isn't just about what happened today," she admitted quietly. "I was with Austin when he passed. I was holding his hand and I swear I felt the moment he died. Seeing Trey like that brought me back to the moment. I'm not pining over him. I loved him and I processed the loss a long time ago, but in that moment it felt fresh, like it had been ripped open again. Now that I think about it, I feel selfish. I was thinking about me."

Almost like he'd felt when he'd lost Lynn. He hadn't been in love with his wife at the end. Too much had gone on between them, but when she died, he'd mourned what she represented—his youth, a hoped-for family, the light she'd had back then. "It's okay. Whatever you felt in that moment wasn't selfish. It was real. Isla, you have to stop trying to be a rock. If you really want to work with me on this, you'll have to promise me you won't bottle it all up."

"So you expect me to cry a lot. I'll try not to. I'll be professional most of the time. And I do want to work with you." She yawned, covering her mouth with her free hand.

"I want to work with you, too." He didn't say the rest of what he wanted to say. It was there in the fact that she'd stopped crying and they were still sitting here. He wanted to see where this would go. He wanted to follow the thread he'd found today and find out if it led all the way back to her.

"Good." She went silent.

They sat that way for a while, their arms around each other, chest to chest. And then her breathing turned rhythmic and deep and he knew he had to put her to bed. He didn't want to but he doubted he could sleep like this. He stood, moving back toward her bedroom.

She didn't wake as he walked carefully to the bed. She was a sweet weight in his arms and he thought about the fact that he hadn't carried a woman like this, not ever. He wanted to make the moment last, but he laid her gently on the bed.

Her eyes came open, looking up at him, innocent and wide. "Please stay, David. Not on the couch. Stay here with me."

She wasn't asking for anything physical. She was tired and likely wouldn't sleep without the comfort of another body in bed with hers. The events of the day weighed on her and she looked like some of the victims of violent crimes he'd met. Haunted. Afraid that nothing would be normal again.

He made his decision in that moment. "I'll stay."

He might not be able to leave her again.

FOUR

David shifted and sighed, a shaft of sunlight crossing his face. Something smelled so good. Actually it was a couple of smells, like layers of goodness. First there was the scent of flowers and citrus. It clung to the sheets and the comforter. And then there was that other smell. The one that always got him excited, the one that made him sit up in bed.

Bacon. Someone was cooking bacon.

Okay. He wasn't in his own bed. Nope. His sheets smelled like whatever bland industrial detergent the cleaners who did his laundry used. And they weren't as satiny soft, and his bedroom wasn't a frothy confection of feminine comfort.

And no one cooked bacon for him.

Isla. God, he'd ended up in Isla's bed. Of course, he was also fully dressed. Well, he was still wearing his undershirt and slacks. He'd even kept his belt on, but he'd slept with her slender body wrapped around his, her head on his chest most of the night.

She'd been lost after she heard that tribute to her boss on the news. All her carefully placed walls had dropped, and he had been left with the soft, caring woman she was, and it floored him how much he felt for her.

He hadn't felt much for anyone or anything since Lynn had passed. They had that in common. They'd both lost someone.

Not that she knew that. He was almost ready to talk about his wife when he'd felt her sag against him, her body going slack.

Please stay, David. Not on the couch. Stay here with me.

He'd gone and made sure her door was locked. Checked in on his parents. Did the dishes and cleaned up the kitchen. And then he'd climbed into bed beside her. He'd left his clothes on because he didn't want her to think he expected anything from her.

She'd rolled over and sighed, and wrapped herself around him like he was a teddy bear and she needed comfort.

Oh, he wanted to give her more. Isla Shayne had gotten to him. She'd gotten to him in a way no woman had in years. He'd dated since Lynn had died. He had a healthy sex life, but he hadn't wanted a woman with a singular passion. He'd wanted sex. He liked the women he'd dated and the sex flowed from that.

He wanted Isla and he was damn glad she wasn't still in bed because she might have noticed that he'd woken up with a terrible erection.

Damn it. She was hurting and he was an asshole because he couldn't control his own dick. And an asshole because he admitted to himself that it felt good to want someone. The last few years had been about work and nothing else. He'd welcomed it because sex had become a biological function. What he wanted from her was something more.

But she'd lost her family the day before.

And she was younger than him. Not by much in years, but she was lovely and young in spirit. She wasn't covered in scars and held back by a knee that never quite stopped aching.

She wasn't facing the chance that her brain would deteriorate like his might from a thousand hits he'd taken since he was a kid in a youth football league.

What were the words from yesterday? Damn it. He'd forgotten to do it. Noah had hauled him out of his apartment before he'd done his daily memory exercises. What were the Friday words?

Mockingbird. Jalopy. Bottle.

It was a silly thing, but he did it every day. He started the morning with three random cards, each with a picture and a word. At the end of the day, he wrote down the three words he'd read at the beginning. At the end of the week, he tried to remember as many as possible.

He did sudoku, crosswords, anything to keep his brain working.

Anything to put off the time when he had to take that test to see if he would be one of the 28 percent of all pro players who succumbed to CTE.

Well, it was good to know he had an off switch. His erection was completely gone. It was damn good to remind himself of the real reason he should stay away from Isla Shayne. Beyond the fact that they'd just met and under terrible circumstances, more than keeping up a wall of professionalism because they would be working together, he could be a walking time bomb waiting to blow up her whole world.

A feminine laugh floated in from the kitchen. He liked the way she laughed. She was unselfconscious and . . . was that a snort? It was cute on her. What was she laughing at? Had she turned on the TV so she didn't have to deal with silence? Or was she on the phone with a friend who was lifting her spirits?

Was the friend a guy?

Nope. He wasn't going there because there was no relationship between them. He wouldn't get jealous because that was illogical.

He told himself that as he used her bathroom. As he went about washing his face and trying to get his hair under control, he decided he would thank her for dinner the night before, sit down, and decide on the schedule for the day. They would need to go by the hospital and see if they could get anything out of Trey. Hopefully the initial police report had been finalized. They would need to make some kind of statement to the press from the family. He would get Margarita on that. She knew some seriously good PR people.

What he wouldn't do was walk out and put his arms around her again. He wouldn't hug her and breathe her in like oxygen. He definitely wouldn't kiss her. He would do his job and get out of her hair.

And be deeply grateful that no one knew he'd spent the night with the client. He would catch such hell.

He stepped out of the bathroom and heard her laugh again. Maybe it would be easier to leave if she had a smile on her face.

"That was when I realized the prosecutor was the woman I'd slept with the night before and, dude, she was pissed. I might have slipped out of her bed and not left a note," a familiar voice said.

"You are terrible," Isla shot back, but there was sunshine in her tone.

"In my defense, I thought she was a model," Noah replied. "She looked like a model. She pretty much had the brains of one. She did not look like an ADA who would hold a mean grudge. How was I supposed to know?"

"Well, first off, models aren't stupid. Stereotypical much? And second, you should have known the name of the ADA you were going up against." She sounded prim and proper in her admonishment.

Noah sighed, a guilty sound. "Yeah, I did, but I didn't actually catch *her* name. It was loud in that club."

"Ewww, it's no wonder you have the worst reputation. You're lucky you're cute."

Some dark instinct flared inside him and he found himself suddenly in her kitchen staring at the younger man. Cute? No one ever accused David of being cute. Was cute what did it for Isla? "Cute won't stop syphilis. What the hell are you doing here, Noah?"

Noah put a hand on his chest as though his heart hurt. "Syphilis? Couldn't I get something that sounds more youthful?"

"I don't know. Are there millennial-specific venereal diseases?" It irritated him wildly that Noah was sitting there. He was wearing a perfectly pressed suit, looking exactly like a young, professional lawyer who also happened to have a billion dollars at his fingertips.

"I'm sure Señor Sarcasm would have a comeback for that," Noah replied, a slightly confused look on his face, as though he knew something was wrong, but couldn't quite figure it out.

"Live-at-home-itis," Isla offered helpfully. "Or in Noah's case, Live-off-big-brother-itis."

Noah flushed, the first time David had ever seen him go that shade of pink. "Hey . . . all right, it's fitting. I can't help it. My brother is extremely pushy when it comes to us not living on the streets. I offered to go one hundred percent vagrant, but Drew said no."

"Why are you here?" Had Noah decided to renew his old friendship with Isla once he'd gotten a look at her? Had he seen how gorgeous she'd turned out and decided she would be his next one-night stand? Because they would have a long talk about that.

"Would you like some coffee?" Isla stared up at him, a quizzical look on her pretty face. She was holding a mug in her hand. She was also still dressed for bed. Her legs were covered in the pj bottoms she'd worn the night before and she wore a tank top that barely covered her breasts. She'd put on a bra but they were still beautifully on display, as was the long, graceful line of her neck. Her honey-brown hair was piled on top of her head. She looked sweet and soft and so sexy it made him ache. "Do you want cream and sugar?"

He took the mug from her. "Thank you. I appreciate it."

"It's my favorite, French vanilla biscotti," she said with a smile.

Noah's eyes widened. "Oh, hey, one of the things you should know about David . . ."

Damn it. He was not going to let that satisfied smile on her face get ruined by Noah. He hated flavored coffee. Flavored coffees were horrible, the single worst invention since someone thought, *Hey, let's put a set of circular escalator steps on an endless rotation and call it a stair stepper*. He hated that thing, too. But he hated the thought of hurting her more. "David loves vanilla. Loves it. Especially in his coffee." He took a sip. Yep, that was flavored coffee. He forced a smile on his lips. "So good. That hits the spot. Thank you."

He swallowed that sucker. No spitting it out.

Noah stared at him. "Are you serious?"

"I'm very serious about coffee," he replied.

Noah was the one laughing now, and he definitely got in a snort or two. "I did not see that coming."

David sent him the look he used to send players across the line from him, the one that said he was coming to get them and they should back the fuck off.

Noah's hands went up in the universal symbol for *I surrender*. "Hey, I get it. And I am here because you're here. Henry called a team meeting but you didn't answer your phone, so we decided to bring the meeting to you. We were lucky that address turned out to be Isla's and not some random hooker you picked up for the night."

"I've never picked up a hooker." Though he had thought a hooker was a fan once at a championship game party. He'd ended up paying for that mistake. Literally.

"That's good to know." The sexiest smile curled up her lips as she tipped her coffee mug back. "I don't pick up hookers either."

The nasty taste in his mouth was worth that smile. But he had another question. He turned to Noah. "How the hell did you know where I was?"

Noah's smile faded. "Would you believe I'm a touch psychic?"

Son of a bitch. Well, he'd known Noah used to be a hacker, and it couldn't possibly hurt that his brother's firm wrote the software all their phones ran on. "You put a trace on my phone."

He shrugged. "Yours. Henry's. Win's for Henry. Margarita's. All my siblings and in-laws. I have issues with people disappearing on me so I keep tabs on you all. You're boring actually." He looked back to Isla. "The most interesting place I've caught him at was a strip club on Fourth, but it turns out Sneaky Cheeks was the place of employment of one Lula Linoleum. Not her real name."

"Her real name was Harvey Stone." Now it was his turn to blush a little. Not that he wasn't proud of his work. "Lula's trans. She got arrested protesting. Her mother is a friend of my mother's, and that's how I ended up representing her."

She totally went gooey on him. "Really? I thought you were some high-powered, take-only-the-most-money kind of lawyer."

He chuckled. Most people thought of him as a bloodsucking predator and not the champion of the underdog. He could be both. "I make plenty of money."

Noah was off his seat, a hand on his shoulder. "But he's also known as the softy. Once he'd repped Lula, he became the lawyer everyone at Sneaky Cheeks called when they got in trouble. And then there was the actual vagrant he repped."

"He was a homeless vet who got accused of robbery. It was a case of false witness identification. He looked a lot like the actual perp and he was an easy target," David explained.

"You take care of the underdog." She said the words like they did something for her.

Pro bono got her hot? "I will admit to using the money I make from high-powered clients to fund some of my other work."

"Heart of gold, this one," Noah said with a nod.

"Who's got a heart of gold?" Henry strode in, carrying a shopping bag. His eyes found David's. "Are we talking about the fact that

Bleeding Heart there can't handle a sob story? It's sad. I swear we have a never-ending line of sad sacks on pilgrimage to my upscale office."

"Henry?" Win was behind him.

Henry stopped, his face in a grimace. "I meant I love all the good work David does. The smell doesn't bother me at all. It's the smell of social justice."

"Forgive my husband," Win Garrison said with a shake of her head. "He's a helpless snob. But David is kind of awesome when it comes to helping the helpless. We got the pancake mix, Isla. Let me help you out. That bacon smells heavenly. You cook it in the oven?"

"I do. I find it cooks more evenly and makes way less of a mess. I'll show you. It's supereasy." Isla glanced his way. "I hope you don't mind. They showed up about thirty minutes ago. I didn't have enough pancake mix, but apparently your partners really like breakfast."

And being supernosy. There was no way Noah hadn't figured out this was Isla's building and so he and Henry had shown up to investigate. "It's okay. It's probably good that we're all together. I should be apologizing to you for my nosy friends invading your apartment."

"I don't mind. It's good to have something to concentrate on, and I love to cook. I usually do it for one. Having people to feed makes me happy. And thank you, David. Thank you for last night. You are a kind man."

Yep. Kind was not what he wanted to be known for with her. "You're welcome."

She turned and moved back into the kitchen with Win. He stayed in the living room with Henry and Noah.

"Turns out Win knows Isla pretty well," Henry said. "I couldn't leave her at home. They met on the charity circuit and Win likes her a lot." He gestured to Noah. "Weirdo over here keeps tabs on all of us, so we knew where to go. Was a little surprised you stayed the night."

"And didn't sleep on the couch," Noah pointed out. "I happen to know this is a one bedroom, so unless she stuffed you in a closet somewhere . . ."

"Can we discuss the fact that Noah invaded all of our privacy?" What the hell was happening?

Henry shook his head. "Nah, he's got childhood issues, and honestly, isn't it good that someone out there knows where we are in case, say, a murderer decides to chase one of us down and we almost float away in the ocean? Besides, I don't go anywhere interesting and it is kind of cool to see the app he built for it. It's got little avatars and everything. You can watch yourself fly slowly across the screen."

So Henry still had PTSD when it came to what had almost happened to Win. It likely wasn't a good time to point out that Win hadn't had her phone that terrible night and Henry definitely hadn't been in a smart enough headspace to have tracked her by it. "Fine. I did spend the night, but these clothes stayed on. I stayed here last night because Isla was having some trouble processing. She found the body."

Henry grimaced. "That was a hell of a scene. I brought you some of the paperwork and the crime scene photos. Don't ask how I got them. I have my sources. I haven't managed to get the autopsy report, but they might not have started yet. It's still early. They'll have to give them to us soon anyway. If they don't arrest Trey Adams for this within forty-eight hours, I'll eat my hat."

"You don't wear a hat," he murmured, taking the file. He moved more firmly into the living room where Isla and Win wouldn't be able to hear them. They were tough, strong women, but they knew the victim and they would have to dive into this soon enough.

"I'll buy one and then eat it," Henry replied. "This does not look good for your guy. Did you know about the CTE?"

He sighed. "When did that get out?"

"They were talking about it on SportsCenter early this morning.

They had a roundtable and it was the first thing they talked about. One of his old teammates brought it up." Henry sank down into one of her comfy chairs. "It was inevitable that someone would ask the question. I actually think this is a good thing."

"If I go with a mental disorder plea." He opened the folder and immediately wanted to close it again. It wasn't that he had a weak stomach. This wasn't his first murder case. But he couldn't help looking at the photos and thinking that Isla had seen this live and in person. She'd walked into that scene, into a place where she'd likely been comfortable, and she would never see that room the same way again. That lovely queen suite had been turned into a killing field, and Isla had witnessed the outcome.

So much blood.

"Tell me you're going with mental disorder," Henry said, staring at him with dark eyes.

"I don't know."

"David, the man tried to kill himself in front of a bunch of cops, and if you don't think they can twist that and make it look like he was trying to take a few of them out when he went, you're not thinking straight," Henry explained.

"That's a separate charge."

"Excellent. We're running up a hefty tab here." Henry sat back, studying him carefully. Sometimes when Henry's eyes narrowed, his focus closing in, David thought he knew what it meant to be a bug pinned down and examined by a curious scientist. "You're the one who asked for the emergency motion on his mental health."

"I'm trying to keep him out of jail. I don't think he'll do well there. And where are we on that front? I got a message late last night that they still hadn't done the eval." He wouldn't feel comfortable with Adams behind bars with the general population of a prison. All it would take was one asshole who hated the Guardians to start something serious. The last thing they needed was Trey getting involved in a prison beatdown.

"I think our best bet is to get that eval, and if he's crazy pants, we cut a deal as fast as we can," Henry said.

He'd known that would be Henry's advice. This case was the kind that would do their firm a world of good if it went to trial. It would put their faces on TV every night. It would get them incredible press coverage. It would put them on the map.

But going to trial might not be the best thing for the client. Especially a mentally ill client who couldn't defend himself properly.

And despite all the lawyer jokes and Henry's moniker, their first job was to do right by their clients.

But what if the client was innocent? Didn't a mentally ill man deserve some kind of trial? Of course, all that might be a moot point. "I don't know the DA's office is going to bargain on this one."

"We need to paint Trey as sympathetically as possible," Noah added. "They can't want to put a mentally ill former football hero on trial."

"For killing his wife? I assure you they can and they will. There are about a million political reasons for them to want this trial," David pointed out. "They can look good because they're not giving a rich white celebrity any more privilege. They can represent this like they're coming out hard against domestic violence. In this climate, this case could check off a lot of boxes for a man looking to run for higher office."

"We have to squeeze him." Henry paced, a thing he always did when considering a problem. "We have to get the public on Trey's side, and we use the CTE to do it. He's a wounded warrior. The DA is the monster here for not seeing he was out of control and needs professional help."

He needed to get control of this and fast. "You know simply

because he has CTE doesn't mean he committed the crime. I haven't even talked to him yet. I know what it looks like. I know what the police are likely to do, but we've got some time to figure this out. I'm going to take it. I don't care what the press has to say about it. I'm taking my time and doing this right."

Henry sat down, crossing one long leg over the opposite knee. "If you don't go with mental disorder, what do you go with?"

He held up a crime scene photo. It was one of the less bloody pictures. It showed the scene of the chaos that was the victim's bedroom. "I seriously doubt the victim routinely kept her room in this state. Our perp was looking for something and they were serious about finding it."

"Or Trey Adams found out his wife was having an affair and he lost his shit," Henry replied.

"Not according to Isla." He could still hear her talking about how perfect their marriage was. Well, not perfect, but loving and true. "Portia stood beside him even as his mental health deteriorated. Again, I haven't investigated, but Isla seemed quite certain."

"Given what I read about CTE last night, he would likely have suffered from paranoia," Noah said. "She could have been perfectly faithful, but if those voices in his head started talking, he might not listen to her at all. Early onset dementia is one of the outcomes. The question is, does the family want this thing to go to trial?"

He thought they were moving too fast. "Can I talk to my client first?"

"Is he truly your client? Isla's got power of attorney," Henry pointed out.

"She's not the client. Trey is." For some reason he needed to make that plain. He didn't want to put her in a position where she had to choose between putting up a defense for her employer or sparing his kids a lengthy and expensive trial where the outcome was uncertain.

And there might be other reasons he didn't want to go into.

Henry looked at Noah, his brows high.

"You want to know the truth?" Noah asked.

Henry's lips curled up slightly. "Can I handle the truth?"

"Watch this," Noah said before turning to David. He leaned in. He gestured toward the kitchen. "Dibs."

Was Noah Lawless actually calling dibs? Like they were fucking teenagers? And why did David suddenly want to throttle him? He knew Noah was trying to goad him but the kid was annoying as shit sometimes. He should mind his own business and keep his hands off . . .

"Whoa, I've never seen him turn that shade of red before," Henry was saying. "And I've known him a long time. We used to drink together in college. That's a serious red."

"I've never seen him drink French vanilla coffee before and claim to love it," Noah replied.

"Seriously?" Henry's jaw was hanging open. "He actually drank coffee that wouldn't grow hair on his chest?"

"Are you both twelve? First of all, we're supposed to be discussing a murder trial. You two are acting like gossiping high school girls. And secondly, dibs? You know she's a human being, right? You can't call dibs on her." David was well aware he was getting backed into a corner.

"How else do we decide who gets to go after the girl?" Noah asked, his eyes perfectly innocent. "We could rock, paper, scissors for her."

"She's a woman, not a girl, and how about I just shoot you and the problem is solved," he said before he could think.

"Shit," Henry said.

Shit was right. If he didn't watch himself, he would get taken off this case, and all for no reason. "I'm not going to do anything about it."

"And I'm not calling dibs," Noah said, more sober now. "Not

really. She's an old friend. I was merely pointing out the obvious. If it helps at all, I think you could be good for her. She's been alone for a long time."

"And technically she's not the client." Henry sighed. "Not that I should talk since I married a woman who technically wasn't the client, but she absolutely was the client. But, David, there are things you need to think about. This woman could be in serious trouble. There's rumbling at the DA's office that she could be charged as an accessory after the fact."

They were moving quickly if they were already talking about a charge like that when they hadn't technically arrested Trey for the murder. "She didn't do anything."

Henry winced. "Let's look into getting her an attorney just in case."

His stomach knotted at the thought of someone coming to arrest her. He had to make Henry understand. "I'm telling you that she didn't do anything."

"For twenty whole minutes," Henry said gravely. "That's a long time to not do something."

"She panicked." Noah shook his head. "I would have panicked, too. That kind of loss of time is normal for people in a state of shock. I can get twelve forensic psychologists to testify to that fact."

"And Royce Asshole will get the same amount to tell a jury something different," Henry replied. "You know how these things go. A case like that all depends on a sympathetic jury, and juries don't tend to be sympathetic to wealthy attorneys. I'll have Margarita start to ask around to see who's available."

"And I'll keep Isla close. I don't want to worry her, but I also don't want her caught off guard. Something about the way the ADA hauled her in yesterday made me think this is personal. Usually there's some professional courtesy between lawyers. He had none for her. He paraded her in front of the press like he was asking them to charge her in the court of public opinion."

Noah frowned. "I think I know why he's behaving like an asshole. Isla dated him very briefly. It didn't go well and she was the one to break it off. I'm not terribly surprised he's being a jerk."

She'd dated Royce? Was that the kind of man she was attracted to? Then she was going to make it easy on him because he couldn't be further from the kind of self-obsessed dick Royce Osborne was. Sure he wore designer suits, but only because he had a guy at Bergdorf Goodman who picked them out for him. When he wasn't at work, he was a jeans and T-shirt kind of guy. "Can we get him recused?"

Henry shrugged. "We can't even try until he's done something."

"Well, as to the court of public opinion, his tactics are working," Noah said with a shake of his head. "There were all kinds of questions on the morning talk shows. It ran the gamut from the reporters accusing Isla of trying to clean up after her client to the more salacious stories."

He should have known they would go there. "So there's a rumor Isla was sleeping with Trey?"

"Of course there is," Henry shot back. "She's a young, beautiful woman. He's an aging jock. I could have told you it wouldn't take any time at all for that malicious bit of gossip to surface. You and Isla should go out to the Hamptons and see if you can get the kids to do a couple of photographs with her. You know, the three of them walking into the hospital together. A show of family unity."

He wasn't sure how well that suggestion would go over. It might be better to simply arrange for it to happen. "I certainly think we should go and talk to the kids."

"Good." Henry's lips curled up in a faint smile, and he glanced toward the kitchen. "Seriously? I thought you had a thing for redheads."

God, he wished they hadn't shown up. "I told you, I'm not going to act on it."

There was a knock on the door.

"I'll get it." Noah bounced up. "It's probably Margarita. I texted her where we were. She's bringing cinnamon rolls."

He practically ran to the door.

David nodded their way. "You want to worry about a problem? Worry about that."

Henry waved it off. "Nah, Margarita's too smart to fall for his puppy eyes routine."

But David wasn't so sure.

"I brought cinnamon rolls." Margarita walked in looking perfectly ready for anything. She was superstylish in jeans, over-the-knee boots, and a chic sweater that complemented her skin tone. David was fairly certain if he went to Margarita's place at three in the morning, she would find a way to be fully made up without a hair out of place. "I also brought butternut squash soup and the makings for tacos. I'm sorry. I'm Mexican. Food is how we deal with grief."

"I thought food was how you dealt with stress," Henry pointed out. She'd said that on many occasions.

"It's how we deal with everything," she replied with a smile. "I also have the McKay-Taggart report from their profiler. The new hot one. Not that Eve isn't hot, but the new guy is superhot."

"I didn't think he was hot." Noah followed her into the kitchen. "He looked kind of like a nerd to me. You really thought he was hot? I was pretty sure he was gay. I mean, I know when a guy's hitting on me."

"He was totally hitting on me, you infant," Margarita replied.

"See, nothing to worry about. She'll hook up with some testosteroned-out McKay-Taggart operative who'll beat Noah to death if he even looks her way," Henry said. "Problem solved."

Win bounced in, a huge smile on her face. She sat down next to Henry, resting her head on his shoulder.

Suddenly the Monster of Manhattan was wearing a soft expression on his face. "Did you have a nice talk, sweetheart?"

She nodded up at him. "I did. I feel better knowing we're going to take care of this. I would hate for her to get dragged into this mess more than she already is." She turned to David. "I like her. I think you should call dibs or Noah might."

He sighed. Yep. His problems were just beginning.

FIVE

sla handed over the last plate. She'd been surprised when David insisted on cleaning up. He'd explained that he'd been taught to honor the person feeding him by doing the dishes.

He'd done them last night, too. There was something about a man who didn't mind a little housework that did it for her. She kind of wondered what he'd look like sorting laundry. He could even take his shirt off because, hey, it needed to be clean, too. Then she would know exactly how cut he was. Yep, him doing the wash could be pretty hot.

What was wrong with her? She was sexually objectifying her lawyer? Not hers. Trey's. When she thought about it, they were really more like teammates. And everyone knew getting emotionally involved with a teammate was also a bad idea.

"Did Henry get everything he asked for?" She stepped back and poured herself one more cup of coffee. Not that she needed it. She'd actually gotten good sleep the night before. Every time her unconscious brain had gone to a bad place, she would wake briefly and realize he was there.

She would miss him tonight.

"I think so. It's good that you kept all the records here. Too many times we have to wait until we can get the base information from the police reports or other family members. It was nice to have it all in one place." He worked diligently cleaning each plate and putting it into the dishwasher to sanitize. "And it's good that you have power of attorney because with him in the situation he's in, it could have required a bunch of court appearances and still left Trey's fate in the hands of a judge."

"When we realized Trey's mind was starting to deteriorate, Portia and I decided to try to cover all the bases we could," she explained. "I know he's in his late forties and that's not really the time when people think about powers of attorney or living wills, but we've had to consider it all."

"Did you write his will?" David asked, wiping down the countertop.

"Not myself. I found an attorney who specializes in them." It wasn't much of a leap to know what he would ask next. "Obviously if he went first, everything went to Portia."

"And if she went first?"

Then it got a bit trickier, but Portia had been insistent. "All of the money and the businesses go into a trust administered by an executor until Trey dies, and then everything is split between Miranda and Oscar."

"And who's the executor?" He asked the question like he already knew the answer.

"That would be me. And before you go into it, yes, I now have full control of the money. All financial decisions are made by me. I have the option, if I feel they're ready, to place ten million in a trust for each child, but honestly, they would both spend their way through it at this point. I also have to ensure Trey gets everything he needs." She studied David carefully. "I'll get you a copy of the will."

"Thank you." He folded the towel. "And I'll share what I can with you, too. Henry left a bunch of reports. Mostly background information, but if you could look through it and tell us if it lines up with what you know, that would be very helpful. Our investigators are already on their way. Noah is going to pick them up from the airport."

"Shouldn't we use NYC-based investigators?"

"We have one on staff and he's working, too, but these guys are the best. By 'guys' I mean a woman and an Irish dude. They're puzzle solvers, and they can also kick some serious ass if we need them to," David replied. "I'm going to meet with them this evening."

"I'd like to be there if that's possible."

"Of course." He smiled her way, and she couldn't help but think about how sexy he was when he smiled.

"I like your friends." She had to stop thinking about him that way or she might make a complete fool of herself.

"I'm glad *you* do because I'm giving them all another look," he said. "Turns out they're all nosy busybodies. I can't imagine what you thought when you opened that door the first time."

She shook her head. "It was nice to have people over. I'm afraid I've become a hermit in my old age. I'd forgotten how fun it is to sit and have a meal with new people. Although if I'd known there was going to be company, I might have put on more professional attire."

She'd entertained the Monster of Manhattan while wearing pajama bottoms with tiny champagne bottles all over them and a tank top that said *Cheers to Sleep*. She was putting out some seriously sexy vibes with that ensemble.

"Well, we get involved in our work. We usually end up eating together and fighting over some small point of law or how to handle a case. It's normal for our firm. I don't spend nearly enough time with my parents. They live out on Long Island. I only get out there once a week."

He saw his parents every week. That was another point in his favor. "I miss my parents. They died in a car accident when I was in high school."

"I'm sorry to hear that. Any siblings?"

"Nope. Just me. You an only, too?" *Only.* There was a reason it rhymed with *lonely* that went beyond how the two words were spelled.

"Yes, I'm afraid my brothers are all of the non-blood type."

"Those can be pretty awesome, too." She felt like she should say something, talk about the elephant in the room. Ever since the others had taken off, they'd been tiptoeing around the subject. "About last—"

Her words were cut off by the sound of her doorbell ringing. Her eyes locked with his before he glanced toward the door.

"Shouldn't you have gotten a call that someone was here to see you?" David asked, drying off his hands. He started for the door.

"They only lock down the building at night. We're open from seven A.M. to ten P.M." She followed him, anxiety starting to bubble inside her. She'd never had to worry about security before. The building had always seemed perfectly safe. Now she had way more than mere crime to consider. Privacy had become incredibly important to her overnight. "You think it's the press?"

"I think I would rather you had better security," he replied as he looked through the peephole. His shoulders came down from around his ears. "It's okay. You'll want to talk to this one."

He unlocked her dead bolt and she smiled. This was one visitor she should have expected.

Carey Kendrick was larger than life, and turning seventy hadn't slowed him down one bit. He stood in her hallway wearing his typical designer suit that he paired with a wide-brimmed Stetson and cowboy boots. He'd lived in New York for years, but the Oklahoma oilman was still there in every move he made. He'd never lost his accent and refused to fit into Manhattan's high society. He always told her that if money couldn't get him into a place, he didn't want to go there. He held his arms wide. "Come here, darlin'. I'm sorry for what you had to go through."

She noticed Amber standing beside him, looking glamorous. She was a trophy wife and always made sure she was polished to a shine.

Isla found herself enveloped in a bear hug. She had to take a deep breath or she would start crying again. God, she'd thought she'd cried so much the night before that she wouldn't be able to today, but there she was, right on the cusp. "Hello, Carey."

He'd almost been her father-in-law. He was the one to take care of her after Austin died. He had a terrible reputation. The press hated him, and she could admit one of the reasons she'd left the Guardians' front office was that she preferred not working with the man. He could be an overbearing boss, but she would never be able to forget how he'd cared for her even through his own grief. When he wasn't working, he was a jewel of a man.

"I'm sorry about Portia," he murmured. "I couldn't believe the news when we heard it. Shook me to the core. You know we all loved that woman."

"Oh, that woman was a saint," Amber said with a shake of her head and a sad sigh. She looked sleek and beautiful, but then that was rather her job as a trophy wife and she was good at it. She was placed on the pageant circuit as a toddler, and sometimes Isla thought she'd never truly gotten off it. Amber had gotten as far as Miss Tennessee, but she still waved like a beauty queen.

"I wouldn't say a saint, but she was definitely a kind and lovely woman." A woman who would scold her for thinking unkindly of

Amber. Portia had been the one to talk Isla into accepting the second wife. She'd pointed out that Carey had started smiling again after Amber came into his life. The problem was Isla remembered the first Mrs. Kendrick. Austin's mom. God, Austin would laugh his ass off at the idea of his dad married to someone who would barely be older than him had he lived.

Funny how thinking of him lately brought her pleasure and not pain. Like a fond memory rather than the loss of her life.

Carey released her and she stepped back to let him in the apartment. He seemed to realize she wasn't alone. His gaze found David and he held out a hand. "Cormack, good to see you're here, and on a Sunday. I like a man who takes his job seriously."

David shook his hand. "And I thank you for the recommendation. I assure you my firm is ready to take this case on."

Carey chuckled as they shook hands. "Well, I'd rather have someone who understands both sides of this field, if you know what I mean. Besides, your partner kind of scares me and I'm not easily intimidated. And your other partner is a puppy dog whose balls haven't dropped yet."

She gasped, a sound that was echoed by Amber.

David simply laughed. "Oh, I assure you his balls are fully matured. His brain when it comes to anything but work? Not so much. Noah uses his equipment on anything that will let him. I expect he would hump the fire hydrants if he got hard up. But he's smarter than he seems. He's going to be second on this. I think you'll find he's an excellent lawyer."

Carey nodded. "As long as you're on top of things. No way the Trey Adams I know would hurt any woman, much less his own wife."

Amber shook her head. Somehow her hair managed to not move at all. "Never. They were in love. They stood by each other. Portia taught me a lot about what it means to be a wife and the female head of the family."

"Matriarch," Isla prompted and then winced. She shouldn't correct the other woman. Not when it didn't matter.

Amber shuddered delicately. "No. That's an old word and I'm obviously a young woman. I like to think of myself as a domestic CEO. Though I am very maternal. I've taken those cheerleaders under my wing. Poor little birds. Most of them don't have time for a man."

As if that was the worst thing that could happen to a woman.

"You knew Portia well?" David asked, looking at Amber.

"She was the best of the best," Amber said. "Such an amazing woman. We were working on several important projects together. Portia was one of the only women in the city who wasn't horribly mean to me. I suspect it's because she was a model at one time, so she wasn't intimidated by me." She glanced over at Carey as her cell buzzed. "Baby, you need to take your meds. It's time."

She reached into her massive designer bag and pulled out a monstrosity of a pill dispenser. She carefully opened Sunday and pulled out two small white pills and then dove back for a bottle of water.

Carey grumbled slightly but took his medication. "Sorry about this. She listens to doctors too much."

"It is my mission in life to have as much time with you as I possibly can," she said with a shake of her head that told Isla they'd been over this all before.

And that was why she put up with Amber. She might be an airhead former beauty queen who had no place marrying a man thrice her age, but she tried. She took good care of Carey, and she'd made a career in the last few years out of protecting the family business and name.

"So many pills," Carey said with a shake of his head. "Don't get old, you two. And, David, if you're asking if Amber knows anything, I assure you she doesn't. She would have told me if Trey and Portia were in trouble."

Amber nodded. "I would have. I know how important they are

to my husband. Carey watches out for his players long after they've stopped playing. They're our family and we love them. I was working on several projects with Portia. We were on a couple of charity boards together." Tears sheened Amber's green eyes. "I saw her last week. I had lunch at the penthouse. She was mentoring me."

Carey put a hand on his wife's shoulder, patting her gently. "She's still in shock."

Amber sniffled and seemed to pull it together. "Portia was helping me put together a charity luncheon for the Humane Society. I was helping her put together some of the media for a party she was going to throw when Trey turns fifty."

"Portia wanted to put together a short film about Trey's career. I opened the Guardian's vaults for her," Carey explained. "We keep films of the games and all the media we get."

She knew the vault well. It was like a library and it contained thirty years' worth of films of everything from training camps to the Super Bowls they'd participated in, to commercials the players made. And all the media. The vault was huge and not the most organized of libraries. Portia had wanted to hire an actual librarian for the vault, but Carey had left it to the publicity department.

"Didn't you do a reality show for a couple of years?" David asked.

Isla had ducked the cameras anytime she could while everyone else in the office tried to get their fifteen minutes of fame. "*Holding the Line.* For three years we had a film crew follow everything from what went on in the front office, to training camp, all the way to the Super Bowl in our final year. It got great ratings, but Carey nixed a fourth season."

"It was too much," Carey said. "And don't look at me like that. You hated the idea. You nearly threw up every time you had to be on camera."

Because she was not that girl. "I was born to be behind the scenes."

Amber wiped her tears and gave her a watery smile. "That's not true. If I'd been around back then, I would have styled you and you would have been a big star. Think about it. You might have had your own show now. *The Real Lawyers of Manhattan*."

The mere thought made her shiver. Amber liked a lot of cleavage and used more glitter than a craft fair. Besides, she was fairly certain people would get bored with that particular show since nothing exciting ever happened . . . well, most of the time. "I think I'm happier with my current job. Speaking of, did you get the contracts I sent you?"

She still took care of Carey's personal business. He always had something going on behind the scenes. Though she no longer dealt with the massive legal tangles that came with a professional sports team, she was happy she could still help out in some small way.

"I did and sent them in to be filed." He winked at her. "Thank you for catching that mistake. Would have cost me a pretty penny. Now tell me what's going on with Trey. How can I help?"

She gave him the general rundown and David explained that he'd gotten an emergency motion for an evaluation. While his friends had been in the apartment, they got a call from the doctor telling them Trey hadn't been conscious enough to answer questions when he went by. They were still hoping for news today, but it would very likely be Monday before they knew anything.

After a while, David stepped back. "I'm going to head home for a bit, Isla. I'll be back in a couple of hours and we can take it from there. I'll call and see if we can get into the hospital this afternoon. Why don't you set up a time to talk with Miranda and Oscar?"

She nodded, weirdly at ease with the idea that they would spend another day together. "I will do that. And thank you again."

"Mr. Cormack?" Amber stepped up. "I need to know when I can get into the penthouse. I called over there and the police were being entirely unreasonable about letting me in."

One brow rose over David's eyes. "Why would you need to do that?"

"Because I'm in charge of the media presentation at Portia's funeral. Excuse me, at her memorial service." She flushed but carried on. "I talked to Miranda and volunteered to do it, but I need access to family photos and their personal videos."

Isla sighed inwardly. She could practically hear how that conversation would have gone. Miranda was in mourning and Amber—while trying to be helpful—was being entirely too pushy. "It's a crime scene. We don't know when the police will let the family back in, much less anyone who doesn't actually live there."

Her eyes widened. "But the funeral will be soon. I need time to make this movie. I've already contacted a couple of country music singers about a memorial song. I want it to be a new 'Candle in the Wind,' except way more meaningful. I'm going to have a Hollywood director help me put it all together, but I need material."

David grabbed his briefcase and his suit coat, the same one that had kept her warm much of the day before. "The good news is they were very public figures. You should be able to find plenty of material because I don't think they'll let anyone who's not working the case in there soon."

He said goodbye and left, and she stared at the door for a moment.

"I can't use all the old stuff people have already seen. I can't," Amber huffed. "Well, I have to start making some calls. I have to get that material. I can't fail Portia with a subpar memorial film. I'll be right back." She took out her bejeweled cell phone and started dialing. "Jay, I need you to get the whole team together."

She walked toward the kitchen, leaving Isla alone with Carey.

"She has a team?" Isla asked, forcing herself to turn.

Carey stood looking down at a picture on her end table. It was one of her and Austin at his high school graduation. She wore a yellow sundress, and he looked young and healthy in his cap and gown. "She's been working with a publicist. She says she needs to revamp her image. I don't see what's wrong with her image, but she wants people to like her and I don't care. Anyway, this publicist person is supposedly teaching her how to better fit into high society. You have no idea how much that is costing me. I know she can be pushy, but she cares about this family."

The fact that he still called it *this* family and not *my* meant the world to her. Her heart ached because their family was smaller today. "Are you okay?"

He picked up the picture and held it to his heart. "No, I am not. I want to go back here, to right here. I want to be in this damn picture before I realized how fragile it all is. I want to go back to when I thought I could handle anything with willpower and money. I was invulnerable when I took this picture. Now I'm an old man who longs for the past."

She moved over to him. This man had been like a father to her. Even after his son died, he'd taken care of her when he should have been in mourning for himself. "I still think you're invincible."

He leaned into her when she put an arm around him. "No. No, I am not. I've made mistakes, done things merely to feed my ego. You would be shocked if you knew some of the things I've done. But my sins are my own. God, I pushed him. I pushed Austin hard."

"He loved you." She'd always been in awe of how well father and son worked together, but then they'd survived the death of Austin's mother. She'd died of a heart attack when Austin was in high school, and as a result, his teenage years had been more thoughtful than most. It was how she'd bonded with him. They'd met at a grief counseling session. Their respective boarding schools had joined together so they would have a group. Two sessions in and one long talk at the café just off campus, and she'd been in teen love.

She often wondered if that love would have survived the harsh adult world.

"I wanted him to be the best," Carey was saying. "I knew what it was like to come out of poverty. Until we found the oil on our land, we were worth nothing but dirt. It's a hard life. I never wanted him to know that feeling."

"He didn't," she replied. "Even at the end, he was smiling and happy for the life he'd had. You gave him that life."

"And you gave him love. He got to experience that," Carey said, placing the picture back down. "But I have to wonder."

She took his hand and led him to the couch. Despite his bluster and bravado, he was getting up there in years. He would be more comfortable sitting down. "Wonder about what?"

Carey sank down, stretching his legs out. "I wonder if I would have done to him what I did to Trey."

She straightened her spine, leaning in. She'd talked to him since they'd gotten the diagnosis, but she hadn't heard the guilt in his voice until now. "You didn't give Trey CTE."

"Didn't I?" He stared straight ahead, as though seeing something else, someplace else in his head. "Didn't we all? The owners I mean. We ignored that research for years because we didn't want to believe it. The players got bigger and the hits got harder, and all we cared about were ratings and cash. How many concussions had Austin gotten before he even finished high school?"

Not that it mattered. "I only remember one."

"And how many did we miss? I think even if the cancer hadn't come, I would have lost him. I would have lost him to this game the way we've lost Trey. I can't believe this happened. I know what I said to David, and I'll say it to every single person who asks. I'll stand beside Trey through everything, but god, Isla. How could this have happened?"

A chill went down her spine. "Trey didn't kill Portia."

"He didn't mean to kill Portia. I understand that, but he doesn't know what he's doing half the time. Sometimes he thinks he's back on the football field. He nearly killed me two weeks ago because he thought I'd made an interception and was running for the end zone. My knee is still in a brace from that tackle." Carey turned toward her. "I love that man like he was my son, and you know what I mean by that."

Austin had been his only child, his precious son. "I do, but I saw Trey that night. He held her after she was gone. He was devastated. I'll never forget the sound he made."

"Ask yourself if that was the sound of a man who'd lost. Or of a man who'd made the worst mistake of his life. I know you want to see the bright side of everything, and that's one of the reasons I adore you, darling girl, but there's a darkness inside every man. There's something primitive and vile inside us, and how we handle that wicked piece of our souls, well, that's the measure of a man. Trey can't push it down. The disease robbed him of that control. I'm sure he regrets what he did. If he can even remember it."

She couldn't bring herself to believe it. "But why? I can't wrap my head around it. And why destroy her room?"

"He could have thought anything. He's delusional." Carey frowned. "And there are some things going on that you don't know about. Things no one would tell you."

"Like what?"

He paused for a moment and Isla waited, her hands in fists in her lap. He finally leaned in, his voice going low. "Like Portia was meeting with a man. Regularly."

"Who?"

He shrugged. "I don't know. That's the rumor. I do know I ran into her a couple months back. I had a meeting with a friend of mine who was staying at the Algonquin. She was in the elevator coming down when I was going up, and she was rattled to see me there."

"What did she say?"

"Not much," he replied. "She muttered something about the fact that she was seeing a friend, but I think she was lying. She looked almost scared to see me. I didn't understand it. We were friends and she practically ran. I watched her as the doors closed and when she turned back, there were tears rolling down her cheeks. I think she thought I would tell someone, but I never would have. I didn't even tell you. But I did ask the person who worked the desk if they'd seen her before. I was told she'd been coming in every Thursday for a few weeks at that point, but I couldn't get them to give me the name of the person she was meeting. Since the room wasn't in her name and she hadn't stopped to ask for a number, all they knew was she went to the seventh floor."

Portia? She couldn't have been cheating on Trey. It wasn't in her. "She had to have been there for some other reason."

"Then why look guilty? Why not stop and talk to me? She practically ran out of the place," Carey pointed out with sympathy in his voice. "And honestly, do you blame her? The last couple of years have been hell on her. After Oscar practically ran away, she was alone in that huge place with Trey, and no one knows how bad it got."

"Oscar didn't run away. He's a grown man. He needed some space." And he and Trey had butted heads often, and after Trey started getting worse, so did their fights.

Because Trey wasn't able to control himself anymore. Because he had problems with his violent impulses.

"Oscar should have stayed home and taken care of his mother," Carey replied with some fire. "He knew what was at stake and he wasn't man enough to handle it."

"There's more reason there and you know it. He and Trey had trouble before. Teenage stuff. Portia encouraged him to get his own space. She rented the place for him."

"He took the coward's way out and now his momma is dead, and I wonder if he knows he could have changed that."

Isla couldn't believe what she was hearing. "You can't blame Oscar. Miranda left, too."

"Miranda went to college," Carey argued. "That's completely different. Miranda was off making her parents proud and securing herself a future. What the hell was Oscar doing except milking his parents for cash?"

Oscar was an artist. He was twenty-two and while he hadn't sold anything yet, he certainly had the artistic temperament down. Oscar could be unpredictable, to say the least, but he wasn't responsible for his mother's death. Carey had very old-school thoughts about family. They stuck together no matter what, and even when the son and father fought constantly, in Carey's mind, the son should defer. In Carey's world, Oscar should have listened to everything Trey said and been a dutiful, if miserable, son.

Thank god Austin had loved football or he would have spent his childhood in the same misery as Oscar had by not conforming.

Still, she felt the need to defend him, even if she found him difficult to deal with. Portia would have wanted someone to defend her son. "I know he loves his parents."

"And you loved them, too. Hell, Isla, I didn't come here to argue with you. I came here to see if there's anything I can do to help you. I wanted to see if you would come out to Connecticut for a couple of days. Maybe by then the press will have calmed down a bit."

"I'm a material witness." She didn't mention the fact that the DA was gunning for her to be more. "I don't think I should leave the city right now, but I thank you for the offer."

He frowned slightly. "Are you sure? Because I hate the thought of you staying here alone. If you're alone."

Embarrassment made her flush, and she told herself that she was a grown woman and didn't need to explain anything, but he was a lot like her dad. "David stayed last night because he was worried about me. Nothing happened."

Nothing except warmth and kindness and the intimacy of her head resting on his chest, her ear hearing the steady sound of his heartbeat. Nothing but his hand smoothing down her hair and the way he'd cuddled her close when he was sleeping.

She loved the fact that she'd caught him staring at her a couple of times over breakfast and that his friends kept whispering and smiling. This morning she'd felt like she was part of a team for the first time in a long time. Not merely the helpful outsider.

"I was afraid of that," Carey said. "His clothes were far too wrinkled for a man of his class to be seen in unless he was doing a walk of shame."

The idea of big, strong David Cormack doing a walk of shame nearly made her giggle. "They were wrinkled because he slept in them. Like I said, he was worried I wouldn't sleep if I was alone. He's a good man."

"And he's a damn good lawyer. Sometimes that has to take precedence over what kind of man he is," Carey said quietly. "Don't get me wrong. I sent you to him because I believe he's the one who can deal with this and help Trey, but I don't want you involved with him. Honey, if you're ready to start dating again, let me set you up. I know some of the nicest, best men in the business."

"David is nice."

"David is a shark. He might be a very nice shark, but you can't ever forget that he's a predator at heart. He'll do anything to win, and if that means manipulating you, he'll do it. If he thinks you'll be easier to deal with by romancing you, he'll do it. Like I said, there's a reason I wanted him brought in, but I wouldn't want my daughter to date him. And I definitely wouldn't want my daughter to come between him and work. That man is all about work."

That wasn't the David she'd met. The David she'd met was startlingly compassionate, kind. He'd been quite tender as he held her the night before, and the chemistry between the two of them had been off the charts. That wasn't something a guy could fake. She'd been alive long enough to know that kind of chemistry didn't come around often, and she would be stupid to let it go without at least exploring what it could mean.

"I'll be careful." She wasn't going to sit here and argue with him. She wouldn't win. He was trying to look out for her and she doubted anyone would be good enough for her in Carey's mind.

"No, you won't," he said with a long, disappointed sigh, but his hand came out and covered hers in a gesture of paternal affection. "Let me tell you one story I've heard about him. You know he was married, right?"

"He didn't mention it." But it didn't surprise her. He was in his midthirties. A lot of people she knew were already divorced and looking again at that age. They hadn't spent a ton of time talking about personal things. Well, he'd spent a lot of time listening to her, not talking about himself.

"He married his wife a week after the draft. He went late, sometime at the end of the seventh round. He barely missed taking on the Mr. Irrelevant. That's what we call the guy who's drafted in the two hundred and twenty-fourth position. Now, there were a lot of scouts who thought he looked fragile, but he performed well that last season at Harvard. His stats were good enough to get him into a higher round, but it was his history of injuries that made me hold off. But Seattle was having coaching problems and David was known as a leader. I honestly think they brought him in for his brains. Anyway, he got a decent deal. He played backup but had to take over in the second half of his fourth season and he was on fire. He was definitely one of the reasons they made it deep in the playoffs. There was talk about moving him into a starting position and renegotiating his contract."

Isla could guess what happened next. "He got hurt."

"Two games into his fifth season, he tore his ACL and was out for the rest of the year. He did rehab and came back strong. But he blew out his knee again and he was done. He was on the roster for another half year and then they released him."

She wasn't sure where he was going with this. "None of that makes me think I shouldn't date him. I don't choose my dates based on the state of their knees."

He sent her that look she was sure had worked on Austin as a kid. He softened it with a little smile. "Smart-ass. I'm getting to my point. After he realized his pro career was over, he decided to go to law school. Unlike a lot of pro players, David actually completed his undergraduate degree. Got a degree in history. He ended up returning to the Northeast, and I believe it was Henry who convinced him to go back to Harvard for law school. They'd become close friends when they did their undergraduate studies there. David's grades and LSAT scores got him in. His marriage started to crumble."

"That's a lot of change. It would be hard on anyone." And they'd married young.

"His wife got cancer. Breast cancer."

God, even the word made her a little sick to her stomach. "That's terrible."

"She fought for roughly eighteen months," Carey continued. "As far as I can tell, he went to her bedside exactly once. According to her parents, she had to beg him not to divorce her. Oh, they hate him, Isla. They claim he's very cold. He had the insurance in his name and he tried to leave her high and dry. They managed to convince him not to divorce her, that it would be better for him financially to stay married, but he moved out of their apartment. The day she died, he was in court. He didn't bother to go to her funeral."

That sent a shiver through her. It was hard to reconcile the kind man who'd held her all night long with a man who couldn't find the time to go to his wife's funeral. But she had to wonder why Carey knew so much. "You talked to his wife's parents?"

"I have a dossier on him as well as his business partners. I have the same on two other firms. I can never be too careful, and I want to know who I'm comfortable calling in case I need a criminal lawyer. Not that I think I'm getting indicted anytime soon, but I have enemies and they're capable of trying anything." He pulled away, relaxing back. "Just think about it. I'll send you his dossier this afternoon. Read it over and think about it before you do anything that could lead to more heartbreak. Now, if you ask my opinion, which you did not but you should have because I'm old and wise, that Noah fellow is a much better bet."

She actually shuddered. Noah was definitely in the friend zone. "He's far too promiscuous for me. I don't think I want to join the model population of Manhattan. And I don't want to think about how many women he slept with in Texas."

Carey was grinning in a way that let her know he wasn't serious. "Now, we can fix that. I've found shoving a shotgun up against a man's nuts makes him think about how he wants to use those things again. And can you imagine having the contacts his brother must have? Baby girl, it would be a royal American wedding."

She groaned. He was always thinking business. "Pass."

He chuckled and got to his feet with minimal trouble. "Well, I had to try. But you know, I do like the idea of you dating again. It's time, sweetheart. Austin wouldn't want you to be alone for the rest of your life. He would want you to find a good man and marry and have babies. I would love to see you have a few babies before I die. You're all I have left of him. But you were a damn good part of my boy."

There were those tears again. They were always there at the surface these days. She hugged the man who would have been her father-in-law, deeply grateful to have had him in her life. He was bombastic and over the top, and he'd been nothing but kind and loyal to her.

"Think about what I said," he whispered.

Think about what he'd told her about David. "I will."

She doubted she would be able to think about anything else.

"Well, Jay says unless I get those videos, the world is going to think I'm a terrible friend. I can't use recycled video. I have to show the private side of the woman." Amber had tears in her eyes as she strode back into the room, her sky-high heels clacking on the floor. "What am I going to do? I can't be a terrible friend."

Carey turned and held his arms out again. "Now, darlin', we'll work something out."

She walked into her husband's arms. Isla had to hope this was Amber's grief coming out in different ways. She prayed the woman wasn't seriously thinking about her own reputation at a time like this. And she also didn't say what she was thinking. Portia wouldn't want the public to see her private side. That had been reserved for her husband and children.

Amber looked over at her, still sniffling. "Please let me know when I can get into the penthouse. I need those private photos and video. Miranda said I could have them. It's just that I want to make this perfect. Portia was so kind. It has to be perfect."

And then Amber seemed to lose it, crying against Carey's shoulder.

Isla put a hand on the other woman's back. They were all too emotional.

And that was precisely why she should do what Carey had asked her to. She should be careful around David Cormack.

SIX

Frustration welled as he looked out over the beach. He shoved his cell phone back into his pocket.

"No luck?" Isla asked as they waited in the pretty sitting room of Portia Adams's sister's Hamptons home. It was one of the larger spreads directly on the beach. He looked out and couldn't help but think about how much he preferred Henry and Win's tiny cottage on Martha's Vineyard. It had none of the glamour of this place, but he felt at home there.

This place was a lovely museum dedicated to high fashion and to two beautiful sisters. The sitting room was dominated by a painting of Portia Adams and her sister, Cressida Bardsley. That painting had to be four feet tall and almost as wide. It showed the two sisters during their youth, wearing garlands in their hair and sheaths of white and pink. They looked slightly surreal.

Every other surface held pictures of one of the two sisters with famous people. Cressida was a slave to celebrity it seemed. And to delicate furniture. There wasn't a single chair in the place that looked like it could handle his weight.

"No luck. They said there's no way they can get our doctor in until tomorrow morning. They had to sedate Trey twice. He's on lockdown and on suicide watch." He turned, staring as she paled, and wished he hadn't mentioned that part. But she deserved to know.

And something had changed between that moment when he'd walked out of her apartment to get his car and when he'd picked her up to make the trip to the Hamptons. When he'd left, there was something in her eyes, something that told him she wasn't particularly happy to see him go. That soft looked had been replaced, as had her pajama bottoms and T-shirt, with a slightly frosty professionalism. She now wore a power suit and some killer heels, and she hadn't looked at him once during the lengthy drive to the Hamptons.

They'd talked, but she'd carefully steered everything toward the case.

He needed to stop thinking about what had gone wrong with Isla and start thinking about the case. He wasn't trying to date her. Except he'd thought about it the whole time they were apart.

Isla's jaw tightened, but she made no move to leave her place on the couch. "I'm going to see him tomorrow. They can't keep me out forever."

"I'll try to get us in."

She nodded and went back to staring at the ocean.

He was about to do something stupid—like asking her what had gone wrong—when he was saved by the tempestuous artistic tidal wave that was Oscar Adams. The young man stormed in wearing loose-fitting jeans, a T-shirt with some sort of "fight the power" message on it, and hair that looked like he'd just rolled out of bed but had likely taken an hour in front of the mirror to achieve. David had no idea why today's masculine youth thought they should wear a bear claw over their foreheads that brushed over their line of vision, but he'd seen this trend all over.

"What are you doing here, Isla? I thought you would have the good sense to stay away at a time like this." Oscar was a good-looking kid, or might be if one forgave the sulky expression on his face. Had he been sucking on lemons? It would be the only way to explain that pouty mouth and pained look in his eyes.

"I called your aunt." Isla stood. "I called Cressida and told her I was coming out."

"And she promptly took a couple of Xanax and passed out," Oscar replied. "It's how she reacts to everything. I take it the housekeeper let you in? Because that bitch is fired."

"Oscar, I thought we agreed I would handle this." Miranda appeared at the bottom of the stairs looking world-weary, her eyes red as though she hadn't slept, but she'd dressed for the occasion. She wore black jeans and a dark sweater, her hair tugged up in a ponytail, and red-soled flats on her feet. "Isla, I'm sorry. Don't pay attention to him. Do you have any news on Dad?"

"What she's asking is, have they hauled our loving father to jail, and if not, why?" Oscar asked, anger feeding every word that came out of his mouth.

Miranda glanced at her brother, eyes narrowed. "That is not what I mean. Do you want me to leave? Because if you don't stop talking about Dad like that, I will. I'll leave you all alone with Cressida and you two can figure out how to handle everything."

For a moment he thought the kid might tell Miranda to fuck off, but his shoulders slumped and he sank to the couch with a sullen huff. "Who's the suit?"

Isla sighed and sat down across from Oscar. "This is David Cormack. He's handling your father's defense."

"Of course he is," Oscar said, his face flushed. "I'm sure he's the best money can buy."

"He's the best," Isla assured him. "I wouldn't get anything less for your dad."

"Even though he killed my mother?" Oscar asked.

"Oscar!" Miranda strode across the room, standing over her brother with a look of fury on her face. "I told you he didn't do it. You can't say things like that. You can't."

Oh, but David was interested. Here was the first real crack in the family line. "Why would you say that, Oscar?"

The young man turned to him, his eyes assessing before he spoke. "Well, Counselor, I say it because my father is a powder keg waiting to go off, and it looks like he blew. Who else would hurt my mother? My mom was one of the most loved people in the city. She . . . she . . ."

Miranda sat by his side, her hand finding his shoulder. "She was an amazing woman who did amazing things. She was well loved."

Beneath all that rage was a young man who'd lost his mother. He needed to treat Oscar that way. There was enough hostility coming off the kid that David didn't need to inject more. He needed to listen because it was obvious Oscar had zero filter. "Your mother did a lot of good work."

He nodded, taking a deep breath. "She cared about people. She wasn't like lots of rich assholes. Mom thought we had a responsibility to the people around us because we had more than they did. She was very involved in the community."

"She had a lot of friends?"

Oscar laughed and sounded a bit less like a tool. "Yeah. Tons. She was one of those people everyone wanted to be around, you know. She accepted everyone."

There was something about the way he said *accepted* that made David home in on the word. "But not everyone in your family did? Accept you, right?"

Oscar turned sullen again. "No. My dad . . . my father was an intolerant ass. Is an intolerant ass."

Miranda sighed. "He's not really. You're forgetting everything from before and focusing on the bad stuff."

Oscar turned to his sister. "Well, when was the last time Dad called you a fag?"

Isla gasped. "He did what?"

Oscar laughed again, but there was no humor in the sound. "Don't know everything, Isla? That's funny. I thought you did. You didn't know dear old dad was a closeted homophobe?"

"He threw you a coming-out party," Isla said, shaking her head and looking at David like she desperately needed to explain. "When Oscar was sixteen, Portia and Trey threw him a coming-out party. Trey would talk about the fact that his son was gay and how much he supported him. There was never any question of not accepting him."

"He only did it because of Mom." Oscar sniffled, a disdainful sound. "I guess his real feelings finally came through."

Oh, but David understood. "When did he start showing these homophobic tendencies?"

Oscar shrugged. "I don't know. I guess he decided to stop hiding it a couple years ago."

"When his memory started going?"

"Don't blame this on some mental illness," Oscar replied, rolling his eyes.

David held a hand out, attempting to stop an argument he couldn't win. "Look, you're a smart kid, do some research. CTE like your father has can cause poor impulse control, dementia, confusion. He might not have understood what he was saying or who he was saying it to. Has he directly told you he hates gays?"

Oscar went quiet.

Miranda sat up straighter. "No. He was having a bad episode and called Oscar a faggot. I don't even know that Dad was calling him that. He said the word. That was all. Oscar's held on to it for two years now. Dad called me a whore once. I was wearing a super-low-cut dress. It was weird though. He spat the word out a couple of times and then he was back to normal. He told me I looked pretty, but it was cold and I should wear a sweater."

"You can't know what he means in those moments," he explained. "He could have looked at you and thought something about how others might view you in that low-cut dress, and the word he spat out wasn't a pleasant one. It didn't mean he thinks you're a whore. His brain is a storm of competing information, some real and some made up. In this case, you have to look to his actions before he got sick to find the real man."

Oscar didn't look convinced, but he sat back and showed no signs of fleeing. "Are you some kind of expert?"

"I used to play. Believe me I've spent my time studying up on CTE," he admitted.

Isla's eyes flared as she looked at him, and that softness was back momentarily.

Compassion. Sympathy. It wasn't what he wanted from her. He focused on Oscar. "Do you have any other reason to think your dad would have hurt your mother?"

"He wouldn't have," Miranda interjected. "Dad loved Mom. She was the only one who could calm him down when it got rough. She was his rock."

"I was asking Oscar."

The young man looked away. "I don't know."

He couldn't give up. It was obvious something was brewing inside Oscar, and he needed to know what it was. "I think you have a theory. I would love to hear it."

Oscar huffed. "No, you wouldn't."

"If you intend to tell the DA, I need to hear it."

Miranda shook her head. "He's not telling the DA anything because there's nothing to tell."

Oscar's head swiveled and he took Isla into his gaze. "Is there anything to tell, Isla?"

Isla's eyes widened. "What do you mean?"

"I mean it's going to come out no matter how hard you try to hide it," Oscar said.

"What are you talking about?" Isla looked at him, confusion plain on her pretty face.

But David was fairly certain he did understand. "I believe he thinks you're sleeping with his father."

Her face drained of color. "What?"

"You think I haven't seen you sneaking out of his room?" Oscar said, his voice rising. "Or all those nights you stayed over? I know I've been in my own place for a year and a half, but I bet nothing's changed."

"I stayed over because your mother asked me to. There were nights when she felt she couldn't handle him by herself," Isla replied, but her voice was shaking. She looked to Miranda. "Tell me you don't believe this."

Miranda looked away. "I don't know. I don't hate you, if that's what you're asking. I figure if Mom was okay with it, I couldn't be too angry. I know she was seeing someone."

Yep, a mental illness defense was looking better and better. "Your mother was seeing someone?"

"You don't know that for sure," Oscar said.

His sister frowned. "Well, you don't know that Dad was boffing Isla either."

"I wasn't." Isla stood up, every muscle in her body tense. "I have never touched your dad in anything but a friendly way. On occasion I've helped him get to bed because the meds got to be too much and sometimes your mom got emotional. So if you saw me coming out of his room, that's what I was doing. I didn't do it because I wanted to crawl in with him. I didn't do it because I was his lawyer. I did it because I was his friend, and I kind of thought I was close to the family."

"Yeah, you always intruded," Oscar replied. "I get it. Everyone who could have loved you is dead, but that doesn't mean you get to play around at being in my family. You're the help. That's what you never once understood."

Isla stood for a moment, her body completely still, and then she turned. "I'm going to wait outside. When you're ready, I'll be in the back."

She turned and walked away, her movements lacking her normal grace.

"You're such an ass." Miranda started to go after Isla.

"She wants some time alone, Miranda," David said, his voice deep. "And I would like to know why you think your mother was seeing someone. I need to know everything. Your brother might not care what happens to your father. From what I can tell he doesn't care about anything at all, including himself, but I rather thought you were concerned."

He was worried about Isla, but he couldn't run after her. He didn't think she would want that given the distance she'd kept today. They were back in a professional setting and he would honor that, but oh, how he wanted to take Trey Adams's son and show him a thing or two about respect and behaving like a gentleman.

But first he needed to get every bit of information he could out of the little ass and his sister because there was zero doubt Royce Osborne would be out here very soon. David had to know what they would say so he could figure out how to turn it to his advantage. Or at least mitigate the damage.

"I care about things," Oscar said. "I certainly care more about my mom than anyone else does. All you people want to talk about is Dad. My mother is dead. Does anyone care about that? My aunt is no help. I haven't seen her sober since we got here. The only one who seems to give a shit about my mom is Uncle Carey's gold digger."

"Her name is Amber," Miranda said between clenched teeth.

"I don't care. She's using Mom's funeral as some kind of social stepping-stone," Oscar replied flatly. "Shouldn't you be dealing with that?"

"I can't when I'm spending all my time keeping my asshole of a brother in line," she spat back. She turned to David and visibly calmed herself. "As to why I think my mother was having an affair, well, the last few months she's had a weekly appointment at the Algonquin in Midtown. My mom was obsessed with planners. Not the online kind. She was old school."

"She would get excited when it came time to get a new one." Oscar sounded softer than before. "She kept a couple actually. One for business. One for family stuff. One for the personal appointments."

"Which one did she mark the meetings at the Algonquin in?" He would need those planners, though they were likely already in police custody.

"The personal one." Miranda wouldn't look him in the eye. She was focused on the carpet in front of her. "I only saw it because I was dropping off some stickers I'd had custom made for her. She liked to decorate the planners. She would start each week by reviewing what she'd written down and then she would decorate. She had stickers for everything. Little coffee mugs for coffee dates. Stickers for doctors' appointments. Stuff like that. I made some travel ones. We were supposed to go to London next month after Dad's party. I snuck up to her office and I saw the appointment on the calendar. It's not a hotel she would use for a function. It's nice and historic, but not Mom's style. I was curious and I spied on her a little. I noticed she'd been there every Thursday for a month."

"Did you ask her about it?"

She shook her head. "No. I didn't want to know. I left the stickers and I went back to my dorm. I tried not to think about it, but I understood. It can't be nice having your happily ever after turn into a nightmare. My parents are young. They shouldn't have to deal with this now. In my mind if Mom was getting something she needed, then I was okay with that."

"Mom wouldn't cheat on Dad," Oscar insisted. "No matter how miserable he made her."

"He wasn't trying to make her miserable," Miranda argued. "He's sick. Why can't you understand that?"

"It doesn't matter." Oscar sat back. "I know Mom wouldn't cheat. If she was going to a hotel, she was meeting a friend there."

"I'll put an investigator on it," David promised. "Can you tell me when you last saw your mom?"

"I was at her place that morning," Oscar admitted. "We had breakfast. Well, I had breakfast. I had to force half a grapefruit down her throat."

"She seemed out of sorts, or did she normally skip breakfast?"

Oscar seemed to think about that for a moment, or perhaps he was thinking about how much information he wanted to give up. He finally sighed and seemed to settle in. "Mom always stopped eating when she was upset about something. I would have to make food myself to get her to eat. She wouldn't turn me down if I put it in front of her. It was obvious to me that she was upset, but she wouldn't tell me what it was about. I figured it was about Dad. It almost always was. I wondered if she'd found out about Isla."

David had to stop himself from cringing. "You know, talking that way about your father won't help his case. Unless you have serious evidence that your father was having an affair, you shouldn't mention rumors."

"Fine. He's probably too crazy to have an affair. I just don't like how Isla hangs around all the time," Oscar admitted. "She's bossy and she pretends she's like my big sister or something."

"She's been a big sister to you," Miranda replied. "You pretend like she's never done anything but lawyer crap for us. She's the one who stayed with us when Mom and Dad were traveling. She would order pizza and play games with us. I don't understand why you hate her now."

"She's trying to help." It seemed obvious to him.

"She sticks her nose in where it doesn't belong." Oscar wasn't having it. "And who hired you? Shouldn't that be my and Miranda's decision? Obviously dear old Dad can't make one since he's crazy. I don't know that you would be my choice."

"Unfortunately, Isla is the one making the decisions here. You don't have power of attorney," David replied. "Do you know what that means? Your mother set it up in the event that she was incapacitated or died. Isla makes the decisions for your family now and for the foreseeable future."

"What?" Oscar stood up. "Why? We're freaking adults."

"I told you," Miranda said under her breath. "I told you Mom wouldn't leave it in my hands. She certainly wouldn't leave it in yours."

Oscar turned to her, his face flushing. "What about the money?"

She shrugged.

It appeared he would have to explain all the legal ramifications to them. "Isla controls it until such time as your father can handle it again. That's highly unlikely. Or until you reach the age of twenty-seven, and even then all you get is the trust they set up for you. If you were expecting an inheritance, try to remember your father isn't dead. The money all went to him."

"But he could go to jail." Oscar couldn't seem to understand.

"That's why Isla is there to make sure the money is properly taken care of and everyone gets what they need." It was kind of fun to watch the little shit squirm. Not that he would squirm for long. The sad part was he was certain Isla wouldn't abuse her position in order to squeeze someone out of pettiness.

"I thought she would leave the power to Aunt Cressida." Oscar sat back like he'd lost something. "She's Mom's sister."

"She's also an alcoholic," Miranda replied. "Aunt Cressida would spend it all. Mom did it to protect us. You're not going to lose your apartment."

"Unless that bitch decides I don't need one," he shot back.

And he'd had enough of Oscar. "All right, you can leave. I need you to understand that if you decide to go public with how much you hate your father, there's a clause in your trust fund that covers drugs. If you're caught with drugs or arrested for any violent offense, you can potentially lose your trust fund."

His eyes went wide. "I can lose my money for smoking weed? You know it's not even illegal most places."

"I didn't write the trust, son. However, I will use it to fuck you over if you continue to behave like an angry toddler," he promised. "It's my job to make sure your father gets the best outcome possible. If you get in my way, I'll deal with you. And I'd be kinder to Isla because she's the one who holds your balls in the palm of her hand. You don't want her to have to make a fist, do you?"

Oscar stood. "We'll see how long you last, asshole. And tell Isla I can get a lawyer, too. I'll fight her over this. I won't let her steal everything."

He stormed out, his sneakers squeaking on the stairs.

Miranda sighed. "Well, that went well. He can't break the trust, can he? Mom was right to structure it the way she did. He would blow through it all and then come asking for mine, and I would be a dipshit and help him."

"No, he won't be able to break it unless he can prove Isla is using it to serve herself. What he can do is cause an even worse scandal." It was time to head back. They had a long drive ahead of them. "Will you at least let me know if you're contacted by the press or the DA? It's never a good idea to talk to police without a lawyer present."

"Someone will come with us? Because I know they'll want to talk," Miranda said.

"Yes, I'll have someone from my firm go with you and advise you," he promised. "And your brother. I'm worried about him intentionally incriminating your father."

"I'll talk to him." Miranda glanced back to the door where Isla had disappeared. "He's not usually this nasty. He doesn't handle change well. And I'll make sure he studies up on the disease Dad has. Maybe it will help him understand. Is my dad okay?"

"He's safe in the hospital. I'm going to try my hardest to ensure he stays there."

"But he's going to die from this thing, right?"

There was only one answer to that. "Yes."

"I'm going to be an orphan soon." Her voice had gotten soft. "That sounds silly since I'm an adult and orphans are kids who can't feed themselves. I can take care of myself. I'll have all that money waiting for me. But I would give it back to have my mom. She won't watch me get married or hold her grandchild. My dad won't walk me down the aisle. I wonder, if he could go back, would he do it again?"

His heart clenched because he thought he knew what she was asking. "Play football?"

"Yeah."

"I think it depends. For some of us, it was the only way out of poverty. I think it was that way for your father. If he had to choose between where he is now and not having you and your brother, I bet he would do it all over again." How many times had he asked himself the same question?

"What does any of it mean if they're not here?" She sniffled and stood. "Please tell Isla I'm sorry. I'm sorry I said the things I did. If she says she didn't have an affair with my dad, I believe her. And please let her know I don't feel the same way my brother does. I always considered her a big sister and I . . . I'm going to need her badly. Will you do that?"

He nodded, sympathy welling inside him. She was young, and such a burden had been placed on her shoulders. "Yes and, Miranda, if you need anything, anything at all, call me. I mean it."

"Thank you. Do you mind letting yourself out? I think I'll take a nap. I didn't sleep much last night."

He watched as she walked up the stairs, his heart heavy.

~

"Are you all right?"

It was the first time he'd talked to her since she'd gotten into his Audi and they left Oscar and Miranda behind. She watched the shoreline as he drove, the waves rolling in. She'd sat outside while David talked to the kids, but she hadn't cried, wouldn't cry. She'd done enough of that. "I'm fine. I always knew I wasn't Oscar's favorite person, but he surprised me today. It won't change the way I do my job. You don't have to worry about that."

His hands tightened on the steering wheel. "I wasn't worried about you doing your job."

He fell silent again.

She hated the tension between them, hated how the whole afternoon had gone, hated that she hadn't been able to take his hand when he'd offered it to her. He'd walked out onto the back porch and held a hand out to help her up. She'd wanted to take that hand and let him pull her until she was against his chest, his arms around her. Instead she'd stood on her own and tried not to think about how hurt he'd looked.

Now he was staring at the road, and the distance between them was her fault.

The worst part was the guilt descending on her as she seriously considered what she'd done. Carey had told her some things he'd heard about David and she'd simply believed him. Or perhaps she'd taken his advice so he wouldn't think poorly of her. No matter what he said, she would always be his son's fiancée in his mind.

She felt guilty about David because he was different. Her feelings for him were stronger, more compelling than anything she'd felt in years, and she was coming to him as a woman, not the hero-worshipping girl she'd been. If Austin had lived, that worship would have been tested. They would have evolved as a couple, but because he'd died, he remained perfect in her mind, and guilt swamped her at the thought of truly giving herself to another man.

Was she willing to live the rest of her life like this? Being alive and yet not truly living?

David had heard a lot of gossip about her and how she'd had an affair with Trey, and yet he'd been warm and open. She wasn't giving him the same consideration. She'd heard that word—cancer—and it triggered a reaction. She'd pulled in on herself. She'd judged him for not behaving the way she thought he should, and it was wrong of her not to give him a chance to explain.

"Do you think I had an affair with my client?"

His eyes were steady on the road. "No."

"Why?"

"Uhm, because you told me you didn't. I assume you don't have a reason to lie to me. I'm fairly good at knowing when someone's lying. It's a criminal defense skill. Unless you're telling me something different now."

"No. I've never had an affair with a married man. I've barely had affairs with single men." She was a heinous bitch. She'd soaked up his faith and given back none of her own. "Carey had a talk with me. He thinks it would be a bad idea for me to get involved with you— and not on a business level."

He nodded slowly, not looking her way. His tone was even as he spoke. "I assumed there was a reason for the sudden chill factor. It's okay. We don't have to be superfriendly to work together. I hope whatever he said doesn't make you worried about my skill. If you're trying to find another attorney, I'd like to know now. We're already spending money on the case and we're a small firm."

A small firm funded by a billionaire, but she wasn't going to argue with him. "Not at all. He thinks you're absolutely the best man for the job and I'll send you a sizable retainer when I get back to my computer. I'm sorry I haven't done that yet."

"I know you're good for it. I was merely trying to figure out what Kendrick's problem is with me. Now I know it's personal," he replied. "Well, like I said, we're adults. I think we can handle a civil working relationship. I appreciate you coming out with me today, but I'll take it from here. I'll keep you up to date on everything."

He wasn't going to make this easy on her. "That's not what I want. I know the smart thing would be to take Carey's advice and pull away, but I've hated sitting beside you and not talking."

"You want to be friends?" His tone was perfectly bland, polite.

"Are you going to make me say it?"

"Oh, yes. You're definitely going to have to say it." He slid a long look her way. "I'll be honest, I'm not sure what *it* is."

She took a deep breath. In for a penny . . . "I'm very attracted to you and I don't know what to do about it. Well, I do know what I should do, but I'm finding it hard to follow through. It's complicated."

His eyes back on the road, he smoothly turned toward the city. "How about you start by asking me about whatever it was that Carey told you."

She was quiet for a moment, feeling like a complete idiot. She'd kind of laid herself bare and he hadn't said anything. Was that some form of punishment? Or was he being supercareful?

"I'm attracted to you, too," he said quietly. "And you're right. It's very complicated."

Something settled deep inside her and she knew she owed him an honest explanation. "Carey talked to me about your wife."

"He knew my wife?"

Wow, they did not need the air conditioner. His tone alone could chill the car. "I believe he was telling me what he'd heard."

Another beat of chilly silence passed. "And you didn't think to ask me about it?"

"David, I was wrong. I'll be honest, I'm a little turned around and I'm not making the best decisions right now. It's been a hard couple of days." And that was an excellent reason to not go through with this. She should take what he'd offered, a civil working relationship, and maybe that could change somewhere down the line when they'd put some distance between themselves and the case.

His hand came out, covering hers. "I'm sorry, sweetheart. It's a touchy subject, but I shouldn't take it out on you. You've had a rough afternoon. I don't want to make it worse. Do you want to hear my side? It's okay if you don't. You need to understand that you're in control of this. I'm not going to push you. Even if I want to."

Why couldn't she have met him at some other time? He was the absolutely perfect combination of smart and sexy, confident enough in himself that he didn't need to always be in control. She flipped her hand over and tangled her fingers with his for a moment, letting the warmth of his skin sink into hers. And then she pulled away. "Yes, I would like to hear your side. Carey talked about how she got cancer. I know a little bit about that."

His hand moved back to the steering wheel. "I married Lynn because we'd been dating for a couple of years and we decided it was time. Jocks were Lynn's thing and when she realized I was going to actually get into the pros, she started pushing me to commit. And it's to Henry's everlasting credit that he never tells me he told me so.

I thought I was in love so we got married and everything was good for a time. We struggled to get pregnant, found out she had endometriosis. I wanted to adopt, but she was insistent. She became utterly obsessed with having a baby. We spent every dime I made on IVF and I'll be honest, I got tired of being treated like a sperm donor. I know infertility is hard and it was hard on Lynn, but after a while it didn't feel like we had a marriage anymore. We had a project and she was determined to finish it. I didn't understand why we couldn't adopt. There are all these kids out there and they need parents. I didn't get why we had to put ourselves through hell when we could go out and open our arms and have what she said she wanted."

"Did she ever manage to get pregnant?"

"No. It never worked for us. Then my first major injury happened. For the first time in years I spent more than a few days at home with her and I realized we lived two completely different lives. But she begged me to keep trying and we went to counseling. I wanted to retire from the game. I wasn't ever going to be an exemplary player. I went into football because my dad loved it and it was a good way to get a scholarship. I didn't want to go pro at all, but Lynn insisted that I would make a ton of money and set us up for the rest of our lives. She convinced me I could go to law school after my pro career was through."

She couldn't imagine anyone walking away from football, but then she'd spent much of her teen years and adult life surrounded by the culture. "I thought it was every boy's dream to be a professional athlete."

"It was when I was a kid. But the older I got, the more I wanted to do something different. Maybe it was Harvard and Henry. I got to be friends with Henry and he was incredibly passionate about the law. It rubbed off on me. Anyway, I let that go to please my fiancée and my parents. But the second injury—I knew it was career ending." His voice was gravelly with emotion.

She wanted to have her hand in his again. "And you decided to go back to school."

His head nodded slowly. "I did. That was when Lynn left me. She explained that she never wanted to marry a boring lawyer and that's all I would ever be. She told me she was leaving me for one of my teammates and she'd been having an affair with him. I didn't see her again for six weeks. I was ready to start divorce proceedings when she showed up and told me she'd been diagnosed. We needed the insurance and that's why I stayed on the roster. I know everyone has this idea in their head that if you play pro ball you're an instant millionaire."

She knew the truth. "Not at all. Don't forget I spent a lot of time working in the Guardians' front office. Unless you're a superstar, you don't make millions until late in your career."

"I made the league minimum most of my career," he admitted. "Back then it was almost three hundred thousand. At the end I was up to six hundred. I know that's a lot of money . . ."

She interrupted him because it was obvious he hated explaining money to her. "Your agent takes a cut. The IRS takes a big cut. And then there's living expenses."

"I bought my parents a house. That wasn't cheap. My wife didn't believe in living within her means," he replied. "I still managed to sock money away. I made some good investments, but those IVF treatments were expensive and they were nothing compared to her medical bills from the cancer treatments even with good insurance. When the team booted me, I got to keep my insurance for a couple of years. It's why we didn't divorce. I went back to school and she chose to go to her parents' home for treatment."

"Why would you pay her medical bills?" She had to ask the question though she already knew why. Because he was a good man.

He shrugged slightly as they started through the Lincoln Tunnel. "She was my wife. I couldn't leave her with nothing."

"It sounds like she left you with nothing."

"Well, I couldn't have lived with myself if I hadn't helped her. But I didn't love her. At that point, I knew I'd never honestly loved her. I shouldn't have married her. If there's one thing you learn as a defense attorney, it's that there's always two sides to any story and no one ever thinks he's the villain."

"Why would her parents hate you? Carey apparently spoke to them. He told me he has dossiers on people he might have to hire."

David chuckled, though it wasn't an amused sound. "That does not surprise me. As to why my in-laws hate me, that's simple. Lynn wasn't good at telling the truth. She told her parents I was the one who had the affair and that was why she left. She was dying at the time and I wasn't going to defend myself. It was better they hated me than be disappointed in her."

"So that's why you didn't visit her."

"She didn't want me around," he explained. "She never loved me. She loved my potential and the life I could have provided for her, but never me. So that is my truth. I'm sure Lynn would have something else to say. I didn't go to her funeral but I paid for it. It wasn't the same as what happened between you and Carey Kendrick's son. There was no young love involved. Just a whole lot of regret."

It was easy to see it still affected him, and she wished she'd never reopened that wound. "I'm sorry."

He looked a little ghostly in the lights of the tunnel. Remote. "There's nothing to be sorry about. I wish she'd lived. I didn't want anything bad to happen to her, but I prefer my life now. I wish I'd followed my gut in the first place and borrowed the money for law school. All I ended up getting from years of playing was a beat-to-hell body, arthritic knees, and a potential sword hanging over my head."

"A sword?"

"I spend every day of my life worried I'll end up like Trey," he admitted.

The thought made her heart ache. "Not every player gets it. Most don't. Trey had a much longer career than you did."

"Well, I still do everything I can to hold it off. That's my side of the story. I don't know if that changes your mind about me or reinforces your decision, but it's the truth."

She shifted in her seat, turning toward him. "It changes my mind, but I don't know what we're doing. I want to ask you on a date, but I don't know how wise that is."

"If it helps, I would say yes," he said, his tone warmer than before. "You're not my client. We share a client, so it's more like dating a coworker. If you have a hard line against that, I'll have to work to soften that up because you're the only woman I've wanted in years."

The words alone made her body heat up. He wanted her. "Do you want to come up and we can talk about . . ." She laughed, her first genuine laugh in hours. "I was going to say we can talk about whatever you found out from the kids today, but I swear if I have to even think Oscar's name again I might scream."

"Okay, well, how about we go back to your place and talk about anything except the case. I could do without thinking about it for a while, too. Although I would feel better if I'd punched that kid."

She laughed again, her heart light at the thought of spending another night with him. "I'm glad you didn't or I would have to play *your* lawyer. Let's order pizza. I'm in a comfort-food mood. And wine. I could use some wine."

They would talk. They would get to know each other better. They would decide if they would go to bed together. God, was it wrong that these normal choices excited her? That she felt real for the first time in years?

He turned down the street that led to her building and stopped at the red light.

"What do you want on your pizza?" she asked. "I know you'll need some kind of meat. Let me guess. You're an Italian sausage guy. Extra cheese. Please tell me you don't mind mushrooms. I can't live without them. It might be a deal breaker."

"Is that your building up ahead?" David asked, paying no mind at all to her flirty tone.

She sat up straight. There were two big news trucks outside her building.

A horn honked and she realized the light had turned green. The traffic was heavy and there was no way David could move to one of the outer lanes before they stopped at the next light.

"Why are they here?" She sank down in her seat and wished she'd brought a hat or something.

"Just be cool. We'll drive by and head someplace safer," he promised.

The car rolled another few feet and that was when someone noticed her. The camera crews turned like predators scenting an easy meal and they were all over the car. They swarmed all around the Audi and she heard the click of a button as David checked to make sure the doors were locked. Knuckles rapped on the windows and suddenly people were shouting questions. If there was any thought that this was some kind of a mistake, it was tossed away as they started shouting her name.

"Isla, what do you have to say about Trey's incarceration? Is it true you were his lover and he killed his wife for you?"

"Isla, how much money will you get if you manage to help keep your lover out of jail?"

"Did you know Trey planned to kill Portia? Or was that a surprise? Did you help him set her up?"

"What?" She couldn't believe what they were asking.

"Don't acknowledge them." David's words came out in a hard tone. "Don't even look at them. Stare straight ahead. Give them nothing. Don't you dare let them see you cry. Keep your face as blank as possible."

"An insider said someone else was in the penthouse that night," a reporter said. She was in a form-fitting suit, a wireless microphone in her hands. "Was that you? Were you there when Trey Adams killed his wife, and did you help him clean it all up?"

She started to turn, but his hand came out, stopping her.

"Not a word."

"But she mentioned a witness." If there was a witness, shouldn't they get that name?

"Their witness is very likely some crackpot who called in to the station. Look out the front window and stop reacting right now, Isla. You can't give them anything to use. And don't cry. You can cry all you like when we get someplace safe."

They kept yelling their questions and the day was crashing in on her. This was how her life was going to be. This would always taint her.

"Noah? I'm going to need Drew's place. Can you call and have it prepped?" He had his cell phone pressed to his ear. "Of course it is. No. That won't be a problem. Yeah, we have a press invasion at Isla's. Same old, same old. Thank you." He moved the car forward an inch, but the reporters were standing in front as well. His jaw tightened and he dialed the police. "Yes, there's a car surrounded by reporters on Fifth outside the Tranor Building. It's holding up two lanes of traffic. Thank you."

"What do we do?" She hated the fact that her voice was shaky.

"We wait for the cops and pray my temper holds because I would really like to mow down a couple of reporters right now." Despite his words, he put the car in park. "When we get to our new destination, I will be filing several suits against a couple of media firms."

Somehow the fact that he was brutally angry calmed her down. He was here with her. "I don't think you can sue them."

"I'll find a way." His hands were tight on the steering wheel.

"Well, right now all they have is me looking confused and staring out the front window. I think we'll be okay."

"You want to give them something else to talk about?" His voice had gone husky, his eyes still on the reporters in front of them, but his jaw had softened slightly.

"What would that be?"

He was silent for a moment as though thinking about what he was going to say next. "They think you're involved with Trey Adams. Show them you're involved with me."

Her heart rate ticked up and it wasn't all about the situation they were in. "Seriously? I thought we were trying not to make news."

He finally turned her way and his lips curled up in a grin. "I'm boring. If you're having an affair with me, you'll be boring, too."

"That might be the worst line I've ever heard." Even with the barbarians at the gates, he made her smile. "Is it going to work?"

"Hell, yeah, it is. Let me lead." He reached over and put his hand on hers, drawing it up and bringing it to his lips. He kissed her hand and then held it to his chest as though giving her comfort or taking it for himself.

As though? No, she felt so much comfort in the touch of his hand. She leaned in and let her head find his shoulder. Under the thin material of his shirt, she could feel his heart beating against her palm.

Sure enough, the reporters were documenting every move they made.

"It's going to be okay, Isla. This is going to go away and life will be back to normal again," he whispered.

Those weren't the words she heard though. She heard what his heartbeat was telling her. *I'm a rock. You can hold on to me and I won't break. You can count on me.*

Slowly she calmed down. "I can't stay at home right now. They'll be here for a couple of days. I would be a prisoner here and I would put everyone else in the building in their way, too."

They kept knocking on the windows.

David ignored them. "You're right. They'll camp out here, though the police will try to stop them. They'll try to hunt us down, but I'm taking you someplace safe. We'll have a few minutes while the cops are sorting everything out. Is the parking garage secure here?"

"Yes. They keep a tight lid on the garage." She started when the car was jostled. It was strange to think that a few minutes ago she'd felt perfectly safe in the car. Everything could change quickly, and she had to remember that.

"It's all right. The cops will be here soon."

She took a deep breath. They were blocking out the sun now. She tried to concentrate on what he'd said on the phone. He'd called Noah and asked about his brother's place. "Drew? Lawless? You're taking me to hide out in Noah's brother's place?"

"Well, I certainly wouldn't take you to Noah's. He wouldn't stop hitting on you, and god only knows who he would drag home at two in the morning. Seriously, Drew's place is empty right now. We won't be imposing and he's got the best security in the city. They would look for us at Henry's. I don't want to bring this down on Win's head."

She let out a shaky laugh. "Noah's not that bad and you're right. Win's been through enough press to last a lifetime. And I'm curious about seeing how a reclusive billionaire lives. You certainly know how to show a girl a good time, Cormack."

"I try."

In the distance she could hear sirens.

"See, there they are. They'll have this whole crew cleared out of here in a couple of minutes, we'll run up and pack a bag, and then we'll hunker down and see what's on Lawless's Netflix list." He squeezed her hand.

The sirens were loud now and the road suddenly cleared.

David breathed a massive sigh of relief and turned into the parking garage. "Okay, we've got two following us."

"The guard should keep them out." She hoped. "Let me off by the elevator and I promise I'll be superfast. If you want to wait with the car, I won't be more than five minutes."

He glanced around, obviously looking for a slot. "I should go with you."

Unfortunately it was a Sunday and everything was taken. If it had been during the week, there might have been some tenant slots open, but there was nothing on the weekends.

"The guest spots are taken." She unbuckled her belt. "I'm grabbing my toothbrush and some clothes and my laptop. I bet the cops won't be here for long. We have one shot at this."

She could see in his face he wasn't happy about the plan, but he nodded shortly. "Hurry."

He stopped the car and she was out in a shot. Her shoes thudded, echoing through the concrete garage as she raced to the elevator.

What had she done? She'd pretty much announced to the world that she was seeing David Cormack. There would be pictures tomorrow of them huddled together in his car, her hand over his chest. Carey was going to be upset that she hadn't followed his advice.

The elevator opened and she waved at David. It didn't matter. This was her life and she wanted to see where it went with him. Hell, she wanted him period. While she was shoving her laptop into a bag she would shove some lingerie in there, too. She'd bought a couple of pieces from Victoria's Secret when she'd decided it was way past time to get out there and start living again, but she'd never worn them for a man. Most of her dates hadn't led to sex, and the few she'd had sex with hadn't cared about anything but their own orgasm.

Would it still fit? Would he like her in it? Or was he sitting down there right now figuring out how badly he'd screwed up by getting involved with her?

She watched as the floors counted off, her heart rate ticking up. *Please don't let there be a reporter at my door.*

It was quiet in the elevator. She'd never noticed that before. It was almost eerily silent.

It was stupid that the elevator doors opened and she was slightly afraid to walk down that hall. It seemed longer than it did normally. How many doors from the elevator to her apartment? Six. She was the seventh apartment on the right. It was a thirty-second walk. Why was she hesitating?

The doors started to close and she stopped them. Something prickled along her spine, but she ignored it. She wasn't going to call David and tell him she was afraid to walk her own hallway alone.

But suddenly she remembered what it had been like to walk down the hallway of Trey and Portia's penthouse. She remembered how low the lights had been, how her eyes had to focus in the dark. God, she remembered the sound of Trey moaning, low and from somewhere deep inside.

Isla forced herself to walk out of that damn elevator. She forced herself to walk down the hall, reaching into her purse for the keys. When she got to the door, she forced her shaking hands to unlock the door and walk inside.

Okay, she was inside and safe and now she had to move. Five minutes. That was all she was going to give herself. She would shove whatever she could into her Longchamp and race back down to David.

And she would kiss him. She wouldn't go another moment without knowing what it felt like to kiss him.

She turned and stopped again.

Standing there in the middle of her apartment was a man dressed all in black. Long and lean and deadly. All she could see of him were his eyes, and they were cold orbs staring right at her.

He was on her before she could scream.

SEVEN

D avid watched the elevator doors close as a car ahead of him pulled out of its parking space.

Bingo.

He didn't give a shit that it was a tenant space. He wouldn't be there for long, but he didn't like the idea of Isla alone upstairs. It looked like the reporters had stayed outside her building, but one or two might have snuck in. They could corner her and she wouldn't be able to fight her way out. It was best that they didn't get split up at this point. She didn't have the training he did to deal with difficult journalists.

Like the ones the guards were holding back.

"Are you involved with Isla Shayne, Mr. Cormack? Are you representing her as well as Trey Adams?" a deep voice yelled from the guard station.

"Is it true Isla called you the night of the murder? Were you there?" The second reporter was a female. She looked like she was ready to hurdle over the guardrail if someone would let her.

He had to give it to them. They were persistent. His cell trilled as he slammed the car door. At least it looked like the Audi had come through all right. His poor baby. He swiped a thumb across the screen to answer.

"This is Cormack." He started toward the elevators, keeping his voice low. The whole place seemed to echo.

"Hey, Romeo, how's it going? I hear you're heading to a very special love nest," a familiar voice said.

He should have known Noah couldn't keep his mouth shut.

"Fuck you, Henry. We got swarmed by the press when I tried to drop her off at her place. I had to call the cops. We couldn't move. She can't stay here. Has this character assassination been going on all day? We've been out to the Hamptons to talk to the Adams kids. I haven't watched the news." No, he'd been watching a nasty soap play out right before his eyes.

"Oh, you have no idea. They're all over your girl," Henry replied. "The regular news shows aren't bad, but the tabloid shows won't let it go. They are all over this story and they smell blood in the water. I've got the investigators dealing with her alibi. I want it so tight no one can question it. I'm worried Royce is going to start feeling some pressure and he'll arrest Isla when he formally charges Adams."

Shit. He couldn't deal with the idea of Isla getting shoved into jail because of some rumors, but people had been arrested for less. "Have them request her phone records. There were lots of calls made that night. Depending on which cell tower picked up the phone, we should be able to figure out if she was in her neighborhood or Trey's when the crime was committed."

"We're already working on it and the investigators asked her building for records. At that time of night she's got to buzz in and out. They've got a security cam on both doors. She didn't take her car so we're also running down her cabdriver." Henry said. "Not that it will help us with Adams's building. Bad news there."

He winced, glancing down at his watch. How long had she been gone? He needed to get up there. He could lose the call while he was in the elevator, but he was getting antsy about her being alone. They needed to move. He didn't want them in the same position they'd been in earlier. Once the cops left, the reporters would be right back to their old tricks, and they knew he was in the garage. "Are you telling me we don't have any video footage from the night of the murder? That's one of the most expensive buildings in the Upper East Side. They don't have security cameras?"

"They have one on the front door and one on the side, but the penthouse has a servants' entrance and that camera had been down for two days," Henry explained. "They were waiting for parts. It gets worse."

Fuck it. He was going to risk it. He pressed the button to call the elevator. "How?"

"I've finally got the official police report. No signs of forced entry. If someone got in that night, they either had the code or Trey or Portia let the person in. Now do you want the good news?"

He was surprised there *was* good news. "I would love any good news you could possibly give me because talking to the kids was a complete bust."

"The police found the murder weapon and they think they have a usable print," Henry said.

"Chef's knife?" That would be his bet given the types of wounds she'd had. It was a weapon of convenience that could be found in most homes. It also led him to believe that whoever killed Portia hadn't gone there with murder in mind. Otherwise he or she would have brought a weapon.

Henry hummed his agreement. "Oh, yes, and it looks like it had been cleaned and placed back in the butcher block, which means our perp stayed behind after the murder. Even more interesting, the police now believe the fight that led to Portia's death started in the kitchen. They found drops of the victim's blood starting near the island in the kitchen and then trailing from there to the hall and to her bedroom."

That was not a good thing. "Which reinforces the idea that it was Trey and they had an argument, or it was someone she knew quite well and again they had an argument that led to the murder. Do we know if anything was missing?"

"According to the police, there was a necklace worth roughly two million dollars sitting on the vanity in Portia's closet. There was also a couple of hundred bucks in her purse and any number of random ridiculously expensive items that would have been easy for the perpetrator to take with them."

"I'm getting in an elevator. I'll call you back if I lose you," he said, stepping in and pushing the button for Isla's floor. The doors closed as he continued. "So what's the police theory?"

He had a few of his own.

The cell signal seemed strong in this building. Henry's voice didn't even waver. "They think Trey Adams went crazy and did that damage himself either before or after he murdered his wife. They could potentially say he wasn't crazy at all and that the damage in the room proves that he knew what he'd done was wrong and he was attempting to cover up the crime."

"And since he would have known exactly where the knife was, premeditation could still be on the table. He's the one with the most to gain if she dies, although we can mitigate that with the fact that while the money goes to him, Isla is the one who controls it."

"And we're back to the beginning. We have to prove Isla isn't involved with Adams."

He wanted to punch something. "She's not."

"How sure are you of that?" Henry asked, his voice low, and there was a creeping sympathy that made David wince.

"I'm sure." He couldn't back down on this.

"Is your brain sure or your dick?"

He practically growled because Henry could be sarcastic at the worst times. "Don't you bring my dick into this. My dick is incredibly smart. My dick is picky."

"Your dick has had a long dry spell and that might be affecting you." Henry sighed over the line. "Will the kids help? We could use some good photo ops. If the kids stand beside her, that might help mitigate the damage the press is doing."

The elevator doors opened again. Thank god. There was a man standing and waiting for the elevator. David brushed by the man who was dressed in all black, a baseball cap pulled low on his head.

"Excuse me," the man said, his voice deep.

David nodded, stepped out, and started toward her door. She had a completely different version of what five minutes meant. He should have driven her to Drew's and prayed she fit into Drew's wife Shelby's clothes, but no, he wanted her to have her things around her.

Maybe his dick wasn't so smart.

"The kids are a problem we shouldn't talk about on the phone." Despite the fact that he seemed to be alone, he had to take into account that someone was always listening. "I'll fill you in when we get to Drew's and I can be sure we have a secure line."

He got to Isla's door and knocked.

"That bad, huh?" Henry asked. "Well, I've read the dossier on the son and it seems like he and Trey had a few public arguments."

"That doesn't surprise me." Why wasn't she answering? He touched the doorknob and the door opened. He stopped. "She didn't lock her door."

"What? Are you up at her apartment?"

He stepped into the small hallway. "Isla?"

The place was incredibly quiet. He couldn't hear her moving around and that was when he noticed her bar. When they'd left this morning, it had been perfectly neat, with a basket of mail to one side. Now the basket had been turned over, the insides dumped across the bar.

"Isla?" Something was wrong. Very wrong.

He moved into the kitchen and saw something that had him panicking. "Henry, I need you to call the cops. Send them up here. Someone's in Isla's apartment and she's down."

Isla was facedown on the floor, her body still. His heart damn near stopped and he let the cell drop to the ground as he hit his knees. He could hear Henry shouting, but his whole being was focused on her. He reached for her hand. Warm.

Her eyelids fluttered. "David?"

He pulled her into his arms. "I'm here. Stay with me."

He held her and prayed the ambulance was fast enough.

～

"I'm fine. I didn't even have a concussion," Isla was saying as he set her down on the couch.

If he never heard the word *concussion* again, it would be far too soon. "I still think they should have kept you overnight. And I definitely don't think you're up for guests."

Detective Campbell had been waiting for them when they got to Drew's place along with Noah, the two McKay-Taggart investigators, and that slimeball Royce Osborne.

Campbell slid out his notebook. "I only have a few questions."

"I have many," Osborne promised. "And you should be happy I'm willing to do this here and not in the hospital where the reporters were. I don't think you would like it if my line of questioning got out." He stood over her like the bully he was for a moment and then stepped back, glancing around the magnificent Upper West Side penthouse. "This is certainly an upgrade. It's even nicer than what Trey Adams could provide for you."

Her jaw clenched, but the detective got to speak before David could.

"Counselor, I allowed you to come along. Don't make me regret it," Campbell said.

"Oh, I can make him regret it," the new guy said in a lyrical Irish accent. Liam O'Donnell had met them at the hospital along with his partner, a pretty but tough-looking redhead named Erin Taggart. From what David understood, Erin was a Taggart by marriage.

"Please let him," Erin said, sitting on the couch beside Campbell and giving him a wink. "Li's been behind a desk too long. He needs some physical work, if you know what I mean."

Li huffed a bit. "Like you don't. You've been behind a desk as long as I have."

Erin shrugged. "What can I say? Age has mellowed me out. Besides, I kind of want to see what the douchebag says. He seems to know everything."

Osborne turned on her. "I'm an assistant district attorney for the city of New York. You should pay me some respect."

"Yeah, I'm not good at that," Erin admitted.

Noah moved in. "I don't understand what the ADA has to do with the fact that someone broke into Isla's apartment."

But David could guess. "The ADA thinks we set all of this up to make Isla look sympathetic and perhaps to get rid of some evidence."

Isla groaned. "I wasn't sleeping with Trey Adams. I don't have any reason to have killed Portia."

"I've got a hundred-million-dollar estate that says you do," Osborne replied quickly.

"And I've got a binding contract that states plainly I can't touch that money for anything except to dole it out to the kids and Cressida, business purposes, or to take care of Trey."

"And if you marry him?" Osborne asked.

Li held a hand up. "I'm sorry. Am I mistaken? Because I thought she was sleeping with this lawyer person who isn't a Lawless."

Erin nodded. "She's totally doing the lawyer. Good choice, girl. I love me an ex-athlete." She poked her partner. "And I told you. His name is David Cormack. I gave you his stats and everything."

The Irishman rolled his eyes. "I told you. American football ain't a real sport. Real footballers don't wear all those pads."

Osborne shook his head and looked to David. "Is there a reason they're here?"

"I go where Big Tag tells me to," Li replied.

"Could I ask a couple of questions of Ms. Shayne?" Campbell asked, looking a bit haggard. "First of all, I need to ask it for the record. Do you have an intimate relationship with Trey Adams? Have you ever had one?"

"I do not now, nor have I ever had an affair with Trey Adams," she replied, her head held high. "I interned in the front office of the New York Guardians when I was in law school. That's how we met. Our relationship was friendly in the beginning. At the end, I helped his wife take care of him from time to time. He often doesn't remember who I am."

David sank to the couch next to her, hoping her closeness would keep him from doing something to Osborne that would have the detective hauling him out of here in cuffs. He would rather they waited until she had a personal attorney with her, but he worried Osborne would use that as an excuse to arrest her. "She's said that a dozen times. Can that be the last?"

"And I should believe it, why?" Osborne asked.

"Because if you people would ever leave us alone, I would be having a relationship with David," she said with a frown. "I can't start one because you're all here and you have been for freaking days."

He had to muffle a smile. It was good to know she was eager.

The MT investigators bumped fists and nodded.

Osborne paced, his thousand-dollar loafers clapping against the marble floor. "That seems awfully convenient. You didn't know him a couple of days ago."

"I work fast," she replied. "And I find it interesting that you would believe I would have a relationship with a man twenty years older than me but not that I'm attracted to one who makes sense to date."

"I don't think it makes any sense that you would date him," the ADA replied. "And he's older than you, too. By a lot."

"By five years," she shot back.

"Four actually." He watched Osborne carefully. It was interesting that the man couldn't quite stop poking at Isla. "And by tomorrow the fact that we're in a relationship will be news. I'm sure the pictures the press took of us will be everywhere tomorrow."

"Thank you for clearing that up," Campbell said, obviously sick of the personal stuff. "Now, what happened tonight? Do you remember anything about the attack?"

"He was dressed in all black," she said with a weary sigh. "He had one of those things on his head. Not exactly a ski mask."

"A balaclava?" Erin asked. "It's the military equivalent, though a bit more high-tech in some cases. It covered everything except his eyes?"

She nodded. "He had blue eyes, but I don't remember a lot. Before I could scream he had his arm around my neck."

"Ah, the choke out," Erin said with a smile, as though remembering good times. "I know it well."

"It could have killed her," David said.

"Not when it's done right, and that makes me think," Li mused.

The detective turned to him. "You're thinking professional, or at least military."

"She doesn't have a mark on her, but he managed to knock her out for a good five minutes," Li replied. "That feels like a pro to me. The question is why."

"I can think of a few reasons." Osborne couldn't keep his mouth shut. "Feeling the heat, are you, Isla?"

David looked up at him. "What is your problem?"

"My problem is with your client. First she lies about how much time passed and now she's acting very suspicious," Osborne replied.

Isla sighed. "His real problem is that I slept with him once, figured out what a horrible mistake I'd made, and refused to go out with him again. Can we get him recused? Also, can I apologize for my horrible taste in men? I was going through a douchebag phase."

He'd already heard she'd briefly dated him. He reached for her hand. She'd been through the wringer and he wasn't going to put her through more. "I'll see what I can do. First he has to actually have a case."

Campbell was staring at the ADA. "If what Ms. Shayne says is true, I'm going to have a problem with you using your office to get back at an ex."

"Prove it," Osborne dared under his breath. "We'll be formally arresting your client in the morning after the psych exam. You've got your expert and I've got mine. We'll see what the judge says. Good night. Enjoy your time here, Isla. If I can prove you're in on this, I will. I'll wait by the elevator, Detective. If you could hurry this along, I would appreciate it."

He stomped off.

"I hate that man," Noah said, speaking for the first time. He'd been quietly observing from his place at the bar.

"You're not the only one," Isla replied. "Do we have anything on the guy who came after me except that he was a professional and I should somehow be thankful for that?"

Campbell looked over at the Irishman and the redhead. "I suspect you two know something I don't. Care to share?"

"When David mentioned he'd walked past a man wearing all black coming down Isla's hall, I decided to look into the security cameras." Li leaned back, looking exactly like a man who knew something.

"I did that, too," Campbell remarked. "We didn't get anything other than his Yankees cap. He was smart, kept his head down. I checked the one in the garage, too. We know he walked out, but the CCTVs on the street couldn't pick him up."

Erin smiled. "Ah, but the one at the bodega around the block did. We talked to a couple of the reporters and one remembered a hot guy in black turning around the corner. She followed him into the bodega and got a cup of coffee. He purchased a burner phone and left. Used cash, but we have a very nice picture of his face."

"And we will email that to you," Li offered. "But I also emailed it to my friends at MDWM."

Campbell's eyes widened. "You're getting a report from Mass Destruction?"

In the last few years the firm technically known as Miles-Dean, Weston, and Murdoch had been shortened to MD by law enforcement, and once Adam Miles's facial recognition software had proven what it could do, the cops just called them Mass Destruction. Because they'd managed to massively destroy a bunch of criminals. The software redefined the search for both criminals and missing persons.

"I love that you guys call it that," Erin said. "And yes. We expect to hear something from them in the morning and yes, we will share it with you."

Campbell stood up, sliding his notebook into his pocket. "I thank you, and, Ms. Shayne, if you remember anything else, give me a call. As far as we can tell he didn't take anything from your apartment, but we think you interrupted him. We don't know exactly why he was there. I think it's an excellent idea that you stay here for a bit."

He held a hand out to Liam and then Erin, shaking both of theirs. "And it was a pleasure to meet the two of you." He started to walk away before he turned back to Isla. "And, Ms. Shayne, stick with this one. He's got a terrible job, but he's a good man. The other one, well, he's proof that you can have the most righteous job in the world and still be a giant ass."

"I heard that," Osborne yelled from where he was standing, waiting for the elevator.

"I'll put it in writing if you like," Campbell yelled back. He walked away, shaking his head. "I'm too old for this."

David waited until the elevator doors closed to laugh. Then he remembered why they were here. Isla had a half smile on her face, but she was still pale. "Are you all right?"

She nodded. "But I was serious about getting that man recused. He hates me for some reason."

"Likely because you won't date him anymore," David replied. "You were the one to break it off, right?"

"Yes." Her hands were folded in her lap, fingers tangled together. "I don't understand why he cares. It wasn't like it was a long relationship. It was a mistake. We didn't even get along. We mostly argued."

"I promise, I'll see about getting him booted." He looked to the investigators. "Tell me what you've found out."

Noah moved in. "Erin just said they wouldn't know anything until morning . . . of course. You already know who we're dealing with."

"Adam sent us a name and a dossier about ten minutes after he got a picture of that pretty face," Erin admitted. "And we'll hand it over to the NYPD tomorrow. I find when dealing with the cops it's best to let them think we aren't as good as we are. You're the client. I wanted to make sure you could take a look and see if there's anything you need to handle before we turn it over to the cops."

Li reached into the messenger bag he'd brought with him and

pulled out a printout of a man standing at a convenience store counter. "Is this the man you saw, David?"

Yep. He'd only seen him briefly, but he remembered the Yankees cap and the sharply defined jawline. "That's the man who got on the elevator after me." He looked to Isla, who was staring down at the picture. "Do you recognize him at all?"

"It happened very quickly," she admitted. "And all I could see of him was his eyes. You can't tell what color they are in this picture. They were blue. I remember striking blue eyes, and then I got up close and personal with his elbow."

Li pointed to the picture. "Meet Mr. Kristoff Paloma. He's a Dutch national and he's wanted by Interpol and several European governments for everything from fraud to burglary to attempted murder, but what he mostly loves is the long con. He likes to romance older wealthy women and swindle them out of their cash. From what I've read he's pulled it about ten times, to the tune of six million dollars. Unfortunately, he has some expensive tastes, and every time he comes into his ill-gotten funds, he spends them and has to find another mark."

His stomach turned because this didn't bode well. Isla didn't need all of her illusions smashed. She'd loved that family and it looked like he had to be the one to bring out all the dirt. "Can we track his movements? I would like to know where he's been for the last, say, six months or so."

Noah sat up, his intelligent eyes narrowing. "What do you know that we don't know?"

Isla frowned. "You can't think this is the person Portia was meeting on Thursdays. I still can't believe she was having an affair, much less one with a criminal. She was careful. She had me vet her caterers."

That tidbit had Noah pacing. "An affair? Does the DA know? Well, that's going to make our job harder. Apparently the DA is planning on saying Isla was in a relationship with Trey. Now we think Portia had an affair?"

Unless Portia's manicurist did her work from a suite at the Algonquin, David wasn't sure what else it could be. "All we know is she had a standing Thursday appointment with someone at the Algonquin hotel. According to her daughter, she's been going every Thursday for at least the last six weeks. The DA hasn't talked to Miranda yet, but they will, and I don't think she's going to lie."

"Well, we know where we're going in the morning. Erin and I will take this picture and a couple of hundred bucks and see what we can find out." The Irishman stood up, looking back at his partner. "I'm going to call Avery and head to bed."

"I'll lock up after Noah leaves." Erin glanced over at Isla. "We thought as long as you were already here, we might as well stay, too. We were going to stay with Noah, but after what happened at your place, he thought it might be best we hang around here at night. The security system is tight, but we don't like someone coming after you so soon. I don't suppose either one of you is carrying?"

David shook his head. "I'm not."

"No whipping out a pistol for me either," Isla admitted. "I generally prefer to talk my enemies to death. I appreciate the help."

"There's something going on and I don't think it's about jealousy or an affair," Li said. "I think Paloma was looking for something. The police report indicated the victim's room had been tossed. Perhaps he was looking for something there, too. That something is what this is all about. Someone thinks you might have it."

"It? What could I have?" Isla asked, her voice a bit shaky. "I have a ton of important documents. Maybe it's one of those."

"Perhaps," Erin allowed. "I think we should go over them. I would bet there's money at the bottom of this. There usually is."

David wasn't sure about that. "I don't know. This crime feels personal. We'll talk to the ME tomorrow. Between the ME and finally getting to talk to Trey, it's going to be a big day. We should get some rest."

They weren't going to be alone. It was good Li and Erin were staying. Isla was obviously in danger and they were both far better trained as bodyguards than he was.

But he'd wanted to be alone with her.

He stood up, reaching down for her hand. "Come on. We should definitely get some rest."

"I put the bag I packed for you in the master bedroom, David," Noah explained before looking to Isla. "Since you weren't able to bring anything with you, my sister-in-law said to feel free to raid her closet. I think you're pretty close to each other in size."

Isla seemed to perk up at that idea. "You want me to raid the billionaire's wife's closet? I can do that."

Noah smiled. "Good. Shelby has excellent taste. I've also put out all the toiletries you should need. We're fully stocked for guests here. I'm going to my place, but I'll be back in the morning. The fridge is stocked, too." Noah sent him a knowing look. "So is the nightstand, if you know what I mean."

Isla went bright pink, proving she knew exactly what he meant.

"Yeah, thanks, man. That's great." David put a hand on Noah's back, starting to lead him to the elevator. The faster he got Noah out, the sooner Isla could forget what they'd been offered.

"I'm talking about condoms," Noah said in a hushed voice.

There were days he was happy he was an only child because Noah was one obnoxious little brother. "I know what you're talking about. Now please stop talking about it. And thank you for giving us a place to stay."

"No problem." Noah pressed the button to call the elevator. He got in and turned as the doors were closing. "They're in the right-hand nightstand along with lube. You're welcome."

He stared at the closed doors.

"I will set this alarm and then leave the two of you. Li and I are taking the two guest rooms in the east wing. On the other side is the master and three other rooms, but two of them are kids' rooms. Have fun with that," Erin said, an amused expression on her face. She quickly had the whole penthouse under the high-tech protection Drew Lawless had provided. "'Night, you two. If you need to leave, wake me up. You don't want to know what happens if the alarm goes off. I've heard Lawless is into lasers."

And then they were alone. And it was awkward. Somehow it had been easier when they were in the car surrounded by reporters. Then it had seemed perfectly natural to take her hand and bring it to his lips. Now he wasn't exactly sure what to say.

Well, he could start with the obvious. "I'm sorry about Noah. He's an ass."

She couldn't quite meet his eyes. "He's joking around. It's normal male behavior from what I understand. Did they put us in the master bedroom? Or was he talking about you?"

It appeared she'd lost her bravado. Damn but he'd liked it when she boldly told Osborne she would be more involved if he would stop cockblocking her. "I think if one of us takes the big bedroom, it should be you. It's okay. If I remember correctly, there's a perfectly nice guest room down the hall from the master. I think it belongs to the nanny. I'll sleep in there."

She stared for a moment, her expression blank. "Oh, okay."

She was probably still afraid to be alone, but that wasn't a good reason to sleep with him. He didn't want that. He wanted her to want him, and that might take some time. "I'll be very close in case you need anything. I'll leave the door open if you like. So you know I can hear you if you call out. And I bet the McKay-Taggart duo are light sleepers when it comes to this type of thing."

She shook her head. "I'll be okay."

"Is there anything you need? We could sit up and talk for a little while," he offered. He wanted to get that blank look off her face. It was killing him how fragile she looked.

"No, thank you. I'm talked out."

Well, that was all he had. "If it's okay though, I would love to take a shower before I go to my room. The other shower is decorated with ducks and bunnies."

"Of course. Feel free. I'm going to make some tea before I go to bed." She started to turn and then stopped. "So the thing in the car was all for the press?"

"Not at all." How to explain this to her? "We can take it slow. I don't want to rush you. You're going through something emotional and I don't want to add to that. I am incredibly attracted to you and I don't think that's going to go away anytime soon. It's okay to want to take things slow."

"You want to take things slow?"

He wanted to slam her down on the bed, get her naked, and eat her up like a starving man at a buffet. But he had to think about what she needed. He had to be better than some of the men she'd dated before. "I think it's probably for the best. The last thing I want to be is the guy who took advantage of you. I'm not interested in a one-night stand and I don't want to be a tool you use to lock the world out for a while. I want to be important to you. I'll step back and give you some room. But know I'm down the hall if you need me." He walked up to her, leaning over and kissing her forehead. "Good night, Isla."

It took everything he had to walk away. He forced himself to grab the bag Noah had packed for him and head to the shower. The master bathroom was probably as big as his whole flipping apartment, and that shower was a room in and of itself. It was completely decadent, and he wished he wasn't going in there alone.

He would be quick because she was tired and needed sleep more than anything else. He was being the good guy.

Being the good guy sucked.

It nagged at him that Osborne knew what it was like to kiss her and touch her. Not because he thought she should be some virgin. God, no. But he was absolutely certain that massive ass hadn't taken care of her in bed. He would bet she hadn't had a good sexual relationship since her fiancé died.

He shucked his clothes after turning the water on. Hot. He needed a ton of hot water after the events of the day.

Of course, he hadn't had a good *emotional* relationship maybe ever. He should take that into account. Maybe he wasn't such a great guy. Maybe he was protecting himself from the gorgeous, smart woman who could easily rip him apart like he was made of tissue paper.

What exactly did she see in him? He wasn't as famous as Henry or as rich as Noah. He was the guy in the middle, the one who was lucky to have found powerful friends or he might be some public defender.

She might have the wrong impression of him. White knight syndrome. She'd needed someone to save her and he'd rushed in, a couple of times now. What would she see in him when her world normalized? Would she wake up and realize what a bad bet he was?

He'd said he didn't want to be used, but god he wanted to forget about everything that had happened today, even if only for a little while.

He stepped under the hot water. What were his words for the day? Monkey. Drum. Bicycle.

Still had it. He chuckled but he wasn't truly amused. It was sad that he counted every day he could remember three new words a win. A day when his knees worked and his back didn't ache was one of the good ones.

Hot water sluiced off his body, the jets coming from two different directions. Of course he didn't want to think about what would happen the day he couldn't remember those words anymore. A day when he understood Trey Adams more than he could ever want to. Yeah, he wasn't such a great bet and she might be smart to listen to all of Carey Kendrick's warnings about him. Not because he would treat her poorly but because he might not have much of a future ahead of him.

"David?"

He nearly jumped out of his skin but managed to stay upright. The shower was a massive walk-in and suddenly he wasn't alone.

Isla was standing in the mist of the shower, not a stitch of clothing covering her beautiful body. "I don't want to go slow."

EIGHT

Isla couldn't believe she was doing this, but the minute she got a good look at David Cormack without his suit on she knew there was no going back. She'd been ready to make a pot of tea and wait for him to come out of the shower when Erin Taggart had appeared in the kitchen.

"Not jumping his bones, then?" she'd asked as she dragged a bottle of water out of the fridge.

"He wants to take it slow." She was aware of how disappointed she'd sounded.

"No man who looks at a woman the way that one looks at you wants to take things slow. He's scared you're too good for him or something stupid like that," she said. "I should know. I held off my gorgeous hottie for way too long because he was a tiny bit younger than me. Don't waste time. Take command. And then when he's all in, give that control up. That always works for me. 'Night."

There was something in the way the redhead smiled, something intimate and soft. Something Isla wanted for herself again. She'd had it as a girl with Austin. She wanted to know how it felt to have that connection as a woman.

So she'd made the decision. Maybe for the first time in her life, she'd genuinely made the decision to be brave, to go after what she wanted with a singular purpose, to put herself out there and see if she was bait enough to catch the one fish she wanted.

Though first she needed some fishing gear. According to Noah, that was in the nightstand drawer.

She'd stepped in and taken off her clothes. All in. Just like a poker game. If he refused to play, she would be devastated and potentially never be able to face the man again, but she'd felt almost compelled to undress and walk to the entry of that sexy natural stone shower. She'd stood there and looked, really looked at David Cormack. He'd been turned away from her, his back on full display. He was beautifully male, his muscles defined by years of athleticism. His back was strong, his butt practically perfect, and he was held up with strong legs. But his head hung low and she could swear she felt how lonely he was.

She hadn't realized how lonely she was until she'd met him. "David?"

He started, every muscle tensing, and then he turned, though he mostly moved his torso as though trying to keep his private parts private. His eyes latched on to her, but he didn't say a word.

Oh, she wanted to run. He was far too gorgeous. She wasn't in his league. She knew she was attractive, but she wasn't even close to being in the same condition he was in. He'd been an elite athlete and he'd obviously never stopped working out. She could stand to lose a few pounds.

And if those pounds and the roundness of her hips ran him off, then so be it. She was done sitting around and hoping she got what she wanted. At least she would know. "I don't want to go slow."

For a second, she was almost sure he would tell her to go. Then he turned and he was standing there in his full glory, as though letting her see what he had to offer. When she simply stared, he crossed the space between them and, without a word, his hands cupped her face and his mouth was on hers.

The minute they touched, something sparked to life inside her, something wild she'd never felt before. It seemed to start in her toes, making them curl as the sensation rushed through her system. Heat and anticipation and pure joy.

It had been forever since a man kissed her like this. Maybe never. The only thing that compared was the sweet high school fumbling between her and Austin. He'd been eager, but he had no idea what he was doing.

David Cormack knew how to kiss. He mastered her mouth with his, soft when he needed to be and then rough, sending a thrill through her system that burned a path straight to her pussy. He brushed his lips against hers and then zeroed in on her lower lip, biting gently and sucking briefly before another soft kiss allowed her to breathe again. And then when she was ready to beg, his tongue surged in, rubbing soft velvet against her own.

"Tell me you're sure," he said against her mouth as his hands moved down.

"I'm sure," she replied with a breathy whisper. He could throw her up against the side of the shower and take her then and there and she would be perfectly satisfied.

"Because there's no going back. I've been a good boy up until this point. I've been civilized, Isla. I've played the gentleman around you, but if you let me in, I'll invade and you'll see the real man underneath the suit. I'll be demanding and overly protective and I'll want you every fucking minute of the day."

And that was bad, how? She'd been on the outside looking in for so long, the idea of being someone's center, being *the* person for him, made her heart ache with longing. "Please touch me, David. I want the real you, every dirty, possessive part of you."

His hands found her hips and he dragged her against him, their bodies coming together for the first time. He was warm, his skin soft over the steel of his muscular body.

She took a moment, letting her arms wrap around him, her breasts against his chest, that hard erection of his cradled to her belly. This was sweet intimacy. Yes, it would lead to something wild, but for a moment she basked in the comfort of another body against hers.

He stepped back, taking her with him and bringing them into the warmth of the shower. He seemed to understand she needed a moment, and he followed her lead perfectly. One hand held her to him while the other smoothed back her now-wet hair as he brushed light kisses over her forehead and down to her nose, lavishing her with affection she'd been starved without. He stood like that with her, learning her body with his hands and mouth.

"See," he said with the sexiest chuckle as he leaned over and ran his tongue along the shell of her ear. "We're still taking it slow. I could do this for hours and I haven't even gotten to your tasty parts yet. You're sweet, Isla. I could eat you up. Are you going to let me eat you up?"

She nodded.

One hand tangled in her hair, gently drawing her back and forcing her to look up at him. His eyes were hot, his jaw tight with arousal. "Talk to me. I won't let you disconnect from me when we're intimate. Tell me. 'Yes, David, I want you to eat me up.'"

"Yes, David. I want you to eat me up."

His lips curled up, satisfaction oozing off him. Masculine satisfaction. "You want me to eat this cute nose?"

He kissed her there.

Oh, he was going to make her crazy. He was going to make her ask for everything she wanted, and she wanted it all, but then she kind of liked the fact that he wasn't about to let her lie back and simply enjoy. He wanted her with him all the way. "Kiss me. I want you to eat me up starting with my mouth. I love kissing you. I can't think about anything else when you're kissing me. Nothing but you."

His mouth covered hers, tongue moving lazily. "I don't want you thinking about anything but me. I assure you my brain is shut down to everything outside this shower. God, you're as beautiful as I thought you would be."

He didn't give her a chance to respond. He simply kissed her again. One hand held her still for the leisurely perusal of his mouth while the other ran down her back, cupping her ass. He could almost fit the whole of it in that big hand of his. He made her feel delicate and feminine against his rough masculinity.

He held her hard against him, letting her feel every inch of his cock. She let her hands roam, exploring the muscles of his back while her nipples brushed his chest. Her leg caressed his, coming up to wind around his strong thigh. She wanted to climb up him, conquer him in a way she'd never wanted with a man before.

In the last few years, sex had been nothing more than a way to try to feel close to someone. She'd tried it a few times and almost always backed away the next morning because she realized it wasn't right.

This was right. This was everything she'd been missing in her life.

He broke off the kiss and started working his way down her neck. "Tell me where else you want my mouth. I know where I want to go, but I would never want to disappoint you. You want my mouth here?"

He kissed her collarbone.

Oh, she knew where he was going and that he was going to tease her until he got there. Her nipples were already aching, begging for the pull of his mouth. "Lower."

But she could tease him, too. She didn't want this to end. They could have quickies later on. Later on, he could pull her into a broom closet during a recess in court sessions and she would be blissfully satiated with their three-minute fling, but now she wanted this long, slow exploration of bodies.

He moved down slightly, caressing the upper swell of her breasts. "Have I mentioned how gorgeous these are? How fucking sexy you are?"

"You haven't." She got the feeling he was going to tell her a lot.

He looked down, staring like he was witnessing something miraculous. "You are the sexiest woman I've ever met, Counselor. In, and definitely out of clothes. You make me crazy. And I've been dying to get my mouth on these."

He lifted her up, hefting her with an ease that took her breath away, and then she was right where he obviously wanted her. He leaned forward and licked her nipple with unselfconscious sexuality. He licked and gently bit and sucked her like she was a sweet treat he'd been dying to try. All the while she could feel herself preparing, getting wet and ripe and ready for him. Her lower body pulsed with arousal, but she simply held on to him and let him have his way.

His way led to pleasure. There was no denying it.

Fire licked along her skin as he tormented her. He moved between her breasts, giving them each equal attention.

She couldn't help the moan that came from her throat. She was caged in his arms, his mouth on her, and she couldn't help but think there was no other place she'd like to be. This was exactly where she belonged. All the horror of the past days melted away, and all that mattered was the feel of his mouth as he set her down on the built-in bench.

He sat down and got on his knees in front of her. "Where else, Isla? Where else do you want this mouth of mine? I know what I want to taste, but I need to hear it from you. Tell me I can taste you. Tell me that pretty pussy is mine to take any way I want."

"Yes, David. It's all yours. I'm all yours." There was nothing she wanted more than the heat of his mouth and tongue on her most sensitive flesh.

He spread her knees wide and then covered her with heat. His tongue moved through her soaked pussy, leaving pure pleasure in its wake. He speared her with his tongue, moving in and out of her, his thumb finding her clitoris and pushing at the exact right time to send her flying over the edge.

The orgasm threatened to pull her under the tidal wave of emotions it brought with it. Isla had never felt this way before. The connection between them was a live wire, and she couldn't help but hold on to it. Even if it burned her in the process.

Her whole body went limp as David kissed her one last time.

He looked up her body, his eyes heavy-lidded and his sensual lips glistening. "Tell me I can have you."

There was only one way to reply. "Any way you want me."

She was his and there was no going back.

~

David's hands were shaking by the time he got to his feet. The whole shower was filled with steam and he wondered how much longer they had before the hot water gave way to cold. Not that he would notice. His whole body was pretty much on fire, and there was no way it was going out until he'd had her.

His cock was so close to the edge he was fairly certain a stroke or two would do him in. Control. He needed to find some or this wouldn't go the way he wanted it to.

God, she'd tasted like heaven. Sweet and honest, no playing around to drag him further in. She'd gone with him, letting him see and hear and feel and taste exactly how much she wanted him, and that honest passion had been a revelation.

He should have known it would be like this. She didn't play around in real life. Her every emotion was there on her face and the way she held herself. She should never play poker because she would lose big-time, and he was happy she'd been smart enough to go into business law, because she couldn't front to save her life.

And he liked it that way. But he had to wonder how many assholes like Royce Osborne had taken advantage of her sweet nature.

He looked up at her. Her skin was flushed a lovely pink from the orgasm, and her eyes had gone soft.

"Damn, but you're beautiful."

"Almost never feel that way," she said quietly, her hands finding his hair. "You make me feel like I am, but you're the beautiful one."

And he was lucky she was blind and didn't seem to notice that his nose had been broken more than once, that his body was covered in scars. Sure, he'd kept himself physically fit, but he bore the mark of years of punishing work on his face. "I'm never buying you glasses, baby."

Her lips curved up in the most stunning smile. That was the hard part. That smile not only got his dick hard. It made his heart soft and ready to do anything to keep that smile on her face.

"I think you said something about taking me," she reminded him quietly. "Unless you'll let me return the favor."

The idea of Isla on her knees in front of him, her mouth working him over, nearly made him come then and there. He leaned in and kissed her, loving how she kind of sighed into him and gave over. She opened her mouth and welcomed him in, her tongue playing shyly at first and then boldly dancing with his own.

He broke it off, pressing his forehead to hers. "I want inside you too badly but, baby, Noah didn't leave his presents inside the shower."

She grinned. "Nope, he left them in the nightstand."

She pressed in, standing up. It brought him in contact with her breasts. Pretty breasts. They were a lovely handful and mouthful, and he couldn't help it that one of them was right there, ripe and waiting to be loved. That perky nipple sort of slipped into his mouth, and then it would be rude not to show it how much he adored it.

Her back bowed, offering him more, and he wrapped his arms around her to balance her. He licked her nipple, worshipping each one in turn. Her hands ran up his neck, and he was gratified by the deep sigh that came from her chest as she held him there.

His cock jerked as though trying to remind him it was still there and it needed attention, too.

It wasn't getting any attention yet. Why hadn't Noah realized the sex was going to happen in the shower?

He winced and pulled away, the last thing he wanted to do. He loved it when there was no space between them, adored how she seemed to fit perfectly against his body. "Baby, I have to dry off and run into the bedroom."

From now on he would keep condoms everywhere. In his wallet. In his pocket. He would stash them all over his apartment and hers. Anywhere he might get the urge to have her. Also in his car—and maybe around the city.

The silly thought made him smile, made him feel way younger than he had in years. He suddenly wasn't an old guy chasing his second dream, slowed down by bad knees and potential nasty futures. He was a kid who was whacked-out crazy about a girl.

"I love it when you smile like that." Her hands came up, thumb drawing over his lips as if tracing the expression and committing it to memory. "It's like that smile is just for me."

He could give her that. "It is."

She gave him back a smile that could light up the world. At least his world. "Then let me make you even happier. There's a condom right outside the shower. It's sitting on the towel warmer. Can you believe there's a towel warmer? I think we should stay here. What's he going to do? Throw us out? When Lawless is here, we'll hide in the closets and no one will find us. We'll be squatters."

Oh, she was perfect for him. He liked them weird and well prepared. "We could be the monster in the closet to all those kids. The elder Lawless siblings breed like rabbits. Billionaire rabbits. I think we'll have to enjoy this while we can."

He could barely get the last word out because her hand trailed down his chest and lower, finally reaching his desperate cock and stroking him. His eyes nearly rolled to the back of his head and he had to take a deep breath to get control of himself.

She looked down between them, biting that plump bottom lip as she took him firmly in hand and started to explore. He wanted to beg her to stop, but he couldn't. She looked far too fascinated as she studied him and stroked him.

Pure torture of the absolute best kind. She stroked him over and over, brushing her thumb over his cockhead when she reached the top. He groaned and tried to think about football plays and then legal briefs. Anything, anything to hold off the inevitable.

"Baby, you have to stop."

"I want to watch."

Oh, those words of hers didn't help the situation at all. She wanted to stroke him to finish so she could watch him come? So she could coat her hand in it and watch as he pulsed out every ounce he had to give her? Yeah, dirty Isla definitely did it for him.

But that wasn't happening now. He reached down and stopped her. "I want inside you. Unless you've decided you don't want that."

"I want everything you have," she said with such sweet openness. "David, I haven't done this often. You say you're going to be demanding. I think I might be a handful because we haven't even finished the act and I'm already thinking of all the things we can do in bed."

He was only thinking of one thing. How freaking hard he was and how he could make this last. One thing he was sure of was he knew what he needed right then. If he didn't get inside her soon, he was going to die.

He reached out of their warm space and sure enough there was the solution to all his problems. He grabbed the condom his amazing, gorgeous, thoughtful lover had left for him. He ripped that sucker open and rolled it over his cock.

There was zero need to wait. He'd done everything he could to please her, to make sure she wanted this, too. Now he could let his inner caveman fly because she'd said yes. She'd opened herself to him and he wasn't about to say no.

He crowded her, getting into her space. Without another word, he lifted her up, pinned her to the shower wall, and had his cock right where he wanted it. He could feel the heat of her pussy as he started to push inside her.

Her legs wound around his waist and she gasped. "Oh god. David, please."

He pressed up inside her, her slick pussy accepting him despite the fact that she was exquisitely tight. Tight and hot. So sweet as she held him like she would never let him go.

He captured her mouth with his, his tongue thrusting inside in time to the hard press of his cock. He gave over, letting his body move in time with hers, shifting her until he found the perfect position, until he could grind against her clitoris with every thrust, until her nails found the flesh of his back and she screamed out his name.

Then it was his time. He pounded into her, holding her tight and finally letting himself fly over the edge. It had been a long time since he'd had a woman who made him feel good. Good about the sex. Good about how close they were. Good about himself.

His whole body felt electric as he carried them both under the warm jets. He kissed her, not wanting to stop for a minute, loving this soft moment every bit as much as the one before it.

She was his for now and he was going to revel in every moment.

NINE

⁓

Isla rolled over and sighed as she felt something warm and muscular against her. Her head found his chest and she wrapped herself around him like he was her body pillow. His arm wound around her, holding her close.

Now this was the way to wake up. Lazy. Safe. Warm.

She didn't want to get out of bed. Maybe never. It was way too comfy in here.

"I don't want to get up." David seemed to feel the same way. His hand found her hair, stroking her.

"What time is it?" There was some sunlight peeking through the windows that let her know it was morning. It also let her see the sculpted line of his jaw and the sexy scruff that had grown there overnight. She knew this was the time with her previous attempts that she would be trying to sneak out of bed and run away, but all she seemed to be able to do with this man was sigh and cuddle closer. She shifted, rubbing her cheek against his, his whiskers scratching her lightly.

"You're like a pretty cat rubbing all over me, looking for affection," he replied as he rolled on top of her. His eyes gleamed in the low light. "You're going to get it, you know."

Nope. No desire to run away from this one. She let her arms drift up around his shoulders. "I'm going to get affection?"

He smiled and his brows rose suggestively. "That's not the only thing you'll get."

He moved his hips, his morning erection making itself known.

"You didn't answer my question." She let her hands find his hair and smooth it back. How was it so easy to be with him? Like they'd been together for years and this was simply how they spent their mornings, teasing and flirting and playing in bed.

He kissed her instead, lowering his head and letting his mouth play lazily against hers. "Time is meaningless in here. You were right. We'll stay here. Lawless will get used to it."

She groaned as he kissed her neck and she felt herself getting soft and ready for him.

The night before had been everything she could have imagined. She'd never been as intimate with a man in her life, and it hadn't all been about sex. He'd been tender with her. After he'd pressed her to the shower wall and made her scream, he carefully washed her body, his strong hands not missing an inch. He'd washed her hair, kissing her the whole time like he couldn't help himself.

Then she'd washed him and they got all dirty again.

When they'd gotten to bed, he held her and talked about his new practice and how they were finally making headway. He wanted to know about her work, and she'd fallen asleep talking about contracts and clients.

This was different. This was right. She could feel it in her bones.

And she suddenly didn't care what the clock said. He was right. Time didn't matter in here. All that mattered was the feel of his hands on her body, the way they moved together. Here she didn't have to be a high-powered lawyer. She could simply be David's and he would be hers.

It was a good thing to be.

There was a knock on the door.

David went still. "Be very quiet and whoever it is will go away."

The words had been whispered against her lips. For a few seconds, she thought it might work.

"It doesn't matter how quiet you are," a familiar voice said. "I'm not going away. And I know how to get into this room even if the door's locked. One time when Case and Mia were staying here, Case had handcuffed Mia to the bedframe and then he threw out his back doing something I don't even understand, and guess who got the call to come down and save them? Me. I've seen more of my sister than I ever wanted to see. And my brother-in-law. Though I now know why Mia's always happy. The point of the story is, you've got nothing I haven't seen already. I will open this door and come in if you don't start talking."

David groaned and rolled off her. "You're a pain in my ass, Lawless."

"And you have horrible timing." Isla felt the need to throw her two cents in. She glanced at the clock. It wasn't even eight A.M. Of course, she was usually up by six on a Monday morning, but then she didn't normally spend most of the night having spectacular sex either. She could have stayed in bed all morning dozing on and off.

David sat up, giving her a spectacular view of his back. The man really worked on his glutes. "What do you need, Noah?"

"I need you to turn on the TV," Noah replied. "The remote's on the nightstand. You know, the one you told me you wouldn't need and you totally needed since you're both in that room. You're welcome, by the way."

She couldn't help but laugh. "Thank you, Noah. They came in handy."

"Don't encourage him," David admonished, but he sent her a sexy wink as he stood up and reached for the remote.

He was totally unselfconsciously naked, walking around the room like he'd been raised in a nudist colony. Not that he had a single reason to worry. He was like a Michelangelo sculpture come to vivid life.

"You're very welcome, Isla," Noah said from behind the door. "I'll go make some coffee. It appears we're going to need it."

David sighed and clicked on the large television on the opposite wall. "I don't know why he can't simply tell us what's going on. But no, Noah has to be dramatic."

Anxiety crept up her spine. She shouldn't have thanked Noah. He was bringing the real world into her happy fantasy time and it sucked. If Noah thought they should see something, it was likely about the case, and she didn't want to think about the case this early in the morning.

A commercial was playing and she looked up at David. "Do you think this is about us?"

"Us?"

"About what happened yesterday with the press? They took pictures of us. If this is going to be some roundtable about what a whore I am, I think I'll skip it."

"On national news? I doubt it." He climbed back onto the bed, stretching his body out. "And Noah would have warned us if this was personal. I'm worried Osborne is going to do something stupid before we can try to get his ass kicked off this case."

He was laid out like a sexy man buffet.

"You are seriously comfortable with that gorgeous bod of yours." She felt better because he was right. The tabloids would run salacious details about how Trey Adams's lawyers were involved with each other, but this was a huge cable news network. They would focus on the real story. Unfortunately, the real story was a minefield for her, too.

"You like looking at me," he said with all the confidence of a man who knew he was right. He winked her way again, a sexy smirk on his face.

Two could play at that game. She threw the covers back. "You like looking at me, too."

His smile widened to that joyous expression that kicked her in the gut every time. "I do. I also love it when your competitive nature takes over and I get what I want."

She tossed a pillow his way. "Weirdo."

He pounced on her, pinning her with his weight. "Call me anything you like, baby. As long as you don't kick me out of bed."

He lowered his head, his lips caressing her neck as the commercial faded to black and a well-dressed news anchor took its place on screen. He spoke in low, serious tones.

"New York City police have put out a 'be on the lookout' for former New York Guardians quarterback Trey Adams. Adams escaped early this morning from the hospital where he's been on suicide watch since the murder of his wife, former model Portia Adams."

David rolled off her, his whole body stiff as he got off the bed, hands on his hips as he watched the screen. "They lost him? He was in a freaking mental ward. How the hell did they lose him?"

She sat straight up in bed, her whole being focused on that newscast. Trey was out in the city by himself? Would the cops shoot him on sight? Had he gotten out of the city? Her heart was in her throat as she watched. "How did he get out?"

As if they'd been listening, the newscaster continued. "According to the police reports, Adams was in his bed for a midnight bed check, but the nurses reported him missing when they entered his room at three this morning to change his IV bag."

David grabbed his slacks from the night before. "What the hell was he thinking?"

She could guess what David was thinking. He was watching his whole case go straight out the window. The DA would surely go back to the judge now and argue that if Trey was able to escape, he couldn't possibly be too mentally damaged. "They'll put him in a prison hospital now."

He opened the closet door and handed her a robe. "At the very least. I definitely won't be able to keep him in a private hospital after this. Shit. We were meeting the judge this morning. The timing couldn't possibly be worse. I turned my phone off last night. I bet it's blown up."

She winced. "I left mine on the bar in the kitchen. I can't imagine what it looks like."

She couldn't take her eyes off the screen. The morning anchor had been joined by someone from the hospital who claimed the only way Trey could have gotten away was through careful planning and athletic strength. He had to have climbed out the third-story window and managed to hold on until he made it to the fire escape, two full rooms down from his.

He could have killed himself. He could have fallen and died. Her stomach clenched, and all the relaxed joy from the morning and the night before had fled and her anxiety was back. What was she doing lying around in bed?

Had she made a terrible mistake last night? A stupid girlish mistake? Had she put her libido before her clients?

"Stop." David stepped between her and the television. "Isla, we're allowed to have some happiness. There is very little difference between us knowing he escaped now and knowing it a few hours ago. Don't second-guess yourself. It's going to be okay."

She shook her head in surprise. "How did you know what I was thinking?"

"Because I thought the same thing," he replied. "And it's ridiculous. Nothing we did last night put our case in danger."

She wasn't sure, but she wasn't about to argue with him. "How could he have run?"

"You know the answer to that."

She took a deep breath and tried to calm down. She needed to be logical. "He woke up and had no idea where he was. He was probably terrified and his first impulse was to escape. I thought they had him in restraints."

He put a hand on her head, staring down at her with soft eyes. "I'll have a report on the entire debacle before you're dressed and ready to go. I promise. Do you have any idea where he might go?"

"Besides home?"

"If he'd gone home, they would have caught him by now," he mused. "But I think he would have gone somewhere familiar. He would look for somewhere or someone who made him feel safe."

There was one person he might remember well enough to run to. "If he went to Carey's, there's a chance Carey wouldn't have turned him in until he got legal advice. I'll call him. Though I would bet he's already called me a few times."

There was a knock on the door. David sighed and answered it. He said something, talking quietly with Noah, but Isla was watching the screen. Pictures of Portia and Trey in better days flashed over the monitor, and the hosts discussed what could have happened to such a previously happy couple.

Life had happened. Life and Trey's disease had eroded what once seemed solid. Like a river slowly cutting through a seemingly impenetrable mountain. Portia was strong but recently she'd started vacationing without her husband. She went to Paris for two weeks last year. Isla had been invited along on the girls' trip but had chosen to stay behind because of work obligations.

You have to live a little, cupcake. Life will try to bring you down.

That's when you go to Paris and tell life to fuck off for a while. It doesn't mean you don't love your life. It means you simply need to take a break from it.

Portia had been happy as she got on the private jet, as though the weight had already come off her slender shoulders. When she'd come back, she was quiet and contemplative.

Paris. Was that where she'd met Kristoff? She'd gone with a group of female friends, including her sister and daughter. Isla racked her brain trying to remember who had gone on that damn trip. Someone must have known, must have suspected it if Portia had started an affair there.

Was that what her Thursdays at the Algonquin were about? Escaping life for an afternoon?

Why hadn't Portia told her? They'd been friends. Close friends. She wouldn't have judged. Or maybe she would have. God, it was such a mess and now Trey was missing.

How was she going to handle it if he was killed or, worse, if he killed himself? How was she going to look his kids in the eyes?

"Hey, baby, here's some coffee." David stood in front of her, a mug in his hand. "And your cell. It looks like Carey called a few times. Well, a few hundred times." He passed it to her and stood there for a moment, his expression serious. "It's okay if you don't tell him you were with me last night. This is new and I get it. He's like a dad to you. You don't want to disappoint him."

There was no way she was going to allow David to think he was a disappointment. She might be worried about the case and her own place in it, but the one thing she knew was that he was an amazing man. "Yes, Carey's definitely been a parental figure in my life. I'm going to tell him exactly what I would my own dad. I would tell my dad that I'm an adult and I pick who I spend time with. I hope he can get along with you. He is important to me, but you are, too. I'm not planning on hiding any of this. There are way too many secrets going around. I'm not adding to them."

He leaned over and kissed her. "Okay. I have to go and talk to the investigators. I want them at the hospital figuring out what the hell happened. I don't buy that Trey could get out of those restraints, shove his massive body out a tiny window, and manage to haul himself across the building like he's some kind of rock climber. They're not taking into account how damaged his body is."

"You think the guy from the hospital is lying?"

"I think he's a talking head for a large corporation and they like to cover their asses any way they can," David replied with a frown. "Trey had help getting out and I want to know who that was. I want every bit of camera footage that hospital has."

She nodded, happy one of them was thinking clearly. "That's a good idea. I'll call around to anywhere he might have gone. Do we have something to say to the press?"

"Margarita's working on it. She's going to have the official statement ready before we leave the apartment. She's out in the kitchen working right now. She brought bagels and cream cheese," he explained. "When you're done with Carey, take a shower. I don't dare get in there with you or we'll never get out. Leave me some hot water, baby. We need to be ready to go in about an hour."

She nodded and watched as he walked out.

She wasn't alone. That might have been what scared her most that first night. The whole weight of a family had come down on her shoulders and she'd been all alone. But David was with her. David, who made smart decisions, who knew what he was doing, who would advise her but wouldn't take over.

Her cell buzzed and she looked down, braced herself, and answered. "Hey, Carey. I'm sorry. I left my phone on the bar last night and I slept like a log."

There wasn't even a pause before the yelling started.

"Where the hell are you? You're not at home and your apartment had goddamn police tape on the fucking door. I've been standing out here trying to get someone to tell me if you're dead or alive." He took a shaky breath. "Goddamn it, Isla. I thought someone murdered you, too."

Oh, it was worse than simply not answering him. "I'm sorry. I had no idea you were still in the city. My apartment got broken into last night and everything was crazy for a few hours."

"Broken into?"

"Yeah, I walked in while the man was there," she explained. "He knocked me out, but luckily David came looking for me. I'm perfectly fine. Not even a bruise on me."

"Why would someone break in? Do they think it's because you worked for Portia? What do you have that the killer could want?" The questions came out like rapid-fire bullets.

"We don't know, but the police don't think it was a coincidence. They're going to want to look into the work I did for Portia and Trey." She bit back a groan. "Which means I'm going to need a lawyer because privilege comes into play. God, this case is going to be a boon for Manhattan lawyers. I need to figure out what I can and can't say. They'll try to use the fact that Portia is dead to break privilege, but I rep the rest of the family, too."

A long sigh of obvious relief came over the line. "But you're all right?"

"I'm fine. I'm sorry I made you worry. The police think he was looking for something, but I was lucky he didn't kill me."

"But if the police think this is connected, does that mean they've got another suspect?" Carey asked.

"I think they might have if Trey hadn't disappeared. Has he made any attempt to contact you?"

"No. I came into the city when I heard he was missing. I wanted

to make sure he hadn't come to hide with you. I know how sympathetic you are, but if he shows up, you have to turn him in. He's
dangerous. He could have an episode and hurt you."

So Carey still thought Trey could have killed Portia. "I have no
plans on becoming an accessory after the fact." She didn't mention
that the ADA already thought she was one. "But we have to find
him before he hurts himself. I'm worried he'll kill himself."

"I'll let Amber know to call me if he shows up at our place." He
was quiet for a moment. "Are you still with Cormack?"

She wasn't going to lie to him. "Yes. I like him. I know what you
think, but there are two sides to every story. I asked him about what
happened with his wife and I'm satisfied with his explanation."

"Be careful around him." Carey's Oklahoma accent was a deep
comfort to her. "Keep in touch with me, Isla. I worry about you."

"I promise." She wiped away a stray tear. The truth was she hadn't
been alone the whole time. She simply had to reach out and Carey
would have been there. "I have to get ready. We're going to have to
deal with the press or the ADA will control the whole story."

"You go get 'em, and you let me know if there's anything I can
do." He hung up the phone.

Before she could put the phone down, it rang again. She didn't
recognize the number, but then she couldn't afford to miss Trey's call
if he managed to remember her. "This is Isla Shayne."

"So, do you have him? Was last night's break-in all a cover-up for
you finding a place to hide your client?"

She bit back a groan at the sound of Royce's voice. "No. I was as
shocked as you. Probably more shocked because I know how sick he
is. I would like to know how he managed to get out of the restraints.
He's a strong man, but he's not an escape artist."

"I would agree that he had help." Royce paused as though for
dramatic effect. "I would like to know where you were between one
and three this morning."

Asshole. Well, if he wanted to know, she would tell him. "I was in bed and I wasn't alone. Well, I might not have been in bed, exactly. There were several spots in this penthouse where I wasn't alone."

"Way to use the whore's excuse, Isla. I wouldn't have expected that from you."

"And I wouldn't have expected you could be such a massive asshole. That was a horrible mistake on my part. Now, if you would like to send the police down here to verify my alibi, I'll let my boyfriend know. I'll also get you the report on the alarm system that was turned on after you left last night and wasn't turned off again until Noah came in this morning." At least that would be her bet.

His huff came over the line. "Boyfriend? Are you a teenage girl mooning over the quarterback?"

"He played safety." She belted the robe around her waist and started to walk into the bathroom. "Now, if you're done insulting me, I need to get ready for work."

"Funny, I've already been at work for hours," he chided. His voice suddenly went low. "Isla, don't make me destroy you. I don't want to have to drag you through the mud, but you're making it hard on me."

Like he hadn't already done exactly that. "And what would it take to get you to stop dragging me through the mud?"

"Look, you know Adams is the guy," he insisted. "There's no way this was some random killing. He lost his shit and killed his wife. Hand him over to me. If you do that, maybe, just maybe, I won't get a judge to freeze all of his assets. How are his kids going to get by without Daddy's cash?"

"You are a bastard of the highest order."

He chuckled, though the sound wasn't amusing. "Oh, sweetheart, I'm merely getting started. I also want you to dump the asshole you're playing around with. I get the message. I didn't call and you got mad. Fine. I'm jealous. Dump him and we can start over again."

"I'm hanging up now." She was done with him.

"Isla, don't play this game with me. You can't win. Like I said, I understand I made a mistake. You were kind of a bitch to me and I decided to let you stew for a while, but this is taking it a little far. This is an important case. The DA is retiring in a year. This is the kind of case that puts me on the path I need to be on. I am going to be the next DA and someday I'll be the governor. You don't want a man like me angry with you."

"Wow, threats. That's quite the romantic gesture, Royce."

"There's nothing romantic about this," he replied. "It's pure logic. You know I'm going places and you're the woman who can help me get there. So are you staying with the dumbass, I-defend-criminals lawyer who'll probably go the same route as your friend Trey, or are you going to be sensible? I'm going to be the governor one day. My family has been grooming me for the position since I was born, and moving through the ranks at the DA's office was part of the plan. You can be by my side or I can view you as a speed bump. I don't like speed bumps."

"And I don't like threats," she shot back. "I need you to understand that I realized dating you was a terrible mistake that first night. I let a friend convince me to give you another shot and you weren't half-bad that night or the third date. Do you know why I broke it off with you? Because you were absolutely a selfish bastard in bed. I haven't been waiting for you to call me. I've been waiting to get the bad taste out of my mouth so I could try again, and let me tell you, I won't be letting go of David Cormack anytime soon. He's a man and you're a selfish, overprivileged little boy. And you haven't seen a speed bump yet, you ass."

She hung up, her whole body flush with anger. Though she hated it, tears pricked her eyes because she was stupidly emotional. How had she ever made that mistake?

"Selfish bastard?"

Damn it. She hadn't heard David come back in. She held the phone and didn't turn around. "Yeah, you know how exes are. I wouldn't even call him an ex."

"Did he threaten you?" His voice had gone low, hard.

She didn't want David to have to get involved in her poor decisions. "It's nothing but talk. I can handle it."

His hand was on her shoulder. "Isla, if he threatened you, I want to know. What happened between us last night meant something to me. It definitely means that I get to be the one who deals with assholes who threaten you."

She turned, letting him see her as she was. "He wants me to fire you. He's afraid of you."

David stared down at her, his thumbs brushing away her tears. "He should be. In the courtroom and out of it. I'll handle him. Now, come on. Let's get cleaned up and ready."

"I thought you couldn't take a shower with me."

"I changed my mind." He leaned over and picked her up. "We have time. I'll make time."

He carried her to the shower and she was able to stay in her safe place a few minutes longer.

~

David finished knotting his tie as he watched Henry on the massive TV in the living room. Naturally, Henry looked perfect, the Hollywood version of a lawyer. Henry Garrison was polished, his Ivy League roots showing in how he comported himself. That was a man who'd never once worried his brain would stop functioning. He was a walking, talking legal encyclopedia and he knew it.

Noah and Margarita looked just as cool and collected at Henry's side. They'd left to join him twenty minutes before, wanting to present as much of a united front as they could.

"Yes, I would like to know how the hospital we placed our client in managed to allow a very sick man to get lost." Henry turned slightly as a reporter shouted a question his way. "No, we don't consider this an escape. First of all, our client isn't accused of anything. There has been no arrest. Mr. Adams was being held on a 5150 psychiatric hold due to the nature of his illness and his state of mind following the death of his beloved wife. We are incredibly worried about our client and ask that anyone who sees him calls our hotline. We do not believe Mr. Adams is an imminent threat to the community, but he is very likely disoriented and could be easily upset."

"He's awfully good at that." Isla stepped out of the bedroom wearing a pretty black-and-white dress that clung to her curves but managed to still be professional.

"He's had a lot of practice with damage control," David allowed.

"It doesn't hurt that with him giving a statement to the press, no one will be looking for us. They likely won't notice where we've come from," she said, settling her phone in her bag. "I'm ready when you are. Are we heading to the hospital first?"

"I don't think we have to," he replied. "Liam said he's on his way up and he has news."

"News about what?"

"Not sure, but he went to the hospital this morning." Li and Erin had been up and working while he and Isla were cuddling.

He wished they were still cuddling. There were days when he kind of wished he'd become a boring corporate attorney with a boring job where the press didn't swarm him on a regular basis.

"I was thinking about the fact that Portia took a trip to Paris last year. Then six months ago she went to London, both trips without Trey. She called them girls' holidays," Isla said. "I'm wondering if that's where she met Kristoff Paloma. Is there any way we can see if the dates line up?"

He hated the blank look on her face, hated how hard this had to be on her. "I can have Liam look into it with his Interpol ties. They've been tracking him. They might know where he was on certain dates."

"I also need to talk to Cressida. I called Miranda and asked if she could bring her aunt here. Cressida traveled everywhere with Portia the last few years. If her sister had an affair, Cressy would know. She might try to lie, but after a couple of martinis, she'll give it all up. It's precisely why Portia wouldn't let her do *Real Housewives of New York City*."

The last thing they needed was another reality show. "Did Portia learn anything from the show about the Guardians?"

"It's funny. That show was kind of different. It was definitely more of a documentary. We didn't play out 'story lines.' They really did try to show the inner workings of the everyday professional sports organization. I didn't like it, but Portia thought it humanized Trey. He came off as the hardworking heart of the team. Before that show, he was kind of hated for being perfect. You know, perfect wife, perfect career. That television show drew the curtain back and let the public see how hard he worked, how hard it was to be on the team at all. Suddenly he wasn't someone who'd had everything given to him."

David shuddered at the thought of how they'd humanized him. "Cameras followed him around everywhere?"

"Sometimes, but it was more organic than that. There were places where the crew simply wired the whole room with cameras. There wasn't a camera guy there but they caught a lot of authentic moments. The locker room, workout rooms, coaches' offices were all covered in cameras." She sat down on the barstool. "It wasn't that bad. Yes, they caught pretty much everything, but I made sure nothing was broadcast without Carey's permission. The team had the final cut and let me tell you, we cut a lot."

He couldn't imagine having his every move filmed. Henry's wife had done a reality show years before, but at least that had been heavily scripted. Some things should be private and the locker room was a sacred place. He wasn't sure how he would have handled it if his team had tried something like that when he played.

The elevator opened and Liam and Erin strode in. There was a look on the Irishman's face that told David he'd found something good.

"Tell me."

"Bastards tried to delete the camera footage," Liam said. "Bloody hospital trying to cover its own arse."

Erin smiled and pulled out her tablet. "Luckily I've learned a few things over the years. You hang with the nerds, you're going to get better with computers. They didn't have time to erase the cache. I pulled it down. Watch what happens next."

She handed over the tablet. A black-and-white scene played out on the screen. There had been a security camera trained on the hallway outside of Trey's room. A police officer sat in front of the door. He glanced down at his watch and then looked up and down the hall. He then stood and stepped away from his post.

"We think he went to the bathroom," Liam explained. "But someone was waiting."

A woman dressed in scrubs stopped in front of the door, placing her palm on it almost reverently before disappearing behind it.

"Do we have her face on camera?" David asked.

"Is she a nurse?" Isla leaned into him.

"My gut tells me no," Erin replied. "I think she's a whack job who's been planning this. And yes, we've got her face. I've already got a name, but I'm waiting on the candy man to get me a location."

"Candy man?" He had to ask.

"It's what we call our tech guy," Liam replied.

On the screen, the door opened again and the woman led Trey Adams out. He was now wearing scrub pants and a T-shirt, a ball cap on his head and no shoes on his feet. She held his hand and he shuffled behind her.

They turned toward the camera and then walked off the screen.

"This woman has Trey?" Isla shook her head. "She walked in and took him?"

On-screen the police officer returned, settling into his chair. He didn't check the room, merely took his station back.

"From what we can tell," Li agreed. "The question is what do we do with this? You want us to turn the footage over to the cops or deal with this ourselves?"

He needed to figure out how Trey walking out of his own volition affected the case. How could he use this to strengthen his argument?

"We can prove he didn't perform heroic feats of strength and agility to get out," Isla said. "But none of it matters if we can't find him. Do you think he's still with this woman? I don't recognize her."

"I think she's either a fan or a reporter looking for a story," Erin said.

David groaned at the thought of either.

Liam's cell phone trilled and he looked down. "Hutch has her name thanks to Adam and he's found her cell phone. I've got a longitude and latitude." The Irishman looked up, a frown on his face. "It looks like she's in Central Park. Not five minutes from here."

Then that's where they needed to be.

~

He held Isla's hand as they raced across Fifth Avenue toward the entrance to Central Park. At this time of day, the streets were teeming with commuters trying to make it to work on time. Liam led them past the long line of open-air carriages waiting for tourists. They pressed on into the park, the world behind them fading away with each step inside. David loved the park, loved the fact that concrete and steel gave way to a lush green world.

"What happens if he runs when he sees us?" Isla asked.

"Somehow I think these two can handle him," he replied. Liam and Erin walked ahead of them. They'd been given explicit instructions to stay back until they were able to assess the situation, but he was worried Isla wouldn't obey that particular order. "Besides, we don't know if he's here. We only know the woman who helped him has her phone here."

"He's here," she said. "And I know where we're going. We're going down this path for a bit. There's an ice cream vendor, and a little behind him there's this set of huge rocks. Trey would bring the kids here when they were young, and he and Portia would sit on the rocks and eat ice cream and watch them play. It's a special place to him."

"Maybe you should stay back." Tears made her eyes shine and he had no idea what she would do if Trey got violent. He didn't want her there if Liam and Erin had to get physical with him.

They hurried down the path, passing joggers and tourists and people out enjoying the morning air.

"I think we're not going to be alone." Li pointed to a spot ahead where two cops stood beside an ice cream vendor cart. There was no vendor there, merely the cops and they were staring at something David couldn't see because of trees blocking his line of sight.

Something was wrong. They were simply standing there.

Isla picked up the pace and he had to nearly jog to keep up with her. A third cop came into view, moving to the side of the first two. They seemed to be surrounding a space.

"That's our helpful fan," Erin said, gesturing to the woman talking to another set of police officers. They were off to the side, the walkway between them and the cart.

Why were they standing there? It was clear one of the three sets of cops was talking to the woman who'd led Trey out of the hospital, but the other four cops were simply standing watch.

Had something happened to Trey? How would Isla cope with that?

"Officer?" Isla dropped his hand and moved in.

The two officers nearest them turned. The larger of the two nodded their way. "Move along please, ma'am. There's nothing to worry about here. Thank you."

David stopped because the officer was wrong. There was totally something to worry about. He could see what he hadn't before. A large man sat on a rock, his head down and bare feet on the ground, a thick line of trees at his back. Trey Adams was why the cops were standing watch. "I can't move on, Officer. My name is David Cormack. I'm a lawyer and I believe that man is my client."

Now he had the officer's attention. "Thank god. Reynolds over there recognized him and called for backup, but Adams hasn't done anything. He sat there and cried for a while. We have no idea how to handle him. He won't talk to any of us. I can't knock out a Super Bowl MVP and throw him in the back of my squad car."

The shorter of the officers nodded. "That man is a damn hero, and I don't buy that he killed his wife. I don't care what the DA tells us to do. I'm not taking him out of here like he's some animal. That man sitting in there is the only reason I have a relationship with my oldest son. We fought about everything except the Guardians. I knew that once a week I could be a good dad, you know. We could watch the game and he would wear his Trey Adams jersey and we would have a good time."

It paid to win the Super Bowl. In far more than simple cash. "Let me talk to him. My colleague is an old family friend. Let us go talk to him and see if we can do this quietly."

The two officers looked at each other and seemed to come to some decision.

"Okay," the first one said. "He's not armed. According to the crazy lady who let him out, he wouldn't go anywhere but here. She was trying to take him out of the city, but he came here and sat down and nothing has forced him up."

Isla started toward the rocks. "Thank you for being gentle with him."

"It's hard to watch that man fall," one of the officers said.

David rushed to keep up with her. "Isla."

She simply kept moving.

If she got herself killed, he was going to be pissed.

He glanced over and Liam and Erin had joined the officers talking to the woman in scrubs.

Isla sat down next to Trey. "Hey."

His head came up. "Isla? Isla . . . Sorry. They gave me so many drugs I can't think straight anymore. I think better here. I always did. I can see them playing here, but I know they're older now."

"It's okay," she replied, her voice soothing. "How are you feeling right now?"

Trey put a hand on his chest. "I feel like I forgot something. It hurts here. Like my heart knows something is wrong but I can't remember. I hurt so bad."

David felt wrong listening in, but he couldn't step away. This was private, a conversation between friends, but he couldn't leave her alone. Wouldn't leave her alone. No matter how kind Trey Adams had been, he had an illness that made him unstable.

"And where are my shoes?" Trey asked and suddenly laughed. He looked up and caught David's eyes. "You. You're the lawyer." He took a deep breath and his head hung low again. "You're the lawyer Isla brought in for me. God, I wanted it to be a bad dream. She's gone. Portia's gone."

Isla looked past him, as though trying to judge whether or not the cops were going to run in.

He thought they had some time. The cops seemed very willing to try to bring this to an easy, no-drama ending. "I am your lawyer and I'm going to help you. Do you know where you are?"

He nodded, not looking up. "In the park. We liked this space. The kids could run around. Miranda would get a Popsicle and Oscar liked ice cream sandwiches. We have lots of pictures from this exact spot. Why is my wife dead? Did I kill her?"

He hoped the cops were far enough away that they didn't hear that. He knelt down, getting to the same level as his client. "Do you remember anything at all about that night?"

"I remember she told me she would get them. She would take them all down." He frowned. "I don't know who she meant. She held me for the longest time and she was angry. She stayed in bed with me until I went to sleep. She does that a lot. Did that a lot. She would tell me stories about us, stuff I forgot. Sometimes it helped me remember. If it didn't, then at least I can remember the story. You know what I mean. She liked it here. Now, Portia wouldn't get ice cream. Said it went straight to her hips, but I thought they were beautiful hips. She was pretty when she was pregnant."

Isla put a hand on Trey's bulky arm. "She was always beautiful, but let's talk about what happened that night. She was angry about something?"

"Yeah, but I can't remember what," he said, his expression contorting to a mask of pain. "She said something about how I couldn't do it so she would. Do you think she knew someone was coming to hurt her and that I wouldn't be able to protect her?"

"No," Isla said quietly. "She knew you would do anything to protect her."

"Did you hear something that woke you up?" He wasn't sure how Trey would respond to being back in the hospital, especially since they would move him to a prison hospital. This might be his best time to get some questions answered, though the cops wouldn't wait forever.

"I thought someone was screaming, but when I got up, I didn't hear anything. There was a light on downstairs. I thought maybe Portia had made tea or something. She does that when she can't sleep. But when I called out she didn't answer. I wish she could sleep with me, but I have bad dreams. I move around a lot when I sleep."

He couldn't hold a thought for more than a few moments. His eyes would dart around, looking for threats. Trey's hands shook, likely from withdrawal since they kept him doped up every few hours.

Was this his future? Drooling and unable to catch a single idea?

Would Isla be the one trying to get him to hold on? Who held him until he could sleep and then went to her own lonely bed because he was too unstable to sleep next to?

"You said there was a light on downstairs?" Isla prompted him.

"I think it was from the living room. It puts shadows on the stairs when you leave it on. They can make me think I'm seeing things. Portia never leaves it on. She turns on the hall lights before she goes to bed."

"The hall between the upstairs bedrooms? The one that runs by the stairs?" David asked, shoving those old fears to the back of his head.

Trey held his head like it was hurting him. "Yeah, those. But they weren't on that night. I heard something move downstairs. I thought I should check on her."

Had Trey walked in as the killer was walking out?

"Counselor?" The tall police officer stepped up, a pair of shoes in his hand. "I'm sorry. The press is coming. We need to get Mr. Adams in a car and back to the hospital. I had some shoes in my gym bag. Like I'll ever actually hit the gym. I think I'm the same size."

Trey's head came up. "That's very nice of you. I don't know what happened to my shoes. I must have left them in the locker room. I'm such a dummy sometimes." He took the shoes and socks and started putting them on. "How can I lead the team to victory without my shoes?"

He gave the cop a brilliant smile and started talking about the game to come. Apparently he thought it was Sunday and he was playing the team from Miami. He started talking about stats and potential plays. He was calmer.

Liam joined them, leaning in to speak quietly. "Erin and I convinced a couple of people to get on social media and talk about how they've spotted Trey Adams by the fountain."

Smart man. They weren't close to the Bethesda Fountain. It could buy them a bit of time if they could get the press to the wrong spot. He didn't want Trey or Isla to have to deal with a crowd of rabid reporters. "Thank you."

"Can I ride with him?" Isla asked the second officer.

He shook his head. "Ma'am, we've already broken too many protocols and rules. I can't allow that, but I promise we're going to do everything we can to keep him calm. We're taking him back to the hospital and arresting the crazy chick who got him out. She was a fan. She thought if she 'saved' him, he would fall in love with her. Yeah, she's going on a psych hold, too. Lots of crazy going around this morning."

"You're taking him to the hospital and not prison?" Isla asked.

"He's not under arrest for murder and the counselor here has a restraining order until a judge decides where he's going. I'm sure the ADA thinks I'm hauling him out to Rikers, but the ADA is an asshole. I don't even want to think about what Sunday dinner would be like if I was the one who tossed Saint Trey in the clink. Ain't happening. Not when they've given me an out." The officer looked over to where Trey had gotten to his feet and was still talking about the big game. "The way I see it, Mr. Adams got a police escort more than once during his career. We'll keep him talking about the game. Why don't you go on ahead and meet us there?"

Isla looked up at him as though asking him if they could.

"Of course. We'll leave now and meet you there," he said, shaking the cop's hand. "And thank you for your kindness and discretion."

He stepped back, Isla's hand in his. Erin and Liam joined them. "What do you want me to prioritize?" Li asked.

There was no question about that. "The Algonquin. I need to know who Portia was meeting there. And I need to know what, if anything, was taken from the penthouse. I think the reason the DA's office hasn't arrested Trey is because they don't want to have to share intel with us. They want time to prove their theory before letting me start to work on my own. I need to know what they've got on forensics, too. If what Trey told us is true, he might have been in the same room as the person who killed his wife. He said he heard something downstairs. I bet that something was a someone. The kitchen is below those stairs. We know the police believe the chef's knife from the butcher block is the murder weapon. What if he interrupted the killer while he was cleaning up?"

A shudder went through Isla. "That's close to the servants' entrance, the same one whose security camera mysteriously went out."

"I need to know if the police found prints on that knife." Even if they had and they'd matched them to Trey's, he wouldn't put it past Osborne to have buried it to buy himself more time before he started the clock by arresting Adams.

"We're on it," Erin promised.

"Hey, Isla!" Trey was smiling and looking more like the man he'd been. "I'm going to the stadium. You going to be at the game?"

She nodded, her face flush with emotion. "Yep. I'm going to have David take me, but I'll be there. I promise."

Trey gave her a thumbs-up. "Awesome." He stopped in front of

David. "She's a great kid. You should be careful with her or you'll have to deal with me. She's important to my family. We understand each other?"

He'd completely forgotten that they'd just met. David nodded. "I'll take good care of her. I promise."

Trey walked away, amiably talking to the officers. If he thought it was weird that he had a procession of six officers surrounding him, he didn't let on. Likely because he was firmly in some world that existed only in his memory, one where his wife was alive and his family was whole, one where he was still the hero and not utterly broken.

Isla turned into David, tears on her cheeks as she watched her boss walk away.

He held her, his brain turning even while she cried.

TEN

Two days later Isla stared at the piles of folders currently taking up space on the gorgeous dining room table. The police had finally released her apartment, and David had all her paperwork transferred to the penthouse. She was in the process of matching the original documents to the copies she'd kept on her laptop.

So far nothing. Everything was here. There wasn't a contract out of place. Her safe hadn't been messed with.

From what the police could tell, Paloma had gone through her mail. He'd opened several boxes that had come in from various places she shopped, but he hadn't taken her new shoes or the new sheet set she'd bought online.

What the hell had he been looking for?

"Anything?" David stepped out of the bedroom, dressed for work.

She couldn't help but stare for a moment. A couple of days in bed with him had done nothing to get her used to how handsome he was, how masculine and protective he could be. She kind of hated that he was going into the office, but after two days of dealing with Trey's state of mind and the question of where he would be held, she understood that he was ready to be in the office for a while. He was good at making her feel like she was the center of the universe, but he did have other clients.

He was wearing a designer suit and she was in jeans and a T-shirt, her hair up in a messy bun, and she hadn't put on makeup yet.

"Nothing's missing. I'm going over to Trey's place in an hour or so. The police released it last night and they sent over the key. Don't worry; Erin's staying with me until Margarita gets here. She's going to Trey's with me," she explained. "Erin is going to escort us over there and then she wants to interview a couple of people in the building about what they might have seen or heard. Liam is meeting with the reservation manager of the Algonquin this afternoon."

"Are you sure you want to go?" David crowded her, but she was kind of used to it. If she was in a room with him, he liked to be close to her.

This would be the first day they'd spent apart, and she wasn't exactly looking forward to it. But then they had to find some normalcy. She couldn't cling to his hand for the next forty or fifty years. "Absolutely. The police know Portia's laptop and phone are missing. They've inventoried all the expensive stuff, but I want to see if there's anything else. How about you? What are you doing today?"

"I've got a couple of things I have to do on other cases," he said. "But I could put them off if you need me today."

She reached up and straightened his tie, resolute in her decision to not cling. "You have to go back sometime. Now that the question of where Trey is going to be held has been answered, we have to move on."

The doctors had been clear. He shouldn't be kept in the general population of a prison, but the judge had compromised and shifted him to the high-security psychiatric facility at Rikers. Thinking of her sweet employer in some dark place where they kept him cooped up and drugged made her heart break. They'd allowed his children to visit briefly, but only Miranda had shown up.

"Speaking of moving on," David said. "I still think we should stay here until they catch Kristoff Paloma. I talked to Noah, and his brother isn't expected in New York for a couple of weeks. We've been invited to stay as long as we like."

"You don't want to go home?" That was the decision she'd truly been dreading, that moment when he decided they were safe enough to go their separate ways. Oh, she had no doubt he would keep up with her, but she wasn't sure what time and distance would do to them. They were both dedicated to their jobs and spent most of their time working. Could they keep this relationship alive?

"I think I should stay close to you," he admitted. "The McKay-Taggart investigators are heading home for the weekend tomorrow and I want someone with you. Now that Erin and Liam have positive proof that Paloma was in both Paris and London when Portia was, we have to consider that he'll be back. He was looking for something, likely something she promised him. My working theory of the crime at this point is that their relationship went wrong and he killed her, but she had something on him. He's looking for information."

"You think that's what Portia meant when she told Trey she would 'get them'? That's what he said. Them. Not him." That talk with Trey in the park haunted her. She couldn't get him out of her mind, couldn't stop thinking about how hollow he'd looked.

"Maybe Paloma has a partner," he offered. "Though according to everything the investigators found on him, he works alone. I don't know how much we can trust what Trey remembers. I've also got a call in about a bail hearing for Trey. Right now the only count against him is reckless endangerment from the incident with the policeman's gun, but now we're waiting on the new psychiatric report before the judge will hear us."

"At least the press has calmed down." She tilted her head up and he leaned over to kiss her.

"At least we have that. I believe they've moved on to a happier story," he said, his arms around her waist. "Some Hollywood star recently had a baby, I think."

He was out of the loop. Of course, he'd fallen asleep while she watched TV the night before. He'd put his head in her lap and was asleep within minutes. She'd sat there stroking his hair and was so content she wished it would never end. "Not exactly. Josh Hunt's wife had a baby. It's their first. Did you know Erin and Li know her? She used to work at McKay-Taggart years ago. She was hired as his bodyguard and they fell in love. Isn't that romantic? Anyway, apparently Hollywood's hottest action star having a baby boy trumps our troubles for the moment."

"Let's hope Liam is able to find something today." He stepped back. "Even if I'm able to get all of this thrown out, you know what you have to do, right?"

He seemed so serious. It made her nervous. "Do?"

"If I can get the case thrown out for lack of evidence, they'll release Trey. They won't keep him unless we file a motion to keep him," David said, his words seemingly carefully chosen. "That wouldn't be difficult."

"I have to find a round-the-clock nurse for him," she said.

His jaw tightened. "I don't know that's going to work."

She couldn't see why it shouldn't work. "There's plenty of money in the estate. I can hire three and they'll work in shifts."

"And when he decides it's time to play football and tries to walk out to go to the stadium?"

He could potentially overpower the nurses. "A bodyguard, too."

David looked down at her. "You need to speak with Miranda and discuss what's best for all involved."

She'd been avoiding having to think about this. There had been so many other troubles, she didn't really want to consider what would happen if they won, but she knew a couple of things. "Miranda will likely try to take her mom's place. That could help a lot. He'll listen to Miranda."

"And she'll give up her whole life to take care of a man who might not remember who she is half the time?" David asked.

"She's his daughter." It should be clear to him. Family was important.

David stared at her. "Yes, she's his daughter. Think about what he would want for her. Would he want her stuck in that cage with him? She could maybe handle school, but could she have a job? Or would he become more and more dependent on her?"

His words were making her antsy. "I would help."

"And still take care of your other clients? What happens when you're in the middle of a meeting and you get a call that he's lost? Because no matter how many bodyguards you put on him, if he's not in a hospital, he's likely to get out." David's tone had lost a lot of the sympathy it'd had before.

"You want me to confine him to one of those terrible places? I thought that was what we're fighting against."

"No, I am representing him in a criminal case. My job is to give him the best defense I possibly can. You need to understand that if it comes to it, I'll recommend he takes a deal that would at least let him stay in a hospital where he can get help. You have to think about this. I know what I would want if it was me, and I would absolutely want to be somewhere I wasn't a burden and I didn't hold the people I love back."

He sounded cold. "How can you say that when you've met him? I don't think I could live with myself if I shoved him in a home. It certainly isn't what Portia wanted."

"I seriously doubt Portia would want you to give up your career in order to watch over a man who will rapidly not care what happens to himself. Do you understand where this disease is going? He will become violent over time. He will need people around to stop him from hurting himself and others."

She shook her head. "You still think he did it. No matter what you say, I can see it in your eyes. After everything we've uncovered, you still think he killed her in a fit of rage."

He held his hands up and stepped back. "I don't want to fight with you."

She didn't want to fight either, but his attitude was the first red flag she'd had. They'd been in perfect harmony it seemed. Of course, they'd also been in a pressure cooker. Sometimes it was easy to cling to each other when the times were bad.

Would they be able to make it in the real world? A world where they both went to work every day and might make it home for dinner a couple of times a week? Could they work if they had such a difference of opinion on how to treat someone like Trey?

"Isla"—he prompted her to look at him—"let's talk about this later. Like I said, it's nothing for us to worry about now. I have to see if I can even get him in front of a judge first. From what I understand Miranda and Oscar went in for interviews yesterday and I was told Oscar refused his attorney."

She winced. "Yeah, he was being an ass about it. Miranda told me the ADA didn't ask anything out of the ordinary and that her story corroborated my own."

"And we have zero idea what Oscar said, but we have to think he implicated his father."

"And maybe me." She didn't like to think about Oscar telling

Royce she'd had an affair with Trey. Royce would believe him without any kind of proof. Of course they would try to get him recused from the case, but until there was an arrest, there wasn't a lot they could do.

"It's going to be okay," David assured her. "Let me know if you find anything, and think about what I said. You don't have to make decisions now, but you might have to soon. Kiss me goodbye. I've got to hop on a call on my way to the office."

She nodded and let him kiss her again, but she needed time to think. He strode away, putting the phone to his ear, and she watched as he disappeared.

How could he be so heartless? What did she really know about her lover? He was good to her, but she'd been shocked at his callousness with Trey's future.

She could handle it. There was plenty of money. Surely that would make things easier.

Although she'd seen the toll it had taken on Portia. Still, she couldn't imagine making the decision to leave him in a home that wasn't his own.

She stared at the elevator. David was overwhelming. He was smart and kind and something didn't sit right about his reaction this morning.

Was he having second thoughts?

And what would she do if he recommended taking a plea? Could she fire him and still have a relationship with him? She knew the stupidest thing she could do was ignore the advice of an incredible criminal lawyer because she was too emotionally involved with her client.

She was in such a tough position and she had no idea what to do, but she'd been placed in this exact position because Portia had trusted her, believed she would do what was best.

The problem was that what was best for Trey might not be best for Miranda and Oscar.

She turned back to the work at hand, staring down at the pile marked *Adams*. A whole family's life and choices, their future and past, in one neat stack. Those papers represented everything from private school records to last will and testaments.

It hit her then that she was responsible. She was the one responsible for Miranda and Oscar and Trey, and they would likely fight her on a lot of the decisions to come.

All the pain of motherhood and none of the joy.

Erin strode in looking cool and confident in her slacks and white button-down. She would put on a jacket when they went out, the better to cover the Beretta she carried at all times. "We've got guests. According to the front desk, Cressida Bardsley is downstairs and she has Oscar with her. You want to see them?"

She should text David, but he was in the middle of a conference call.

If Oscar was here, she wasn't sure how that could be good. Still, she wouldn't do herself any favors by not seeing them, and she had a few questions for Portia's sister now that she'd apparently woken up from her Xanax stupor. Isla had been calling for two days to see if she could set up an interview. "You can let them up."

She wished she was better dressed but it was still early. She'd barely finished her second cup of coffee. She hoped David didn't get pissed that she took this meeting without him, but she wasn't sure Cressida would make herself available again.

Within a few minutes, the door opened and Cressida Bardsley walked through. The woman liked to make an entrance. She was dressed in black from head to toe, her mourning translated into fashion. Her makeup was impeccable, but she looked gaunt, a bit haunted. Oscar was by her side, his hair slicked back and an arrogant look in his eyes as he entered the penthouse.

"Well, Isla, it looks like you've traded up in the world. This place is even better than ours. Who are you fucking to get this?" Oscar asked.

Erin's brows shot up. "Hello, young asshole. I don't know that I like how you're talking to my client."

Oscar was about to say something, when he seemed to notice that nice-sized gun in Erin's shoulder holster. He backed down quickly. "Sorry."

It was good to know someone could handle Oscar.

"You wanted to talk to me, Isla?" Cressida's heels clicked along the floor. "You left enough messages. Between you and that disgusting gold digger, my phone is full."

"Gold digger?" Isla asked.

"Carey's wife," Cressida replied with a long-suffering sigh. "She keeps calling me looking for pictures for the funeral. Who the hell put her in charge of the memorial? I suspect it was you."

"Amber kind of takes charge and you weren't exactly up and around," she started. "Apparently, Miranda told her she could do it."

"Well, I was in mourning," Cressida shot back. "I'm sorry that I miss my sister so much that I couldn't handle planning her funeral thirty minutes after her death. You can tell that woman that she'll plan my sister's funeral over my dead body."

The morning was going great. "Can I get you some coffee?"

"You can get me some answers. Why is my brother-in-law in a hospital instead of jail?" Cressida gracefully sank to the couch.

"He's in the hospital because he's sick and you know he's sick," she replied.

"Sick enough to kill my sister," Cressida said.

"I told you she doesn't care." Oscar shrugged. "She only cares about controlling our fortune."

"And he's in a high-security hospital. It's rather like a prison. I couldn't keep him out." David couldn't, but had he done everything he could or had he agreed with the judge and thought it was better to lock Trey up as tightly as possible? She hadn't considered that until he'd talked to her this morning.

Cressida frowned her way. "I don't want that man walking around free. Who knows who he'll come after next? I tried to warn Miranda away, but she won't listen to me. I'm afraid she'll be his next victim."

"He wouldn't hurt his own daughter," Isla replied, but she could see it was a losing argument.

Oscar leaned forward, his eyes narrowed. "Is that your plan? You let him kill off me and Miranda and then you get all the cash?"

Erin leaned in, too. Oscar frowned and sat back.

She was tired of being the bad guy. "If you and Miranda die, all the cash goes to a charity. I don't have any way to use the money on myself. I get paid for the legal work I do, but nothing more. I'll let you read the contract if you like."

"I already have a copy, thank you," Cressida said. "My sister stored a copy of her important legal documents at the beach house in case she ever needed them. Believe me I've forwarded it to my own lawyer. I find you use extremely technical language."

It was called legal terminology, but she bit her tongue on that one.

She needed to get her answers before she lost control of the situation. Defending herself wouldn't mean a thing to Oscar or Cressida. "Do you know a man by the name of Kristoff Paloma?"

Cressida's elegant brow rose. "No. I can't say I have heard of him. What does he have to do with anything?"

"I think Isla and Miranda are so desperate to save Dad they've made up a fake lover for Mom," Oscar answered. "They don't care about her reputation at all. You don't mind dragging her through the mud, do you?"

Erin reached into her bag and came back with a picture. "He's a Dutch national, wanted all over Europe for his various frauds and cons. He would likely have been going by another name."

"He broke into my apartment the day after Portia's murder," Isla explained. "We think he's looking for something. We also suspect he might be the person your mother's been meeting every Thursday."

Cressida took the photograph, studying it. "Honestly he does look familiar. I've seen him. I can't say where though. London, perhaps. No, it was Paris. This man was in Paris the last time I was there with Portia and her friends. He was staying at the same hotel as us and we spent some time in the bar together. But he certainly wasn't romancing my sister. She never did have eyes for anyone but her husband. And she'd been meeting with an old producer friend for the last month of her life. I do believe it was on Thursdays. He was splitting his time between New York and L.A. Thursday mornings were free for him. What's his name? You know, the one who produced that football show."

She knew exactly who Cressida was talking about. "Gary Keller? Why would she meet with him?"

"It was all very hush-hush. She wanted it to be a huge surprise. She was putting together a documentary of Trey's life and career," Cressida explained. "I thought it was a waste of time since it's not like he'll remember it anyway, but she was quite insistent. It was her labor of love. I think she thought it could remind him. Gary was teaching her how to edit. She'd bought a bunch of software that would help her create the movie on her laptop."

And there went her best lead. "You're sure?"

Cressida seemed softer talking about her sister. "Absolutely. She wasn't having an affair. She would have told me." She turned to Oscar. "And I highly doubt your father was having an affair with Isla." She looked up, a frown on her face, but not an unsympathetic one. "You'll have to forgive our dear Oscar. I think his parents made a terrible mistake by accepting him so easily. He's an artist, and struggle is important to artists. They should have pretended to be horrified when he came out. Then he could have used that as fuel for his fire. He's been forced to make up drama. I assure you, I told that terribly arrogant Mr. Osborne that my sister's marriage was practically perfect, with the single exception of her husband's mental illness, which, yes, I believe absolutely led to her death. I didn't say I thought he meant to do it, but he's capable of it. The man always was a barbarian on the inside."

Isla struggled to keep up with Cressida's mercurial opinions. She'd always been like this, always changed her stance to keep the drama going. "I wish you would have talked to me before you went to the ADA."

How could David fight this if most of the family was willing to testify against him?

An unamused smile crossed Cressida's perfect face. "Why, dear? So you could convince me to lie to the police and the DA? You wanted me to plead for my brother-in-law's life? The truth is my sister was far too good for some athlete. She should have married someone with real talent, but Portia would never listen to good advice. Now, do you have anything else to ask me in your desperate attempt to save my brother-in-law's pathetic life?"

She wanted to tell Cressida to fuck off and get out, but that wouldn't solve her problems. She still needed answers. "Do you know of anyone Portia would have wanted revenge against?"

A blank expression crossed her face. "Revenge? That sounds awfully dramatic. I would expect that to come out of Oscar's mouth, not my sister's."

Oscar huffed and sat back. "You don't know her as well as you think you did. My mom was a saint unless you messed with her family. Then she could be ruthless."

"Trey said the night she died she talked about getting back at someone, taking them down," she explained.

"My father could have been talking about a conversation from my childhood," Oscar said, waving her off. "Mother used to talk about bullies like that. She would cuddle me and tell me she would take them down and then she would lean on the mothers and explain that they would have no social life at all if they continued to allow their brats to mess with me. Mom took care of us. Always."

"He was very certain." She didn't want to lose this. "He also said he heard someone moving around downstairs that night."

"And two months ago I had to call a service because Dad decided to go scuba diving in the bathroom," Oscar said with a shake of his head. "He tried to fill the whole of the bathroom so he could do it. He's insane. You can't trust anything he says. Look, if Mom was talking about taking someone out, it was likely someone who said something shitty about Dad. Hell, it could have been me she was talking about. We had a fight that morning."

"The morning you made her breakfast?" She needed to get a timeline of the day.

"Yeah, like I said, she would only eat if I did the work and put it in front of her. Then she would eat it out of pure guilt. She was worried about Dad." Oscar's arms went over his chest in a protective gesture. "I didn't make things easier on her. I told her she should put Dad in a home. He was making her miserable."

Cressida patted her nephew's leg. "We all tried to talk to her about that. He was a danger to himself and others. He needed to be somewhere they could handle him."

Well, wasn't that the argument of the day. "I don't think she was talking about you. Your father said she used the term 'them.' She said she would take them down. And I seriously doubt she would talk about revenge on you. No matter what happened, she adored you."

For once Oscar looked like he gave a shit. "She was a good mom." He was quiet for a moment. "She was a little off that morning. Like

I said, she wouldn't eat. When my mom was upset, she wouldn't eat, but when I asked her what it was about she said she didn't want to discuss it. She said I would know soon enough."

That was mysterious. "But she gave you no indication at all why she was upset?"

"I can tell you some of the things she was worried about," Oscar offered. "She was worried about me being out in Brooklyn. She was worried about my lack of a boyfriend. She thought Aunt Cressy was drinking too much."

Cressida shuddered. "Like she should have talked."

Oscar continued. "She was worried about Miranda because she thinks my sister is screwing one of her professors. She is, but it's nothing serious. She doesn't . . . didn't give Miranda enough credit for having a level head. The man's not even married or anything. It's barely a scandal. But mostly she was worried about Dad. Always, always worried about Dad."

"Maybe she was finally going to put him in a hospital," Cressida mused. "That would certainly make her tense. I know she wasn't feeling up to our girls' trip."

"You were planning another one?"

"We wanted to go to Milan for a week with the usual women. I personally would have been happier without Portia's friends, but she believed in having a group of friends. I found some of them extremely gauche, but she tried to mentor some of the younger wives she met at various functions. She was always taking in strays, you know."

"Can you get me a list of who went with you on that Paris trip?"

"If I can find it," Cressida replied in a tone that let Isla know she wouldn't make this a priority. "I've got it somewhere. I was responsible for the private jet and had to have everyone's passport numbers. I'm sure I kept it since we used the same list for London. I was surprised she canceled Milan. She told me we would still go but quietly. I think she finally got tired of having a procession of obnoxious bitches around her. Speaking of one of them, will you get that Amber thing off my back? The medical examiner hasn't even released my sister's body yet. I don't know when we want the memorial service to be. It certainly won't be public."

"Yeah, I think family only." Oscar was back to being a brat. "That means no interlopers. And I hear the penthouse was released by the cops. I'm going over this afternoon. There are some things I need to pick up. Try not to be there when I am."

Oscar stalked off toward the elevator.

Cressida rolled her perfectly done eyes. "Of course you'll be welcome at the memorial, Isla. But you should understand that I intend to challenge the will and you as executor. I don't have a problem with you except that you're not family. It's nothing at all personal, but my sister wasn't thinking about what was best at the end."

And now she would have to fight Cressida and Oscar. She would need to pay a lawyer and spend all her time trying to maintain control.

"You can certainly try," she replied.

"Goodbye, dear. I'll let you know when we plan the memorial. And I'll get you that list. I know you're trying everything you can to convince yourself this isn't Trey's fault, but I think you're wasting your time. Still, it's what my sister would want. She did see you as something of a daughter."

She turned on her heels as the elevator was opening. Isla felt like she'd gone a couple of rounds with a boxer. The doors closed.

Erin shook her head. "Wow, she's a bitch, and I don't even know what to call the kid."

"Asshole," Isla said. "He's an entitled little asshole."

And she had to deal with them all. The day was not looking up.

~

David sat back, his eyes tired. The damn words were all kind of meshing together at this point. He'd read the brief about a thousand times and he still wasn't sure it was right. That might be because his mind was somewhere else. He kept going back to that moment when Isla looked at him like he was a monster for even suggesting that Trey belonged in a hospital.

She'd looked a lot like his mother had when he suggested the same thing for his father.

His mother had barely spoken to him for two weeks after he'd tried to get her to see that she was killing herself taking care of him. She'd merely said that was what people in love did.

He wondered if she would go back. Had his mother known how her fairy tale would end—with Alzheimer's dominating her husband—would she have chosen a different path? Was he taking Isla down the exact same path his mother had walked? Would he fall for her? Marry her, have a couple of kids, and then leave her when the CTE kicked in? Hell, it would be better if he would leave her, but that's not what would happen. He would become her dependent. He would suck the life out of her and their children. He would drag them all down. At least if he fell apart at work, they could fire him and not look back.

"That's a bleak look," Henry said from the doorway. "You know something I don't know?"

He shook off the dark thoughts. He needed to concentrate. It had been days since he'd actually been in the office. "Not at all. I think we went over everything earlier today. Although we did clear up who Portia Adams was meeting every Thursday."

"McKay-Taggart come up with that?"

"No, Isla did. She finally talked to Portia's sister." Isla had texted him roughly an hour before, letting him know she was sending him a report on the conversation and he should look for it in email.

Very polite. Very professional. He'd obviously fucked up quite badly with her.

"I've forwarded her email report to you. She's going to follow up with Cressida because she also found out that Kristoff Paloma was definitely around during their Paris trip but he wasn't hanging out with Portia. The sister is adamant she wasn't having an affair."

Henry studied him for a moment. "What are your thoughts right now?"

"I think we're not in a position to do a whole lot of thinking."

"But that never stopped you," Henry pointed out. "You've been brooding in here all morning."

He knew he was in trouble when the broodiest person he knew called him out. "I've been thinking about probable outcomes. I know what Isla wants me to do."

"And that is?"

He sat back in his chair, his brain threatening a truly impressive headache. "She would go to trial. I think she would want me to go to trial even if there was footage of Adams stabbing his wife."

"And you?"

He hated what he would have to do. "If we don't find conclusive evidence that someone else was in that apartment the night of the murder, I think we have to plead this out. I think insanity is our only defense and we'll have to admit to the crime in order to have a prayer of it working and our client not going directly to jail. The crazy thing is, it's Isla testimony that will likely put him there if I let this go to trial."

Henry sank into the seat in front of David's desk. "Is there any purpose in me telling you that this is exactly why we don't get involved with clients?"

"She's not the client."

A dubious huff came from Henry. "She might as well be. Legally, she now makes all the decisions for the client. She can fire you if she wants to, and Trey doesn't have a say. Look, I can easily see you're into this woman. The best thing might be to hand the case over to me. Let me be the bad guy."

It wouldn't work. "And when the inevitable happens? She's going to turn to me and ask me to take over and I won't be able to. I'm in a position where I can't win. If I take this case to a jury right now, I better hope I get twelve crazed Guardians fans because otherwise, Trey Adams is going to jail for the rest of his life."

"She's not exactly some wide-eyed novice," Henry pointed out. "She's an attorney. I can't imagine she doesn't understand the implications of the evidence we have and how that's going to affect an actual trial. Unless we come up with something concrete, I'm with you. Mental incapacity is our best defense, but I wouldn't take this to court unless the DA's office simply won't deal with us."

Ah, but there was the other issue. "Well, we've got a problem with that. The ADA handling this thing had a prior relationship with Isla that didn't end well. It looks like he's using this case to punish her. And I can't get him recused because he hasn't actually had Trey arrested."

Henry shifted, his irritation apparent. "They're playing for time. They don't have to turn anything over until they arrest him. Technically they've only got him on the reckless endangerment charge and they can avoid bail because he's being held for his mental state. It's a nice little package they've tied him up in. If we didn't have such good police contacts, we would know next to nothing."

At least someone understood the problems he was facing. "She thinks I'm some sort of legal superhero."

Henry's expression softened. "She's obviously in that first stage of a relationship. You know the one, where you can't stop thinking about your partner and you need a couple of reminders that someone less interesting is talking to you."

He groaned because that had happened a couple of times during the morning meeting. Henry had to poke him to get his attention and apparently Noah had started talking for him at some point. All in all, not his best performance. "I told you I was thinking about the case."

"Yeah, but you also have a couple of tells when you lie, and no, I'll never describe them because I like winning at poker." Henry sobered. "It's okay to think about her. God knows I still think about Win all the time. We're the old married couple now and I still can't get her out of my head. It's a good thing."

Old married couple was a bit of an overstatement. They were basically still honeymooners, but David got his point. They were settled, and he and Isla didn't even know what they were yet. If they were anything at all but a bunch of chemistry and need. "It's not in my case."

"Because you think she's going to dump you if you can't get her client off on a murder charge? I'm going to sound an awful lot like my grandfather now. If she requires that you get all her friends off their murder charges in order to maintain a relationship with you, she's not worth having a relationship with."

David groaned and let his head fall back. "It's not that."

But he couldn't tell Henry his real worry. He couldn't admit it out loud. Twenty years he'd known Henry and not once had he told his best friend his deepest fear.

He sure as hell wasn't going to bring it up with Isla. No, if she hadn't figured it out . . . did he have any right to put that on her? On anyone at all?

Heart. Bottle. Zebra.

His mantra for the day. Did she deserve a man who desperately held on to three random words as proof that he wasn't losing his mind?

"It's hard once the pressure's off," Henry said. "I know that sounds crazy, but it is. Win and I went through all that drama and then we were living together out of necessity. It would have been easy to skip steps. You know there's not a lot of going back after you live together, especially not if you care about her, but you can fix a couple of things. You can take her on a date that has nothing to do with the case. You can take her out to meet your parents."

The thought turned his stomach and then made him flush with shame. He loved his parents and yet he was hiding them away.

Henry's eyes narrowed. "There's no shame in your dad having a disease."

Oh, but there was such anxiety and fear in knowing that it was one more fucking strike against him. "He can be difficult to deal with. Maybe I could ask Mom to let me know when he's having a good day."

"Or you could understand that you've managed to find a woman who gets it, who won't be afraid to deal with your situation. She could be great for your mom because she wouldn't be afraid of what's happening with your father."

But maybe she should be. However, there was no point in arguing with Henry. "I will see if I can make that happen."

Henry stared at him for a moment and then sighed and stood up. "Like I told you before, David. You have tells. I would hate to see you ruin something that could be good because you're scared of something that might not ever happen."

Or maybe he didn't need to tell Henry what he was afraid of. "Yeah, well, I've got a damn good shot of it happening. I have to think about it."

"And you could also get hit by a bus. She could have some unknown heart defect," Henry argued. "The world could come to an end tomorrow and there's very little we can do about it. You've got a twenty-eight percent chance of developing CTE. You're my best friend. You think I don't know that?"

That shook him up a bit. "It's more than twenty-eight percent. You have to add in the factor that a close relative of mine has Alzheimer's. It ups my risk factor considerably."

"I don't care if you have a fifty-fifty chance. What are you going to do? Stop living because the coin flip doesn't go your way?" Henry paced as though this was a topic that unnerved him, but he was going to plow through. "Because that's not the David Cormack I went to school with. He was a full-ride kid who worked his ass off to make his life better, his parents' lives better. He didn't fucking give up because things might go bad. He fought and he fought like hell."

"I'm not lying down, man," he replied with some fire of his own. "You have no idea everything I do to keep my mind sharp."

"Good, then put the same effort into the relationship with Isla. I know this case is what brought her into your life. Don't let it be the thing that takes her out of it, too. You need to talk to her about what you want outside of the case. Firm boundaries. Explain to her that she's more important than any one case, even this one. Tell her you need those boundaries or you need to pass the case off to someone else."

It wasn't a horrible plan. "I'll talk to her."

He pointed David's way with a relieved sigh. "Good. That I believe. You talk to Isla and I'll have Noah call his mole in the DA's office to see if she's heard anything. We'll try to get ahead of them if we can. I hate this cat-and-mouse shit."

Naturally, Noah's mole was a female, one he very likely paid for information with his body. Noah was a giver. But he still had one question. "Come on, man. You're not going to tell me how you know I'm lying?"

Because Henry seemed to have excellent instincts.

A smirk lit his friend's face. "Nope. Like I said, you suck at poker and I'm not going to change that for you. I've got a wife now. I need the extra income."

Noah showed up at the door, his face flushed and chest heaving because it was obvious he'd run from wherever he'd been. "Guys, you aren't going to believe this. They've made an arrest in the Portia Adams case."

The world seemed to stop and David prayed whatever came out of Noah's mouth next didn't change his life forever.

ELEVEN

"Are you sure you want to go in?"

The sound of Margarita's quiet question brought Isla out of her thoughts. How long had she been standing here staring at the door to the penthouse? They'd left Erin downstairs talking to the guard about the protocols of the building and security. They'd gotten in the elevator to the penthouse and she'd kind of zoned out. She didn't remember walking down the hall.

She remembered that night. She remembered how she could practically hear the pounding of her heart as she'd stepped up to the door.

"I'm fine," she managed.

Margarita stepped in front of her. She was a lovely woman in her midthirties, the kind of woman who looked stylish even when she was working out. Today she was wearing a drapey sweater, slacks, and boots that came up to her knees. Her deep brown hair was highlighted with sections of honey blond. "You can't possibly be fine. The last time you were in this place, your friend had been murdered. It's okay to not want to walk in."

She wished it were that simple. "I don't want to, but I have to. I don't have a choice. It's my job."

"Okay, then let's talk about what we need to do in there, and that might help us focus. I'm going to take some of my own pictures. Until we get the crime scene photos, these will have to do. You are going to look for something."

Isla took a deep breath, trying to shake off the feeling of dread she got from standing outside the door. "Anything, really. Anything out of the ordinary. I know whoever broke in that night took her computer, but she kept up with her schedule a couple of ways. I have to wonder if the police found all of it."

"Do you know if she wrote in a journal? Maybe a diary?" Margarita asked.

"No, but she used a small voice recorder to document ideas that came to her. I want to know where that went. It wasn't on the log of what the police processed."

"Then the killer might have taken it."

"Or Portia misplaced it. She kept a few around in places where she was most likely to come up with ideas. Like she kept one in the bathroom because she thought a lot in the shower or the tub. She said she always had the best business ideas while soaking in the tub." Isla could feel herself calming down as she talked about what she needed from this trip. Focus. She needed to focus and not get lost in the nightmare.

Still, a vision of all that blood struck her.

A perfectly manicured hand reached out to touch her shoulder. "They'll have cleaned up for the most part, though there might still be some stains. You don't have to do this."

But she did. "I'm not going to be able to be one hundred percent cool. I might as well use it to see if I can remember anything else about that night."

"Are you sure? Because that might be incredibly helpful but David will kick my ass if you end up a shivering heap in the corner somewhere," Margarita said. "Not that anyone would blame you. Like I said, he would totally blame *me*."

"I'm going to try not to," she replied. "Okay. Let's start at the beginning."

Margarita pulled out her phone. "Do you mind if I record this?"

She hated being recorded but understood the need. "No. We definitely should. The door was unlocked when I got here. I remember asking the doorman if anyone had come up."

"And what did he say?"

She took a deep breath and proceeded. "He had no one using the private elevator after six P.M., which was when Portia returned. He didn't know where she'd been. I can only hope it was in her day planner. She left the building at four P.M. Before that the only visitor they had that day was Oscar. He had breakfast with his mother. He claims he simply came by to spend time with her, but I bet he needed money."

Oscar always needed money, which was precisely why he would be upset about the will. He had years before he could blow through his trust fund with impunity. Isla was certain the idea of having to come to her for cash didn't sit well with Oscar, but he would find that the will was going to be impossible to break.

"The door was unlocked. Was that unusual?" Margarita asked.

"Yes. Though Portia considered the private elevator to be the real security. You had to be allowed up. I opened the door and walked in." *Deep breath. Don't let your hands shake.* She pulled the key out and opened the door. The police tape was gone, but she could see where the adhesive had held it to the exquisite custom door.

"Was there a security system on?"

She frowned. "No. I guess I didn't think about it at the time. It wasn't usually on when I came by during the day. I didn't come by a lot at night, but it should have been active. I stepped inside and everything was quiet for a moment."

Margarita followed her in. There was a foyer that led to the grand staircase.

"I called out but no one answered."

"Were there lights on?"

"A couple." She closed her eyes and tried to remember. She'd walked down the foyer and stopped. "The living room had a lamp on. They have lights that lead up the stairs, but they were off and that wasn't normal. As you can see it would be difficult to navigate in the dark." She stood at the edge of the stairs. "The bedrooms are upstairs. There are five of them, but the two largest are on either side of the penthouse. There's also an office and a workout room. I went upstairs and checked on Trey. He wasn't in his bedroom. That was when I heard it."

"What did you hear?"

"I heard Trey screaming." She could still hear it, that horrible sound. It was ripped from the soul. "I ran up the stairs."

"You know a lot of people would have run the other way."

"I wasn't thinking. I heard that sound and I needed to get to him. Trey's been like a big brother to me. I've known him since I was a teenager hanging around the Guardians' front office." She climbed the stairs much more slowly than she'd done before. "I helped them buy this place. It was one of the first deals I handled for them."

"You've been with them a long time."

"Yeah, I like this kind of legal work. I like helping clients build businesses and lives and families. I make sure they're safe." She stopped at the top of the staircase. "Not that I did a good job this time."

Margarita stepped in front of her, the phone down now. "You are not responsible for this."

"Aren't I?" She hated to say it, but she had to. They'd found noth-ing. Why would Kristoff Paloma murder Portia if she was the target of his latest con? He would want her alive so he could potentially blackmail her. "If Trey killed Portia, I am absolutely responsible. I helped make the decision to keep him out of an institution. I sided with Portia when Oscar and Cressida wanted to put him in a hospital. I think if I'd argued with her, Portia might have been persuaded. She wouldn't have wanted to, but I could have swayed her that it was best for her family. If I'd done that, would she be alive today?"

Margarita shook her head. "You can't ask yourself those questions. Look, I've been an attorney for a long time. Well, it feels that way at least. I worked in corporate for years. I helped Drew Lawless build his business, but I wanted something more. When the chance came to move over into criminal law, I took it. And it is fascinating and invigorating, and I've never felt as low as I have when I fail. It's inevitable because sometimes we're representing criminals. But they're human, too. One of my first cases was a woman with two kids. She'd been brutalized by her husband, but she didn't make a move on him until he slapped their son one night. She waited until he fell asleep and she shot him."

Isla could guess the rest of the story. "She was convicted because he was helpless when she attacked."

"Oh, yes. I brought in everyone I could. I threw every expert I could find at that jury. The sad thing is, if he'd been awake he likely would have fought, and he had a hundred and fifty pounds on her. If she'd run with the kids, he could have taken her to court to get them back. She had no money, no resources, and only one way in her mind to protect her children. And all my schooling, all my passion and expertise, couldn't keep her out of jail. I couldn't keep her children from being raised by her in-laws, who produced an abusive son of a bitch in the first place. I always wonder if I screwed up during jury selection or if I should have pressed her harder to take a plea. I tried, but she couldn't stand the idea of being away from her kids."

"It sounds like you did everything you could."

"And you did, too," Margarita insisted. "We make decisions at the time that later seem wrong, but you can't know what would have happened. If you do your job with all good intent, with all your heart and soul, you have to be at peace with the results of your work. Maybe not happy or content, but at peace. A smart man taught me that."

Isla could guess. "David."

"Yeah, he was like me. He had one career and decided he needed something that fed his soul more. The trouble is when you put your soul out there, you get hurt as much as you get fed, but it's worth it because at least you know you're doing something important."

She nodded. At the time her instincts had told her Trey was harmless to anyone but himself. It was the heavy weight of others' suspicions that pressed on her. She was being forced to think like David would be and coming up with nothing that would sway a jury.

"Okay, let's keep going." Margarita brought the phone up again. Isla started walking. "By the time I checked Trey's room and came back out, I knew the sounds had to be coming from Portia's room. I ran down the hallway. Again, I wasn't thinking about anything but getting to whoever was screaming. I had to hope it was a cry for help. Oh, I knew deep down it was grief, anger, pain. But I pushed through. I guess I thought knowing was better than not knowing."

Margarita nodded encouragingly. "And all of this happened in a couple of minutes?"

"Yes. I would say it was no more than a moment or two between me entering the penthouse and getting to Portia's bedroom door. I did stop there."

"Was it open?"

She nodded and stared at that door ahead of her. "It was about halfway open. I did pause because the sound was so much closer. I think this was the first time I was really scared."

"But you went in."

She pushed the door open and though the place had been picked up, the carpet pulled out, and the marble cleaned, she could still see the blood everywhere. "Someone had trashed the place. It was like a bull in a china shop. They removed drawers from her dresser and desk. There were papers everywhere and clothes all over the place. I kept moving because the moans were coming from the bathroom. That's where I saw him. And her. He was holding her and there's no question in my mind that she was dead. No one could lose that much blood. It was savage."

"Did you say anything to him?" Margarita kept the phone steady.

"No. He didn't look up. He was holding her close. I don't think he knew I was there. I kind of lost it and I ran." She turned and started to back out. "I meant to go and call the police. It's weird but I didn't think about my cell. It was in my pocket, but what I was going for was the landline in the kitchen. I don't know why. It was first thing I thought of. I hate that I panicked."

"But you didn't make it to the kitchen."

She stepped back out and suddenly remembered what she hadn't before. The light. That light had been coming from the wrong place. The hair on her arms stood up as she remembered why she'd retreated. "I threw up in the potted plant and then I saw that light. God, why didn't I remember it? I can't remember if it was on when I came in, but it was definitely on when I ran out of Portia's room. There was a light on in the kitchen. The overhead in the kitchen is very bright. The living room is all lamps. You can't see the actual kitchen from here. It's under the stairs. But there was a light down below and I remember that it suddenly went off and I went still. God, Margarita, I think the killer was still here."

"And if the killer was in the kitchen, he couldn't be Trey."

"He couldn't have done it." Guilt swamped her. "God, why didn't I remember that until now? No one is going to believe me. They'll think I'm covering for him. How could I have forgotten?"

"Because you experienced a traumatic event. We can get the best psychiatrists in the country to testify about lost time. Your brain shut down in the face of pure fear. It's how you could have been frozen but not remembered the time passing. This is something we could work with. Can we go down to the kitchen? I want to see where the killer could have gotten out. Is there any way you caught a glimpse of him?"

The terror of the moment hit her. "Not that I remember. Now that I'm here, I recall trying to make myself very small. I shrank back against the wall like I could hide. I could smell my own sick because I was trying to put that plant between me and him. I thought he would come back up the stairs and take me like he'd taken Portia."

What she didn't say, couldn't say, was that she'd known no one would cry for her. No one would wail the way Trey had wailed. No one would miss her like they'd lost a piece of their soul, and that meant she hadn't truly lived. She'd stayed there because she was afraid. So afraid that she'd missed something and couldn't leave this life without it.

Now she knew what she'd missed. She'd cared about Austin, loved him in a girl's way, but what she felt for David went beyond. Beyond youth. Beyond crush. Beyond yearning. There was a connection that came from a mature soul, that came from knowing this was the part of her that was missing and now made whole.

Margarita was right there with her, a hand on hers, letting her know she wasn't alone. "It's okay. You're all right. And, Isla, you've given us a lot. I'm going to call Erin. You've given us a time. We can request the CCTV footage around the same time and see what we come up with."

Isla moved down the stairs. It wasn't at all what she'd done that night. No, that night she'd cowered, but now she was moving. Now she wasn't afraid, though she felt a deep guilt in her gut that she'd hesitated that night.

Margarita followed her. "Did you call the cops on your cell phone?"

"I did. It took me a while, but I called them. Miranda messaged me. That's what brought me out of my stupor. I have the most ridiculous text message sound and it brought me out of it. Then I got up and called the cops. I couldn't leave Miranda down there waiting."

She needed to stand in the kitchen and know the killer had been there, too.

She got to the ground floor and stopped because she heard someone at the front door. It came open and Oscar walked through.

"I should have known you would be here." Oscar came in all swagger, but he stopped and looked around, momentarily silent.

Miranda was behind him. She stopped, too, glancing up at the stairs as though she could see her mother's bedroom. She shook it off quickly, plastering a smile on her face that didn't reach her eyes. "Isla, I'm glad you're here. Are you okay? I can't believe how the press is fucking you over. Are you seeing that hot lawyer guy?"

"She is," Margarita said with a smile.

"I am." She felt the need to speak for herself. Somehow David was hers. She'd spent years and years on the outside and David was something different. David was more. It was insane how possessive she felt about him, how much she believed he belonged to her.

"Awesome, Isla's got a boyfriend. That's not what we're here about. We came to grab a few things and one of those things is Mom's copy of the will. It should be in the safe. I'm going to prove you manipulated Mom into writing that will so you could steal our inheritance." Oscar was still an asshole.

Isla didn't engage the crazy. It was her new mantra. She turned and walked down the long hall that led to the kitchen. Margarita followed her.

It didn't matter what Oscar did. She needed to follow this through.

"What are you doing here?" Oscar wasn't letting up.

"I'm going back over that night." It was good Miranda was here. "Miranda, did you get worried when I didn't come back?"

"I panicked when you didn't come back," she admitted. "But I waited. I thought you were talking to them, dealing with something crazy my dad had done. I broke down when you called and told me the cops were coming."

"And what did you think then?" Oscar asked. "What did you think had happened?"

Miranda shook her head as she looked at her brother. "I thought something terrible had gone wrong and there had been an accident."

"Bullshit," he shot back, getting into his sister's space. "Tell me the truth, damn it. Stop lying to yourself."

Miranda held her ground. "Fuck you, Oscar."

"Tell the truth," he insisted. "What did you think? In the moment that Isla told you Mom was dead, what was the first thought that went through your head? Don't fucking lie."

"I thought he'd killed her. Is that what you want to hear? Yes. Yes, I did. I thought he'd finally gone insane and killed her," Miranda shouted.

Isla started to move toward Miranda, but she held a hand out, stopping her.

Oscar pointed his sister's way. "I knew it. I knew all that shit about how much you love Dad is nothing but a front so Mom didn't get upset with you. I knew you did it to make me look bad."

"I said it because I love my father," she shot back. "I said it because I didn't abandon him the minute he became human. I have no idea what's wrong with you. He says one thing in all the years of loving you, of taking care of you in a way very few people on this earth get taken care of, and yet it wasn't enough. No one could ever love you enough. You needed . . . god, I don't know. Drama. Strife. Well, guess what. If you feed off negativity, I'll give you some. I hate you, Oscar. I'm going back to my dorm. You can stay at Cressy's or whatever. I don't care."

Oscar stopped, the arrogant look fleeing his face. "I'm not trying to piss you off. I just think you should face the truth."

Miranda turned and kept walking. She never once looked back.

Oscar turned on Isla. "You had to be here, didn't you?"

Isla was done with Oscar. "Don't you pin this on me. You know, I've watched you since you were a teenager. You've never once taken responsibility for anything that goes wrong with your life. When you wrapped your brand-new car around a tree, it was the deer's fault. When you got caught smoking pot, it was your friend's fault. Anyone but you. The time is coming that you'll do something or say something that you can't take back, that nothing will fix, and you won't have anyone to blame but yourself."

"I'm sure you would love that," he replied.

Anger thrummed inside her. At one point, she'd looked at Oscar like a little brother. Now she just wanted to punch him. "I wouldn't. That's the crazy part. I don't hate you. I simply no longer care. And you need to think seriously about fighting me on the will. It's iron-clad. Your mother made sure of it. If you decide to fight me, everything freezes. That allowance you get, frozen. The apartment that's paid for out of your parents' account, frozen. I suggest you get on board with the plan and be a good boy and when you're thirty, I'll happily hand over your trust fund and you can blow through it in a year or two, and when you come back to me for more, I'll send you on your way with nothing. You see, what you forget, but that your mother remembered, was how important it is to make something of yourself. That trust is all you get."

"But there are millions extra. And the companies . . . they're worth a ton," Oscar said.

"And your sister will inherit them because she'll run them, and not into the ground," Isla replied. "You won't see a dime of that money because you've never once worked for it. Miranda helped your parents set up most of those companies. She'll be in charge of all of this someday and you pissed her off. That day I talked about might be here sooner than anyone could have imagined."

There was a chime of the private phone that connected the penthouse to the doorman. Margarita stepped away to pick up the call.

Oscar squared off with Isla. "My aunt's lawyer will have this fixed in no time."

She had him in checkmate. Portia had loved her kids, but she'd known their flaws as well. "And if I told you your mother put a clause in the will that states plainly that if you challenge the will, you get nothing, will you still roll those dice? Because it's there. Like I said, she knew you. She loved you, but she knew she had to protect you from yourself."

His face had gone red. "She wouldn't have done that. You did it."

He had no idea how these things worked. "I didn't write the will, Oscar. I can't be the executor of the will and write it, too. That would be a conflict of interest. You think you're suing me, but what you're doing is suing your own estate. And I hope Cressida has the money for a lawyer because I won't allow the estate to pay to sue itself. Good luck with that."

His lip curled up and his hand flashed out in a hard arc. Pain shocked through her system as he slapped her. She gasped, her hand going up to cradle the left side of her face. She looked up at him. "Back off. You back off right now and I might—and I mean might—not call the cops and charge you with assault. I understand that you're under a lot of stress, but if you even move my way again, I won't be responsible for what happens. I won't slap you, Oscar. I'll break a couple of bones and then we'll see how you feel about hitting women."

Oscar's eyes widened and he took a step back. "Isla, I'm so sorry. Oh my god. I didn't mean to do that. I've never hit anyone before." His hands were shaking. "Ice. I think I should get you some ice."

"Maybe you should leave before I lose my temper." She was holding on by a thin thread. The need to strike back was right there, but it wouldn't solve anything.

Oscar turned, his eyes wide. "I'm hurting everyone. Ever since Dad got sick, I can't stop lashing out. I don't know how to handle it. And my mom . . ."

"Would be ashamed of you right now."

He nodded. "She would be ashamed of me for a lot of things."

Margarita walked back in, her eyes going from Isla to Oscar as if trying to figure out where the tension was coming from. "The police are on their way up."

Oscar went white. "How did they know?"

Isla rolled her eyes. He could be overly dramatic, but at least he'd backed down. He looked like the kid he was now, scared and unsure of what happened next. Like the Oscar she knew when he was a kid. He hadn't always been this way. Once they'd been friends. Once they'd felt like siblings. "They're not here because you hit me."

"He hit you?" Margarita asked, looking from one to the other. She stepped in when she saw Isla's cheek. "He hit you. Do you have any idea what David's going to do when he sees this? He's going to lose his shit."

"I did it. I hit her. It's my fault. All my fault." Oscar pulled the cold pack out of the freezer. He wrapped a kitchen towel around it. "I'm sorry. I'm . . . I've lost my damn mind the last few weeks. I'm so sorry, Isla. Like I said, I've never hit anyone in my life. I can't believe I did that. Here. Mom kept them around for Dad when his elbow flared up."

She put it to her face, glaring his way. "You better be happy the cops are on their way up and I'm a good attorney. We can't let them see how divided we are, but don't think for a second that we're done talking about this. When they leave, I'm going to explain how this will go from now on."

Oscar nodded. "Okay. Okay." His eyes teared up. "I'm . . . damn it, I'm sorry. You can punch me if you want to. I've been a complete dick."

She might have, had the cops had better timing. "I'll hold that in my back pocket." She turned to Margarita. "Do we know why the cops are here?"

"They claim they were looking for Oscar," Margarita said with no small amount of relish.

Isla put a hand up because this wasn't the time or place to continue the argument. "I'm sure they simply want to talk to you. I'm going to ask you to at least let me sit in."

Oscar nodded. "Okay." His eyes closed and when they opened again, there was somber truth in them. "I'm strung out, Isla. I'm hurting bad and I took it out on you. I take it out on everyone."

"What have you been on?" At least they were getting to the heart of the problem. Before her death, Portia had been worried about Oscar and drugs.

"Coke, X, pot, you name it." He stared at the floor. "And I'm out of cash and I . . . god, I thought about buying H because it's cheap. I think I need to go to rehab. Would you help me go to rehab?"

That she could do. Some of her rage quelled. "I think you're definitely going to rehab. And you need some damn therapy, Oscar. You can't go on like this. You're going to lose everyone who cares about you."

His hands were shaking as he ran one through his hair. She hadn't noticed how thin he'd gotten lately. "Anything you want me to do. I can't believe I did that. I said some terrible things to Miranda."

She didn't have time to start his therapy now. "Let's get through this interview and we'll talk about it."

"I'm so sorry." Oscar couldn't seem to stop repeating his apology. "I need to talk to my sister. I . . . hate myself right now."

That was what they called hitting bottom. She had to hope he'd made a breakthrough because she wouldn't be so magnanimous if he pulled something like this again.

The elevator doors opened and Royce stepped through, leading the two detectives on the case and another two uniformed officers. Her spine straightened out of pure instinct. This wasn't about an interview. She watched as the uniformed officers took spots by the elevator and Detective Campbell stepped up, a pair of cuffs in his hands.

Margarita moved in front of Isla. "Think before you do this, Osborne. You've got nothing on her. If you arrest her, I swear I'll have you in front of a judge for malicious prosecution before you can sit down and enjoy your very temporary victory."

Royce's lips curled up. "No, I don't have anything on Isla. But I do have something on that little bastard."

Campbell moved in. "Oscar Adams, you're under arrest for the murder of Portia Adams. You have the right to remain silent."

Oscar was pale as a sheet. "What?"

That was her reaction, too. "You're arresting Oscar?"

She looked over and Margarita was already on the phone. She heard her say the name "Noah" and knew they would get here ASAP.

"I am." Royce stared at Oscar. "You cleaned off the blade, but forgot to wipe down the handle, dumbass. Next time be a smarter killer. Not that there's going to be a next time."

"What are you talking about?" There was something wrong here. He was a pain in the ass, but Oscar couldn't have killed his mother. He loved his mother.

"We have his prints and his prints alone on the handle of the murder weapon, and his alibi doesn't check out," Royce explained as the detective Mirandized Oscar. "Given some of the things he's recently said on social media, I'm not surprised it's him."

"I didn't mean any of it," Oscar said, not paying attention to the words coming from the detective's mouth. It wouldn't matter. The detective was doing it all by the book. "Isla, I was high. I didn't mean what I said."

"And the deeply deranged artwork?" Royce asked. "We went by your place before we came here. Your landlord was happy to help with our search warrant."

"You searched my place?" Oscar looked desperate. "Can they do that?"

Her stomach was in knots. "I'll take a look at the warrant. If anything's out of place, I'll have absolutely everything they find thrown out."

Royce glared at her. "He has a painting of himself killing his mother."

"No, it was a nightmare I had. It wasn't Mom. Maybe it was, but it's not literal. It's art. It's practically therapy. I dreamed she found out about the drugs," Oscar said.

"Drugs? Yeah, we found those, too," the detective replied. "Son, I'm going to suggest you keep your mouth shut for a while. Don't make this too easy on an old man."

"Oscar, don't say another word unless it's to ask for a lawyer," Isla said. "Do you understand? You answer no questions without someone at your side."

"I'll meet him down at the station." Margarita was already putting her cell in her handbag and getting ready to go. "I'll be there before they bring him in for processing. Oscar, my name is Margarita Reyes. I'm going to be there and so is my partner Noah Lawless. Do not say a word unless one of the two of us tells you it's all right."

Oscar started to open his mouth and shut it very quickly, nodding.

"Good. Detective, I'll see you at the station. I promise I won't make things easy on you, and you're not an old man. Prime of life," Margarita said with a wink.

The detective sort of half smiled as she walked away. "I like her even better than Cormack." He nodded to the uniforms. "Come on. Let's take him to the station and get him processed. I wouldn't want to keep the lady waiting."

David. What was David going to say when he realized he was going to have a saner and oddly less mature client?

Oscar looked back at her as they took him to the elevator. All his arrogance was gone and he was nothing more than a terrified kid.

Royce stood over her, his eyes staring down. "What happened to your cheek?"

"It doesn't matter." She wasn't giving him more ammo. "Oscar didn't kill his mother. I think this was an outside force. Have you ever heard the name Kristoff Paloma? He's the man who broke into my apartment and he was looking for something. We handed over that information to the police days ago. I think whatever he was looking for is what got Portia killed."

Royce stepped back. "You're reaching, Isla. Go out and look at your boy's social media. He talks about how much easier his life would be if his parents were dead. He talked to a friend about how he was going to get cut off if his mother found out what he'd been doing. I suspect that's coke and whatever the hell else rich, dumbass kids do rather than work these days. I thought you would be thrilled with me. Now you only have to deal with the firearms charge on Trey and he can happily be drugged up for the rest of his life. I hear you're the executor of the estate. Bet Oscar didn't know that."

That wasn't the point. She'd just seen what happened when Oscar got violent. He'd been horrified with himself. Either he was an incredible actor or he'd never hurt anyone like that before. "You're not listening to me. I don't know how his prints got on the murder weapon, but he was over here that morning. He had breakfast with Portia. Obviously whoever killed her wore gloves."

"Or the easiest explanation is the best and it was Oscar who had means, motive, and opportunity," Royce replied, his voice flat. "Now, tell me if your new boyfriend did that to you, because I can have him hauled in, too."

Her hand went to her cheek. She was sincerely hoping that had gone away. It didn't hurt anymore. "Is it that bad? I put ice on it."

"Not Cormack, then. And I don't suppose the lady lawyer thinks you're a punching bag, so I'm going with our little shit murderer," Royce said. "I'll give it to you. When you represent a family you're dog loyal even when one of the assholes hits you. Say what you like about me. I never would have done that."

"Royce, think this through before you ruin his life more than it is." She reached out and touched his arm. "I remembered something. The killer was still here when I got here. Whoever it was didn't flee after killing Portia. He was here and he was looking for something. Oscar had no reason to do that."

He looked down to where she held his arm and his hand went over hers. "Okay, you're so sure. Let's talk about it over dinner. Dump the meathead athlete and we can talk."

She pulled her hand away. "I wasn't offering up my body."

"It might be a good way to get me to do what you want," he said quietly. "God knows you don't have logic or evidence on your side. Look, this works in your favor, babe. Have you thought about that? With Oscar gone, no one is going to contest the will and you're in charge of this entire empire. I can make sure he never comes back. Hell, I think I can likely scare the shit out of the aunt enough that she'll stay away. This is good for you. I'm going to make this work. I can do it with your help or without it. I still haven't decided whether or not you knew something about this."

"What are you saying?"

He stepped back as he heard the elevator doors open. Royce smoothed his expensive suit coat down. "I'm saying you have a choice. Make it a wise one. Why, hello, Cormack. Looks like your primary client gets to roam free and crazy. I'll be in my office ready to talk about what life in prison is going to look like for that other Adams boy. I got this one locked down."

David was standing there. He hadn't bothered with his coat. It was obvious he'd basically run from the office to here. It wasn't more than a block and a half, but still he'd gotten here fast and he wasn't out of breath. Erin had come up with him, but she stepped back as though allowing things to play out as they would.

David's eyes flared as he saw Isla.

Royce's hands came up. "Wasn't me. Ask your client about that lovely handprint on your girl's face. And then ask yourself how long you're going to be able to keep her because she's about to be the undisputed head of a five-hundred-million-dollar foundation. You should probably try to upgrade your suits. Too bad you can't upgrade yourself, huh, buddy? I give you six months before she realizes you're not what she needs."

David's shoulders squared. "I give you ten seconds to get the hell out of my face."

Isla moved to him, getting between the men. All she'd wanted since she'd walked into this place was to have David's arms around her, and Royce had ruined even that.

David stopped and looked at her, really looked at her. And in the matter of a breath, she was in his arms. Those big strong arms held her tight and she was okay for now.

"Yeah, you should probably leave," Erin was saying as she held the door for Royce.

He stepped inside the elevator and she saw him look her way.

He wasn't done with her. Not even close. He would come back for her and it wouldn't be nice.

"That guy is an ass," Erin said. "I'm going to look into him. It's cool. Totally gratis. Fucking with asses is kind of a hobby of mine since I've been told I can't shoot people anymore. Apparently it's not good for my kids or something. My husband is a very uptight person. It's good he's so hot. So it was the kid? Because that doesn't make a lot of sense to me."

David held her for a moment before stepping back and looking down into her eyes. "Did Oscar do that to you?"

She sighed. "Yes, but that doesn't mean he killed his mother. And, Erin, I think the cops are wrong. They think the killer left the penthouse shortly after Portia's time of death. I believe he was here when I was here. He didn't leave until then."

David turned to Erin. "Could you please take a look at Oscar's alibi? We need something, anything that places him somewhere else. And perhaps look at any CCTV cameras within a few blocks. He doesn't have a car if I remember correctly, so he had to walk, have someone pick him up, or take the subway. And no, I'm not convinced he did this either. Look for any connection between Oscar and Paloma. I know you're heading home for the weekend."

Erin nodded. "I can put some feelers out and I'll be back on Tuesday. You'd be surprised what I can do from Dallas. I'll go look around and see what I can find CCTV-wise at that time. I'm going to make some notes and a few calls back home. I'll be back at the penthouse if you need me."

"Why did he hit you?" David said when they were alone again.

She wasn't sure why they had to deal with this when they had way bigger problems. "He lost it and then he practically got on his knees to beg my forgiveness. He admitted he's strung out and having problems with drugs. He'd asked me to help him find a rehab when Royce walked in."

"That had to have hurt." David was still staring at her face. "I know you're fair, but he had to have hit you hard to leave that kind of mark."

"And I explained what would happen if he ever touched me again. What was I supposed to do? Shoot him? Kick him in the balls? It would have been easier if he hadn't broken down in front of me. I'll see if I can cover it with makeup." She didn't want to spend the whole day explaining.

"That is not the point, Isla." David's jaw tightened and he shoved his hands in his pockets as though he was trying to keep from reaching for her.

"No, the point is I have a client who was hauled away by the police and now they're going to ignore any evidence we find," she returned. "They'll rush this through as fast as they possibly can and Royce will use it to try to get himself elected to god only knows what. I don't trust him not to bury any evidence that might help us."

"Have you thought for a second that perhaps Oscar did do it? He was upset about the will. He didn't realize it had changed, had he?"

"He didn't do this, David. I know him."

He stepped away, turning from her. "Well, I'll see what I can do to get Trey out of prison. Now that this isn't hanging over our heads, perhaps I can get him moved to someplace nicer. But you have to understand that they won't allow him out until they're satisfied he's not a danger to himself or others."

Why was he putting so much distance between them? "What's wrong, David?"

He took a deep breath. "I'm starting to wonder if you're actually capable of seeing the bad in people. You seem to have these rose-colored glasses on about everything. I have to wonder if you're capable of saving yourself."

Rose-colored glasses? "What the hell is that supposed to mean?"

"It means I don't know how much I can trust you." The words

came out of his mouth on a weary sigh. "Not to be loyal or kind. You'll do that a hundred percent of the time, but you won't save yourself, and I need to know you'll do that if it's necessary."

She wasn't sure what he was talking about. "Of course I would save myself."

"You're willing to give everything up for a family that isn't even your own. What would you do for a man you truly loved?"

That was easy. "Anything."

"And that's my problem." He walked to the elevator. "I'm going to the station. I assume you want me to represent the man who left his handprint on your face."

"I'm not a doormat, but I'm also not going to react to every little thing that happens, David. I act. It's something I was taught to do. I don't allow bad things and people to change the core of who I am. Would I defend myself in the event that someone attacked me? Yes, I would. Am I going to get into some kind of hand-to-hand fight with a kid who slapped me and then started crying? Is that what makes a person strong to you? Do you keep a ledger of everyone who hurts you so you make sure everything is even?" Maybe they weren't as close as she'd thought.

He didn't take the bait, merely waited for the elevator. "I'll be back later and we can talk."

She stood silent because she wasn't sure she wanted to know what he would say.

As he disappeared behind the elevators, she wondered how much she was going to have to give up to keep her promises.

TWELVE

Hours and hours later, David walked up to the building that housed the Lawless penthouse, his whole body weary. He couldn't help but wonder if he had made a terrible mistake with Isla. The problem was he couldn't figure out which mistake he'd made.

Had the mistake been getting involved with her in the first place? Or pushing her the way he had this afternoon? All he knew was he was tired and he wanted to see her, and he might have given away the right to her comfort.

Though god knew she gave it to people who didn't deserve it.

"Are you sure you're okay? Noah and I can handle Oscar," Margarita said, stepping beside him.

"I think Isla wants David to take the lead on everything about this particular case," Noah pointed out.

"I don't think that's a great idea." Margarita held her notes against her chest. "You can't properly represent someone you hate."

"Oh, I assure you, I can." The fact that Margarita could say that reminded him that she hadn't been in the criminal game for long. "I've hated several of my clients and it worked out quite well."

Noah shook his head. "I agree with her. I know what you're saying, but it's not the same. This is personal, David. He hit your girlfriend."

God, that was a silly word. Girlfriend. It was something to describe a couple of teenagers, and he was so much older than that. Lover. Companion. Sanctuary. Those were far better words to describe her. In a few short days, she'd become all of those things, but he had to wonder if he was the same for her. He might be in control now, but all he could think about was how his mother had to endure his father's spasms of abuse after the disease had taken over. How Portia had spent her last days loving her husband and having to be apart from him, too.

They stood at the bottom of the building they'd been living in for days and he wondered if he shouldn't go back to his place. Isla made decisions with her heart. She didn't think about the consequences. She was lovely and naive, and hadn't enough people used that against her?

And yet, he had to admit that she might be right about his newest client. Oscar Adams had been quiet and contemplative the whole time he was questioned by police. The arrogance he'd shown before had been stripped away and he proved he knew what manners were. When David had a moment alone with him, before he could even threaten the little fuck, he'd asked about Isla, begged for forgiveness.

He wanted to throw Oscar to the wolves, but something about the way he'd spoken, how remorseful he'd been about the crime he *had* committed, made David think Isla was right.

"I can handle Oscar. I'm not going to ruin my career because I hate the kid," he said. "However, I would rather not think about it tonight. I need to work some things out with Isla."

They had to talk, but the thought of where that talk could go made him feel sick inside.

"Of course," Margarita said. "I'm going to hang at Noah's and go over some of this paperwork. I'll look for anything we can use, but I'm betting the arrest was by the book. We might have better luck with the warrant to search. The bail hearing is Friday morning."

"I'm handling that. We'll take his passport, but I'm worried about this one," Noah explained. "He's got resources and he wouldn't be the first privileged kid to run from his crimes."

"Yeah, he doesn't have the resources you think he has." David pressed the button that would take him to Isla. "I'll shoot you a copy of the will. Isla holds the keys to his cash, and there are numerous clauses to control who has access to the estate and the money. He has no right to any freely held money until he's thirty. He's not going anywhere. We'll agree to house arrest. I'm worried about what happens to that arrogant ass if he hits the general population at Rikers."

Margarita shuddered. "They'll eat him alive."

"Then we've got some work to do." Noah put a hand on Margarita's back, an oddly possessive gesture that she didn't seem to notice. "Let's pick up some dinner and head back to my place."

She was nodding as Noah started to lead her off. He said something that made her laugh, her head thrown back, and for a moment they genuinely looked like a couple. Not work partners. Noah leaned in, whispering to her, and it felt far more intimate than anything between coworkers. One of these days, Noah would make a move and Margarita would have a decision to make.

He didn't think that was what Drew Lawless had intended when he set up one of his best corporate lawyers to watch over his baby brother. Or perhaps it was exactly what he'd wanted. The eldest Lawless played some deep games.

He didn't want to leave Isla. He didn't want this thing between them to be over. The truth was she still wasn't safe. Until they figured out how Kristoff Paloma fit into this new paradigm, he shouldn't leave her.

Or he could play it smart, hire a bodyguard for her, and walk away. He could explain that it had been a nice affair, but that they both needed to rejoin the real world and it simply wouldn't work out.

Yeah, he kind of wanted to kick his own ass for even thinking about it.

He didn't have to make the decision. Not yet. He could have a few more days with her, maybe a week.

And then what?

He wasn't listening to his conscience. His conscience sucked and wouldn't get him what he wanted.

God, he wanted her. He needed her. The whole lousy day was crashing down on him and the only thing that would make it better was to get his hands on her.

Would she welcome him or tell him to go to hell because he'd been so crabby with her earlier? Would she hold him off until they'd had that talk that would inevitably crush them both?

His body hummed the whole way up to the penthouse. They would leave here soon, and he had no idea what would happen then. This place had become a sanctuary where they didn't have to think about the future, where they only had to be.

He shoved the thoughts out of his head. None of it mattered because they could have tonight and tomorrow. They could have until it was safe for her to go home.

The doors opened and he strode in. Isla was sitting on the sofa, talking to Erin and Liam. He got the feeling they might have found something, but he didn't care. He needed more than the case. He needed her.

She turned to him, her eyes lighting up. "You're back. Hey, we found a couple of places with CCTVs that might have picked up someone moving around at that time of night. Li and Erin are going to check them out before they head home for the weekend."

"I don't think he cares," Li said with his thick accent. There was an amused smile on his face.

Erin glanced up and mirrored her partner. "Oh, yeah. I know that look. We'll get takeout. I don't think she's cooking tonight."

"David?" Isla stood up and looked so damn sweet and sexy in jeans that hugged her every curve and a sweater that showed off her breasts.

He didn't bother to speak. He'd tried that earlier and screwed everything up. If she wanted to talk, she could do it in the bedroom without her clothes on. He would try to listen while he drove himself deep inside her. That was what he needed, what he'd craved all day. Connection.

He picked her up and started for the bedroom.

"David," she said, completely surprised. "What are you doing?"

"Decompressing. Relaxing. Finding my sanity after spending hours and hours locked in a room with two people I would rather see dead than waste my time on. I'm involved in this shitty case with that shitty prosecutor because I can't stand the thought of letting you down. The very least you can do is let me find some peace at the end of a long day."

Her arms went around his neck as he turned down the hall. "Maybe we should talk about this."

"I'm all talked out."

She held on to him. "But earlier you seemed so mad at me."

"Not mad. I can't get mad at you. Scared for you, yes, but never mad. I want the best for you. But right now, I just want you," he admitted. He kicked open the door and eased her to the floor, turning and pulling her into his arms. His mouth found hers, and something eased inside him when she sighed and flowered open for him.

Her body softened against his. "You don't have to be scared. I can take care of myself."

He doubted that. Oh, she was competent and smart, but she was so wide open and willing to be vulnerable, so willing to give of herself. That was what scared the crap out of him.

Still, he didn't want to fight. Not tonight. She was safety and pleasure and joy all wrapped up in one gorgeous package, and the selfish part of him wanted to take everything she had for himself. She would accept him. She would make vows with no idea of what was coming and then be foolish enough to keep them, to keep him.

He could wrap her up before she knew how damaged he was. If he could get her in front of a judge and have her sign that piece of paper that would bind them together, she would never leave him.

His tongue found hers and tangled in a sensual dance, his body ready and wanting. All it took was a thought of her, a glance from her, a single vision skimming across his brain and he was ready for her. No woman in the world had ever taken hold of him the way she did. Mind and body and soul. He was hers, and there was nothing more he wanted to be.

Her hands moved on him, restless and searching. She moved her hands down his back to cup his ass as she pressed her body to his. "I thought you would be angry with me for making you rep Oscar."

"I hate Oscar and he's a little shit, and if he ever hits you again I'll put him through a window," he admitted. "Take off my shirt. I want your hands on me. Did I mention the window I'll shove him through is not on the ground floor?"

Her hands immediately moved and her fingers started working their way down his shirt. "I know it was upsetting, but it was also something of a breakthrough."

Because she thought Oscar had finally admitted what the real problem was? He didn't care. All he could think about was showing the young man how a real man hit. With a fist and pure fury.

Only the oath he'd made to the New York State Bar Association kept him from tanking Oscar's chances at freedom someday. "I was a very good boy today. I made sure our client didn't incriminate himself, but you have to know I want him in jail for hitting you."

She pulled his shirt free and shoved it off his shoulders. Her eyes roamed his torso, and the light he saw there made every rough hour at the gym so fucking worthwhile. "I know you do. For the record, I would feel the same way about you. How about next time you can be the one who gets smacked and you can try to tamp down my crazy?"

God, he loved her. "I would greatly prefer that."

He wanted to be the wall in front of her, keeping out all the people who would take advantage of her sweet nature. Everyone but him.

Her hands moved across his shoulders and started down his chest. He was well aware he was a beast and she was soothing him with her affectionate petting. He didn't care. All that mattered was it worked. In the past he would have hit the gym or run a few miles to burn off the bad energy of the day, but now he knew it wouldn't work. None of that shit would ever work again because he'd found his peace and it was with her.

Her hands went to the buckle of his belt and then the fly, opening his slacks and easing them down.

His heart rate tripled. Yeah, this was way better than the gym.

She looked up at him, her eyes wide and shockingly innocent. Even as her hands moved down to stroke his cock, there was nothing dirty about her stare. Just that clear gaze that kicked him in the gut every time. He thought about what she'd said before. She acted. She didn't react. She kept the core of who she was pure and didn't allow that precious soul space to be infected with anger or pain.

Was that how she could open herself? Even after everything she'd lost?

"I don't understand you." But he wanted to.

Her hand moved over the stalk of his cock, taking his breath away. "I'm simple, David. There's nothing complex about me."

Oh, but there was. She didn't act like anyone he'd ever met. She was capable of things he couldn't dream of. "You care about me."

Her lips curled up in the sweetest smile. "What makes you think that?" She stroked him with a firm grip, from right above his balls to the head, where her thumb moved over him, lubricating her hand with the liquid she found there. "There's nothing complex about how I feel about you. It's simple and easy to care about you. I started pretty much the moment I met you. You're a lovable man. You're smart and kind, and I don't know if anyone has ever mentioned this but you are incredibly hot. Also, you're amazing in bed and I want to fuck you all the time. It's really hard to concentrate."

He put a hand on the wall behind her because he needed balance. He wanted to put his hand over hers and force her to go faster, rub harder, but he was determined to let this go at her pace. "That's not what I meant. I need to know how you can care for me after what happened. After what happened to your fiancé. How can you offer yourself up again? I want to understand."

Her hand came off him, but she didn't move away. He gritted his teeth and bit back a curse. Why did he have to push her? Why couldn't he simply accept that what they had was something that would last as long as it did and be happy to have had it at all?

But no, he had to take that good thing and poke it and prod it. He had to push it until it broke so he knew this good thing was like all the rest. Temporary. Unreliable.

Her hands came back up to his chest, one right over his heart. "David, I was in a shell for a long time after Austin died. I didn't date for years. Austin and I had gotten close in high school. We had sex but only after he got sick. We were waiting for our wedding night. I know that sounds silly and old fashioned, but we wanted it to be special. And then he refused to marry me because he was going to die. I pretty much seduced him into sleeping with me, but he wouldn't marry me. He tried to get me to leave him. Told me he didn't love me. Basically all the stupid things a guy will do to try to save the delicate female of his choice."

Heat flashed through his system because he was that guy. He started to step away from her, but her arms wound around his waist and she cuddled up against him.

"I'm not delicate, David. I'm stronger than you can imagine. I took all his pain and I lived through it because I loved him. Because I watched how my parents loved each other and I wanted that. You can't have that kind of love if you're always afraid of losing something. That kind of love is brave. That kind of love knows that it's worth the trouble, worth the pain. I went into a deep depression, but Carey was there. He gave me the internship, helped me with law school. He gave me something to focus on. And after a while, I was ready. I was ready to live some more. I kissed a couple of complete frogs. I tried sex again. And then I found you and I was *really* ready. I don't want this to be some short-term fling. If that's what you want, you should tell me now. It won't change my mind. I'm still about to get on my knees and worship that cock of yours, but it will give me a chance to process that this isn't going to go how I want it to."

He let his forehead rest against hers. With any other woman, this would be a fight, not some intimate discussion where she politely asked if he was going to leave her. "See, that, that right there. I don't understand. If I'm unwilling to give you what you want, why would you do that? Why would you reward me for failing you?"

"Because I wouldn't consider it a failure. Not everything lasts. Not everything is meant to be, but it can be beautiful anyway. Maybe Austin was the love of my life or maybe he was merely my first love, the one I had to learn from so I could find you. Maybe you'll end up breaking my heart, but I wouldn't change a thing. I wouldn't spare myself the heartache because loving you, even if it's only for a little while, makes me feel, and that's the best we can hope for. To feel and love and be connected. To know even for these brief moments that we are not alone. So yes, I will take all the time with you I can, and I'll thank you for it even if you choose to walk away."

To feel? God, she made him feel. So fucking much. Too much, but he wouldn't change it. He cupped her face and looked at her, connecting with her. "I don't want short term. I don't want a hookup or a booty call or anything that isn't committed and serious, but I don't know what happens when we're back in the real world. There's so much you don't know. Risks you might not want to take."

"There's very little I wouldn't risk to feel like this, David," she said with that beatific smile of hers.

"You don't know what you're saying."

"Yes, I do. I know exactly what I'm saying and I mean every word. You, Mr. Cormack, have never been properly loved. Your wife married you for your career and she wanted babies more than she wanted the marriage. But the marriage is everything. I can show you. I can teach you. You can be the badass who protects me at every turn, but I get to teach you how to be properly and completely and wholly adored." She sank down and this time he let her.

He knew he was a bastard and that he should tell her no. He should walk away and not look back and know that he'd done the right thing, but she was his Kryptonite. Yearning that had nothing to do with sex wound its way through him. He wanted to know how Isla Shayne loved a man. He wanted more than anything in his life to be that man.

She eased him out of his loafers and then pulled his slacks and boxers down. He was naked in front of her but there was nothing awkward about it. Lust and love were right there in her eyes. She settled in and took a long breath. His cock strained as though the damn thing knew how close it was to heaven. Isla leaned over, her eyes up on him, and that sweet pink tongue of hers came out and swirled around his cockhead.

Pure desire lit his system, and it took every bit of willpower he had not to fist his hands in her hair and force his dick deep.

Instead he took a long breath and let the sensation wash over him. All of his life he'd worked toward a specific goal, ignoring everything else around him. It was how he'd been taught. Eyes on the ball, the prize, the case. But what if there was another way to be happy? What if his eyes should be on her? For so long it was about lifting his family out of poverty, out of the daily battle that raged from paycheck to paycheck, but money hadn't made him happy or content. He enjoyed his career but there had to be something more.

She was something more.

He let himself give over to the glorious feel of her mouth on his cock. She played unabashedly, licking and sucking, leaving not an inch of him untouched. Her tongue ran over him, dancing across his skin. Her small hand came up to cup his balls, rolling and playing. She squeezed him gently as she sucked at his cockhead, the sensations making his whole body shake.

He looked down at her. She was a gorgeous goddess of a woman, giving him everything he could possibly want. He reached down and pulled her hair out of the bun she'd pinned up at the back of her head. His fingers tangled in the soft stuff, and he loved how she groaned against his skin. That throaty sound reverberated over his cock.

If he let her, she would be the one tangling around his soul, making herself a necessary part of his every day. If he gave in, she could be the best part of his days, of the rest of his life.

If he could only trust that his future would be one he wanted to give her, to share with her.

He let it go. She wanted what he could give her in the here and now. She'd promised him she could be satisfied with finding joy today and in the tomorrows they might have. He couldn't walk away from her. Not now. Maybe not ever.

"Harder. Suck me harder, baby."

She took him deep, forcing her mouth around his cock and then drawing back only to start the process once again. Over and over she worked him, taking him deeper each time. Her tongue danced over his cock with playful licks and then she blew his mind by sucking him to the back of her throat.

Soft. He was lost in the soft heat of her mouth, in the vibrations she made as she drew him in and dragged him back out. He came almost out and then her lips would capture him again. Her hands ran up his legs and then she settled in, stroking him as she sucked.

There was so much joy inside her. Even this was suffused with her unique energy. After that first day when she'd been traumatized, he found out that there was a core of wonder inside her that made him look at the world differently. She found the good in what was bad, the beauty in the weeds of the world. She turned responsibility into satisfaction.

Could she turn him into something joyful? Could she teach him to embrace the now and not let the future intrude on happiness?

Could she be the one woman in the world to find those small moments of pure love that came even with tragedy?

He stopped thinking about anything but how much he wanted her, how happy she made him. He let go and allowed the pleasure to take over and, within a moment, he was on edge.

She looked up as she took him deep and swallowed solidly around him. That connection was all he needed. He gave up and gave in, letting his instincts take over. He thrust into her mouth and let the orgasm roll through him.

Isla didn't falter. She sucked him, taking all he had to give her.

When he was done, she sat back on her heels, a perfectly satisfied look on her face. Her lips curled up like the cat who'd gotten all the cream. It was one of the sexiest sights he'd ever seen.

He held his hand out. "Come up here."

She took it and rose to her feet, coming up on her toes.

He still had to lean over to kiss her. "I'm not through with you. Come here. You want to teach me? I'll be your best pupil."

She wrapped her arms around him. "I'll teach you. First we start with all the kissing."

God, she made him smile. "All the kissing."

She nodded even as he lifted her up and started for the bed. "All of it."

That, he could do.

~

Hours later, Isla rolled over, her every muscle deliciously sore. Used. The word normally meant something bad, but she felt like she'd used her body in the way it was supposed to be used—to worship, to connect, to become something more than she'd been alone. Yeah, she loved the ache.

She glanced at the clock and winced, sitting straight up. It was ten. They'd been in bed for hours, making love and cuddling and talking about things that had nothing to do with work.

David's hand came up, trying to catch her, but she knew what would happen if he did. He would drag her back and he wouldn't let her go and more hours would fly by and her belly would still be empty even if all her other places were totally full.

"Come here." He rolled on his side, the sheet barely covering his hips. He let his head rest on his palm and watched her with hooded eyes. Bedroom eyes. That's why they called them that. Those eyes were lazy with satiation, and yet she knew he would be on her in a second. "I just want to cuddle."

Cuddling would lead to him falling directly into her vagina and not coming out for a really long time.

She rushed across to the dresser and pulled his dress shirt on as a robe. "No. I know what you want and it requires calories, mister. I skipped lunch. You don't want me to pass out in the middle, do you?"

He growled and rolled on his back. "Baby, you remember how I represented that little asshole I hate and faced off with your ex?"

She knew exactly what was coming. Lazy man. "Yes, I'll make you a sandwich. I have a legal degree and a high-powered career, but I'll be a good little woman and make you a sandwich."

She wouldn't tease him if he hadn't spent much of the week catering to her. He'd brought her coffee and made sure she had everything she needed.

He refused the bait, smiling up at the ceiling and looking ridiculously sexy as he lay there tangled in the white sheets. "Good because I totally need calories, too. Lots of them."

"I will add extra meat to yours." There was some ham in the fridge. Hopefully. Otherwise she would have to find someplace that delivered. "Be right back."

His head came up. "You better or I'll come look for you."

That was what she liked to hear. She winked and slipped out into the quiet hallway. He'd been so hungry for her earlier. There had been a desperation to his lovemaking that pulled at her soul. It seemed to her he was trying to make a decision, and she worried that choice was about her. But he'd settled down. He was a magnificent beast and sometimes he needed soothing.

The key was to get him comfortable. He was inside that head of his too much. When he stopped thinking, he was all in. He'd made love to her over and over again, telling her how beautiful she was, how much he wanted her, how much he wanted to be with her. A few weeks of living together, making a home together, and he would be telling her exactly what she wanted to hear.

His wife had done a number on him, but all he required was some patience. And apparently a sandwich.

"Hey." Erin looked up from her laptop. She sat at the bar, a beer at her side. "I thought you two were down for the count or I would have asked you what you wanted for dinner. There's some noodles left but Li tends to inhale everything the women around him don't eat. Seriously, I have no idea how his wife manages to feed him."

Strangely, she didn't mind being not completely dressed. Erin was easy to be around. She didn't take shit from anyone, but she was also open and honest. "It's okay. I think we have some sandwich stuff. What are you still doing up? Don't you have a flight in the morning?"

She looked up, her green eyes clear in the light of the laptop screen. "Yeah, but something's bugging me about this. That arrest went down awfully fast. I don't like the kid."

"No one likes the kid."

Erin grinned. "I meant for the killing. He's too soft. This was done with purpose. Yes, there's rage in there, but to then stay around and look for something? That's cold. So I'm looking for someone who could get angry enough to stab a woman many times, and cold and practical enough to then clean up and stage the scene. I don't think that's Oscar. The trouble is his alibi is shit."

She'd been worried about that. Oscar's alibi hadn't been important yesterday. "He said he was with a friend. We can't find the friend?"

"Oh, I found him. I'm also fairly certain I found a good deal of Manhattan's cocaine users."

That was bad. "Seriously? Please tell me there weren't drugs lying around for everyone to see."

She opened the fridge and grabbed the ham, some lettuce, a tomato, and the mayo.

"I know what to look for but then the cops would, too," Erin explained. "There's no way they see this guy as a credible witness. And even with me he was reluctant to get involved. He'll throw Oscar under a bus to save his own butt."

"What did he say?" It wouldn't be anything good. She concentrated on making the sandwiches while Erin spoke.

"The friend says he passed out around nine o'clock and didn't wake up until the next morning, and Oscar wasn't there anymore. He lives in a Brooklyn walk-up. No security to speak of. Again, I've got feelers out, but I doubt I'm going to find much. I have to see if I can pick him up on a camera somewhere." Erin sighed. "It's a lot, but if the cops think they've got him, they won't do this work for us."

The police would only be interested in serving their own narrative. Oh, they would consider evidence that went against their theory of the crime, but they wouldn't go looking for it. And once the case was firmly in the ADA's hands, Royce wouldn't even consider anything other than the explanation that would win him the case.

"Tell me what to do and I'll do it," she offered, slathering the mayo on before making sure David's sandwich had a ridiculous amount of ham on it. The veggies were more of an afterthought, but at least she knew he would eat something green.

"I can do most of the work from Dallas," Erin said. "My son has a soccer game and we've got a big family dinner at my brother-in-law's on Sunday, but I can still get some of this done. I'll update you when we get back Monday. Until then you should work on your boy. He's got something going on in that head of his."

It was good to know she wasn't the only one who saw that. "I know. I think something about this case is getting to him. Or it's me."

"If it's you, it's not a bad thing," Erin said. "I know something of his story. His wife died before they could divorce."

"I've lost someone, too."

Erin shook her head. "Not the same. You were in love. Your lover died. His feelings for his wife changed long before she left this world. He likely considered himself divorced. I've had both happen to me. Oddly enough, the divorce shook me worse. See, the funny thing was I knew Theo loved me. I was in a dark place for a long time after he died. I was angry at the world, at him. But there was this core of strength I got from loving him that didn't go away. It was the opposite of what happened when I got divorced in my twenties. It felt like that core I believed in had been a lie. Does that make sense?"

Isla shook her head. "Not at all. I thought your husband was named Theo."

Erin laughed, a musical sound. "He didn't stay dead. That happens sometimes in my world. But like I said, it was a different pain. One made me question the world, God, everything. The other made me question myself—every decision, emotion, step I took was suddenly under a microscope because I couldn't trust myself."

"So you think David is worried that this thing between us is going too fast? Is it about the pressure cooker we're in? Because it's nothing I haven't asked myself."

"And what was your answer?" Erin asked.

That was a hard one. She cut the sandwiches in two and started putting the ingredients back up. "I suppose I don't have one yet. But I'm making plans. I care about him. I think this is a man I could love, really love."

"And he's wondering if he's lovable at all."

The thought hurt her heart. "He's entirely lovable."

"Make him understand that and you've got a shot," Erin replied. "I like Cormack. I like working for him and with him. I haven't seen him this animated since he and Henry and the Lawless puppy started the firm. Be patient with him and when he's a dumbass, and he will be a dumbass, don't go too hard on him."

Isla closed the refrigerator door after grabbing two bottles of water. "I hope we have some more time together before we have to go back to our own lives. I think I might be able to convince him to give us a shot."

At least she hoped so.

"I agree." Erin glanced to the end of the bar. "By the way, while I'm gone, if you get a chance between bouts with the boy toy, why don't you look through that and see if there's anything we can use."

A medium-sized box sat at the end of the bar, marked with black numbers denoting a case file. "What's in there?"

"The police released some of Portia Adams's belongings today. It's mostly books and some journals, though she didn't write much past business plans and lists. She was super into lists." Erin slid the box across the bar. "They released it back to the lawyers. Henry sent it over here. He thought you might want to look through it. See if it could jog your memory."

Isla took off the top of the box. Inside were some familiar items. Portia's most recent day planner in the familiar pinks and blues and greens of Lilly Pulitzer. There was a stack of notepads and Portia's large tablet. "I will go over them with a fine-tooth comb."

Portia made a lot of notes, and some of them wouldn't make a lick of sense unless one was familiar with Portia's shorthand. Luckily, Isla was quite good at reading her boss's handwriting and her code words.

"Also, you owe me," Erin continued. "Some crazy lady wearing more jewelry than a Tiffany store came by. Amy? Something like that. I don't know. All I know is that chick believes in hair spray. She wanted to talk to you about the memorial."

Oh, she didn't want to think about the memorial or all the problems it would cause. "Amber Kendrick. Thanks for covering for me. I know she can be a lot to handle."

Erin nodded. "You could say that. She was extremely focused. She told me to tell you that she'll expect you at the offices tomorrow, and she wants to know if you can bring some of the photos you have. She was adamant about that. Told me you should bring all the boxes and she would go through them. I think she thinks I'm your assistant or something."

"She kind of treats everyone like that. And she's going to make some new enemies if I can't talk her out of this crazy scheme." Isla grabbed a couple of paper towels. "She and Portia weren't exactly the best of friends and yet Amber is insisting on hosting the memorial. Portia's sister isn't a fan and will likely do something nasty to block it."

"Huh, I thought I saw the same chick in one of those pictures at the penthouse. She was in there with a group of women," Erin mused. "I recognized her from the photo. It was the only reason I let her come up in the first place."

The woman was good with details. "You're talking about the eight by ten in the living room. That was taken on one of Portia's many girls' trips. I think that was either London or Paris last year. I should actually take a look at that. We need to talk to those women and see if any of them remember meeting Kristoff. Cressida remembered him but she said he didn't hang around Portia. She couldn't remember who it was. Of course, she rarely remembers anyone past her sister and Oscar. She probably doesn't even remember Miranda went on those trips."

"Yeah, I've had some family members like that. So it might be one of the other women he became involved with," Erin mused. "I would like to know who. I'll get a list of the ladies who went on both trips. But I'm curious about Amber. You said Portia was a big deal. Why would she invite the gold digger along?"

"It was a big thing in Manhattan society to be invited. Portia was kind of the queen of her people, if you know what I mean. She took Amber under her wing because Carey, Amber's husband, was important to her and Trey. Carey's first wife was beloved. He, not so much, but even the jaded ladies of the Upper East Side came to love Marilyn Kendrick. You couldn't not. She was kind. She would forgive you for being mean to her and then explain how much better the world would be if everyone was nice. That was her version of confrontation. The mean girl or lady who was making fun of her accent or where she came from would then find herself laughing *with* Marilyn rather than at her, and then the world did seem a little nicer place."

Erin swiveled in her barstool. "She was a great lady and after she dies her old man marries someone half his age? I can't imagine that went over well."

"Oh, I don't think it's even half his age. Amber's only a year older than me. And the ladies of society did not take it well. She was labeled a gold digger and a stripper. She's probably the first one, but I don't think she's coordinated enough to be the second. They met when she was trying out to be a Guardians cheerleader. She pretty much kicked herself in the face and didn't make it through the first round, but Carey felt bad for her. Or he was horny and he asked if she'd like a tour. Four months later they were married. I think he had no idea what to do without a woman managing his life, and to her credit, Amber does a good job with that."

"You like her?"

That was a tough question. She'd loved Marilyn like her mom. And yet, she'd seen how Amber took care of Carey. She had to admit that Carey seemed happy. He wasn't in love the way he'd been before, but he also wasn't in a dark place, and Marilyn wouldn't have wanted that for him. "I don't hate her. It's hard to see a new person take the place of someone you love, but I had to ask myself if he should be miserable for the rest of his life. In a way, it's almost perfect. She'll make his senior years happy and then she'll have a lot of money to find happiness of her own. I don't have a problem with that."

"You are a unique soul, Isla Shayne," Erin said with a smile.

"She's also a slow food maker." David stood at the end of the bar, wearing only his slacks. His hair was mussed and he looked deliciously sexy. "I got cold waiting for you."

Well, she wanted him to want her. "Sorry, babe. Here's your sandwich. I got caught up in what happened while we were napping."

He took the plate with a heated look. "Oh, there was no napping involved."

Erin smiled his way. "I kind of got that, buddy. I ran interference against all who would cockblock you."

"And that is why I intend to tip." David took a healthy bite. "And tip well, Taggart."

Yep, she was going to be a permanent pink. "The police released Portia's day planners and journals. Henry sent them over. And Amber showed up."

He frowned as he swallowed his second bite. The way he was devouring that sandwich, she would have to make him another one. "How did she know where we are?"

"I told Carey," she admitted. "He worries."

"You know he doesn't like me. I'm going to have to figure out how to change that if he's going to continue treating you like a daughter," David said. "I'm not used to parents not liking me. I'm freaking awesome. I went to Harvard and I'm a lawyer. Oh, I don't tell them I'm criminal defense. I simply tell them my salary and they no longer give a shit. I'm not used to the billionaire potential father-in-law."

She liked that he was using those particular words. "He's a sweetheart. You'll come to love him."

"I don't know about that," he said. "So we have her journals and day planners. They had to be sure they're going after Oscar if they sent those back."

Erin slid off her barstool. "I'm fairly certain they have no plans on looking for another suspect. That's good for Trey, but bad for Oscar. I'm heading to bed. We have a super-early flight so I'm going to say goodbye. Call us if you need anything. You're sure you don't want a bodyguard? Paloma is still out there."

The last thing she wanted was someone on her 24-7. Well, except for David, but that was different.

"It's not a bad idea," David mused.

"I'm good," she said quickly. "Paloma didn't even try to kill me. As long as I stay out of his way, I think he'll leave me alone. And if I go out, I'll be careful."

David stared at her.

"I don't want a bodyguard," she said with a frown. "Besides, I'll spend the weekend going through these journals. I need to go out to the Guardians' offices tomorrow and talk to Amber, but other than that, I'll be a very good girl and stay in the gorgeous penthouse I will never be able to afford."

"All right, but I'm going with you to the stadium," he said. "And if you have to go somewhere, I expect you to take Noah or Margarita with you. She's surprisingly good at self-defense and Noah can scream louder than any teenage girl at a boy band concert, so they'll keep you safe."

"Agreed."

Erin gave her a thumbs-up.

"Good. Now that we're done with that." David finished the last of his sandwich. He leaned over and hauled her up against his chest.

"Hey," she protested. "I didn't eat."

"Nope, you spent your eating time talking," he said, but he let her grab her plate and the waters. "It's my time again. You'll have to be fast."

She smiled as he strode back to the bedroom. It looked like his time was going to last a long while and she was fine with that.

THIRTEEN

David stood outside the prison. Rikers Island was a pit, but then it was basically one big prison in between the Bronx and Queens. They'd driven in through the private bridge from Queens, and every time he made the trip he felt the world go a bit darker the closer that he got.

"Are you sure you want to do this? I could handle them both and you can get back to Isla. She's going to the stadium, right?" Henry had left his coat behind. It was best to leave anything a person didn't absolutely need to function when entering a maximum-security prison.

"He asked specifically for me." He pulled at his tie. Isla had made sure it was perfect before he left, but he couldn't quite breathe in the damn thing now. Ever since he got word that Trey Adams wanted to see him he'd been antsy, anxious in a way he hadn't been in a long time. He had the feeling that Trey would ask him to do something he couldn't do. He was getting in deep with this family and it worried him.

Or maybe it was because the night before weighed on him. It felt as though he and Isla had settled something between them the night before. He knew damn straight things were settled in Isla's mind, but he hadn't told her the truth about himself. She should know, but she didn't know the extent of the risks she was taking.

Could he keep her in the dark like that? Was it fair to her?

He'd forgotten to memorize his words this morning.

"Yeah, I know, but you're on edge," Henry pointed out. "I'm worried about you. I don't see you like this often. I think the last time I saw that look on your face, you were telling me about the separation. If you need to spend some time with Isla, I get it."

David frowned his way. Henry had been a lot easier to deal with when he simply yelled at everyone and didn't expect him to discuss his feelings. Win had turned him into a touchy-feely guy. "What happened to the Monster of Manhattan?"

Henry smiled in a way that David had never seen him smile before he'd met Win. Henry slapped him jovially on the shoulder. "I'm still here, but I only let the monster out when the case requires it. Otherwise, I'm more than happy being Win's husband and potential baby daddy."

David felt his jaw drop. "What?"

Henry smiled like a man who couldn't be happier with his life. "We're trying."

Henry Garrison with babies. It was hard to imagine it. "I did not expect that."

"Why not?" Henry asked softly. "You know it's because of you."

"I didn't introduce you to Win. You found her all on your own."

"Her clumsiness was my salvation," Henry agreed. "But I wouldn't have met her if you hadn't answered my call. If you hadn't flown out to L.A. to pick up an old friend who you hadn't even talked to in a year, who kind of treated you like shit."

"You were going through a bad time. I knew that." Henry had

married an actress and got caught up in the Hollywood scene. Unfortunately the marriage had quickly fallen apart and Henry found the bottom of every bottle he could.

He'd called one night and asked David to come get him. He was drunk and probably didn't really know what he was doing. But when he'd been at his lowest, he reached out for David and there was no way David would blow him off. He'd gone straight to the airport, found the next flight out to L.A., and was at Henry's side the next day.

The day after, he'd dropped his best friend off at rehab and started Henry's divorce proceedings. Three weeks later, they'd headed back to New York and started their lives over again.

"I'm just saying that anything you need to make things work with this woman, I'll do it," Henry said. "You need time, take it. You need a reference, I'll write one up. She's not cooperating, I'll hire some kidnappers and get you alone time with her."

He laughed because Henry might do it. "I don't need to kidnap Isla. She's happy where she is."

"Then it's you."

Yes, it was him. "It's early. I care deeply about her, more than I should at this point."

"Stop overthinking it. Trust yourself. I like her a lot. Win adores her. You deserve some happiness."

He forced himself to continue. "And if my mind starts going?"

"Then I'll do my duty, shoot you and put you out of your misery," Henry said with a pat on the back. "See? Problem solved. You don't have anything to worry about. Besides, once your mind goes, you won't even know it. I don't get why you're worried about this. If you think about it, it's not your problem. It's kind of ours."

"That doesn't help." He turned to walk up the path to the prison doors.

Henry followed hard behind him. "Come on. I'm joking, man.

You have to keep a sense of humor about these things. I have a ton of cancer in my family line. I'm not going to spend my life worrying about it. Hell, I'm not even going to change my bacon intake, and that is precisely why I don't tell Win about it. She would flip out and I would find myself eating kale, and *then* I would be the Monster of Manhattan."

"It's not the same."

"It's exactly the same," Henry insisted. "If Isla told you she's got a fifty-fifty chance of dying of breast cancer, would you dump her?"

"Of course I wouldn't. But again, it's not the same. Cancer is horrible, but at least you get to still be yourself. It doesn't rob you of your memory and personality and control."

"Oh, I think a lot of cancer patients would completely argue with you about at least two of those. Pain can rob you of a lot," Henry pointed out. "Talk to her about it."

The doors opened and he was assaulted by the blandness of the space. It was all concrete and bars, fluorescent lights and industrial smells. "I'll think on it. Can we work now? I have to inform a man who didn't kill his wife that he's going to stay in prison for a while for a crime that would never have been committed if the police hadn't thought he killed his wife. Which he didn't do."

No matter the circumstances, the reckless endangerment and weapons charges weren't going to go away. And no bail would be heard until the psychiatrist was happy with Trey's mental state. David had been told Trey was stable today and the meds seemed to be doing their job. It was a good time to talk to him. He'd asked if Trey wanted to see Isla, but he'd turned down speaking to anyone but his lawyer. He'd turned his own daughter away.

Not that David would want to bring Isla out here. It had been a relief that he didn't have to try to talk her out of coming with him. This was privilege. She might have power of attorney, but if his client wanted to see him privately, she had to respect the choice.

"I'm working on getting him moved to a private facility," Henry explained. "I'll get Oscar ready for his bail hearing. Let's take this one step at a time. We get Oscar out on bail. We get Trey moved to a private facility, and then we figure out our next move. I hear the ADA is giving a press conference this afternoon."

"He's interested in getting on camera as much as possible." He hated Royce Osborne, but at least he thought the ADA was no longer looking to make Isla some sort of accomplice. He would stand in front of the reporters, explain that he was the smartest man in the world and that New York City was once again safe because of his investigative techniques and say, hey, vote for me when I run for DA next year.

Henry approached the first of many barriers, pulling out his wallet to show his ID. "Maybe we should hold our own. I'm going to think about it. I would like to get Kristoff Paloma's face out there. Shake the tree and see what falls out."

"Do it but wait until Monday. If we can have Oscar standing next to us, I'd like that," he replied. "I think he'll look far less arrogant after he comes out of here. We need to show how young he is, how vulnerable he is, try to get some public sympathy going. We'll get him nice, normal clothes and make him look like every troubled kid you know."

Henry nodded. "All right. Whoever finishes first waits out here. Good luck."

David was going to a different part of the prison. It might be the only thing more disturbing than gen pop. He was buzzed through by a thoroughly bored guard to an even more bored guard who proceeded to pat David down with absolutely no enthusiasm.

"You can wait in here." The guard pointed to a small interview room. There was a table and a light overhead that blinked. Not off and on, but enough to let him know it could go dark at any moment. The whole place was unnerving. Isla was right about one thing. This was not the place for Trey Adams to end his days.

His gut clenched at the thought. Trey Adams had everything. The best doctors. More money than he knew what to do with. All the treatments he could buy. He was still here. He'd lived a life most people couldn't even dream of. But he was still here. He'd had talent and drive and work ethic.

He was still here.

Would he change it? Would he go back, knowing where it would end? Would he have never picked up a football?

Fuck. He had to get control of himself. He wasn't here as Isla's boyfriend. He had to give this man some hard information and make certain he understood.

The door buzzed open and a massive figure stepped through. The guard didn't look so bored now. He was smiling and animated as he led Trey into the room.

"I didn't think anyone could throw a ball like that, man," the guard was saying.

"What? That ball was a desperate plea to the universe. It was the Hail Mary of all Hail Marys," Trey replied. "Don't be impressed with me. It was Douglas who caught that sucker. Fastest wide receiver in the game and a damn good man."

The guard put a hand over his heart. "Still is. Though not as fast on his feet anymore. Here we are, Mr. Adams."

"Trey, please. And thank you." Trey Adams turned to him. He looked thinner, as though the last few days had stolen something from him. His eyes were weary, but surprisingly clear. "Mr. Cormack, I would shake your hand, but that's a bit difficult at this time."

The guard looked down at Trey's cuffed hands. "Oh, let me . . ."

Trey shook his head. "Absolutely not. I appreciate it, but this is safest. We don't know how long these meds are going to work. Could I have a moment alone with my attorney?"

It was a complete change from the last time he'd seen Trey.

The guard stepped back, glancing David's way. "The docs seem to have found a cocktail of meds that gives him a couple of hours. We don't know how long they'll work though. He still reverts at some point in the day, so you should be quick. But he's not violent unless he's threatened. If he starts talking about the past like he's there, go with it. He won't hurt you. Trey, I'll be right outside."

The door thudded closed and he was locked in.

"You played for Seattle, right?" Trey asked, his cuffed hands on top of the table.

"I did, safety, and mostly I played backup. I blew out my knee and gave law school a try," he explained.

"That's impressive. I was never much good at anything but football and . . . well, I was a good husband when I was sane."

"I'm sorry for your loss. I know that doesn't begin to cover it, but I am."

He nodded. "I appreciate it. Now I need something else from you."

"Of course." He was going to explain that it would take some time, but they would get him out of here. "We're working on getting you a bail hearing on the endangerment charge."

Trey shook his head. "No. I don't want that. I want you to represent me. I murdered my wife. I would like to confess."

Yes, that was what he'd been waiting on. Because not only was he a good husband, he was a good father.

"It won't work," David replied quietly. "They have too much evidence on Oscar."

Desperation lit Trey's eyes. "Please. You have to make them believe that it was me. Oscar wouldn't do this. I know he's a pain in the ass. I know he hates me because I'm a symbol of everything that's wrong with his world, but he's my boy and I won't ever stop protecting him. But I forget sometimes and Portia . . . my wife wouldn't want this. Please let me take his place."

He did the one thing he knew he shouldn't but he had to ask. "Did you kill your wife?"

A hollow look came into his eyes. "I don't know. Maybe. I know I found her. I woke up and I knew something was wrong. But that doesn't mean I didn't kill her because I thought she was an intruder and then went back to bed."

Had he been living with this guilt? "There was no blood on your sheets or in your room. There was no blood trail to your room. If you woke up in your own bed and then walked to find your wife, there is no way you killed her."

The scene had been far too bloody. There were no footprints tracing back to Trey's room.

Of course, there hadn't been any going to the kitchen either. So whoever had killed Portia had to have cleaned his shoes. He made a mental note to ask the police if they'd found anything that the perpetrator could have cleaned himself up with. Or odd footprints in the room.

Why hadn't he thought about that in the first place? If Oscar had gotten high and angry with his mom, would he have had the presence of mind to clean up after himself?

"I can't let my son stay here." Trey's eyes closed as though he could feel what his son was going through.

"We're working on his bail right now," David assured him. "I think I can convince a judge to let him wait out his trial at home. We'll have to surrender his passport and put him under house arrest, but he'll be safe. As for you, we're going to get you a bail hearing and move you to someplace more comfortable. Given your mental health history, I'm going to push the DA to settle."

"You don't understand." Trey's hands fisted and then he seemed to force himself to relax. He leaned over, whispering the words. "I want to say I did it so Oscar doesn't have to stand trial."

He did understand. If he and Isla had a kid, he would do almost anything to protect him or her. Had that thought run through his head?

Had he thought about having a child with Isla? He forced himself back to the problems at hand. "The prosecutor isn't going to believe you."

Trey frowned. "But if I say I did it, they have to let Oscar go."

"That's not how it works. Otherwise most kids would never go to jail. Their parents would confess and they would take the blame. The problem is the DA, for the most part, wants the right person in jail. In this case, they would make you prove you did it. I don't think you can. It wasn't your fingerprints on the murder weapon."

"I could have worn gloves." Trey's jaw went tight. "Oscar's print was there from that morning. He cut up a grapefruit. Portia wasn't eating. Something was off and had been for a week or so. Since a week or so before she died."

"Did you know she was seeing a director every Thursday?" While he was able to, it would help to ask him a couple of questions.

Trey leaned in, nodding. "Yeah, she was making a movie about us. I mean, it was a lot of football stuff, but I like to think it was about us. I know she was hoping she could show it to me when things got bad. She was hoping it would help me remember how much I loved them all. Love them all. Does that ever go away? She's dead but love isn't in the past. Just because she's not here doesn't make me love her less."

"I can't imagine how hard this is." David pulled out his notepad, jotting a few things down. "Did she say or do anything that stood out?"

"She canceled a trip," Trey replied. "She said she canceled it because of something that was going to happen. But I can't remember. I'm sorry. Even on the meds, I can't remember everything. My head's still foggy. The last thing I remember vividly talking to her about was how she could get the best footage of the last championship game."

"The one where you got knocked out and the Guardians were down at the half?" He remembered that game well.

He nodded. "Yeah. My swan song."

"Hell of a swan song. You came back despite the injury and led them to a twenty-one-point comeback victory. I would think that would be easy to find."

"Yeah, but the best footage is in the vault at the stadium," Trey explained. "We were filming *Holding the Line* at the time and when they were done, they donated all of the footage to the Guardians. There was probably a hundred hours of footage of that game alone. They had cameras everywhere. Most of it's never been seen before. That's what she wanted. I set her up with one of the media specialists, but I can't remember if she ever went."

He'd been hoping there was something with the director that might lead somewhere, but it was hard to have an affair when you kept telling your husband where you were going and what you were doing. That seemed like a dead end.

"Could she have had an item or knowledge someone wanted?"

A smile played across his face as though remembering something good. "She was real good with fashion. And she had lots of jewelry, but other than that we were pretty normal."

"You can't think of anyone who fought with her?"

He shook his head. "Not who would kill her."

"But there was someone."

He sighed and for a moment David wasn't sure he would reply. "Miranda was upset about the will. Oscar didn't know. When Miranda found out she wouldn't get her money until she was thirty, she and Portia yelled a lot. She didn't hate Isla or anything, but she didn't think Isla should have control of the money. But she's only been in college for a couple of years. It might be different if she wasn't so young. Portia didn't want that burden on her."

"Did Miranda know the will had been filed?" This was interesting. Miranda had been on Isla's side every single time. And she was the one who'd called Isla the night of the murder. What if she'd done that to cover her own tracks?

"She knew it was being written," Trey explained. "I don't know if Portia told her we'd finalized it. I hated disappointing her, but I follow Portia's lead when it comes to this stuff. I'm not as smart as she is." His face went blank for a second. "God, what am I going to do without her? I don't know how to live without her. How do I make decisions? How do I take care of my kids?"

He wouldn't. Isla would until they were ready to deal with the companies and the money themselves. This man shouldn't be feeling guilty. "You put your children in a position where they never have to worry about money or how to keep a roof over their heads. You did everything you could. And your wife hired Isla."

Trey breathed a deep sigh of relief. "Isla. Thank god. Isla is a good woman. She's been like another daughter to us, but like the most reasonable daughter a couple could have. I hate that she sees me the way I am now. Did she think . . . ?"

"Not once. Not even when all the evidence was against you. And she doesn't believe Oscar did it either," he explained. "She's on my ass to get him out of here as soon as possible. Believe me, she won't stop until you're both out of here."

Trey went still for a moment. "You sound like you admire her."

He was more than half in love with her. "I do."

His eyes went a little steely. "Does it go beyond the professional?"

It looked like he would have to get through more than Carey Kendrick if he wanted Isla. "I'm seeing her, but don't think that will have an effect on my defense. She's not the client. You are. Oscar is. I'll take care of you both."

"How long did you play?" Trey asked, his fingers tangling together.

When had this become an interrogation of him and not Adams? "A few years."

"How many hits did you take?" Trey's tone was soft, but the words lashed at David.

"More than I can count."

Trey kept it up. "How many concussions?"

He wanted to stand up and walk out, but he forced himself to answer the question. "Serious ones? Three, but you know as well as I do, it's not the serious ones that count. Not for what you're asking. You want to know if I have CTE. I've got the same chance as everyone else, maybe worse odds because my father's been diagnosed with Alzheimer's."

A shudder went through Trey. "So you know what you could be facing?"

"I know it's a possibility. You don't like a football player dating Isla?" Even though he'd thought the same thing, he couldn't help but feel something about the fact that a man he admired didn't want him around his daughter.

"She's been through a lot and now she's going to do whatever it takes to help me. I wish she wouldn't. I wish you would let me do this one last thing for my son. If I'm not around or locked away in some prison, what does it matter?" Trey asked softly.

"I think your family would say it does."

"Portia doesn't say anything." The words came out on a grim huff. "She won't say anything again and I might not have killed her myself, but I didn't save her. I wasn't there when she needed me the most. I was so drugged I didn't hear her crying out for me. I couldn't save her because I'm not here anymore. Not really. Do you know?"

"Know?"

"They can test you now. Do you know?" Trey asked.

"I haven't taken a test." Testing for CTE in a live patient was fairly new.

"You should think about it. Take the test and if you have it, walk away from her," Trey said, his tone firm.

"What?"

Trey put his hands on the table and leaned in. "Walk away from her because all you'll do is bring her pain. It might be good for a couple of years. Hell, we had a lot of good years, Portia and me, but I should have died. She should have let me go, kicked me out when I started getting mean. When I would get paranoid those first few times, she would be so calm. She didn't even know what was happening, but she would take all the abuse I would spew at her and tell me she loved me."

His stomach was in knots. Every word coming from the man's mouth reinforced his nightmare. "She knew something was wrong."

"Yes, and she knew I should have saved her. She knew in her last moments that I was a hundred feet away and I did nothing. I was useless. I've been worse than useless to her. I've been . . . you ever read that poem? It's funny, I don't remember a lot from school, but I remember reading about the albatross."

He did remember a lot from school. "'The Rime of the Ancient Mariner.' Samuel Taylor Coleridge."

"She had everything. She had a future." The words sounded tortured coming from Trey's lips. "But she kept me when she should have saved herself. I was the albatross around her neck."

"I don't think that's what he meant," David argued. "The albatross was good luck until the mariner shot him down. It was in not showing kindness that the mariner lost everything and brought bad luck down on his crew."

"And yet I was the bad luck. She didn't see it." Trey looked down at his hands and when he looked back up there was no mistaking the confusion in his eyes. "I . . . I'm getting fuzzy. I know I know you and you're supposed to be here, but could you remind me why?"

"I'm your attorney," David replied patiently, but he knew this was the end of Trey's good portion of the day. How long before there were no more good parts and Trey's whole personality was devoured by the disease eating away at his brain? How long before his soul wasted away?

And how many people would he take down with him?

Trey started to cry as the tragedy hit him again. It seemed to be fresh, as though the memory was something he lived in the here and now.

When he screamed his wife's name, the guards came in to take him away and David was left to think.

⁓

Isla stared down at the day planner. She'd spent hours going through them and now it was almost time to head over to the stadium. It was kind of sad that she was looking forward to spending a couple of hours listening to Carey talk about the new season and trying desperately to convince a crazy lady that she should let family handle a memorial. It wasn't going to be easy, but she had to convince Amber to let Portia's sister handle it. She'd gone over the argument in her head about a million times, trying to figure out the best way to get Amber to understand.

Being stuck inside day after day was starting to make her stir-crazy. It wasn't so bad when someone else was around. Okay. It wasn't horrible when David was around and he took her mind off things, but when it got quiet all she could think about was what had happened. What might happen.

When it was quiet, she could hear those footsteps on the floor. In her mind she could hear the water come on and somewhere deep inside a set of whispering voices. Was she remembering more or was her mind playing tricks on her? If she closed her eyes and tried to put herself back there, she could remember the feel of bile in her stomach, rushing up to escape. She could remember finding the big potted palm and how she'd hit her knees in front of it, her hands against the rim as she was sick.

And then the sounds. Even sitting in the safety of the penthouse a chill went up her spine as she remembered the sound of someone walking across the floor. Then the light from the kitchen filtered in, casting shadows on the hall below her. That was when she'd shrunk back, trying to evade the illumination like it was a searchlight and she was prey.

If she concentrated very hard, she could hear the whispers.

Why?

I had to . . .

Stupid bitch . . . hurry . . . that asshole isn't going to stay up there forever . . .

She started as something in the background creaked and she nearly screamed.

Deep breath. She was going to make herself crazy if she kept going like this. Now that she knew she'd sat there outside of Portia's bedroom for twenty minutes, her mind was trying to fill in that time. Nature abhorred a vacuum and apparently so did her brain. How could she tell David she suddenly remembered not one but two voices? It didn't make sense. She would have run into the killer if he'd still been there. Wouldn't she?

Or had they been in another part of the house looking for whatever they were looking for? Had they done that search more quietly, calmed after knowing Portia was dead and wouldn't be able to say anything about what she knew?

She glanced up at the clock. There was an hour or so before she needed to leave, and as far as she knew David hadn't left Rikers yet. She had a bad feeling that he wasn't going to make it back in time.

Should she call and reschedule? David wouldn't be happy with her if she went out by herself.

Maybe she should have taken that bodyguard they'd offered her. At least then she'd be able to go outside these sacred walls. She would be able to drive around and think. Perhaps working at David's office would provide her with enough of a change of scenery that she could concentrate.

Despite the memories playing through her mind, she'd gotten some work done. She'd managed to get the director Portia had been working with on the phone. He corroborated everything Cressida had told her. He'd been meeting with Portia to help her edit the film for her husband's fiftieth. She'd canceled their last meeting in an abrupt fashion that didn't seem to mesh with who Portia was, but he hadn't been able to tell Isla why. He'd told her they'd worked on the family films first, editing some beautiful wedding footage and some footage of Trey's college and early career. The week of her death they'd been ready to start on the latter portions of Trey's career, but she wanted to find rare footage.

And then she'd told him she couldn't make it. And then she was dead.

Isla turned the page and stopped. There in Portia's handwriting was a series of letters and numbers.

09–19–AVI1–5

What did that mean? There was also a name under the letters and it was underlined three times. Garrison. And what was obviously a phone number.

Henry Garrison? David's law partner? If he'd talked to Portia before her death, surely he would have mentioned it. It had to be someone else. If Henry had talked to Portia, he could potentially be a material witness and therefore would never have allowed David to take the case.

Of course, there was one way to find out. She dialed the number. "Garrison, Cormack, and Lawless, how may I direct your call?" She hung up, her heart skipping a beat.

Why on earth would Portia have called Henry Garrison? Why would she need Manhattan's top criminal attorney?

Why hadn't Henry said a word?

She glanced down. The words were written on the date page before the day of her death. There was only one meeting noted the day after she died and that was a meeting at nine in the morning. It read, *Isla 9 A.M.?*

What was that question mark about?

Her phone trilled as a text came in. It was from David, saying they were back in the city but he was going by the police station to check something out. He didn't want her leaving without him.

She sighed and texted back.

Should I reschedule?

A moment passed.

If you can. We have a lot to talk about.

Anything good?

Why don't you order us some dinner and we'll talk.

Wow. That didn't sound promising. He'd left this morning in a good mood. What had Trey said to him?

The answer hit her square in the gut. If Trey was truly stable now and if he knew Oscar had been arrested, he would have confessed. He would have done anything he could to save his son.

How would David handle that? She wasn't exactly sure, but she knew from a legal standpoint it would be difficult to do anything. Trey could confess all he liked. If the evidence didn't back him up, the DA wouldn't send him before a grand jury. They would keep their eyes on Oscar.

She could handle a nasty talk if it had to do with work. But she'd seen his eyes as he left her today. Oh, he'd done and said all the right things, but that storm Erin had talked about was swirling inside David, and she wasn't sure she could handle it if he asked her to make a choice.

He was upset that she intended to take over Trey's care. That had to be it. When they'd argued over what would happen with Trey, that was the moment she felt some distance between them.

It hurt that he couldn't understand this was her problem now. She couldn't foist it off on the kids. She'd been hired so the kids didn't have to deal with this, so they could find their footing before they did have to take over.

What was she going to do if he made her choose? She thought he wouldn't like her decision. She couldn't be with a man who made her choose between him and her job. It wasn't fair. She would never do the same thing to him.

If he did this, he would rip a piece of her soul out when he left. She was in far too deep with this man and she wouldn't be able to shrug and move on the way she had with Royce.

Isla stood and dialed a number she didn't want to dial, but it was always better to rip that bandage off.

"Hello?" Carey answered immediately, but then she was calling his private line. He always carried two cell phones. One for business, which he could easily ignore, and one for family, which included his wife and Isla and a cousin he liked. "Isla? Is everything all right?"

She needed to call him more often. If she'd realized one thing from all this horror, it was that she needed to stay in touch with the people she cared about. She'd skipped Portia's girls' trips because she decided work was more important, and now she would give a lot to have those memories of her friend and mentor. Carey was like a dad to her and yet she called him so infrequently that he worried something was wrong when she did.

"Nothing's wrong. Well, everything is, but I suspect you know that."

A long sigh came over the line. "How is Trey? I've asked if I can see him, but they said no one but his attorney can right now. You know what he's going to do if those meds work and he can think straight, right?"

Anyone who knew the man could guess. "I think he already did. David sent me a text about needing to talk. I think Trey confessed to him."

"And you're sure he didn't do it."

"I am, Carey," she replied, trying to be patient. "I heard someone moving down in the kitchen. I know it sounds crazy, but the killer was still in the apartment when I was. And I know where Trey was. He was holding Portia."

Carey paused. "Are you absolutely sure?"

"I'm one hundred percent sure that someone turned on the light to the kitchen and turned on the water," she explained. "I know that happened. The rest is fuzzy. I apparently had a panic attack."

"Okay, but the memories are there," Carey said. "We can get a therapist. I'll find the best in the country. We can put you under hypnosis and prove that Trey couldn't have done this. I can't let him spend the rest of his life in jail. But what about Oscar? The news is saying the case against him is strong."

The news liked to overstate things. "They have one very good piece of evidence against him and I can explain it away. Once we get through his bail hearing, we'll start on his case in earnest. I know what Trey is going to do, but it won't work even if we allowed him to do it."

"Good, because I can't stand the thought of this being the end of Trey's life. I'll start looking for a therapist. And maybe you could use someone to talk to. I can't imagine what that scene was like."

Yep, he was like a dad. "I promise I'll talk to someone. Right now it's easy to sleep because I'm working like a dog and my brain shuts off. I think it's going to get worse as I put some distance and try to normalize. But I actually called because I need to cancel tonight."

"Cancel?" There was a pause on the line. "I'm sorry, honey. Did we have plans tonight?"

"Amber asked me to come out to the stadium. She wanted to go over some of the memorial plans and said we would have dinner afterward."

A long-suffering sigh filled her ear. "That damn memorial. I'll deal with it, Isla. I've already had two calls from Portia's sister. You have to know that Amber is trying to do something good."

At least he understood. She had a shot at getting Amber to let go if she had Carey on her side. "I do. She's trying to do something nice for a woman who was nice to her. I get it, but Cressida has the right to control this. I would appreciate it if you would talk to her."

"I will. And I'm sorry you couldn't make it tonight. She didn't mention it to me, but she knew I was free so I suppose that's all right. She's busy. She's in the city today. I'll give her a call."

"Thanks. And I'll talk to you soon. Maybe we can have lunch."

"Absolutely not," he said in a firm tone. "You'll have dinner with me next week and bring that young man of yours out here. And, Isla?"

"Yes?"

"I love you, sweetheart. I know my boy was stubborn and he didn't want you to be a widow, but in my heart, you'll always be my daughter-in-law," he said, his voice filled with gruff emotion.

Tears pierced her eyes. "And you'll always be my second dad."

"You don't ever forget it."

The line went dead and she sniffled a bit. She'd gotten too involved in work. What did she want out of life? If she wasn't careful, she would look up one day and all she'd have would be a fabulous list of clients and a fat stack of cash, and that didn't seem like a complete life.

She wanted David. She wanted him more than she wanted her next breath. She wanted a life with him, a family with him. It was time and she was ready to take the chance again.

Was he?

He was right. They had a whole lot to talk about. From Portia's day planner to whatever Trey had said to where they went after all this was over. It would be a long night.

She called in a couple of orders for later in the evening and then contacted the front desk so they would know she had people coming up. They would unlock the private elevator and make things easy for a few hours. After all, no one knew where she was staying with the exception of the people closest to her. Well, except Oscar, and his butt was in jail. Damn. She was putting on a good front, but she was still angry with the young man she'd cared for like a brother.

After the deliveries were made, she'd put everything back on lockdown.

Perhaps some of his favorite Scotch would help the situation. She'd noticed how much he enjoyed a good single malt and he seemed to prefer one over all the rest. And some of the best Thai he'd ever had. Booze and noodles. And a low-cut blouse. That was her plan of attack. She still had an hour or so until the deliveries would come. She could clean up both the living room and herself.

Isla started stacking the journals back in the box, when the doorbell chimed indicating someone was coming up.

That was fast.

The elevator doors opened and Miranda stepped out, her face blotchy from crying. Maybe she shouldn't have told even the people she was closest to where she was staying.

Yes, it was going to be a very long night.

FOURTEEN

"What exactly are we looking for?" Henry asked as David pushed through the police station double doors.

"A couple of things," he said, nodding to the sergeant at the front desk. "Could you please let Detective Campbell know David Cormack and Henry Garrison are here to see him?"

The woman stared for a moment before picking up her phone and calling for Campbell. It wasn't more than a moment before someone walked out.

"Gentlemen, what can I do for you?" The man standing in front of them wasn't Campbell. Royce Osborne stared at them through the gate that led to the squad room. He made absolutely no move to open it.

The last person he wanted to deal with was Osborne. "You can allow us to speak with Detective Campbell."

"He's busy. He's got criminals to put in jail. He doesn't have time to deal with people who actively work against him," Osborne replied.

"We need access to the crime scene photos and the inventory the police took of Portia Adams's closet." He wasn't going to argue with the asshole. He had rights as the defense attorney.

"Then place a proper request through the proper channels and we'll see what happens," Royce replied.

"I need to see those photos," David insisted.

"Unless you want us to go to the press and explain that you've already bungled this once and now you've arrested a second person with very little evidence." Henry stared the man down.

"I didn't ever actually arrest Trey Adams for murder," Osborne pointed out. "That was all about reckless endangerment."

Henry shrugged. "That probably won't come up."

"Talk away, Garrison," Osborne said, a smirk on his face. "Oddly enough, I don't think the public is going to sympathize with an overprivileged brat of a kid who's had everything in life handed to him. I understand that Trey Adams is a hero to many in the community, and that is exactly why the DA's office took its time investigating. It's why we treated Mr. Adams with such careful concern. See, I can play the game, too."

Bastard. "You're not looking at this reasonably. You found one tiny piece of evidence and you're ignoring the rest. If Oscar killed his mother, why leave his father alive? Oscar had problems with his father, not his mom."

It was obvious from the nonchalant sigh that Osborne didn't care. "I've got a couple of people who tell a different story. Don't ask me who. I'm not doing your job for you."

The ADA obviously wasn't thinking. "Where are the tracks? That scene was bloody. I want to know where the tracks are. Whoever killed Portia Adams had to have walked back out of that room. Are you telling me someone could have done that kind of damage and not gotten blood on his shoes, on his clothes?"

"So he cleaned up," Osborne replied. "Or he took off his shoes."

"The carpet was soaked." Henry backed him up. "And we now have reason to believe the killer was in the kitchen when Isla was there."

Osborne's eyes rolled. "Good luck selling that one to a jury."

"Come on," David cajoled. "You're going to have to give it to us at some point. I want an inventory. The police took one, right? They inventoried everything in that closet to match it against the insurance."

There was a loud buzz and the gate opened. Osborne glared over at the sergeant. "I didn't tell you to let them in."

"You don't actually work here," she replied with a shake of her head. "And I know damn well Campbell is still working on this case. I was one of the officers who helped inventory that closet. There were some beautiful things in there. And a couple of things that didn't fit. Check out the shoes, Counselor."

"What are you doing?" Osborne asked.

"I am an officer, not a politician," she replied. "No cop wants the wrong person in jail. None of us. So I don't play sides and neither do my detectives. Campbell will be more than happy to talk to you boys."

"I'll have your job," Osborne vowed.

"You can certainly try," she said. "Campbell's in the back."

David strode through, ignoring the fact that Royce was hard on his heels.

"You can't think a judge is going to allow Isla to change her story," the ADA said. "She never said she was there when the killer was still in the penthouse."

"She recently remembered. But I don't think I'm going to have to bring Isla into it at all," David said with some confidence. The sergeant had seen something out of place. She'd likely said something about it but was ignored because it didn't fit with the DA's theory of the crime. "I think this is about to turn into a Cinderella story."

"You think?" Henry asked, his eyes lighting the way they always did when he thought he'd caught a thread he could pull.

"I think this is going to come down to who fits the shoe." It was what had struck him when he talked to Trey. There were some bloodstains from the downstairs going up to the bedroom, likely as Portia had tried to flee her attacker. But nothing coming down. The killer hadn't cleaned up the footprints going toward Portia's room. That made David think all those were made by Portia herself, having been attacked but only lightly, not enough to make her bleed out, but enough to send her fleeing, looking for a place to hide. And not enough to get on the killer's feet.

But that bedroom was a completely different story. No one could have walked in and out without bloodstains. Isla had them on the bottoms of her feet but they'd discounted those.

So how had the killer avoided leaving tracks behind?

"You think the killer took off his shoes, or her shoes," Henry said, catching up.

"That's ridiculous." Osborne stalked behind them as they turned down the hallway that led to the detectives' desks. "You can't think the killer took off his shoes and left them there."

"It might have been easier than cleaning up." The idea had been humming in his head the whole way back from Rikers. "If Trey isn't the killer, there should be some evidence that the killer left. The killer would have to have cleaned up the shoes or left them, or gone back and cleaned up the path from the kitchen to Portia's bedroom."

"But if he did that, why not clean up the evidence that was left there? They left the same way they came in," Henry said.

"There was a mop," Osborne said. "It hadn't been used. Damn it. How would he have kept his feet clean?"

David stopped in front of Campbell's desk.

The detective looked up and peered at the ADA. "One of the

many questions I felt we hadn't answered, but you pressured me to arrest the kid."

"And I stand behind that choice," Osborne insisted. "His fingerprints are on the murder weapon. The ME matched the chef's knife in their kitchen to the wounds on the victim."

"We gave you a plausible explanation for that." Campbell sat back in his chair, looking over his glasses at David. "You have something new?"

"He thinks the killer might have left his shoes behind," Osborne explained.

"There were over sixty pairs of shoes in that closet," Campbell said with a shake of his head. "I thought it was odd that they were tossed around the room. Ms. Adams was a very organized woman. Her shoes were boxed and in those bags high-end shoes get stored in."

"Dust bags," Henry offered.

"I'm looking for anything out of the ordinary. If the killer was worried about time because he was looking for something, he might have slipped his shoes off and then been forced to leave them behind when Isla showed up. Or when he heard Trey moving around. Were there any men's shoes found in Portia's closet or her room?" He was onto something. He knew it. Some instinct deep inside told him this was the thread that would lead them where they needed to go.

Every killer made mistakes. Some big. Some infinitesimally small, but the key to solving a murder was to locate the mistake.

The killer might have thought chaos was his friend, but if the cops had been careful enough, they could still find the mistake.

Campbell shook his head. "If I'd found a man's shoe, I would have been all over that. I assure you there was nothing like that. I'll pull up the inventory. We were careful about taking pictures of everything."

"See, you're wrong," Osborne insisted. "A man's shoe would stick out like a sore thumb."

"Then our killer is a woman." Shit. He'd been thinking of an angry husband or lover or son. But there were women in Portia's life who could be just as angry as any man. "Did we put sizes in the inventory?"

Campbell sat up, his attention suddenly caught. "My team is thorough. When we inventory clothes, we describe each by color, size, and label, if we have one. Hold on."

"A woman? You think it's the daughter," Osborne said. "Damn it. I didn't consider the daughter because she fucking called it in."

"Killers often come to the scene of the crime," Campbell was saying as he typed on his keyboard.

"So she finds out about the will, kills her mother, goes to look for the will, and when she can't find it, she takes the laptop and phone and flees the scene." Osborne had picked up on the argument.

It was a plausible scenario, but he wasn't sure he believed it. Although, Miranda had gone on the girls' trips with her mom. She had access to Kristoff Paloma. But he would not offer up any theories beyond trying to find that shoe.

He glanced over and Henry's jaw was tight. He would rather do this back at the office, but the ADA was right about one thing. They would have to jump through some hoops to get copies of the inventory, and he needed to know now. He needed to see it for himself.

"Here's the shoes." Campbell pulled the file up on the screen. "Who needs so many shoes? And what's a Louboutin anyway? I think our victim must have been that company's biggest investor."

"I'm fairly certain that's my wife," Henry grumbled.

There it was. Halfway down the page. "Women's thirty-six. Louboutin ballet flat, black with ribbon detailing. Portia wore a forty."

"In American that's a six and a ten, right?" Osborne asked. "So we're looking for someone smaller than the victim. Where's her daughter?"

Campbell shook his head. "No. You are not having me arrest

another member of that family until I've got some serious evidence. I'm calling my partner and a forensics team and we're going back over there. We're going to examine that shoe and figure out who the hell it belongs to. And then we'll talk about another arrest. Now you boys take this fight somewhere else and let me do my job."

Henry drew David back. "I'm going to get the paperwork started to get that list ourselves."

"You know this doesn't mean Oscar is innocent. Perhaps he stood outside the killing zone or he was busy looking for the will," Osborne said stubbornly. "It merely means Miranda might be in on it, too."

"Or some other woman altogether did it," David shot back. Isla would have his hide if he got Miranda shoved in jail alongside her brother.

But, then, of course he had to consider what would happen if she had done it.

"Well, we'll see, won't we?" Osborne stepped back. "Looks like I have more work to do. And if you want to see our evidence again, I suggest you do it through proper channels."

David stepped back. "See you in court."

"Yes, we'll start there," Osborne promised.

"Damn it." Henry pulled out his phone. "I didn't think about Miranda."

"Neither did I," David said. "But we need to take another look at her. I'm going to break the news to Isla."

Those shoes were too small for Portia's sister. Cressida mirrored her sister. If she couldn't wear Portia's shoes, he would eat his briefs. Of course, there was one other woman he'd met who might fit the shoe. But she wouldn't have a reason. He racked his brain trying to come up with some kind of motive. There was nothing.

Unless Portia had known something she shouldn't.

He hailed a cab and hoped Isla had some answers for him.

Miranda stepped off the elevator, tears in her eyes. "Did you get to see him?"

"No, I didn't. He wouldn't see anyone except for David. I'm sorry." She held a hand out. Talking to Carey had reminded her that she had to be there for these kids. Even when they didn't want her. Even when she was angry with one of them.

Miranda had never had the problems Oscar had. Miranda had always been open and friendly, even as a teen. She went straight in for a full-body hug. "I can't believe he won't see us at all. Does he even know about Oscar? I know he's a dick sometimes, but I can't believe he would kill Mom."

She hugged her back. She'd known Miranda since the kid was about ten, and she'd always wanted a little sister. "I'm pretty sure your dad has been told about Oscar's arrest. I don't believe he did it either."

Her head came up. "You don't?"

Isla shook her head. "Not for a second. I still think the killer is someone outside the family. Cressida wouldn't risk breaking a nail."

Miranda huffed out a bitter laugh. "No, she wouldn't. And she passes out when someone gets a paper cut. She's truly incapable of being around blood."

"David is going to handle Oscar's bail hearing and he's working on getting your dad moved to a private facility, but don't expect him to come home anytime soon. Because of what happened with the police, he'll probably be in the hospital for a while." She wondered if he would ever be allowed out again. The fight over Trey might be moot.

"They're saying terrible things about our family." Miranda stepped back and glanced around.

Isla got her a box of tissues. "You have to stay strong and not react. I know that is the hardest thing in the world to do. Your mother loved you and she would want you to be strong, but in the right way. She wouldn't want you watching those shows."

Miranda brushed back her hair, looking so young and vulnerable. "People at my school are talking about us, too."

"They don't know you. I want you to think about this. Do you gossip about celebrities?"

Miranda shrugged. "Sure, everyone does."

"That's all they're doing," she explained. "And they'll turn their attention to the next scandal that comes along and forget all about this. Things will calm down. The people who know you, know what your family is like, will stand beside you, and you and Oscar and your dad are going to come out of this on the other side and you'll be stronger. I know it doesn't seem like you can be, but if you'll make one decision right now you can get through this."

"What decision is that?"

She looked down at Miranda. Even in heels, Miranda was petite. Which was why she almost always wore them. Something her mother had taught her. "Decide right now that they don't get to break you. Decide that you're stronger than they are and you will come out of this whole. They don't get to break your spirit and take your light."

Miranda sniffled. "God, you sound like Mom."

"Your mom sounded a lot like my mom." Another reason she'd loved working with Portia. "She always told me I made the decision about how I reacted to the things that happen to me. We don't get to choose what happens, but we can stand tall and be strong when the bad things happen. When people are crappy to us, we don't have to hand it back to them. We don't have to let heartache turn us dark."

"But I want to," Miranda said. "God, I want to fuck every one of them over."

"I assure you, life will do that."

Miranda's shoulders squared, the light back in her eyes. "Okay. They don't get to break me. I have to make sure they don't break Oscar either. If we can get him out of jail, can he go to rehab?"

"We can work something out."

"They think he killed Mom because of the will, but he didn't know about it." She moved around to the sofa and sank down. "I did though. I know I told you I was as shocked as Oscar, but I found out a few weeks ago."

That was news. "Your mom said she wasn't going to mention it yet."

A familiar smile crossed Miranda's face. "She caved pretty fast when it came to me. I started talking about when I could run some of the businesses, and she admitted what she'd done. I was so mad at her."

She could understand. "You didn't like the fact that she'd placed me in charge."

Miranda reached over, setting a hand on hers. "I would have been mad about her putting anyone but me in charge. Please understand that."

"I do. I remember how mad I was that my parents had put my trust in someone else's hands." She'd been a high school student when her parents died in a crash. "My trust came into my hands at the age of twenty-five. It wasn't anything like yours, but it was substantial. And I was angry that my mom and dad hadn't trusted me. I know you won't believe it, but I'm happy they did it now."

"Because you realized you didn't need the stress at that point in your life? You weren't ready to deal with all of the problems that came with the cash? Because that's what I've figured out."

Isla breathed a sigh of relief. "Yes, that's what happened."

"I'm not ready yet, Isla," she said. "Not even close. I need to be a student for a while and then I need to learn the business from the ground up. Can I take that time?"

"You can, sweetie." She'd always known Miranda would be the reasonable one.

Tears welled in Miranda's eyes. "I hate that some of my last words to her were in anger. It was so stupid. She would have changed it again if she'd lived."

"Yes, we discussed changing the will again in ten years," she explained. "You would have been mature enough to handle things. You would have been your father's power of attorney. You still will. I'm going to hand everything over to you when the time is right."

Miranda's hand came out, covering hers again. "Thank you for being here for us. Please know that I'll handle Oscar and Aunt Cressy. I'll get them to drop the suit."

"And I'll pay your aunt's bills if she does. It's what your mom wanted," Isla promised.

Miranda leaned over and let her head rest on Isla's shoulder. "Mom understood the need for clothes and shoes." She laughed and then sobered. "I think we should auction off her collection for charity."

"Now, that is something she would love." One good thing had come out of this day. At least she wasn't losing her family altogether. They had a lot to get through, but she was going to be the strong hand that helped to guide them.

"And maybe we could take a memorial trip to Europe. She loved Paris so much."

The mention of Paris jogged something in her brain. "You went on the last Paris trip with your mom, didn't you?"

Miranda sat back up. She'd kicked off her shoes and curled her feet under her skirt. "Yes. I only went to Paris and London. Mom didn't think I was old enough before this last year. After London, I'm pretty sure I won't ever be old enough. It's fine when they're shopping, but I do not need to see old ladies flirt with men I should be dating. It's weird and gross. And it's not like they meant anything by it. Mom wouldn't do that. Aunt Cressy wouldn't wreck her makeup, but some of the others. Well, I walked in on things I can't unsee."

"Like what?"

Miranda shot her a surprised look. "I wouldn't have suspected you would be the one I should gossip to."

Isla shook her head. "No. It's not about that." Where was that picture? She stood and started to go through the stacks she'd made on the coffee table. "You know how my apartment was broken into?"

Miranda sat up. "I do."

"I think the man who attacked me might have hung around the group when you were in London."

Miranda's jaw dropped. "Are you serious?"

The bell chimed, indicating someone was coming up. It was either the booze or the food, or maybe even David. She hoped it was David. This might be the break they'd been looking for. She hadn't thought about the fact that Miranda had gone on the trips with her mom. She'd been focused on Portia's friends. The truth was she'd spent the last week trying to give Miranda some space, and that might have been a mistake. "Yes. His name is Kristoff Paloma. I think I have a picture of him somewhere."

Miranda stood up, frowning. "There was a guy named Kris, though I didn't know him personally. He was this hot guy who was staying at the same hotel we were at in Paris. I thought he was like eye candy for some of the other women, but I doubt my mom would even remember him past the fact that he looked like a male model."

"But someone got to know him very well," she prompted. God, she'd wasted time by not talking to Miranda. "Someone started an affair with him."

Miranda's jaw went tense, her eyes sliding away. "I think so. I should have told you. I know how close you are to her husband."

Her brain found the name even as the elevator doors opened and the woman herself walked through. Amber Kendrick was wearing all black, right down to her shoes.

And she wasn't alone.

A tall man with sandy-blond hair walked behind her, and Isla reached for Miranda's hand, squeezing it.

"Hey, I'm so happy you're here," Amber said with a big smile that disappeared briefly when she saw Miranda. "I came for those pictures. Carey told me you canceled on me tonight, you silly you. Well, it's like they say, if you can't go to the mountain, the mountain's going to show up on your doorstep."

Isla finally knew who had killed her friend. She only prayed she and Miranda weren't about to become the next victims.

FIFTEEN

"I'm so sorry," Isla began, her voice surprisingly smooth despite the fact that inside she was shaking like a leaf. "I haven't picked up the family photos yet. I told Carey I wasn't going to be able to come over tonight. I know you're on a time crunch. We'll go over everything together tomorrow."

Miranda seemed to pick up on her plan. She nodded her head vigorously. "Yes, I'll come, too. Have I thanked you for doing this for us? It's so nice of you to think of my mom."

Amber looked from one to the other, as though trying to figure out if she was being played. "I loved your mom. She was a wonderful woman."

Isla squeezed Miranda's hand, a reminder to not say what they both had to be thinking. *If you loved her so much, why would you kill her?*

Because she knew about you and Kristoff?

"We were sitting here talking about her while we waited on dinner." She needed to let them know they wouldn't be alone for long.

Even if it was still a bit on the early side for the deliveries. David was going to kill her for taking the security lock off the elevator.

And for telling Carey where she was. It had to be how Amber had known to come here.

Amber stood in the great room, glancing around. "Nice place." She seemed to remember she hadn't come alone. "Oh, this is my new bodyguard, Kris. After everything that's happened Carey insisted I have one if I'm going into the city. He doesn't want to lose me."

She nodded the man's way. "Carey's a good man. Kris, it's nice to meet you."

Miranda wouldn't look at him. "Nice to meet you."

"Well, Miranda was about to go," Isla said. "She's running late for a study group."

The least she could do was to get Miranda out of here. She could go for the doorman, who would call the police.

Miranda's eyes came up, shock and then recognition settling in. She went to grab her purse. "Yeah, all that stuff about professors giving you a pass for family tragedies is made up. Mine couldn't care less. I'll see you tomorrow, Amber."

Let her go. Let her go. Please let her go.

Miranda made it almost to the elevator when Paloma stepped in front of her. "I don't think so. I think you recognize me. You think I didn't know you were watching Amber and me? She might have forgotten, but I have not."

"Forgotten?" Miranda stared up at him. "I've never seen you before."

"You're a liar." Paloma's voice held a silky threat.

"Miranda, come here." Isla waved her back. It wasn't going to work.

Miranda shuffled toward her, not taking her eyes off the snake in front of her.

Amber frowned. "What are you doing, Kris?"

He shook his head. "That one saw us last year. I remember her watching us. I didn't say anything because I didn't think she would mention it to anyone, but she knows. And so does Ms. Shayne. Her hands are shaking. She knows it was me in her apartment that day."

Amber shook her head. "Damn it. This wasn't how it was supposed to go. I never meant to hurt Portia. I loved her. She was nice to me, but then she found . . ."

"You didn't want Carey to know about the affair."

"No, of course not," Amber replied, but she wouldn't look at her. Her eyes were on the ground. "I love my husband, but I need to feel young sometimes, too. He can't . . . you know. He can't satisfy me in that way. Kris is an old friend. We met a long time ago when I tried to model in Europe."

Miranda's hand was suddenly in hers, but there was something in it. Something cylindrical and metallic. Isla could feel a chain as though it attached to keys.

And there was a button. She knew the feel of that item well. Mace. Or something like it. Either that or Miranda had an inhaler and wanted her to breathe better.

"I can't believe this." Paloma was pacing behind Amber, his irritation clear. "You went insane on the first one, and now we've got to kill these two as well. They're not the ones we should have killed. Your husband is the one who can get us the money."

"I told you I'm not killing him. He's already sick. He's going to die soon anyway." Amber's eyes shone with tears. "And Portia wasn't my fault. She was going to tell everyone. She was going to ruin it all."

"Ruin what?" She was starting to understand. "Ruin your plan to walk away with all of Carey's wealth even though you cheated on him? I happen to know what was in your prenup."

After all, she'd written it herself.

Amber frowned. "I haven't put up with that old man for as long as I have only to watch one mistake take everything away from me."

"So you picked up a knife and killed her?" Isla asked. Now she understood the game. Somehow Portia must have figured out the affair.

"When Portia wouldn't agree to our demands, Amber went utterly insane. She chased Portia through the apartment and . . . well, I've never seen anything like it," Paloma replied. He sighed. "Well, the doorman saw us walking in. And there's security cameras. I didn't take them out this time."

The security lock might be off, but there would still be video.

Paloma shook his head. "But perhaps we can make this work. I read something about the daughter being upset about the will. It could be a plausible reason for her to kill the lawyer."

One chance. They would have one chance to run. One chance to hide. But first she had to get closer.

"What are you talking about?" Amber's hands were fists at her sides.

"I'm talking about the fact that you admitted to a lawyer that you committed murder, and now you can go to jail or we can fix the situation," Paloma explained. "The investigators believe that Miranda's brother killed their mother over the will. Why wouldn't the sister be in on it? At some point they'll figure out there were two people there that night, a man and a woman. It could have been them."

"Why would the police believe that?" Amber asked.

"Because we'll make them believe it." He reached behind his back and pulled out a gun. Miranda gasped.

"They certainly won't believe that some random person walked in and shot us both in the head," Isla pointed out. She had to stay calm.

"I thought it would be a better story if the daughter kills you and then herself," Paloma corrected.

Amber looked up, still crying. "I didn't mean for this to happen.

I just wanted to make sure I have it all. I can't let someone else get it. I have to do this for Carey's sake. I know you won't believe this but I care about him. I'm doing this for him. Portia was going to tell."

"I believe you," Isla said, willing to say anything. "I know you love him."

"I know you won't believe me, but this is about more than money. Yes, I want the money, but his legacy is important, too." Amber wouldn't look her in the eyes. "Being a part of his family, having that name has meant something to me."

"Me, too. That's why I'll help you protect him."

"You will?" Amber asked.

"Of course." Again, she would agree to anything as long as she and Miranda came out of this alive.

Paloma raised the gun. "Don't be ridiculous. She'll say anything because she knows she's about to die."

Isla couldn't let that happen. "And you need to think about the forensics of the situation. Right now, if you're correct, you haven't killed anyone, Mr. Paloma. I understand you were careful that night you went to see Portia. You went up the service entrance and made sure the cameras were down. Today, you marched through the lobby and the cameras and the doorman will have seen you." She had to get through to him. "All you've done so far is not tell the police what you know. If you walk away now and tell the police what you know, hell, they might cut a deal with you."

"Or they will cut a deal with France or Italy or Portugal. Any one of those countries where I've run one of my little games." Paloma strode forward. "This is the biggest con of my career. Once the old man passes on, Amber and I will have more than enough to last a lifetime. There's no going back for me."

He was close now, pushing past Amber. But he would have to make it look good if he was going to have a shot at getting out of this with his freedom. He had his gun, but the safety was on. He would need them in the right positions to make his plan work.

She wasn't about to go along with any plan. She brought the mace up and pressed down, spraying the chemical all over Paloma's face and eyes.

He screamed and fell back. It was the moment she needed.

She took Miranda's hand and started for the elevator. It should still be at the top. It was a private elevator and wouldn't go back down until someone called for it. Something grabbed at her ankle and she fell face-first, the breath knocked from her body as she hit the marble floor hard.

Miranda was standing over her, helping her up.

"Go, run."

"Not without you." Miranda swung her bag out, catching Paloma's hand and shoving him back.

She got to her feet and realized Amber was standing in front of the elevators. Paloma would be on her in an instant if she went that way. They had to get somewhere and call the police. Isla took Miranda's hand and ran toward the west wing. Thank god Drew Lawless was wealthy and needed a mansion on top of a building. It gave her room to run.

And the last few days had given her time to explore.

"Do you have your phone?" Isla asked.

"It's in my purse. He's coming," Miranda said, fear plain in her voice.

"Come on." She ducked into the first of the three connected bedrooms. She slammed the door and locked it.

This room was painted a vibrant pink, the space dominated with a princess canopy bed. "The kids' rooms are connected to the nanny's room by doors in the back. I think there's a space where I can stash you."

"I don't think I should be stashed anywhere," Miranda said.

"You have to call the police." She dragged Miranda back to the door and into the second bedroom. It was painted a deep blue and stars covered the ceiling. There was a set of bunk beds, the bottom one sitting on top of a pair of large drawers. Noah had joked about only one being full and the other empty because his brother was trying not to spoil his kids. "Get in."

Miranda easily fit in the space.

"Call the police and then stay as quiet as possible." Isla gasped as there was a loud banging sound from the other room. She shoved the drawer closed, praying Miranda could stay silent. The best plan she had would be distracting Paloma so he didn't go looking for Miranda.

She ran through the next door and into the nanny's room, leaving the doors open to lead him where she wanted him to go. She nearly tripped opening the door that led back to the main hall. Paloma was coming up behind her and she would bet he'd taken the safety off now.

"Keep running!" she yelled even though no one was in front of her. She had to keep him on the hook, had to make him think Miranda was ahead of her.

There was a blast behind her and she felt something skim her shoulder, licking fire along her skin.

She had to make it to the gym. There was a whole room in this section of the penthouse dedicated to fitness and filled with stuff she could potentially defend herself with.

Her heart pounded in her chest, thudding like a hummingbird's wings.

"Isla!"

She stopped at the sound of a familiar voice screaming her name. David was here.

"If you move an inch, I'll shoot, bitch." Unfortunately, Paloma was here, too, and he wasn't going away.

She held her hands up and prayed for a miracle.

David glanced down at his phone as he started to worry. He'd called twice now and she hadn't responded. After he'd texted her, he thought about the best way to break the news that he thought the killer was one of two women—Miranda or Amber Kendrick. Either name would likely upset her. Then there was the fact that Trey Adams might never see the outside of a mental hospital again. Any way he looked at it, he was going to disappoint her.

And Trey's words wouldn't leave him alone. No matter how hard he tried to forget them, they crept back into his consciousness, nudging and poking at him. Did he have any right to bring Isla into his life when he couldn't be sure he would be sane ten years from now? Did he have any right to bring children into a life where their father might not recognize them one day?

"Good evening, Mr. Cormack." The doorman opened the gorgeous glass doors, welcoming him inside.

They would have to leave here soon. They would go back to their own places and get lost in the minutiae of normal days if they didn't actively try to stay together. If she was any other woman in her position, all he would have to do was forget to call. Ignore a couple of texts. What was the current term? Ghost. He could ghost on her and she would move on. Not Isla. Isla would show up on his doorstep and demand an explanation, not because she was selfish, but because she would be worried about him. She would need to know.

How could he tell her he wanted her but couldn't allow himself to have her?

Or he could stay quiet and offer himself up to medical science. There was talk of a test that might be able to diagnose CTE in living patients. It was in the early stages and more likely to miss the disease than catch it, but he could try to test and see if he had the protein markers that could lead to CTE.

It wouldn't be enough. Even if they weren't there now, he could develop them.

All you'll do is bring her pain.

"Good evening, Ed." He nodded to the doorman. It wasn't his fault David was having a terrible day. It wasn't the doorman's fault David's past was going to wipe out any hope for a future.

"I'll make sure to send those deliveries up as soon as they get here," Ed said with a smile. "Could you let Ms. Shayne know that I don't mind vetting everyone who goes up there? I think she's worried it's too much work and that's why she took the code off the elevator, but I'm used to Mr. Lawless. Even when he and the missus have playdates over, I make sure they're exactly who they say they are."

"She turned off the security code to the elevator?"

"Yeah, she asked me to do it. She's got a couple of deliveries coming up and she didn't want to have to give them the code, but I'm more than happy to accept the delivery and take it up to her myself. It's why there are always two of us on duty," Ed explained. "She doesn't ever have to give out that code. Please let her know I appreciate what she's trying to do, but I know Mr. Lawless would prefer I vet anyone going up there."

"I agree. I'll have a talk with her. While we're here, that code needs to stay on. Have the deliveries been made?" It was exactly like Isla to try to spare the doorman extra work, but she wasn't thinking straight.

"Not yet." He nodded toward the door. "Ah, it looks like the liquor store delivery is here. A few of the guests have already arrived."

"Guests?" He wasn't aware they were having guests. He knew where Noah, Margarita, and Henry were. They were in the office. Erin and Liam wouldn't be back for days. Henry was probably telling them about the new evidence even as he stood here.

Ed buzzed in the deliveryman, taking the bag out of his hand. David fished into his pockets, pulling out a tip and thanking him.

"Yes, one of her clients showed up. That poor girl. I can't imagine what she's going through," Ed said, handing over the brown paper bag.

A chill went through him. "Are you saying Miranda Adams is up there?"

The phone rang on Ed's desk. He started moving toward it as he nodded. "Yeah, she was crying, too. Not that I blame her. The other one, the wife of that crazy guy who owns the Guardians, she wasn't crying. And I personally think Kendrick should watch his wife, if you know what I mean. I didn't like the looks of that man with her."

Ed picked up the phone but David was already jogging to the elevator. They were both up there. Isla had let the wolves in.

"Hey, Mr. Cormack, I need you to stop," Ed shouted across the lobby. "Mr. Jacobsen just heard screaming above him. Lots of it. The only thing above him is the penthouse. I've called the cops, but they said they're already on their way."

The words didn't make him stop. "Isla's up there."

He rushed into the elevator, Ed running behind him. The security guard pulled the Taser out of the holster on his belt. "Take this. I have to stay down here to let the cops in. We'll be up in minutes. Be careful."

David took the Taser, letting everything else drop. The elevator doors closed and the longest ride of his life began.

He couldn't breathe. Was she already dead? Had she been murdered over that damn will? Or because she might have found out about Amber's affair? His mind played through every terrible scenario as the elevator rose. He had a Taser against a gun. Paloma would probably have a gun. Hell, he'd never even used a damn Taser.

Please let her be alive. Please let her be alive.

The doors opened and he heard a shot and a scream. He stepped out into the foyer. The scream had come from close by; the shot he thought was somewhere deeper in the penthouse. The doors closed behind him, and he prayed the cops would be hard on his heels, but he couldn't wait for them.

"Isla!"

The first thing he saw was a woman hunched over the couch. She'd curled into herself and sobbed into the pillow, her hair wild all around her.

Amber.

Her head came up at the sound of his steps on the marble, eyes going wide. "He made me do it. You have to believe me. I never wanted any of this. I wanted to protect my husband and his legacy. No one can know. It would ruin everything. Can you understand?"

He didn't care. Only one thing mattered. "Where's Isla?"

She shook her head, waving toward a hallway. "She ran."

He took off down the hallway she'd suggested he try. Time was running out and that was when Paloma would get dangerous. The doors to the kids' rooms were open, but he stopped and started down the hallway as quietly as he could. He could hear a deep voice talking and it sounded as though it floated in from around the corner.

"I didn't kill Portia. I was merely there," Paloma said, his accent thick.

"I know, but you won't be able to say the same of this," Isla replied. She sounded calmer than he would expect, but then that was kind of who she was. Unflappable. Stalwart. The kind of woman any man would want watching his back. "Look, your best bet at this point is to put down that gun and blame everything, and I mean everything, on Amber. She was the one who killed Portia, am I right?"

"She went crazy when Portia wouldn't give her what we asked for. I only went with her in case we had to pry the evidence out of her, but she wouldn't even tell us where it was." Paloma's voice went soft. "Amber . . . it was terrible. I've never seen anything like it. She became unhinged. One minute she was crying and the next that knife was in her hand and she'd stabbed Portia with it."

And Portia had run. She'd fled trying to find the safety of her bedroom. David crept along the wall. He needed to take out Paloma before the cops got here and he decided to take a hostage.

"Amber followed her and when I got there, she had Portia on the floor and she was like an animal. A trapped animal. I had to clean her up. We left her shoes behind but no one would notice one pair of shoes with all the others. Amber wouldn't let me take anything. The stupid bitch was upset and not thinking. It would have looked better if we'd taken something other than her laptop and phone. I still think we could have gotten away with it if she hadn't been so paranoid."

"You can mitigate the damage," Isla offered. "Like I said, you haven't hurt anyone. Not yet."

"I need you to get out of here," he said, his voice shaking a little now. "The girl will have called the police. Come here and I promise, once I get free of this building, I'll let you go."

That wasn't about to happen. He stepped out and Paloma's back was to him. Isla was so pale. God, he hoped he did this right. He had to take the focus off her.

"Paloma," he said as he lifted the Taser. The big guy began to turn, the gun coming David's way. He'd never fired a Taser before, but it was as easy as pulling the trigger.

The darts flashed out from the Taser, burying themselves in the right side of Paloma's chest. His body jerked and the gun went off.

Fire blazed through his brain and he was thrown back.

Hit. He'd been hit. His vision started to go fuzzy.

Someone screamed out his name and then he saw Isla's face looming over him. How had he gotten to the floor?

She was crying. His head ached as he reached up to brush those tears from her face. He hated to see her cry.

She was saying something, but it sounded so far away.

Her face was the last thing he saw before the darkness encroached and the world faded away.

SIXTEEN

"I don't understand." Isla stood outside the hospital room door. She'd rushed over as soon as she was able, ready to see David, to hold him again. She'd been met by his best friend standing in the doorway and blocking her path. "I thought he was awake."

"He is." Henry Garrison towered over her, a grim look on his face. "Come with me. We need to talk."

She took a deep breath and followed him down the hallway to the waiting room. At this time of day there were only a few people sitting in chairs and sleeping on sofas, waiting for word of their loved ones. The smell of stale coffee permeated the air as she squared off with Henry. It had been a crazy couple of hours. Maybe she needed to go over it all again. She was obviously missing something important. "What's going on?"

Henry scrubbed a hand over his head, his weariness a palpable thing. "I suck at this. I have no idea what to say. Maybe you could wait until Noah or Margarita gets here and talks to him."

"Tell me what the doctors said first. We'll get to the crappy part in a minute. I'm sorry I wasn't here last night. You have to know I tried to come to the hospital with him. They wouldn't let me. Is that why he won't see me? Is he angry I left him?"

"It's not that." Henry paced over the carpet of the waiting room. "You had to deal with the police. He knows that. It's only been a couple of hours since he woke up. He's not thinking straight."

She was worried about how stubborn the man she loved might prove to be. "I'm sorry I wasn't here when he woke up. Did I thank you for sending Margarita down to the station? She was lovely."

"I know you were only there for questioning about what happened, but I don't like any of my clients talking to the police without a lawyer," Henry said. "It's best to always be represented. Is Miranda all right? Did she get home okay?"

Miranda was forever changed by the experience, but she was safe. "Well, I think she's claustrophobic now, but Noah was kind to her. He convinced the police to let her leave long before I got out of there. He made sure she got home, and he's picking up Oscar as we speak. I think they'll go out to their aunt's place for a while and try to avoid the press. Thanks for getting that done so quickly."

Henry held up a hand. "Oh, thank that idiot Royce. He was thrilled to expedite the process. He thinks arresting Amber Kendrick is going to make him look even better than Oscar. Paloma is already talking about how she killed Portia. Well, after he stopped shaking. David had that sucker on full power. It took a while before that asshole could talk again."

"Do we know what he's saying? Besides pointing the finger at Amber?" From what she could tell, Amber had gone quietly with the police. Not that she saw it happen. She'd been far too busy trying to figure out if David was even alive.

She would never forget that horrible moment when she realized David had been shot. One minute she'd been certain she would be used as a human shield, and the next she heard the sound of the

Taser firing and then Paloma's gun had gone off. It was like time had slowed down as she tried to get to him before he hit the floor. She'd seen the blood and called to anyone who would listen to save him.

In that moment she knew she loved him. It couldn't be anything else. She'd also known that she might never get over losing him. Austin had been her first love, but David was her soul mate, her other half.

The cops had found her there in the hallway, crying over his body. Begging him to come back to her.

And now he didn't want to see her.

"I don't know a lot. I've been here waiting for news on David and then making sure he's got everything he needs."

It was so obvious it had been a long night for Henry, too. "I thank you for that. I wish I'd been here. I hated not knowing what was going on, but the police were insistent."

"The good news is I can't represent Amber Kendrick, so don't even ask." He said it with a sigh of relief. "Since David is going to end up being a material witness, I can happily step back from this clusterfuck of a case."

"I wasn't going to ask you to rep her. I will happily send her to jail. Though I can't imagine what Carey's going through." She'd tried to call him, but he wasn't answering either of his phones. The news cycle was in full frenzy, with every single station talking about the scandalous details. But she was curious. In the long hours she'd been at the police station, a couple of questions had run through her brain, loose ends she felt the need to tie up. "If this was all about an affair, what proof do you think Portia had?"

Henry shrugged. "I don't know. Maybe she took pictures. Or had some video."

"But the affair happened in Europe and, according to the McKay-Taggart investigators, Paloma hadn't been here in the States for very long. I think Erin had them track him to the city the day before Portia's death. So those photos couldn't have been new. Why would Portia have sat on them for so long? The last time Amber had been physical with Paloma was months before on the London trip. The Paris trip was the year before."

"Maybe she didn't know what she had until she started putting together the memorial video," Henry mused. "There might have been something there she hadn't noticed before and she went to Amber about it."

"Why not go directly to Carey?"

Henry crossed his arms over his chest as he thought the problem through. "She probably didn't want to cause trouble if she didn't have to. She might have thought she misunderstood. When Amber couldn't explain it away, Portia decided to tell. She must have had enough evidence to convince Carey. I know they've found the phone and laptop, but the DA's not going to give me anything. I wouldn't either. Not when he knows damn well I'm probably going to sue the city. Lots of false arrests on this one. It's going to be fun."

He had that predatory grin on his face that reminded her this was a man who loved the fight.

Still, he didn't know everything she did. "And why would Paloma have searched my house? I didn't normally store photographs for Portia. If this was a completely personal thing, why bring me into it? There was something. Something about you. Before Amber showed up this afternoon, I found your name written in Portia's day planner."

His eyes widened. "You did?"

"I did. She had the phone number to Garrison, Cormack, and Lawless and your name underlined."

"I never met with her," Henry admitted. "If she called and made an appointment, she did it under another name and never showed up. The firm couldn't have taken Trey's case if we had Portia as a client."

That was what she'd thought. "She had a couple of aliases she used when she didn't want the press to know what she was doing. If she called, she likely used one of them. I can give them to your admin to see if she had an appointment. There was also a code written in the planner. I haven't figured out what that is yet, but it's too odd to be pure coincidence. It was on the same page as your name. It's got to have something to do with all of this. I want to know what they were looking for."

"I'm sure Paloma will talk. He's going to do anything he can to get out of this. Amber, on the other hand, I hear is being very quiet. From what we heard, she lawyered up and shut down entirely. I think she might make a play for insanity," Henry said. "I don't think it's going to work, but she directly told David she did it."

"Me, too. And Miranda." Amber had been so broken. It was like a light had shut off inside her and she was hollowed out. She hadn't looked like a woman who was merely upset that she was caught.

Henry's gaze snared hers. "It was a brave thing you did, hiding her and taking on Paloma yourself."

"Anyone would have done it and it gave Miranda a chance to call the police," Isla said.

"No." He shook his head. "Not anyone would have done it. It was incredibly brave. I hope you know that. I admire you very much."

She glanced back at the hallway that led to the door David had firmly closed between them, the door she meant to bust open. "Good, I'm brave and that means you should try to help me. What's wrong with David?"

"Physically or mentally?"

"Just talk to me, Henry. I know the bullet only grazed him."

Henry seemed to think about what to say. "The bullet wasn't the issue, though it took off a tiny portion of his earlobe. Noah's already started with the Van Gogh jokes."

"Somehow I think I can live with the loss." She knew it wasn't the injury that had sent David into a tailspin, but she couldn't think of why he would shut her out. He'd said they had something to talk about. Had he been planning on ending it then? Then why had he been so desperate to save her?

"It wasn't the bullet that put us here," Henry explained. "He fell back and hit his head pretty hard against that marble floor. The reason he lost consciousness wasn't the bullet. It was the fall and the concussion. You know he played football for years, right?"

"Of course."

"This isn't his first concussion."

She hadn't assumed it was. "But he's all right?"

"He's fine. But it took him a couple of hours. He woke up and he was really upset that he couldn't remember his words."

"His words?"

A long sigh came from Henry. "He uses several mnemonic devices to keep his memory sharp. He couldn't remember the words he'd memorized yesterday and he kind of lost his damn mind."

Why would he care about a few words? Unless . . . They'd talked about this, but he hadn't directly said it. "He thinks he has CTE."

"I know he worries about it," Henry allowed.

She groaned her frustration. Not only had David had a physical setback, he'd also spent a good portion of the day before in the company of a man suffering from the very disease he feared. She could imagine some of the things Trey had likely said to him. Especially if David had asked him for advice. Trey wouldn't have been optimistic. He was in a dark place with a dark prognosis.

All of her conversations with David about Trey had to be re-evaluated and filtered through the new information. She'd thought he was being heartless, but she had to take out Trey's name and fill in David's. This wasn't about shoving a problem away. It was about David being the potential problem. It was about sacrifice.

Idiot. Masculine dumbass.

"I'm going in now, Henry."

He stepped in front of her. "I was told to keep you out. I know he's being difficult, but he's my best friend in the world."

It was time to draw some firm lines in the sand. "And he's going to be my husband one day. Don't doubt me, Henry Garrison. I might look all soft and sweet, but I have a spine like nothing you've seen before. I love that man and I won't allow some potential disease to come between us. So you get to choose how our personal relationship is going to work from here on out, best friend. You can understand that I'm going to get my way in this or you can play into David's insecurities and make this worse for me and I'll remember that for all of time."

Henry stepped out of her way, offering her an easy path to David. "All right, then. I'm more afraid of you than him. You have my full support."

Excellent. She started for the door.

"Isla?"

She turned. "Yes?"

"He's afraid. He thinks he's doing the right thing by you. Go easy on him," Henry said.

"I would love to go easy on him. I would love to walk into that room and coddle him and promise him all manner of filthy sex if he does what the doctors tell him to do. I would take care of him. But I have to break through to him first. He might ask you to file a restraining order against me before all of this is done."

Henry's hands came up. "Not my specialty. I think he'll find Noah and Margarita aren't very good at those either."

Good. One less thing to worry about. She turned again, ready for the fight of her life.

~

He hated Jell-O. And pudding. The next person who tried to give him pudding would get the staring of a lifetime. Could he sue over how shitty the food was? There had to be something he could do because sitting in this bed knowing that any minute now Henry would walk in and tell him he'd sent Isla away was making him fucking crazy.

Would she cry? Would she think it was her fault? Or that he was a complete dick and he was done with her?

How would it affect her?

Maybe she would shrug and move on. Maybe she was way smarter than he was giving her credit for and she would thank him for dodging that bullet.

Except he hadn't. Dodged the bullet. He had a half hole in his right ear to prove that he hadn't even been able to manage that.

He had managed to make her cry. The time in the penthouse was foggy, but he could see her looking down at him and crying. How much would he make her cry if he stayed with her? She wouldn't be smart. She would stand by his side even when it got rough.

She could end up like Portia. Or his mom.

It didn't matter now. He'd done what he needed to do. Isla might try to call but he wouldn't answer. She was safe now. There was no reason to keep things going when they would fall apart. She was safe and free to find someone who could give her the life she deserved.

And he would spend the rest of his life mourning her. Because he knew beyond a shadow of a doubt that this was love. What he'd felt before was a pittance compared to the love he had for Isla.

The door started to swing open. Henry. Maybe it was over and she could get on with her life. She would cry and hurt for a while, but she would see someday this was for the best. He would catch a glimpse of her and maybe hear whispers about her. She would find a healthy man, a good man, and have a family, and that man would take care of her for the rest of her life.

Or he would answer to David Cormack.

Yes, she would be upset and then she would move on.

"You're a coward and it's not going to work."

Not Henry. He managed to turn and there was Isla. She was in the same clothes she'd worn earlier. No shower and change for her. Nope. She'd dealt with the cops and come over here as soon as she could because that was how Isla handled her responsibilities. Even tired and a bit on the ragged side, she was the most beautiful thing he'd ever seen.

Had she gotten around Henry? He hadn't expected her to sneak in. "What are you doing here?"

"Talking to my coward boyfriend." She frowned at him, standing at the end of his bed. Despite how tired she must be, she looked like sunshine to him. He wanted to scoot over and ask her to hop into bed with him so he could cuddle against her and know she was warm and alive and here.

Instead he was going to have to do what Henry should have. "I'd asked Henry to let you know I wanted to be alone."

She crossed her arms under her breasts. It made them stand out more. "Yes, he tried. I explained the way of the world to him."

Was she angry? It wasn't the reaction he'd expected from her. He needed to make himself plain. Apparently, Henry was shitty at breaking up with a woman. "Isla, I don't want to see you anymore."

She groaned and shook her head. "And now you're a liar, too. It's okay. I am actually glad this happened. It was probably inevitable. You've got a martyr complex." She moved to the side of the bed, but didn't reach out to touch him. "Are they letting you out soon? Or keeping you for a while?"

"They're releasing me in the morning." What had she said? "I don't have a martyr complex."

"Oh, you so do." She glanced around and found the lounger. "I guess this will have to work. I'm going to find a blanket. It's cold in here."

He had to regain control. The reason he'd asked Henry to talk to her was because he was afraid if he saw her, he'd give in to his needs. Now he realized she wasn't reacting at all the way he thought she would. "You're not spending the night here. Did you not hear a word I said? I don't want to see you. I don't want you."

She rolled her eyes. "Heard and rejected, Counselor. When I'm talking to David again and not David's completely irrational fear, I'll listen. Until then, I'm going to find a blanket and settle in because I'm supertired. You need to think about whether we're going to move into your place or mine."

"I'm going to call security."

She stopped and moved in close. "You want them to arrest me?"

God, she was gorgeous. She was every single thing he wanted in a woman, and he even liked this aggressive part of her. "I don't want to."

Her lips curled up. "Good, because I do think you need to rest and it would suck for you to then have to follow me down and arrange for bail. It would be messy." She leaned in. "David, it's not going to work. Don't bother to try."

She was close, close enough that if he moved up even slightly, he could press his lips to hers. "I don't know what you're talking about. I changed my mind about us."

"I love you. Don't make this hard on me." She leaned forward, but her lips found his forehead. "Are you supposed to stay awake tonight? Because of the concussion? What did the doctors say?"

She was going to make him crazy. He wasn't sure how to handle her. "You should leave."

"Make me."

"Damn it, Isla." He was on the verge of getting emotional and he didn't want that. He needed to be rational and cold. He needed to remember all the reasons this was the right path.

She stared down at him, her clear blue eyes boring a hole to his soul. "Then tell me you don't love me."

"I don't . . ." Fuck. He couldn't do it. "It's not going to work."

"That wasn't 'I don't love you,'" she said with a sigh. "As long as you love me and I love you, it will work out. Now, do you want me to tell you what I found out about the case? Besides Amber being the bad guy. There's something else going on here. Too many unanswered questions."

"I don't want to talk about the case." The case didn't matter now. "We need to talk about this. You have to be reasonable."

"No, I don't."

He wasn't even sure what to say to her. "If I don't want to see you again, what exactly are you going to do about it?"

"See, this is where you've underestimated your opponent, Counselor. You see my kindness and kind of gooey middle and think it's weakness. I can see it all play out in your head. You can spare me a life of pain. You're going to turn out exactly like Trey Adams one day. Let's not even discuss the odds of that. It's only twenty-eight percent."

He could argue on that one. "My father has Alzheimer's, so my risk is greater."

"Objection."

"This is not a trial."

"Isn't it though? And I object to your bad research." She sat down on the bed, her hand mere inches from his. "If you're going to use the Internet for research, keep up to date. Did you know that a study a few years ago showed there's little impact on a person's chance for getting Alzheimer's if it's the father who has the disease?"

What was she talking about? "We know there's a genetic component."

"There is," she agreed. "It runs through the maternal DNA. Or at least there's strong evidence that it does. Also, there's good evidence that it's only early onset Alzheimer's that's highly inheritable. When was your father diagnosed?"

"He was seventy-six. He's had it for six years now." How did she know so much?

She nodded as though she'd suspected that fact. "Then he's late onset and there's only a slight risk associated. So we're back to a twenty-eight percent chance that your brain is going to go bad on us. Don't test my knowledge. I went through all of this with Portia when we got Trey's diagnosis. I studied up on CTE and Alzheimer's because for a while they weren't sure which one he had. Is your mother suffering?"

His mother was sharp as a tack. "Not from Alzheimer's. But that one-in-three shot that my brain is going to go is enough. You know what it was like for Portia. My mother has to take care of everything. She can't be happy."

"Marriage isn't all about happiness." She took a deep breath and continued on. "So you got another bump on the head and freaked out. You decided to be the white knight. All you need to do is turn me away and I'll be safe. Did you worry about me crying? Maybe feeling bad about myself? Because I didn't and I won't. I won't have to because I will win this war. I've already fought it once. I might not have won every battle, but I was by his side when he died. I held his hand. I got what was my right."

"Isla," he began. She shouldn't have to do this again. Couldn't she see that's what he was trying to save her from?

She shook her head. "No, you've talked enough. Now you're going to listen. I'm not weak. I'm not some fluffy thing you need to protect. I am a grown woman who knows exactly what I want and who I want it with, and I'm brave. I learned at a very young age that life isn't neat and tidy. It isn't fair, but it can be beautiful. Even when it's at its harshest, it can be beautiful if we let it."

"There was nothing beautiful about what happened to Trey Adams."

"But he had a wonderful life before," she said wistfully. "Do you honestly believe he would give that up? I know Portia wouldn't have."

"He would. He would do it to save her," David said, emotion finally getting the better of him. "He would do it so she wouldn't have spent the last years having to be his mother and not his wife."

She stared at him, her eyes clear. "You want some guarantee that life is going to turn out like you want it, but that's not the way it goes. Do you intend to spend the rest of your life without love? Because getting the disease is a tragedy. What you're talking about is pure cowardice. You're afraid you might be a burden one day. What if it was me? I could get cancer. My only aunt died of breast cancer. Should I live in fear and not try to have a family because one day they might have to take care of me?"

How could he make her understand? "It's not the same."

"It's exactly the same, and we obviously have two different versions of family," Isla replied. "Taking care of each other through the good and the bad and the desperate is what family does. And if you don't see that, then maybe you aren't the man for me. I don't know. I'm going to sleep on it." She moved to the small closet and grabbed the extra pillow and blanket.

"We should talk." He couldn't let this go on. Could he?

"In the morning. It's getting late. Wake me up if your brain explodes." She settled in.

"It's not funny."

She lay down, easing the lounger back. "Learn from a pro, Cormack. If you don't laugh about it, you cry, and laughing is way more fun. And just so you know, I was a kid when I let Austin refuse to marry me. I'm a woman now. Get used to it."

Her eyes closed.

It was moments before he could see the way her breathing became rhythmic, her body relaxed.

His wife. His indomitable, take-no-prisoners, leave-no-man-behind wife.

No. He couldn't.

The door opened and the nurse walked in, her eyes widening when she saw he wasn't alone. Her voice took on a hushed tone. "Your friend said you would probably want some more Jell-O."

He was going to kill Henry.

~

Hours later, when the sun was shining, the door opened again. He grimaced. The nurses had been regular in their care, waking him up every few hours even though he'd barely slept at all. He'd turned off the light and lain there, staring at Isla.

Isla, the brave.

Isla, the unrelenting.

Isla, the soundest sleeper in the world.

At seven, he'd turned on the TV to the morning news shows and she hadn't even stirred. He'd watched the coverage as he half ate the mush they'd brought him. He'd even groaned at the sight of Royce Osborne making the rounds and acting like he'd cracked the case.

Asshole.

Isla had slept through it all.

How was he going to convince her to leave? He wasn't sure he had it in him to be vicious enough to scare her away.

He turned in bed and was surprised. The woman who walked in wasn't another nurse, though she'd been awfully good at taking care of him. "Hey, Mom."

His mother smiled, her face lined with age but still lovely to him. He could remember when she was the most beautiful woman in the world. "Hey, baby boy. I'm sorry it took me so long to get here. That nice Noah is sitting with your father for me. They're playing checkers. He's having a good morning."

Isla stirred finally, her eyes coming open. She sat up.

"It looks like you're having a good morning, too," his mother said, staring at her with obvious curiosity. "Hello, dear, I'm Alma Cormack."

Isla's eyes went wide. "Oh, I'm Isla Shayne and now I wish I'd brought a toothbrush. And taken a shower."

This was awkward. "Mom, Isla's a friend from work."

That seemed to get rid of all of Isla's awkwardness. She stood up and held a hand out. "I'm your son's girlfriend. If I have my way, I'm going to marry him because I love him madly. Now, before I end up sounding like a stalker, I'll go and see if the nurses can find me some toothpaste. I'll be back in a while. It was nice to meet you, Mrs. Cormack."

"It was nice to meet you, too." His mother turned on him the moment the door closed. "You didn't tell me you were getting married. How could you not tell your own mother? Oh, David, she's lovely. What does she do? How did you meet? I'm going to set up a lunch with her. We'll invite your aunts. When is the wedding? Spring? I love a spring wedding."

He hadn't seen his mother so excited in years. She was patient and calm. She was controlled because his father was not, but there was pure joy in her eyes now. And naturally he had to be the one to squash it.

"I'm not getting married." Though he needed to watch Isla closely now. She was a bit on the ruthless side. If he let her get together with his mother, he might find himself in a precarious situation. "I'm sorry to disappoint you. I'm trying to break up with her."

Her eyes widened in obvious surprise. "Why would you break up with her? Is she dangerous?"

How was he going to explain this to her without bringing up touchy subjects? "No, of course not. She's . . . she's amazing. She's smart and funny, and I had no idea how stubborn she could be."

His mom moved to the side of his bed. "You sound like you care about her."

Maybe she would understand. "I care about her enough to let her go."

His mom went still. "What does that mean?"

Damn it. He shouldn't have started this. "It means this isn't going to work out the way she thinks it is. She's being stubborn. We had an affair while we were working a case together and now that the case is over, it's time to move on."

"That's how you treat a woman who loves you?"

His mother could still send him a look that made him feel like he was ten years old and caught doing something he shouldn't. "It wouldn't work."

He even sounded like a stubborn kid.

"Why?" She stared down at him as though trying desperately to understand.

"She's a lawyer, too. You know how hard it is to have a marriage and two high-powered careers." He would give logic a shot. "Besides, the firm is just getting off the ground. That means it could be years before I have time to give her. It wouldn't be fair."

There was a moment of heavy silence before she looked at him, grave knowledge in her stare. "This is because of me."

He sat up and wished he was wearing something besides a hospital gown. "No, Mom. It's because of me."

She shook her head and set her purse down. "I doubt that. You know you never asked me. All these years and you've been quite good about taking care of us. We wouldn't have gotten through financially without you. I would have had to put him in a home. Is that why you won't let yourself be happy? Because we're too much of a burden to you? Because we can downsize the house. I saved money."

"It's not about that. How could you even think that?"

"Because the other reason is too terrible to contemplate."

He reached out, pulling her small hand into his. "We both have to face facts. There is a chance that in the next ten or twelve years, I'm going to develop a disease. It's called CTE."

She frowned. "I know about that. Of course I know. What does that have to do with whether or not you marry?"

"It wouldn't be fair to the woman I marry."

"Does she know about the risks?" his mother asked.

"Yes." Apparently Isla knew a lot about CTE.

"But she accepted them? Did she tell you about her risks?" The questions came out in an impatient tone.

"She doesn't have any."

His mother paced the small room, her irritation evident. "She could be killed in a car accident. She could be murdered walking down the street. But that's not what you're afraid of, is it? Did she tell you she could live through that car accident and lose her ability to walk, to feed herself, to do anything? Because that could happen, and here's the easy thing for you to do, son, since you're so worried about it. Leave. Walk away. You can shove her in a nursing home and not look back. That's a risk, too. I wonder, when I get too sick to take care of myself, will you simply euthanize me? Do I lose my meaning to you when I can no longer function as I did?"

Those words shocked him, made him flush with shame. How could she think that? "I would never do that to you. Never. I love you. Can't you understand? Either of you? I'm a walking time bomb. I could blow up and ruin everyone's lives. What if we had kids?"

"Then I would get grandkids and have more joy in my life," his mother shot back. "You were a joy to us and if your father had known his risk and done what you're thinking of doing, then you'd never exist. You are the walking proof of your father's love for me. Of my love for him. I can't imagine a world where you weren't born, but that's what you're asking of that woman who loves you."

He loved his life. He'd loved his childhood, even though it was spent in poverty. There had been a few years when even food was scarce, but his father would always eat last though he was the largest. His father would take the pain so his wife and child could have the comforts. "I miss Dad."

She sat down beside him. "He's still here, baby. That's what you don't understand. I still see him. He comes out in little glimpses. Rarer now, but even when they're totally gone, I won't regret a thing. What I would regret is not taking care of him the way he took care of me. What you see as a burden . . . I won't say it's not hard, but I wouldn't change it. Not for the world. I have had the best life. I had your father for almost forty years. I wouldn't change that simply because the end isn't perfect. Sometimes he thinks it's the seventies again and he puts on Elton John and he asks me to dance like he did then. And we dance and dance. It's not all bad. Some of it is so beautiful if you open yourself to it."

Exactly what Isla had said. There was beauty in everything. Even in the end.

"I don't know what to do." He'd felt this way for so long. He wasn't sure how to change it. "Maybe I should take the test so I would know the real risks. They can tell me if I have the protein marker."

His mother seemed to consider the idea. "If that would make you feel better, but if it would change her mind, then she's not the right girl."

"It wouldn't and that's why I'm trying to spare her."

"And if she doesn't want to be spared?"

He had no answer for that.

The door opened and Isla walked in. She smiled at his mother. "He's getting out today. Don't worry. I'll make sure he doesn't do anything to reinjure himself. Babe, I'm going to grab some breakfast in the cafeteria. They said it would be another hour or so before they release you. Don't run. I'll find you."

His mom stood up. "I think I'll have a cup of coffee with you, Isla. If you don't mind some company."

Isla smiled, that crazy, gorgeous, light-up-his-whole-world smile. "I would love that."

"Hey, I thought you were here to see me," he complained as his mom grabbed her purse.

"I find her infinitely more interesting at the moment. Think about what I said." She followed Isla out.

David sat back. He wasn't sure he would be able to think about anything else. His mother would fall in love with Isla and he would be the bad guy.

The TV caught his eye, a picture of Portia Adams crossing the screen. The news anchor's voice introduced the piece.

We end today's broadcast with newly released footage from a documentary film Portia Adams was working on with renowned director Gary Keller. Mr. Keller is releasing a few minutes of the film in honor of the recently deceased Portia Adams. He hopes to complete and expand her vision later this year, focusing on the highs and lows of being a famous family, and how love was still at the center of everything. Here it is.

Slow music played and a shot of Trey launching the football came on the screen. Portia's voice took over.

It didn't matter that you were the hero of the city. What mattered was you were my hero.

The clips slid into one another, each a precious taped memory. Portia and Trey's wedding. Her cheering him on from the sidelines. Trey Adams holding his newborn son.

You were their heroes.

Trey Adams grinned as he scooped up a toddler girl in his arms as they ran across the green of the park.

And that, through it all, through wins and losses, good and bad, we were a family.

The anchor came back on, but David was transfixed by those simple words.

We were a family.

Portia Adams loved her husband. She loved him truly and deeply and she wouldn't have taken it back.

And that's why it didn't make sense.

Trey had said she was angry. Why would she have been angry about Amber cheating on Carey? Sure, there would have been some self-righteous indignation, but that wasn't what Trey had described that day in the park. He'd said Portia had held him.

I remember she told me she would get them. She would take them all down.

That didn't sound like some affairs. That sounded like someone had hurt her family. Amber and Carey's marriage wouldn't affect the Adams family.

There was something else. Something they hadn't figured out yet.

He slid out of bed and got dressed, eager to deal with a problem that wasn't Isla.

SEVENTEEN

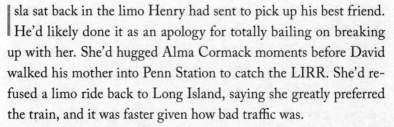

Isla sat back in the limo Henry had sent to pick up his best friend. He'd likely done it as an apology for totally bailing on breaking up with her. She'd hugged Alma Cormack moments before David walked his mother into Penn Station to catch the LIRR. She'd refused a limo ride back to Long Island, saying she greatly preferred the train, and it was faster given how bad traffic was.

Would David run with her? Would he slip on that train himself and disappear in a desperate attempt to get away from his unwanted potential bride?

How the hell was she going to make him see the light? The truth was she only had limited time with him. She could tell him that she wasn't leaving, that she was going to stand and fight, but he could bar her from his offices. He could avoid her. If he truly chose to, he could keep her out of his life. Time and distance would do their work, and eventually she would have to let go.

Give him a little time, his mother had requested. Alma had practically begged her to be patient with him. She'd talked about what a great son David was, how happy she was that he was involved with someone again, how hard the divorce had been.

How hard his dad's illness had been.

David was afraid of the future. Without her, he could cling to the present and ignore what might or might not happen. With her, he had to face it all. She wasn't sure he was ready to do that, would ever be ready to do that.

She'd started the day so positive, but after going back to the penthouse to pick up their things and change, she was starting to wonder if this was a fight she could win. David had been quiet and distant. He was polite, but he allowed her to do most of the talking with his mom. Isla had shown her around the penthouse, got her some coffee while David packed up.

When the time had come to drop Alma off, he asked if he could do it alone. He'd left her in the car. Had he left altogether?

The door opened and David climbed in. "Take us to the office, please."

He closed the door and then hit the button that brought up the privacy wall between the front and back of the car.

"Are you feeling okay?" She was worried about him. He was still pale even after she'd gotten some food in him. "Maybe you shouldn't go into the office. I know Henry was expecting you to go home."

"Henry isn't my boss."

He was going to be stubborn and that was bad news for her. "No, but he cares about you. He wouldn't want you back at work before your body is ready."

"My body is fine. It's my brain I'm worried about. I've got a couple of ideas I want to run by the group and then I'll rest," he said. He sat back and was quiet as the driver managed to make the turn down Lexington. "She likes you. She never liked Lynn."

"I liked her, too."

His eyes narrowed, but there was a small smile on his face that softened the expression. "You like everyone."

Oh, he was wrong about that. "No, I don't. I hope Kristoff Paloma rots in jail. I would say something about him becoming someone's prison bitch, but I'm above that. Rotting in prison is one thing. The complete violation of another's right to be violation-free is something else."

"See," he said, his voice deep, "you're soft, Shayne. I personally would like to fillet the fucker for holding a gun on you. Though I think first I would torture him for information."

"Information? I would think he's giving up Amber as fast as he can."

"Yes, he's admitted Amber is the one who killed Portia and she threatened to blame it on him if he didn't help her," he explained. "Henry sent over some new information this morning. Apparently they're holding a hard line, saying this was all about covering up their affair."

She was happy to have him talking. "You say that like you don't believe it. Miranda told me she knew about the affair. They were definitely sleeping together. She said it started during that girls' trip to Paris and continued to London the next year. I have to think they arranged that meeting."

"It would be too coincidental," David mused. "They either arranged it or Paloma had been watching her and waiting for the chance."

"I don't know about that. I do know Amber took several trips to Europe in the last couple of years. They could have been meeting. I would bet she's been giving him money." But something bugged her. "Amber is always so conscientious about taking care of Carey. She makes sure he takes his pills every day."

"Maybe we should check that those are the pills he's supposed to take," David said with a huff. "She might have been trying to kill him the whole time."

"Then why make sure he goes to every doctor's appointment and has his blood checked once a month? These aren't new doctors. They're the same doctors he's been going to for years," she pointed out. "It's hard for me to believe she's trying to kill him. Black widows tend to try to isolate their spouses, try to keep them sick. She encourages him to have his friends over, to exercise. Honestly, she's a pretty good wife."

"If you don't mind the lover on the side."

"Well, there is that." She looked out the window. Traffic was her friend today. They were stuck at a light, surrounded by taxis and Ubers all fighting to be the next one through. The limo driver would be far more chill. "Why do you still care? You're off this case. Unless Carey called you. Did he? I'm worried about him."

"No, he didn't. I wouldn't take the call anyway. I'm going to have to testify against his wife." David leaned back. "And I can't be bought. I'm not going to refuse. She did the crime and she needs to be in jail."

"I know. But it makes me sad for Carey," she said with a sigh. "I'm sure the news has made him look like a fool. He hates that. He can handle almost anything but looking like a fool. He's not answering my calls."

"He needs some time."

It was right there—the thing he didn't say. He needed some time, too. He needed to figure out what he wanted because he wasn't sure he wanted her.

A long moment passed and she wanted to push him. She wanted to poke and prod and make him decide because she wasn't patient. It would make her crazy. But he'd been on edge all morning and her taking his mom time probably hadn't helped.

He shook his head and suddenly spoke. "I don't think this is about the affair. Something in my gut is telling me we missed something."

"What would we have missed? I'm not sure what else it could be about and why Amber would lie about it."

"Unless there was something worse than an affair."

"She was very protective of her marriage to him," Isla explained. "I remember her talking about how the Kendrick name was sacred and she had to uphold the image. I think she was ready to do anything to keep their name out of the tabloids. She had to know Carey would divorce her."

He looked like he wanted to argue for a moment and then sat back with a frustrated sigh. "I don't know. Maybe she was skimming money from the company and sending it to her lover? Something like that might drive the stock price down."

"She wouldn't know how to do that. She's not the brightest bulb." She felt bad saying it but it was absolutely true. Amber had been great at throwing parties and cheering on her team. She hadn't exactly fit into Portia's circle. Portia had been the smart one. She glanced down at the box she'd brought with her. When they were clearing out of the penthouse, she'd brought along the box the police had sent back the day before. She was still looking through it. Isla told herself she merely wanted to glance through it, but maybe she was also looking for answers.

"You know Henry and I were talking about this last night."

"Before you invaded my hospital room and declared me a coward?"

She winced. "Yes, before I invaded."

His face softened, mouth curling up gently. "Proceed."

She would take what she could get. "I found something in the material the police shipped back. It's what Henry and I were talking about. I know you've been texting back and forth, but did he mention that I found his name and number in Portia's day planner?"

"See, that doesn't sound like something having to do with a

divorce. Henry only handles criminal cases," David pointed out. "If this was about the affair, Henry couldn't do anything at all about it. I know Portia wasn't a client. We checked when we looked for conflicts of interest. The only reason to call Henry would be because she needed an attorney for something she or Trey had done."

"Sometimes she would find experts to answer her questions," Isla mused. "If she had a question about something criminal, she might have called the expert."

"But you're her lawyer. Why not ask you?"

She reached down into the box, pulling out the day planner in question. She turned the pages until she found the one marking the day before Portia's death. "She's got my name written in here, too."

Passing it to him, his hand brushed hers and he held it there for a moment, their skin against each other's. He finally pulled back and she felt the loss of his warmth.

"Any idea what the question mark is about?" he asked.

She shook her head. "No. I talked to her at least every other day. If she had a question, she could always call me, so I have to believe that she was wondering if she wanted to bring me into this at all. I think she meant to contact Henry for some reason and leave me out of it until she'd spoken to him."

David handed it back to her. The car was moving again, turning toward uptown, where he would likely leave her. "And I can't help but think about what Trey told us in Central Park the morning after he escaped. He said Portia held him and promised to get back at someone. Why would she get back at Amber for an affair that wasn't with Trey?"

"She wouldn't. I mean she wouldn't have approved, but I also don't know how involved she would have gotten." Isla thought about it as the car picked up speed. Just a few more blocks. "Trey would have told him, but I don't know about Portia. Miranda knew, but she didn't tell."

They were quiet for a moment, the silence between them anything but comfortable.

"I was trying to protect you," he said quietly.

"I don't want to be protected." She wanted him. She wanted a life.

"No, you want a family."

"I do. But not with just anyone. Don't think I'm using you for your sperm. I love you, David. I think you complete me somehow. I know you don't think you have a future, but I'm going to prove you wrong."

He moved over, getting in her space. "Family sticks together."

Tears filled her eyes and she leaned into him. "Through everything."

His arms wound around her. "I watched part of the video Portia was making and it was beautiful. I think Trey was wrong. He said he wishes he'd died before it set in, but Portia still loved him. My mom still loves my dad. They get through it."

She nodded, her heart speeding up. "That's what people in love do."

Could that video Portia had been making save her and David? Could it be that simple? One cobbled-together video of football plays and babies and wedding videos. Who would have guessed he would be so sentimental?

Football plays. She'd caught that on the news. Portia would have gone through clips in the vault, the AV library the Guardians kept.

"What is it?" David asked. "You figured something out."

She opened the day planner, her hands shaking a little. What could this mean? Why would it mean anything at all? "It's the code."

"The numbers?" David slid across the seat.

"Yes. I think I know what they mean." She found the page again and there they were.

09–19–AVI1–5

"I interned with the Guardians' front office," she said. "One of the places I worked in the beginning was the vault."

"The vault is the media library," David murmured. "'AV' stands for 'audiovisual'?"

"Yes. Zero nine refers to the year and nineteen is the game."

"That would be the championship game," David said, thinking out loud. "That year the Guardians were the number one seed, so they didn't play the wild card game. Two playoff games and the overall championship. This is the game."

It was the game that cemented Trey Adams's status as one of the greatest players of all time. He'd been injured in the first half and no one thought he would be able to play in the second. He'd been heroic.

"This is a specific reel of film we have in the archives. The number tells me this was from the documentary, likely one of the cameras they had throughout the facilities. Most of that stuff has never even been looked through. It was footage from the locker rooms and the offices. Why would she want that?"

David reached for the button that let him communicate with the driver. "I don't know but we're going to find out. Sir, we need to change our destination. We need to leave the city. We're going to the Guardians' stadium. And hurry if you can."

"You want to see the film?" She couldn't imagine what was on it. "This could be a wild-goose chase."

"I want to see it. I want to make sure no one's gotten rid of it." David pulled out his phone. "I'm going to call the office and let them know where we're going."

She sat back, her mind worried.

⌒

David followed her up the stairs that led to the offices of the New York Guardians. The stadium below was quiet, so quiet it felt a bit like a tomb. Through the bank of glass windows, he could see the stands that held a hundred thousand fans and the field where glory had been found. Where Trey Adams had lost his future.

He stopped for a moment. He hadn't played here. The stadium had been opened the year after he retired, but it brought him right back to the places he had played.

God, he could still hear that sound. Sometimes he wondered if it was always with him, like a low buzzing in the back of his head. A remembrance of a life he'd left behind, a life that still might catch up with him.

Isla stepped up beside him, staring out over that field. "Was there anything good about it?"

"A lot. I loved it most of the time," he admitted. "I loved the game, but I hate it, too, because I think it might cost me something I wanted more than I ever wanted to play."

She leaned against him briefly. "Only if you let it."

He wanted to move his arm, to wrap it around her and bring her close. He couldn't help but remember what his mother had said to him before she got on the train.

If you let that one go, you'll regret it for the rest of your life. But I think you'll be doing something worse. I think you'll make her ache the rest of hers. That woman is in love with you. If you love her, even a little, you can't let her go. That kind of love makes everything worthwhile.

Even the bad parts. Even the horrible parts.

His father and mother still danced together. Wasn't that what life was? Moments of pure beauty surrounded with the everyday? No one was happy every moment of the day, but if he had Isla with him, perhaps happiness would be like the sound of the crowd—always in the background, waiting to surge.

That happiness was right beside him. All he had to do was reach out and take it. She was making it easy on him.

"Isla! It's good to see you. It's been too long."

She turned and he moved along with her, the moment lost. A

man roughly her age dressed in khakis and a collared shirt reached out a hand.

"Hi, Mike. This is my friend David Cormack." She gestured toward David. "Mike runs the media portion of the Guardians' empire. He was a great boss when I interned here."

"Yeah, that's easy to be with interns like Isla." Mike shook David's hand.

She reached out to shake Mike's hand, too. "How are you?"

Mike took her hands between his and David had the oddest urge to growl at the younger man. "It's a rough day. Are you here to see the big boss? He's in a bad way. We're all worried about him."

"He's here?" Isla asked.

Mike nodded. "He came in a couple of hours ago. He's in the main viewing room, but he's asked to be alone. I think someone should try to talk to him, but no one is willing to disobey him."

"I would love to see him, but first I need to get into the vault," she replied. "I need access to a specific reel of film."

"Of course," he replied. "Come on and we'll find it for you. I can get you a screening room, but it's going to be one of the smaller ones. What exactly are you looking for? Is this for Portia's memorial?"

"Do you need to hold her hand while you do it?" Yep. That had come out of his mouth. So much for playing it cool and giving himself some time.

Mike flushed but Isla merely smiled and released the man's hand.

"I've got the location of the film." She followed him, waiting a second until she was walking beside David.

And he freaking gave in to his impulses. The minute their hands brushed, he tangled their fingers together. The minute her hand was in his, his heart rate calmed and the world seemed slightly better than it had been before.

Mike walked down the hall toward a big set of double doors.

"Who would have guessed that the boss's wife had that in her? I mean, I knew she'd been anxious lately, but damn."

"How had she been anxious?" Now that Mike wasn't pawing Isla, David could see him as a possible resource. "What was her normal role in the day-to-day running of the team?"

"Next to none," Mike replied. "Don't get me wrong. She was up here a lot. She was always bringing the boss his lunch and sitting with him. We all kind of thought it was nice. Like they were a real couple. She amused him and she seemed to genuinely care about him. And don't let anyone say something bad about the family name. She was hell on the publicity department because anytime someone would make fun of Carey on some show she would try to sue them. I don't think she ever truly grasped the idea of the First Amendment."

"She took the family legacy very seriously," Isla explained as they approached the doors to the vault.

There was a keypad that protected the doors. Mike held up an employee keycard, and the light on the door went from red to green, the lock unlatching audibly.

"Are these doors always locked?" David asked as they moved into the cool, dimly lit vault.

"Yes," Mike replied as the doors shut behind them. "We keep some very old films in here. They're delicate and too much light or heat could damage them, so we regulate who comes and goes."

"Do you have a list of the people who have been in here in the last, say, six weeks?" Isla seemed to catch on to what he was thinking.

"Of course." Mike put a hand on one of the computers in a bank that stood in front of the neatly stacked shelves. "You can check out films here. If you try to leave without checking out, security is alerted. But there's also a list of who's been in here and what they searched for."

Isla looked up at him, her mouth firming in a suspicious line.

He nodded because they had to know. "Could you please tell us if Amber has been in here recently?"

"You know, she did come in a couple of weeks back. She was looking for some footage from the documentary. She asked for the reel, but we destroyed it last year," Mike explained. "It was the weirdest thing because I thought she would be disappointed, but she smiled. She didn't even let me explain what we'd done. Just said since it was gone, she wouldn't worry about it."

"You destroyed film?" Isla asked.

"Obviously not the rare footage ones, but we digitalized the majority of the documentary series." Mike's fingers tapped along the keys. "It's been my project for a while. Carey wanted that documentary done first class. That made for a lot of film. I digitalized most of it, and now you can simply go into one of the viewing rooms and pull it up on a laptop that feeds through to the projector."

He saw Amber's mistake. "And you didn't tell Amber that the film she was looking for still existed?"

"She didn't give me the chance," Mike replied.

"Can you see if Portia Adams had been in?" Isla asked.

Mike stopped. "What is this about?"

"Nothing I want you to mention outside of the three of us, please." Isla leaned in. "We're curious about a few things."

Mike nodded, turning back to the system. "Portia was in here several times. I helped her find a couple of reels. She was interested in some relaxed shots of Trey and his close friends. I told her some of the best stuff came from the locker room, and there are literally hundreds of hours no one ever went through. There was too much. I let her download a bunch of it onto her laptop so she could go over it at home. She was making a movie for Trey's fiftieth birthday. Do you think I'm going to get in trouble for letting her do that? I didn't think anyone would mind."

"No one will mind," David assured him. "Honestly, it doesn't have to go past us. Like Isla said, we're merely curious. Isla has a code. Could you tell us how to find it?"

Isla had written the locator code on a piece of paper before they'd walked in the stadium. She handed it to Mike and he frowned.

"What's wrong?" Isla asked.

Damn it. He was going to punch something if that piece of film was missing. It was right there. They'd come so close. If that film was missing, they might never know the truth. It would kill Isla to not know why her friend had truly been murdered.

Mike was staring down at the code. "This is the film Carey requested for the main viewing room. He's watching this right now."

"I'm going in." Isla turned and started toward the viewing rooms.

"He wanted to be alone," Mike pointed out.

"I am basically that man's daughter-in-law," she replied. "If you don't let me in, I'll bust the door down. Do you understand me? You're going to let me in and then you'll walk away and you won't let anyone else into the vault until I give you the okay. Am I clear?"

Mike stepped back. "Yes."

David knew that look well. "Don't feel bad. She looks sweet, but when she wants to she goes all warrior princess on you and it's a little scary."

Mike was already rushing to do her bidding. In the back of the large library there were three different viewing rooms. David had spent a lot of time in spaces like this. It was where the team would gather to go over game films, to discuss what had gone wrong and get their asses handed to them by the coaching staff.

Isla had spent time in spaces like this, too. She'd grown up around football and football players. She walked into this world like she owned it.

What if she was the one woman in the world who could handle his damage? Who was ready for it?

He already knew she was the one woman in the world he wanted more than his next breath. He knew she was smart and sexy and stronger than he'd imagined.

And reckless.

"Hey, let me go in first." He moved in front of her as Mike got the door opened. Ghostly light filtered out and he could hear the sounds of cheering.

She put her hands on her hips. "You think he's going to hurt me."

"I think we don't know what we're going into at all. We have no idea if we've completely misread the situation."

"I know him." She looked over as though reminding him they weren't alone yet.

But they were about to be. He wanted to go in alone, wanted to confront the situation first and explain it to her later. She was never going to be that girl. She wouldn't be the kind of wife who let him go into danger alone. She would be right there beside him. Through everything.

Any family raised by Isla Shayne would stick together. And if the darkness came, she would be the light.

He had no idea what they were walking into, but he knew he wasn't going to drop her off at the end of the night. He would be there with her no matter what.

He led her down the short hall to the theater. The door closed behind them. It seemed Mike knew when to obey. The theater looked like it could seat roughly seventy-five to eighty people, but there was only one man sitting in the audience. The large screen showed a wild celebration in the Guardians' locker room. The players were jumping up and down, spraying champagne, and in the middle of it all Carey Kendrick held that championship trophy high.

"Carey?"

He was a shadow in the room, his head swinging slowly Isla's way. He was quiet for a moment. The audio went silent all of a sudden, though the team continued to celebrate.

"Isla? Is that you, David?"

Isla moved to the row in front of Carey. "Yes, we're both here. Why this tape? This is what Portia found. This is why Amber killed her. Why?"

Even in the low light, he could see that Carey Kendrick had been crying. His face was lined and he looked even older than normal, as though all the plastic surgery in the world couldn't hide his pain.

"She was trying to protect me," he said. "Or rather the family name. She never had one she was proud of, you know. Her daddy went to jail when she was a baby. She never knew him. He got killed in there. Her momma started putting her in pageants as soon as she could walk. All she had was her beauty, but I saw there was something more. I'm not foolish. I knew she had lovers. I can't . . . I can't take care of her physically. I looked the other way because she was good to me. People are complicated. I didn't love her, never loved any woman but my Marilyn."

"You knew about Paloma?" If anything shocked him, it was this. He assumed Carey Kendrick would be possessive, but the man was right. People were complex creatures.

"Not his name or face, but I knew she took some pleasure from other men," he admitted. "And I knew she cared for me in her own way. I wish she'd come to me. When she found out, I wish she'd trusted me to take care of it. I think deep down she knew I wouldn't. She knew I would let it out."

"What did you do?" Isla asked.

Carey pressed some button on a tablet that seemed to control the footage. The screen went blank and then light filled the room again as the film started. He paused the scene.

It was footage from a locker room. David tried to remember

everything he could about the game. Trey Adams had been hurt in the first half and came out in the second like nothing had happened. The Guardians had won and Trey was named the MVP.

David watched the screen. Trey was nowhere to be seen. The clock was in the background. The championship game started late. This would have been sometime in the first half.

After Trey had won the MVP, he took the plaque and the microphone and then he didn't speak. He shook his head and everyone had said he was far too emotional.

What if it hadn't been emotion?

"What did you do to get him back on that field?" David asked.

It fell into place. Portia's rage, her desire to strike back. She'd called Henry to make an appointment because she wanted to see if there were criminal charges she could bring against the man who'd hurt her husband.

"What do you mean?" Isla stared at him.

Carey was looking at him, too. "Exactly what every owner and coach does when he can smell it. You remember. Don't you remember how you would have done anything to win that one game? When you're in the moment, it seems like everything. It seems like if you can find a way to pull it off, the world will fall into place. Almost like you're in a movie and you'll get to the happy ending if you push through, if you sell your soul. The problem is the movie doesn't end and the characters have to live with what they did."

"And you weren't selling your soul," David pointed out. "You sold his."

"I want to see it." There was a hitch in Isla's voice that let him know she was emotional.

"You have to know I didn't realize this footage even existed. I didn't know where all the cameras were. No one ever mentioned it so I didn't know. I certainly didn't send my fluffy wife out to hurt someone. I wouldn't have. If Portia had come to me instead of her, I would have told her to put it out there, to let everyone see. I would have given her anything she wanted. God, I didn't remember it being this way. I knew I was pushing him, but . . . I'm a monster."

He picked up a tablet, and the scene on the screen started up. Trey, the team doctor, and Carey walked in and they were alone in the locker room.

Trey groaned and held his head. *Everything hurts. I don't want to go back. I know I'm letting everyone down, but I think something is wrong with me.*

Carey got on one knee in front of him. *You took a hard hit. You're fine. We'll get you all the medical care you need after we win. Okay?*

David's gut churned as the scene played out. At one point Carey yelled, screaming about Trey being a quitter. And it ended with the doctor doping Trey up so much that he didn't care if he hurt anymore.

"How could you? You knew something was wrong," Isla said, watching as Trey Adams lay on the bench waiting for the drugs to work.

"We wanted to win." Carey stared at the screen. "It was all we ever wanted. When I was going through it I told myself he would thank me. And he did. That's the worst part. The next day, he thanked me. I sent him out again and again, killing off little pieces of him, and he thanked me. I wonder if Austin would have done the same."

He was an old man, finally facing his sins, and David's heart twisted with the tragedy of it all. None of them had meant to end this way. They'd been children looking to please their parents first, their coaches later on, and that mob of fans at the end. They'd done it for the love of the game, to find glory, to lift themselves out of poverty. None of them had meant to come to this end. Not even the owners. They'd been greedy and shortsighted, and it all seemed so useless.

"David, I need to speak with Carey alone," Isla said quietly.

He turned and realized his cheeks were wet. Damn it. He brushed the tears away and nodded. Carey wasn't going to hurt her. And this was a family matter.

He needed to be out of this room, out of this place entirely, but he would take walking back into the sunlight. "I'll be outside."

He couldn't get away fast enough. Not from her. He needed to get away from this place where he was faced with how useless he was, how utterly helpless he was to do anything.

He hit the door and then strode through the vault. He got outside where the sun lit the whole place up and shone on all those trophies and honors won by warriors who lost. Lost their futures. Lost their hope.

Palms on the railing, he stared out, forcing himself to breathe.

He had no idea how long it was before she walked back out. She'd done her makeup before they'd left the penthouse, but her mascara was ruined. It didn't matter. She was still lovely even in her grief.

"I'm going to ask you to do something for me."

He nodded. "Anything."

"Please don't tell anyone what you saw today. Apparently, Amber never told Kristoff the truth. She told him Portia had video proof of their affair and that she might have sent it to me. What she honestly worried about was the chance that Portia had sent me the tape we just saw. The tape from the locker room. They were terrified I had a copy."

"So you want to let him get away with it?"

"I want to take something horrible and make it better," she said, tears starting again.

"You can't make this better, baby." Maybe she would understand now. He was potentially doomed and there was no reason for her to go to hell with him.

"But I can. After he has his will rewritten, I will be Carey's only heir. I've agreed to sell the Guardians, the stadium, the businesses, everything. I will take all the liquid cash and form a foundation to cure CTE," she said, her jaw firming stubbornly. "Oddly enough I'm keeping quiet for the same reason Amber did. If that tape gets out, the Guardians as a business will take a huge hit, both financially and public relations–wise. I want the company strong when I sell it. I'll put everything Carey worked for into fixing this. That's what we agreed on. I want you to head the foundation."

"You're talking billions," he said, not quite believing the words that came out of his mouth. What she was talking about seemed impossible. No one did that. No one except Isla. "Carey's worth billions."

"And we'll raise billions more because we won't just go after CTE. We'll go after them all. Dementia. Alzheimer's. We'll beat them all," she swore.

She was the single most amazing woman he'd ever met, and she'd done the one thing he thought no one could. She gave him purpose. He'd thought he was useless in this fight, thought there wasn't much of a fight at all, and she'd turned it all around. She gave them a chance. Maybe they wouldn't win, but they could fight.

Wasn't that all anyone could ask for?

He dropped to one knee. "Isla Shayne, will you marry me?"

Her eyes went wide and a smile broke over her face. "I thought it would be harder than that. All I needed was a billion-dollar charity fund?"

He was going to ignore her ill-timed sarcasm. "I promise whatever time we have on this earth together, I'll spend it with you. I'll be your husband and your partner and we'll build a family. We'll build a future."

"Come what may?" She knelt down, getting to his level.

"Come what may." Whatever happened, he would face it with her.

"Then yes, I'll marry you."

He leaned forward and kissed her and vowed to spend the rest of his life being as brave as his almost bride.

EPILOGUE

THREE MONTHS LATER

"Are you sure you want to do this here?" Henry straightened his tie. "We could do it out on the island."

"The press would still find out." David stood outside the judge's office. He didn't want some big wedding. He wanted a big, long marriage, and this was the first step. "Since Isla announced she was selling the Guardians, they've been all over us."

Carey Kendrick had died quietly three weeks after the day they'd gotten engaged. No one was particularly surprised he'd left his fortune to the woman he considered a daughter, but they had been surprised that she was basically giving it all away. Well, not giving it away. His woman drove an incredibly hard bargain. She'd let everyone know she wouldn't take anything less than an incredible offer because she was going to do something wonderful with it.

She'd already raised millions, even without the sale. The Kendrick/Adams Foundation was well funded and he was starting to hire the best specialists for his board.

It was time to fight the good fight.

Was it time to find out his fate?

The envelope had come this morning. His test results. He hadn't opened them, wasn't sure he wanted to. He was going to do what he always did now when it came to important decisions. He was going to talk to his wife.

It didn't matter that they hadn't said *I do* yet. She was his soul mate.

"I'm just saying the justice of the peace isn't where I thought you would go," Henry replied.

"I think he wanted to be your wedding planner," Noah said with a grin. "He had a binder and everything."

Henry's eyes rolled. "Can we get rid of him now?"

"You wouldn't know what to do without me." Noah wore a designer suit, looking every bit the successful young lawyer he was. "Let's get this thing done and get to the reception. Margarita made empanadas. Isla loves them so she insisted on prepping them herself. You should have seen her stare down the caterer."

"What's up with you two?" Henry asked.

Finally someone had found a way to make Noah Lawless blush. "Nothing. We're friends. Just friends. I can be friends with a woman."

Henry shook his head and David knew exactly what he was thinking. This was going to blow up in someone's face.

But he wasn't thinking about anything but his wife today.

He turned and there she was, Margarita and Win at her side. She was in a lovely designer suit, her hair pulled into a bun and a bouquet of tiny roses in her hand.

Henry patted him on the shoulder. "Come on, guys. Let's go inside and give these two their last single moments."

He didn't want single moments, but he did want to be alone with her.

Their friends all entered the judge's office and they were left alone.

God, she was beautiful. She was everything. "Hey, wife."

She smiled. "Hey, husband."

"I love you." It was an easy thing to say. "And thank you for being so kind to my mom and dad. You know our reception is going to have an alarming amount of nurses on duty."

Because Trey was coming along with his kids. And his father would be there, accompanying his mother.

"Everyone's family is crazy in their own way," she said. "I can't wait for ours."

They were trying. And trying and they would try some more. He liked nothing better than trying with his gorgeous woman.

He pulled the envelope out. "One thing before we go. It's here. I know you didn't think I should take the test."

She looked down at the envelope. "It's not entirely accurate, David."

"But I wanted to give you a chance to know," he said.

She took the envelope. "What do you want me to do?"

"Whatever you feel like. This is your choice."

Her lips curled up and she found the nearest trash can and tossed it away. "No going back on me. We're in this together. Now let's get married."

He took her hand and finally found his future.

ABOUT THE AUTHOR

Lexi Blake is the *New York Times* bestselling author of the Courting Justice novels, including *Order of Protection*; the Lawless novels, including *Ruthless*, *Satisfaction*, and *Revenge*; and the Masters and Mercenaries series, including *Love Another Day*, *For His Eyes Only*, and *Submission Is Not Enough*. She is also coauthor with Shayla Black of the Perfect Gentlemen series, including *Big Easy Temptation* and *Seduction in Session*, and the Masters of Ménage series, including *Their Virgin Mistress* and *Their Virgin Secretary*.

Ready to find
your next great read?

Let us help.

Visit prh.com/nextread